# OBI; OR, THE HISTORY OF
# THREE-FINGERED JACK

broadview editions
series editor: L.W. Conolly

Drummond delin.                    Bromley sculp.

*Jack attacked by Quashe & Sam.*

Published as the Act directs Sept.¹ 1800, by Earle & Hemet, Albemarle Street, Piccadilly.

Frontispiece to *Obi; or, the History of three-fingered Jack* (1800),
courtesy of The University of Virginia.

# OBI; OR, THE HISTORY OF THREE-FINGERED JACK

William Earle

*edited by Srinivas Aravamudan*

broadview editions

**Library and Archives Canada Cataloguing in Publication**

Earle, William
    Obi, or, The history of Three-fingered Jack / William Earle ; edited by Srinivas Aravamudan.

(Broadview editions)
Includes bibliographical references.
ISBN 1-55111-669-3

    1. Mansong, Jack, d. 1781—Fiction. I. Aravamudan, Srinivas. II. Title. III. Title: History of Three-fingered Jack. IV. Series.

PS1567.I15S02 2005        813'.2        C2005-902173-X

**Broadview Editions**

The Broadview Editions series represents the ever-changing canon of literature by bringing together texts long regarded as classics with valuable lesser-known works.

Advisory editor for this volume: Kathryn Prince

Broadview Press Ltd. is an independent, international publishing house, incorporated in 1985. Broadview believes in shared ownership, both with its employees and with the general public; since the year 2000 Broadview shares have traded publicly on the Toronto Venture Exchange under the symbol BDP.

We welcome comments and suggestions regarding any aspect of our publications—please feel free to contact us at the addresses below or at broadview@broadviewpress.com / www.broadviewpress.com

*North America*
PO Box 1243, Peterborough, Ontario, Canada K9J 7H5
Tel: (705) 743-8990; Fax: (705) 743-8353
email: customerservice@broadviewpress.com
3576 California Road, PO Box 1015, Orchard Park, NY, USA 14127

*UK, Ireland, and continental Europe*
NBN Plymbridge
Estover Road
Plymouth PL6 7PY UK
Tel: 44 (0) 1752 202 301
Fax: 44 (0) 1752 202 331
Fax Order Line: 44 (0) 1752 202 333
Customer Service: cservs@nbnplymbridge.com
Orders: orders@nbnplymbridge.com

*Australia and New Zealand*
UNIREPS, University of New South Wales
Sydney, NSW, 2052
Australia
Tel: 61 2 9664 0999; Fax: 61 2 9664 5420
email: info.press@unsw.edu.au

PRINTED IN CANADA

# Contents

# Acknowledgements

I am sincerely grateful to librarians at the British Library, the Institute for Commonwealth Studies, and the University of Virginia for making a number of texts available for consultation, and for helping with the construction of this edition. A partial bibliographical list of sixteen different versions of *Obi; or Three-fingered Jack* with comprehensive descriptions can be found in Frank Cundall, "Three-Fingered Jack: The Terror of Jamaica," *The West India Committee Circular* Vol. XLV No. 818 (6 February 1930) 55–56. Cundall's initial foray into documenting the multiple editions of *Three-fingered Jack* is invaluable.

I would like to thank colleagues at the University of California at Riverside, the University of New Mexico, the University of Miami, Florida State University, the American Society for Eighteenth-Century Studies (ASECS), and the Southeastern Society for Eighteenth-Century Studies (SEASECS) for inviting me to give talks that helped me realize and further the implications of the project. Special thanks go to Vincent Carretta, Joan Dayan, David Barry Gaspar, George Haggerty, Jonathan Hess, Shaun Hughes, Deborah Jensen, Thomas Krise, Tom Lockwood, Dennis Moore, Philip Morgan, Felicity Nussbaum, Frank Palmeri, and Charlotte Sussman for answering questions, suggesting resources, and inviting me to lecture on the topic. For research assistance with scanning and computing work early in this project, I would like to thank Amardeep Singh. I would like to thank Hollianna Bryan for expert assistance with proofs. My greatest thanks, however, goes to the diligent cheerfulness and brilliant efficiency of my research and editorial assistant Alice Sarti, whose bibliographical, editorial, and computing skills over the last two years resulted in the speedy realization of this edition. Any faults that remain— whether they are errors of commission or omission, text or context, fact or interpretation—are my own.

# Introduction

The full title of this novel promises the treatment of a number of inter-related topics to those who are interested in the history and aftermath of slavery and abolition, the literature of the Caribbean, and the development of New World religions. As a novel based on a true historical incident that was rendered to the public in a number of different versions, the success of *Obi; or, The History of Three-fingered Jack* depended first on the literary taste of the early Romantic period and then on popular taste during its reception history thereafter. *Obi* met with great success through the genre of performed pantomime with an initial unbroken nine-year run, and also by way of multiple editions in chapbook and pamphlet form. Additionally, the oral dissemination of folklore in Jamaica has made the novel's historical protagonist, sometimes referred to as Jack Mansong, into a recognizable legend even today. An early twentieth-century scholar claims that "few persons connected with Jamaica—probably none except Columbus—have been the subject of so many publications as Three-Fingered Jack, the Terror of Jamaica."[1] This assessment will sound hyperbolic to those who may never have heard of this colorful character before; all the same, this novel's rousing account of a heroic individual's attempt to combat slavery while defending family honor suggests aspects of epic tale and revenge tragedy alongside the history, memory, and syncretic legacy of the New World African diaspora. Jack Mansong, according to several historians of Jamaica, remains one of the country's long-standing folk heroes, and his story continues to be commemorated through multiple retellings and song.[2]

Furthermore, the story of Three-fingered Jack is a key source for information about the Afro-Caribbean religion of obeah (or

---

[1] Frank Cundall, "Three-Fingered Jack: The Terror of Jamaica," *West India Committee Circular* Vol. XLV No. 816 (9 January 1930) 9; continued in Nos. 817, 818 (23 January and 6 February 1930). Cundall also lists sixteen different publications since 1800 that re-tell the story for popular audiences.

[2] Clinton V. Black, *The Story of Jamaica: From Prehistory to the Present* (London: Collins, 1965) 106; Clinton V. Black, *History of Jamaica* (London: Collins, 1958) 114.

"Obi" in the title), a set of practices and beliefs produced by the cultural synthesis of enslaved populations drawn from a number of African locations. For this reason, we might trace obeah as a religious theme treated through several genres during the time—examples of which can be found in the appendices—but we can also consider whether the complex phenomenon of obeah stimulated writers into experimenting with a number of generic innovations when representing it. Earle's fiction also attempts to match the novelty of its content with several innovations of form by combining romance elements, sentimental poetry, mock-epistolary structure, anthropological footnote, and colonial reportage. The mock-epistolary structure, which separates the narrative out into individual letters written by the Jamaican George Stanford to his English friend Charles, mimics the many correspondences maintained between overseers of plantations and their absentee landlords, such as the extensive correspondence between Joseph Stewart, a plantation overseer, and Roger Hope Elletson, the Lt. Governor of Jamaica from 1766–68.[1] The novel's letters, however, are much more informal than a business correspondence would have been. *Obi* is written with a view to eliciting the feeling tear or the melancholic sigh of the sentimentalist reader and the abolitionist activist.

*Obi* is of scholarly significance to students of eighteenth- and nineteenth-century literature, and to historians of empire, colonialism, and slavery, but it is also a highly readable novel with a compelling plot and a breezy pace.[2] While the author had no pretensions to high aesthetics, his use of anthropological and ethnographic footnotes, his resort to poetry, and his handling of suspense alongside a romantic subplot altogether reveal considerable skill, and undoubtedly helped capture multiple audiences for the various versions of the story.

---

1 For the Stewart-Elletson correspondence, see Huntington Library, Stowe Brydges Collection, 1766–68. As Mavis Campbell suggests in another context, there is a structural relationship between two lines of flight from Jamaica, absentee landlordism and marronage. Mavis C. Campbell, *The Maroons of Jamaica: A History of Resistance, Collaboration and Betrayal* (Granby, MA: Bergin and Garvey, 1988) 4.

2 For a fuller account of slavery-related Anglophone fiction between 1760 and 1834, see Srinivas Aravamudan, ed., *Slavery, Abolition and Emancipation Volume VI: Fiction* (London: Pickering and Chatto, 1999).

Not much is known about William Earle Junior, although his writings clearly reveal a predilection for sentimentalist excess and rhetorical flourishes. What is known is that Earle was also the subject of a couple of literary controversies. He was accused of plagiarizing Marie Thérèse De Camp's *First Faults* with his published play *Natural Faults* (1799) (both of which imitated Henry Mackenzie's *The Man of Feeling*), but he defended himself credibly as having circulated his version of the manuscript before De Camp's was performed. He also wrote "The Villagers," a *petite pièce*; *The Welshman* (1801), a novel; and probably compiled *Welsh Legends* (1803). Another known setback to Earle's life was in February 1814, when he was "sentenced to six months' imprisonment in Newgate [an infamous London prison] and a fine of 100 pounds for a most scurrilous and malignant libel on a respectable tradesman."[1]

Whatever notoriety he gained during his lifetime, Earle is now best remembered for this novel, in which the tale of Three-fingered Jack's exploits is coupled with a discussion of obeah (sometimes spelled in the period as *obi*, *obia*, *obeiah*, or *orbiah*). In the West Indies, as Earle suggests in the novel, several aspects of obeah functioned as political resistance by enslaved persons to the economic and racial oppression they endured under the system of plantation slavery. The danger posed by obeah resulted in various attempts to control it through criminal and civil legislation. Observers characterized the practice as a form of black magic, and its opponents took preemptive actions against what was seen as obeah's political agenda against the plantocracy—the white plantation-owners—in the colonial period and thereafter. The anthropology of obeah is still speculative when compared to knowledge about the more famous Afro-Caribbean religious syncretic religion of *voudou* (or voodoo), with which obeah is often confused but from which it differs considerably. This novel puts at stake the meaning, scope, and function of obeah as religious practice and also as literary representation, medical cure,

---

[1] See John Genest, *Some Account of the English Stage Vol. 7* (London, 1832) 417–19; *Biographica Dramatica Vol. 3* (London, 1812) 73–74; and S. Austin Allibone, *A Critical Dictionary of English Literature* (London: Trübner and Sons, 1859–71).

and political resistance. In retrospect, it is very likely that obeah's political power arose from its integration with traditional medical practices. A full understanding of the multiple meanings of obeah can come about only by surveying the different literary genres and media used to represent it. To this end, appendices from related texts have been made available at the end of this volume to serve as background materials. Readers are also invited to consult the comprehensive timeline that features significant historical and literary events of the pre-emancipation British Caribbean. The collection of documents presented in this edition situates the novel in its literary contexts, and also helps readers to evaluate the beginnings of a literary culture created around obeah. Ultimately, a close reading of this text enables a fuller understanding not just of obeah, but also of the broader field of the Anglophone literature of slavery and abolition and the cultural history of the Caribbean.

## The Historical Origins of Three-fingered Jack

The first reference to the historical personage of Three-fingered Jack can be found in the Jamaican newspapers of 1780. In August of that year, the first journalistic item acknowledging his existence emphasized the threat posed by the group he headed:

> A gang of run-away Negroes of above 40 men, and about 18 women, have formed a settlement in the recesses of Four Mile Wood in St. David's; are become very formidable to that neighbourhood, and have rendered travelling, especially to Mulattoes and Negroes, very dangerous; one of the former they have lately killed, belonging to Mr. Duncan Munro of Montrose, and taken a large quantity of Linen of his from his slaves on the road: they also have robbed many other persons servants, and stolen some cattle, and great numbers of sheep, goats, hogs, poultry &c. particularly a large herd of hogs from Mr. Rial of Tamarind Tree Penn. They are chiefly Congos, and declare they will kill every Mulatto and Creole Negro they can catch. BRISTOL, alias *Three-finger'd Jack*, is their Captain, and CAESAR, who belongs to Rozel estate, is their next officer.

This banditti may soon become dangerous to the Public, if a PARTY, agreeable to the 40th or 66th Acts in Volume I of the laws of this Island, or the MAROONS, are not sent out against them; which should be applied for, and no doubt it would be ordered.[1]

Later accounts focus much more exclusively on the banditry (or heroism) of Jack Mansong, but this early notice is important for its recognition of the collective nature of the threat posed by runaway slaves, who were sometimes known as maroons (after the Spanish term *címarron* for mountain-dweller). Fleeing slave society and sometimes attempting to form alternative political communities based on subsistence agriculture and political autonomy in the woods and inaccessible mountain areas, escaped and former slaves experimented with various forms of desertion (also known as *marronage*) especially in eighteenth-century Jamaica and Surinam.

The party of escaped slaves mentioned by the report consists of men and women, and a rudimentary leadership structure is also indicated, with Jack, alias Bristol, at the head, and Caesar as his deputy. The ethnicity of the group, designated as "chiefly Congos," suggests that they are likely Koromantyns, who were characterized since the late seventeenth century as fierce, warlike, and apt at organizing rebellions and insurrections in the Caribbean (although later sources also claimed that Jack was a Feloop from near Gambia whose African name was Karfa and whose father was Onowauhee). Even while the existence of a group under Three-fingered Jack's leadership indicates an attempt at establishing a runaway slave settlement, the newspaper report recommends bringing in already-recognized Jamaican Maroons to quell the rebellion. A treaty between the British colonists and the existing Maroons after various "Maroon Wars" over the eighteenth century in Jamaica stipulated that Maroons who were already free ought to track, capture, and return any runaways in exchange for a recognition of their independence and territorial autonomy. In

---

[1] *Supplement to the Royal Gazette* Vol. II No. 67 (29 July 1780–5 August 1780) 458. This, rather than the passage in Benjamin Moseley's *A Treatise on Sugar* (1799, see Appendix A) as some have argued, is the first published reference to the incident.

addition to returning runaways, Maroons were also sometimes asked to help put down slave uprisings.

Three-fingered Jack's mountain hideout was later identified as Mount Lebanus in the Queensberry ridge of the Blue Mountains in St. Thomas-in-the-East, and two other caves where Jack and his companions may have stayed are to be found at the head of Cane River and Cambridge Hill respectively; there also exists a water-source named Three-fingered Jack's Spring. On 2 December, 1780, the next report on the uprising registers that:

> Three fingered Jack continues his depredations in St. Davids; last week he intercepted three negroes coming to town with loads, and carried them off—A mulatto of Dr. Allen's, with a party, went in pursuit of him and recovered the negroes, who gave him information where three fingered Jack was, and he laid a plan for securing him, but Jack being upon his guard, shot the mulatto through the head and made his escape.[1]

By 23 December 1780, it can be inferred that the rebellious party is almost entirely disbanded after the actions of the Jamaican militia. Three-fingered Jack is on the run, but most of his companions have already been apprehended:

> We are informed that the wife of Three Fingered JACK has been lately removed from Saint David, to the Jail in this town; and that directions have been given, some time since, to deliver her and the other negroes, taken by the Maroons, to be dealt with as the law directs.[2]

The punishment for participating in robbery would have been death. Simple desertion would have been punished with flogging and other forms of corporal punishment, and, if the slave were a repeat offender, by resale or transportation. The same issue and subsequent ones carry the royal proclamation authorized by the Jamaican Governor John Dalling (reproduced in the novel's

---

[1]   *Supplement to the Royal Gazette* Vol. II No. 84 (25 November 1780–2 December 1780) 698.
[2]   *Supplement to the Royal Gazette* Vol. II No. 87 (16 December 1780–23 December 1780) 747.

last letter) offering a bounty of 100 (raised to 300) pounds for Jack's capture or execution and full manumission for the killer if he happened to be enslaved. The conclusion to the incident is reported more than a month later:

> We have the pleasure to inform the public, of the death of that daring freebooter Three Fingered Jack.—He was surprised on Saturday last, by a Maroon Negro named John Reeder, and six others, near the summit of Mount Libanus, being alone and armed with two musquets and a cutlass.—The party came upon him so suddenly, that he had only time to seize the cutlass, with which he desperately defended himself, refusing all submission, till having received three bullets in his body and covered with wounds, he threw himself about forty feet down a precipice, and was followed by Reeder, who soon overpowered him, and severed his head and arm from the body, which were brought to this town on Thursday last.—Reeder and another Maroon were wounded in the conflict.—The intrepidity of Reeder, in particular, and the behaviour of his associates in general, justly entitle them to the reward offered by the public.[1]

According to some sources, the Maroon bounty-hunters were joined by hundreds of their fellows, blowing conchs and celebrating Jack's demise. Accompanied by a large party, the bounty hunters took Jack's body parts (preserved in a pail of rum for identification) along with them on their trip to Kingston and then to Spanishtown to claim the bounty. If government records are to be believed, Jack's killer was exceptionally long lived, as he was still being paid the pension he was awarded as late as 1840, nearly sixty years after the event.[2]

Through the raw material of journalistic reportage, we can discern the rudiments of an episode often violently repeated in the eighteenth-century Caribbean. The first and second reports sound an alarm about a collective threat to the law and order of slave society; the third acknowledges the successful dispersal and

---

[1]  *Supplement to the Royal Gazette* Vol. III No. 93 (27 January 1781–3 February 1781) 79.
[2]  See the records of *Revenue and Expenditure*; also cited in Clinton V. Black, *Tales of Old Jamaica* (London: Collins, 1966) 119.

apprehension of the rebels by police action; and the fourth achieves closure by announcing the death of Three-fingered Jack and praising the intrepidity of his killers. The story of Jack's individual heroism and failure is founded on the suppression of a more complex story, of collective rebellion by many participants whose identities remain unknown, and whose fates were likely violent death, dismemberment, other forms of corporal punishment, or transportation to other islands.

The next published account of Three-fingered Jack's rebellion comes almost twenty years later, in Benjamin Moseley's *A Treatise on Sugar* (see Appendix A). However, by this point, the emphasis has shifted from law and order to obeah. Moseley focuses more prominently on the materials recovered from Three-fingered Jack that demonstrate his identity as a practitioner of obeah, rather than on his political objectives. In contrast to the newspaper reports, Moseley's detailed inventory informs us that Three-fingered Jack's paraphernalia consisted of:

> the end of a goat's horn, filled with a compound of grave dirt, ashes, the blood of a black cat, and human fat; all mixed into a kind of paste. A black cat's foot, a dried toad, a pig's tail, a flip of parchment of kid's skin, with characters marked in blood on it, were also in his *Obian* bag. These, with a keen sabre, and two guns, like *Robinson Crusoe*, were all his OBI.[1]

Moseley's account of Jack's final moments also mocks the obeah elements, describing the failure of his imputed magical abilities and the triumph of his humbler adversaries through raw violence. The context of slave rebellion is downplayed in Moseley's account, which instead depicts Jack as a formidable sorcerer and bandit. At the same time, the long description of obeah exoticizes Jack's power and characterizes it as resulting largely from the credulity of his followers. In contrast, the newspaper accounts in 1780–81 emphasize the immediate threat to civil order, but do not mention Jack's powers of obeah. These complementary omissions are significant, in that they tell a larger

---

[1] Benjamin Moseley, *A Treatise on Sugar* (London, 1799) 173–74. See appendix A, 164.

story about the displacement of the political repercussions of Jack's challenge into the vague threat of obeah as religious practice. Like other writers on obeah, Moseley exoticizes the existence of secret knowledge and its esoteric practitioners, even as he dismisses the practice as a failed primitive belief in the efficacy of magic. Often dismissed as a fraudulent practice, obeah is nonetheless the cause of great anxiety in colonial writing because of the deleterious psychological effects (including disease and death) that it produces on its credulous victims. This focus on a mysterious religious practice shifts attention away from the political intentions and actions of slave rebels.

Besides Moseley's account, published the year before the novel, William Earle Junior might also have had independent sources for the story. The mock-epistolary structure of the novel, subtitled *"in a series of letters from a resident in Jamaica to his friend in England,"* suggests the possibility of first-hand experience, a second-hand Caribbean native informant, or a perusal of the sources cited in Earle's extensive footnotes. Is it possible that Earle, who was the son of a Piccadilly bookseller and a mere nineteen years old when the novel was published, might have made a quick trip out to Jamaica earlier as an apprentice, perhaps in the manner of the novel's William Sebald, Captain Harrop's cousin and bonded apprentice in the novel? Sebald's sentimental views and romantic attachments, expressed alongside an inability to affect the outcome of the narrative, might very well have reflected Earle's brief experiences in Jamaica, if he was indeed there—or at the very least it expresses a fantasy concerning such a trip. Whatever Earle's source of information, it was not very reliable. There is frequent inaccuracy in the description of Jamaican life and topography: the plantation of Amri's master Mornton could not have been in Maroons Town, as that was free of white-owned land; there are no savannahs around it as described; if Quashee was from Maroons Town, he would already be free and not need to hunt Jack to win his freedom; the ability of Jack to traverse vast distances in a single night is not credible and reveals ignorance of the local geography; and there is the odd mention of a priest performing last rites before Amri is to be burnt at the stake when there were no Catholic priests in

Jamaica and Anglican pastors in the colony were never referred to as priests.[1]

At some points in the final chapter, Earle's language echoes Moseley's account of Jack's death, although Earle's celebratory sympathies for Jack are clearly somewhat different from Moseley's laconic and debunking account. Some of Earle's representations are of a highly sentimental cast that situates the novel within its period and genre. The description of the betrayal of Jack's parents, Amri and Makro, into slavery by Captain Harrop after they had saved his life and nurtured him, resembles the plot of the famous sentimental tale of "Yarico and Inkle" that saw so many versions in the eighteenth century.[2] Jack's Caribbean literary antecedents also refer back to well-known eighteenth-century characters such as Aphra Behn's *Oroonoko* (1688) and Thomas Southerne's play adapted from it. Oroonoko seems to be echoed in some of the speeches Earle attributes to his hero. Jack's male bonding with his fellow-warrior Mahali also echoes Oroonoko's friendship with Aboan. Moseley's comparison of Three-fingered Jack to the protagonist of *Robinson Crusoe* also applies to Earle's novel.

Several passing references in the advertisement and the novel suggest that Earle went beyond conventional literary sentimentalism and perhaps held some sneaking Jacobin sympathies.[3] Especially intriguing is the notice that Three-fingered Jack was

> one who, had he shone in a higher sphere, would have proved as bright a luminary as ever graced the Roman annals or ever

---

1  These are some of the inaccuracies spotted by J.J. Williams, *Psychic Phenomena of Jamaica* (New York: Dial, 1934) 124.

2  Yarico, an Amerindian native, gives succor to Thomas Inkle, a shipwrecked Englishman, hiding him in a cave from other members of her tribe. When Inkle is eventually rescued by a passing English ship, Yarico, who has become his lover, agrees to accompany him. Making his way to Barbados, the heartless Inkle sells the now pregnant Yarico into slavery for a high price. See Lawrence Marsden Price, *Inkle and Yarico Album* (Berkeley: U of California P, 1937); Peter Hulme, *Colonial Encounters: Europe and the Native Caribbean, 1492–1797* (London and New York: Methuen, 1986), and Frank Felsenstein, *English Trader, Indian Maid: Representing Gender, Race, and Slavery in the New World, An Inkle and Yarico Reader* (Baltimore: Johns Hopkins UP, 1999).

3  "Jacobin" is a term used to refer to individuals belonging to political clubs that encouraged radical beliefs for the time, such as the ideals of democracy and absolute equality fostered by the French Revolution.

boldly asserted the rights of a Briton. His cause was great and noble, for to private wrongs he added the liberty of his countrymen, and stood alone a bold and daring defender of the Rights of Man (73).

Expressed in 1800, following a decade of British negative reaction to the French Revolution and its Jacobin sympathizers, such sentiments in favor of slave revolt could well have been deemed seditious. After the Irish Rebellion of 1798, a second crackdown was underway in Britain on Jacobin organizations such as the London Corresponding Society. Since 22 August 1791, the ongoing revolt in Saint Domingue was also seen as having been sparked off by the French Revolution, and it is significant that even Moseley describes Three-fingered Jack as having "ascended above SPARTACUS"—the famous slave rebel of classical antiquity. Even after the threat of black slave rebellion and independent Haiti had been contained by the European imperial powers, the notoriously racist Thomas Carlyle was able to write in his *Chartism* (1839): "a sooty African *can* become a Toussaint L'Ouverture, a murderous Three-fingered Jack."[1] While a celebrated contemporary slave rebel such as Toussaint L'Ouverture came to mind to Carlyle much later, Earle may not have had him specifically in mind in 1800 (Toussaint became more widely known as the Governor of Saint-Domingue only in 1801). All the same, Toussaint's simplistic but fearful message to slave society in English is evocative for the context of Three-fingered Jack's slave rebellion—at least when viewed twenty years later. When reported in the newspapers, his message was said to be as follows: "Brothers and Friends. I am Toussaint L'Ouverture. My name is perhaps known to you. I have undertaken vengeance. I want Liberty and Equality to reign in Santo Domingo."[2] Is it possible that Earle was hinting at an egalitarian message of a similar kind regarding the oppressive institution of slavery in Jamaica and the British Caribbean?

[1] Thomas Carlyle, *Chartism* in *Selected Writings*, ed. Alan Shelstone (Harmondsworth: Penguin, 1986) 195.

[2] C.L.R. James, *The Black Jacobins: Toussaint L'Ouverture and the San Domingo Revolution* (London: Alison and Busby, 1980) 125.

### The Insurrectionary Legacy of Tacky's Rebellion of 1760

While there is the distinct possibility that the historical legend of Three-fingered Jack was refashioned in relation to the ongoing events of the 1790s in France and its colony of Saint Domingue, soon to become Haiti, one of its most significant precursors was Tacky's Rebellion in 1760 (see Appendix B). Obeah became the target of legal interdiction and morbid interest in Jamaica soon after the suppression of this rebellion that was organized by obeah-practitioners. According to reports, many of the slave rebels believed that magical powers gained by obeah practices would make them immune to the weaponry of the plantation-owners. Upon the suppression of the rebellion, a large number of obeah-men were executed. A further consequence was Act 24 Section 10, passed by the Jamaican Assembly on 13 December 1760, outlawing the meetings and practices of obeah, specifying death by burning at the stake as the sentence if convicted:

> Any Negro or other Slave, who shall pretend to any Supernatural Power, and be detected in making use of any Blood, Feathers, Parrots Beaks, Dogs Teeth, Alligators Teeth, Broken Bottles, Grave Dirt, Rum, Egg-Shells or any other Materials relative to the Practice of Obeah or Witchcraft, in Order to delude and impose on the Minds of others, shall upon Conviction thereof, before two Magistrates and three Freeholders, suffer Death or Transportation (Appendix A).[1]

Obeah-men had already been executed in Antigua in 1736,[2] but Tacky's Rebellion and the ensuing prohibitive legislation led to the denounciation of obeah as a dangerous religious practice with political implications. The Act never met with Royal Assent but it was an important conceptual origin for subsequent legislation.

---

[1] Act 24 of 1760, clause X, *Acts of Assembly* (1769) 1:55. See also John Lunan, *An Abstract of the Laws of Jamaica Relating to Slaves* (Spanishtown, Jamaica: Saint Jago de la Vega Gazette, 1819).

[2] David Barry Gaspar, *Bondmen and Rebels: A Study of Master-Slave Relations in Antigua With Implications for Colonial British America* (Baltimore: Johns Hopkins UP, 1985).

In his *History of Jamaica* published in 1774, Edward Long discusses obeah-men as "pretended conjurors" who poison their victims secretly even as they claim to prevail by supernatural powers ("conjuring" is indeed a parallel term to obeah throughout this time). According to Long, the introduction of the myal dance (an activity thought to "pull" or counter any obeah that had been "put" or "set") generated the belief in invulnerability to death and the white man. As Long puts it, "many a poor grimalkin has fallen a victim to this strange notion."[1] The objective of Tacky would have been an eventual "partition of the island into small principalities in the African mode to be distributed among their leaders and head men."[2] During the course of the suppression of the conspiracy on the island, according to Long, an old Koromantyn obeah-man was surprised at the rebellion's failure. "With others of his profession," he had "been a chief in counseling and instigating the credulous herd." The rebels were given a powder that ostensibly rendered them invulnerable, and they were also persuaded that Tacky, "their generalissimo in the woods ... caught all the bullets fired at him in his hand, and hurled them back with destruction to his foes." Long reports with satisfaction that "this old impostor was caught while he was tricked up with all his feathers, teeth, and other implements of magic, and in this attire suffered military execution by hanging."[3]

Long's account of the rebellion suggests another connection with obeah. The Koromantyns had "raised one Cubah, a female slave belonging to a Jewess, to the rank of royalty, and dubbed her *queen of Kingston.*" Long acidly follows this information with the news that "her majesty was seized, and ordered for transportation" but executed when found later on the island. Female leadership was not uncommon among Jamaican Maroons, whose obeah leader Nanny is also reputed to have caught bullets and defied weaponry.[4] These strong female figures in the resistance

---

[1]   Edward Long, *History of Jamaica*, 2 vols. (London, 1774) 2: 416, 420.
[2]   Long, *History of Jamaica* 2: 447.
[3]   Long, *History of Jamaica* 2: 451–52.
[4]   In governmental records, Nanny is referred to as "the Rebels Old Obeah Woman." See Jenny Sharpe, *Ghosts of Slavery: A Literary Archaeology of Black Women's Lives* (Minnesota: U of Minneapolis P, 2003) ch. 1.

to slavery suggest an analog for the important role played by Three-fingered Jack's mother, Amri, who instigates, organizes, and conceals Jack when necessary. Amri's trial and execution parallel the intriguing mention of the capture and impending execution of Jack's wife in the newspaper reports; Earle seems to have displaced this aspect of female leadership onto Amri, even as romantic considerations are removed from Jack altogether. Sexual motives are transferred to the novel's subplot, involving the love triangle among the whites: Harriet Mornton, William Sebald, and Captain Harrop.

Earle was not unique in his decision to cast slave rebels in a positive light. Even Long, the virulent racist, has a slightly positive account of Tacky who "was a young man of good stature, and well made; his countenance handsome, but rather of an effeminate than a manly cast." The historical Tacky was killed in hot pursuit by one of the Maroons, Lieutenant Davy, perhaps providing Earle with a historical precursor to Three-fingered Jack's final battle with Quashee. Tacky did not "appear to be a man of any extraordinary genius, and probably was chosen general, from his similitude in person to some favourite leader of their nation in Africa." In justification of this point, Long relates an anecdote that slaves on a particular plantation had fallen down and worshipped a bronze statue of a gladiator that reminded them of one of their princes. Long also reports occasional attempts at conspiracy between the Jews and the slave rebels.[1]

In general, colonial historians of rebellion mingled admiration with fear. Writing of the "fetishe or oath" that, when administered, leads to absolute fidelity and the waging of perpetual war against the enemy, Long is most suspicious of the obeah-men who are the "chief oracles in all weighty affairs, whether of peace, war, or the pursuit of revenge." The oath, once taken, is irrevocable and can be kept even after an interval of several years. This transgressive power is exacerbated by the attention given to the blood-quaffing conspiracies and secret rites of obeah that are remarked upon as preceding slave uprisings. His description hints at obeah's vampiric and cannibalistic associations:

---

[1] Long, *History of Jamaica* 2: 455, 457, 460.

When assembled for the purposes of conspiracy, the obeiah-man, after various ceremonies, draws a little blood from every one present; this is mixed in a bowl with gunpowder and grave dirt; the fetishe or oath is administered, by which they solemnly pledge themselves to inviolable secrecy, fidelity to their chiefs, and to wage perpetual war against their enemies; as a ratification of their sincerity, each person takes a sup of the mixture, and this finishes the solemn rite.[1]

An Antiguan source discussing the 1736 rebellion on that island says that the usual form of swearing was "by a mixture of Grave dirt in rum or beer, which they drank, holding their hand over a white dunghill cock."[2]

In his narrative, Long is unrelenting about the danger posed by the vengeful preoccupations of Koromantyns in particular, who are kept as slaves on plantations despite the danger they pose, alluded to in his remark that "nature does not instruct the farmer to yoke tigers in his team, or plough with hyaenas." His proffered solution is to "break that spirit of confederacy, which keeps these Negroes too closely associated with one another." He is also justifiably suspicious of "their *plays* [which] have always been their rendezvous for hatching plots" and wishes that all obeah-men, whenever apprehended, should be transported off the island.[3] Long's account had a formative influence, even as its implicit contradictions repeat themselves in many subsequent discussions of the role of obeah in slave rebellions of the British Caribbean. Wishing to demystify obeah as trickery and fraud, Long is nonetheless in great awe of obeah's ability to rally the slaves and generate fidelity and loyalty. He veers between ethnicizing it as a uniquely Koromantyn problem that can be solved by assimilation of this group with other slave groups, while wishing for instant transportation of any individual professing obeah,

---

[1] Long, *History of Jamaica*, 473. The corrigendum to the text replaces "solemn" with "horrid," which suggests an interesting displacement of qualification from reverence to transgression.

[2] From Tullidelph Letter Book, 15 January 1737; ctd. Gaspar, *Bondsmen and Rebels*, n.322.

[3] Long, *History of Jamaica* 2: 473–75.

or of anyone who is even dressed with some of the material arti-facts of the practice of obeah. Following in the line of Long's predictions of the mischief-making power of obeah practition-ers, Earle's Three-fingered Jack also learns his own obeah skills from a wrinkled practitioner, Bashra; furthermore, Jack's venge-ful mother, Amri, happens to be the daughter of a formidable obeah priest, Feruarue.

The depiction of Feruarue's death is beholden to Earle's back-ground reading. An important source for the circumstances of Tacky's Rebellion was Bryan Edwards' famous history of the West Indies (first published in 1793). Having occurred in 1760, the inci-dent has receded enough in time to be thought of in sentimental terms. Edwards' account of the rebellion begins by being subordi-nated to an admiring account of his uncle, Zachary Bayley, on whose Trinity plantation the rebellion had actually broken out. The rebellion, according to Edwards, emphasizes the magnanimous virtues of Bayley and his overseer Abraham Fletcher, whose government "of singular tenderness and humanity" led to his life being spared by the rebels "in respect to his virtues." Obeah elements also surface in the account, as the rebels are reported to have drunk the blood of the white servants they butchered after mixing it with rum. Edwards comments extensively on the courage and the appetite for revenge of the Koromantyns, who approach death with stoicism and equanimity after they are captured.

When read in relation to Edwards' account, Earle's novel emerges as a combination of unabashed revenge tragedy and sentimentalist morality tale, borrowing heavily from history but also from fiction and poetry. Reading Earle's novel suggests that he might have been brought up on a literary diet of Laurence Sterne and Henry Mackenzie, as well as copious amounts of weepy anti-abolitionist poetry; at the same time, he has clearly read around in Caribbeana—whether Edwards on history, Moseley and Grainger on sugar, Wright on botany, or Hort on diseases. At several points, the narrator of the letters, George Stanford, is too overwrought with emotion to be able to continue his tale, in the manner of the heroes of sentimental novels by Sterne or Mackenzie. While in Earle's case sentimen-talism is twinned with abolitionist sympathies, it could also be rendered compatible with proslavery ones, such as Maria Edgeworth's novella "The Grateful Negro" (see Appendix C). While abolitionists expressed moral repugnance toward slavery some sentimentalist proslavery enthusiasts took up paternalistic responsibilities.[1]

Both Earle and Edwards were writing when the British West Indies were in considerable ferment, facing internal revolt as well as intensified colonial competition at the commencement of the Napoleonic Wars. While the abolitionist Earle responded to his times with a novel exposing the tyranny and cruelty of slavery, the generalization of torture and inhumanity, as well as the dastardly duplicity of European slave-drivers such as Captain Harrop, Edwards (given his proslavery views) predictably focuses on accounts of Maroon inhumanity and bestiality.

### Obeah as Religious Practice: Confused Perceptions

While the first reference to obeah recorded by the Oxford English Dictionary is dated after Tacky's Rebellion, a recent investigation has concluded that the term "has greater antiquity elsewhere in the West Indies, and by the 1720s and 1730s it was well established in the lexicon of Barbadian English."[2] Much discussion of the etymology of the term "obeah" arose in the late eighteenth century after the practice was proscribed and given much greater attention by the West Indian colonists as a form of black magic. As a result, colonial observers felt a predilection to cite sources from African languages that suggested a close link between obeah and sorcery or witchcraft. The term *o-bayi-fó* meant "witch" or "vampire" in Twi, and to this idea some planters such as Edward Long, interrogated by the British Parliament in 1789, added a confusing and spurious etymology from Biblical sources. According to these white informants,

---

[1] For a more full-fledged account of proslavery sentimentalism, see George E. Boulukos, "Maria Edgeworth's 'Grateful Negro' and the Sentimental Argument for Slavery," *Eighteenth-Century Life* 23.1 (1999) 12–29.

[2] Jerome S. Handler and Kenneth M. Bilby, "On the Early Use and Origin of the Term 'Obeah' in Barbados and the Anglophone Caribbean," *Slavery and Abolition* 22.2 (August 2001) 88.

A Serpent, in the Egyptian Language, was called *Ob* or *Aub*—
Moses, in the Name of God, forbids the Israelites ever to enquire
of the Daemon *Ob*, which is translated in our Bible, Charmer,
or Wizard, *Divinator aut Sortilegus.*—The Woman at Endor is
called *Oub* or *Ob*, translated Pythonissa, and *Oubaious*…was the
Name of the Basilisk or Royal Serpent, Emblem of the Sun, and
an ancient oracular Deity of Africa (see Appendix A).

While it can be assumed that the origins traced to African
languages would be more believable than the eighteenth-century
resort to the Biblical hermeneutics of diabolism, there is still
considerable difference in the meaning of the term depending
on which African language is being cited. In addition to the
meaning of *o-bayi-fó* as sorcerer, Joseph Williams proposes the
more neutral Ashanti term, *obi okomfo*, or priest.[1] Jerome Handler
and Kenneth Bilby propose that malevolent meanings have
predominated because of the colonial vested interest in the
suppression of the practice, and instead they propose a different
etymology from Igbo and Ibibio of *dibia* or *di abia*, a derivation
that literally means "master of knowledge," and eventually signifies "doctor," "practitioner," or "herbalist." The term might then
have been transposed into Caribbean vernaculars with the
English morpheme *–man* as *abia-man* or *obeahman*.[2] Practitioners
in the Caribbean are often given the intriguing sobriquet of
"professors of obeah" by numerous sources. The practice's opponents were very well aware that those who professed obeah

---

[1] J.J. Williams, *Psychic Phenomena of Jamaica* 72; see also J.J. Williams, *Voodoos and Obeahs*
(New York: Dial, 1934).

[2] Jerome Handler and Kenneth Bilby, "On the Early Use and Origin of the Term
'Obeah,'" 91. See also Douglas Chambers, "'My Own Nation:' Igbo Exiles in the
Diaspora," Slavery and Abolition 18. 1 (1997) 74–76; and John Anenechukwu Umeh,
*After God is Dibia: Igbo Cosmology, Divination and Sacred Science in Nigeria* (London:
Karnak House, 1997). Other derivations culled from various sources and listed by
Handler and Bilby are: Nembe *obi* "sickness, disease;" Igbo *obi a* "this particular
mind;" Efik *ubio* "a charm put in the ground to cause sickness;" Edo *obi* "poison;"
Twi *abia* "a creeper used in making charms;" Ga *obeye* "entity within witches;" Akan
*abayide* "sorcerer;" KiKoongo *(o)b-bi* "evil;" and Awutu *obire* "charm" (fn. 14, p. 96).
In contrast, the etymology of myal is probably from Ewe or Hausa, from *maye* "evil"
*le* "to take hold of, or grasp." Ivor Morrish, *Obeah, Christ and Rastaman: Jamaica and
Its Religion* (Cambridge: James Clarke, 1982) 46.

possessed specialized knowledge and experience even if their detractors charged that their repertoire consisted mainly of cheap confidence tricks.

A search for the correct etymology in a specific African language might be a misguided hope for the certainty of cultural origin when the practice clearly underwent considerable dynamic change upon transplantation to the Caribbean. Enslaved Africans from several language groups refashioned their traditional resources into a new syncretic vocabulary that could encompass religious demands as well as medical and psychological needs. Multiple types of obeah might have already converged into an overlapping knowledge complex among enslaved Africans in the century before 1760, and the legal interdictions after Tacky's Rebellion, sensationalized it as sorcery. Hence, the preamble to the Act of 1760 warns,

> Whereas on many Estates and Plantations in this Island there are Slaves of Both Sexes commonly known by the name of obeah-men and obeah-women by whose Influence over the minds of their fellow Slaves through an Established Opinion of their being endued with Strange Preternatural Faculties many and great Dangers have arisen Destructive of the Peace and Welfare of this Island.[1]

In his novel, Earle cites extensively from the House of Commons Sessional Papers on "Obiah Practice" and "Obiah Trials" in his footnote to Amri's first use of the term "Obi-Man." The practice was perceived and defined by colonial discourse, primarily through the criminal cases brought against it. However, in Earle's text we also see the beginnings of a transition, whereby obeah is not just a political conspiracy, but also an anthropological curiosity. The Parliamentary depositions quoted almost verbatim by Earle focus principally on the many political suspicions the planters held about obeah. As suggested earlier, the passages by these opponents reveal a grudging respect for the knowledge of obeah practitioners alongside a predictable fear and revulsion:

---

[1]    J.J. Williams, *Psychic Phenomena of Jamaica* 78.

... the Professors of *Obi* are, and always were, Natives of Africa, and none other, and they have brought the Science with them from thence to Jamaica, where it is so universally practiced, that we believe there are few of the larger Estates possessing native Africans, which have not One or more of them. The oldest and most crafty are those who usually attract the greatest Devotion and Confidence, those whose hoary Heads, and somewhat peculiarly harsh and diabolic in their Aspect, together with some Skill in Plants of the medicinal and poisonous Species, have qualified them for successful Imposition upon the weak and credulous. The Negroes in general, whether Africans or Creoles, revere, consult, and abhor them; to these Oracles they resort, and with the most implicit Faith, upon all Occasions, whether for the Cure of Disorders, the obtaining Revenge for Injuries or Insults, the conciliating of Favour, the Discovery and Punishment of the Thief or the Adulterer, and the Prediction of future Events. The Trade which these Wretches carry on is extremely lucrative; they manufacture and sell their *Obies* adapted to different Cases and at different Prices. A Veil of Mystery is studiously thrown over their Incantations, to which the Midnight Hours are allotted, and every Precaution is taken to conceal them from the Knowledge and Discovery of the White People. The deluded Negroes, who thoroughly believe in their supernatural Power, become the willing Accomplices in this Concealment (see Appendix A).

Obeah becomes a term for resistant knowledge and indeed the wisdom that is an attribute of those who profess it. While slaves are dismissed as credulous victims of the practitioner's cunning, the obeahman is nonetheless credited with being able to manipulate and profit from a sophisticated market in his wares even while he maintains professional secrecy and stays out of the punitive clutches of the white establishment. Obeah is about demonstration of metaphysical and technological mastery as much as it is about the purported hoodwinking of the naïve and the gullible. Hence, the triumphal report of how subjecting obeahmen to torture gets one of them to admit surrender: "[O]n the other Obeah-Men, various Experiments were made with

Electrical Machines and Magic Lanthorns, which produced very little Effect; except on one who, after receiving many severe Shocks, acknowledged his Master's Obeah exceeded his own." Modern forms of torture, using electricity, image manipulation, and bright lights, are mechanisms of metaphysical and corporeal mastery that can be shown to supersede and exceed even the formidable powers of obeah.

John Stewart's 1823 anti-emancipationist tract about Jamaica also relies on this trope of technology as metaphysical mastery that displaces the threat of obeah:

> Negroes are astonished at the ingenuity of the Europeans, and there are some articles of their manufacture which appear quite unaccountable to them as watches, telescopes, looking-glasses, gunpowder, etc. The author once amused a party of negroes with the deceptions of a magic-lantern. They gazed with the utmost wonder and astonishment at the hideous figures conjured up by this optical machine, and were of opinion that nothing short of witchcraft could have produced such an instrument.[1]

As a source of personal power that is obscure, occluded, and otherwordly, obeah represents primitivism and animism, even as here we find that it can be converted, by technological demonstration, into a worship of Enlightenment, modern media techniques, and the white man. Obeah validates and normalizes that very thing which is meant to replace it, and technology can be justified as white magic. While sometimes obeah represents the desire for technology and the need for human beings to manipulate their environment and each other, the substitute for obeah offered by the colonists' culture will be Christianity, or white Obi. Stewart acknowledges as much: "so much do the negroes stand in awe of those obeah professors…that a negro under this infatuation can only be cured of his terrors by being made a Christian."[2]

---

[1] John Stewart, *A View of the Past and Present State of the Island of Jamaica* (Edinburgh, 1823) 258.

[2] Stewart, *A View of the Past and Present State of the Island of Jamaica* 278.

While Handler and Bilby (and earlier critics such as Edward Kamau Brathwaite)[1] take the route of reinterpreting obeah as beneficial to the enslaved black population where the whites saw it as malefic, another interpretation exposes the competitive relationship between the openly practiced myal dance and the more secretive rites of obeah. Joseph Williams speculates that myal was developed as a vehicle by way of which the Ashanti priest, or *okomfo*, transposed old religious rites and became the eponymous myal-man. Myalism was opposed to obeah, even as the *okomfo*, or myal-man, was an adversary to the *o-bayi-fó*, or sorcerer, who correspondingly became the obeahman. The complex Ashanti drumming ceremonies—involving extended collective dance rituals that venerated the all-powerful deity Accompong, other minor deities, and ancestral spirits—were strictly prohibited by Jamaican statute in 1717, 1760, and 1781. Obeah, according to this version, involved the placation of a more diabolical supernatural being, Sasabonsam, who could grant magical powers and fulfill destructive intentions.[2] Also maintaining this distinction between myal and obeah, Orlando Patterson argues that the myal-dance was invented defensively to counteract the nefarious effects already attributed to obeah. Unlike obeah, myal was "not an individual practice between practitioner and client, but was organized more as a kind of cult with a unique ritual dance."[3] If these sharp distinctions between two dueling versions of Ashanti religion as it was adapted to Caribbean circumstances are accurate—one beneficial, collective, and open-air, the other malefic, personalized, and underground—it is possible to conclude that the suppression of myal by the plantocracy para-

---

1  Edward Kamau Brathwaite, "The African Presence in Caribbean Literature," in Sidney Mintz, ed., *Slavery, Colonialism and Racism* (New York: Norton, 1974). Brathwaite divides the functions of the African religious complex into 1) worship 2) *rites de passage* 3) divination 4) healing 5) protection.

2  Joseph J. Williams, *Psychic Phenomena of Jamaica* 70–76. Talking drums were used to send messages back and forth between enslaved Africans on different plantations. The initial regulations enacted in May 1760, immediately after Tacky's Rebellion, still focus on severe penalties against drumming activities; it is only in December 1760 that obeah comes into legal purview. Williams further suggests that in Ashanti, the *okomfo* always maintained the upper hand, but in Jamaica the *obayifó* was made more powerful.

3  Orlando Patterson, *The Sociology of Slavery: An Analysis of the Origins, Development and Structure of Negro Slavery in Jamaica* (London: MacGibbon and Kee, 1967) 188–89.

doxically and inadvertently empowered its much more potent and subversive rival, obeah. These interpretations demonstrate that obeah and myal together formed a loosely related religious complex with shared assumptions but differing applications; as time went on the same practitioner might well have combined roles culled from the rival traditions.

Once Tacky's Rebellion brought the existence of obeah into the colonial consciousness, it continued to be debated and debunked throughout the eighteenth and nineteenth centuries. By the time we get to the final throes of slavery in the British Caribbean in 1827, Alexander Barclay's proslavery tract still defends the punishment of obeah with death. Disagreeing with an antislavery tract's dismissal of obeah as the "ground of a fanciful though fatal imputation on the poor slaves," Barclay suggests that the power obeah had over the superstitious imagination, combined with the use of poison, justified treating it as a capital offense given its insurrectionary potential. Barclay claims to have attended a trial of "a notorious obeah-man" who "had done great injury" by his practice of shadow-catching or manipulating duppies.[1] The most extensive Jamaican insurrection since Tacky's was the Christmas Rebellion of 1831 led by Samuel Sharpe, which caused the death of 207 slaves killed in action and the further execution of 500 slaves. This disaster gave a boost to the arguments that led to the emancipation just a few years later. By this point, Sharpe's Baptist Christianity played a much more prominent role in the 1831 revolt than did obeah, and many of the rebels swore on the Bible rather than take the "fetish-oath" that their counterparts had taken in 1760. The influence of Christianity, Barclay suggests, would ultimately extinguish obeah.

In 1790, the bankrupted planter William Beckford (not to be confused with his more famous namesake) picked up on Locke's discussion of the effect of "ghosts, giants, and enchanted castles" on children in the *Essay Concerning Human Understanding* to discuss the connection between superstition and impressionable minds he saw operating in belief-systems such as obeah. Beckford

---

[1]  Duppies are the ghost-doubles of dead individuals who haunt the living. Alexander Barclay, *A Practical View of the Present State of Slavery in the West Indies* (London, 1827) 190–91.

describes plantation blacks as possessing a childhood dread, reinforced with adult prejudices and passions; according to him, such is the condition of slaves without education.[1] In 1823, William Sells placed the credulity of obeah practitioners alongside various other forms of Western religious belief: "[I]s there more of folly or wickedness in the Obeah of the negroes, than in the witchery and wizardism lately practised in Wilshire to cure fits? Or in the miracles of Prince Hohenlohe, attested by Catholic dignitaries, and the charlatanism of quack doctors?"[2] Published in 1835, R.R. Madden's *A Twelve-Month's Residence in the West Indies* argues in secular modernist fashion: "insanity and supernatural inspiration are frequently combined, and consequently, knaves and lunatics (partially insane) are commonly the persons who play the part of santons and sorcerers." Madden, who was a doctor appointed as Special Justice to the Jamaican courts and who resigned his post after a year, claims that most of the hundreds of poor blacks who were executed for witchcraft in Jamaica were just weak in intellect: "it is evident to any medical man who reads these trials that, in the great majority of cases, the trumpery ingredients used in the practice of obeah were incapable of producing mischief, except on the imagination of the person intended to be obeahed."[3] Writing in 1843, James Phillippo, a Baptist missionary, exults over the fact that "obeism" is in decline, that myal-men have set up as medical men, and that Christianity has thousands of new converts among the recently emancipated slaves.[4]

As historians of Jamaican religion have noted, the resurgence of myalism from 1841–60 led to the subsequent synthesis of myal and Baptism (or Pentecostalism) in the form known as revivalism after the religious fervors of the Great Revival of 1860. An additional re-influence of obeah on revivalism ultimately led to the even newer religious syncretism of Pocomania (*Puk Kumina*) and ultimately, Shangoism (that also includes South Asian religious

---

1   William Beckford, *A Descriptive Account of the Island of Jamaica* (London, 1790) 210–11.
2   William Sells, *Remarks on the Condition of the Slaves in the Island of Jamaica* (London, 1823) 30.
3   R.R. Madden, *A Twelvemonth's Residence in the West Indies During the Transition From Slavery to Apprenticeship*, 2 vols. (Philadelphia, 1835) 2:76.
4   James M. Phillippo, *Jamaica: Its Past And Present State* (London, 1843) 247, 263.

elements). Obeah relied on the collocation of traditional pharmacological knowledges, an enslaved population in need of alternative forms of resistance to slavery, and a white plantocracy intent on identifying, criminalizing, and occasionally romanticizing exotic cultural resources. However, if after emancipation this multiform expression of the creative power of slaves disappears into other syncretic religions, there are also those who argue for the continuous tradition of obeah in Jamaica, where the obeahman continues to be "professor" or "knife-and-scissors man" and scholars of religion can refer to a "Revivalist-Pocomania-Obeah complex."[1]

Some of this varied background over the period helps to explain why the colonial discourse around obeah sounded hysterical and Manichaean at the outset, but turned exotic, primitivist, and condescending once its threat was past. The slaves represented extreme credulity and the obeah-practitioners great cunning; the slaves were genuine sufferers subject to a variety of incurable and serious diseases, and at the same time, depicted as dispositionally melancholic and hypochondriac shirkers. The plantation-owner's idea of fetishistic mystification arose from a denial of the material and pathogenic circumstances within which obeah could operate along with a heightened belief in the slave's psychosomatic susceptibility to suggestion. The 1789 Parliamentary Report was paradigmatic in its suggestion that once a black is led to believe that obeah has been set, "his terrified Imagination begins to work, [and] no Resource is left but in the superior Skill of some more eminent *Obiah-Man* of the Neighbourhood who may counteract the magical Operations of the other." If this superior resource is not found, "he presently falls into a Decline, under the incessant Horrour of impending Calamities. The slightest painful Sensation in the Head, the Bowels, or any other Part, any casual Loss or Hurt, confirms his Apprehensions, and he believes himself the devoted Victim of an invisible and irresistible Agency" (see Appendix A). At the same time, in other venues, the plantation-owner is forced to admit

---

[1]   Ivor Morrish, *Obeah, Christ and Rastaman: Jamaica and Its Religion* 43; George Eaton Simpson, *Religious Cults of the Caribbean: Trinidad, Jamaica, Haiti,* 3rd ed. (Rio Piedras, Puerto Rico: Institute of Caribbean Studies, U of Puerto Rico, 1980) 189; see also Edward Seaga, *Pocomania: Revival Cults in Jamaica* (Kingston: Institute of Jamaica, 1982).

the reality of slave mortality and disease as depredations caused by climate, pestilence, and rebellion rather than this overblown narrative of self-inflicted death by willful auto-suggestion. The medical aspects of obeah were often dismissed as irrelevant, and yet these aspects, if studied, can shed more light on the confused set of perceptions about obeah.

## Obeah as Medical Practice: the Hidden Story

While practices such as obeah and myal shot into prominence because of their crucial role in slave rebellions, they represent evidence of medical and religious activities among enslaved persons that were not merely reactive to slaveowners and their ideology. The stress on enslaved lives was never simply that of the edicts of slave society and the direct brutality of plantation owners and overseers. Physiological suffering, exacerbated by poor diet, overwork, and epidemics led to a battery of psychological responses and metaphysical worldviews. Emphasizing the medical contexts of obeah dispels the canard that its practitioners merely preyed on the credulity of their peers. The combination of pharmacological knowledge and religious belief within the intolerable social structure of slavery could have also led to the rise of obeah as an instance of what some anthropologists have called crisis cults.[1]

Richard B. Sheridan's systematic medical study of British Caribbean slave society reveals a contest between two medical cultures. The brutal conditions of plantation life, combined with malnutrition and lowered immunity, led to a disease-prone population among both the enslaved and the free. European-trained

---

[1]  Colonialism, in a wide variety of situations, has led to the creation of a number of new religious cults, whether shamanistic or messianic. The ghost dance religion of the Sioux studied by James Mooney, the famous South Sea cargo cults studied by F.E. Williams, and the *mau mau* religion of the Kikuyu are clearly analogical instances of religious syncretism forged by colonized peoples under the conditions of colonial rule. According to La Barre, "new projective sacred systems, or crisis cults" arise from "culture shock and the strains of acculturation." However, La Barre's suggestion that the religious "excludes the pragmatic, revisionist, secular responses" does not seem persuasive regarding obeah, as it is a combination of very rational medicine combined with mystical belief structures. Weston La Barre, "Materials for a History of Studies of Crisis Cults: A Bibliographic Essay," *Current Anthropology* 12.1 (Feb. 1971) 4, 11.

plantation doctors, operating under humoral, climactic, and miasmal theories of medicine, often shortened the lives of their patients even further with the usual panoply of now-discredited remedies such as bloodletting, purging, vomiting, blistering, and sweating. A large part of a doctor's income came from the sale of medicine, which at that time meant the prescription of poisonous substances such as mercury, antimony, and opium. Practiced alongside European medicine, African medical practices combined mystical beliefs with the prescription of herbal remedies and poisonous substances. Many of the African herbal remedies were occasionally effective, and, at worst, benignly ineffective, even while "heroic" medicine (Sheridan's ironic term for European remedial practices) more often than not hastened the death of already sick patients. African herbal remedies were widely available and also resorted to by members of the white population who noted their success in instances where "heroic" medicine had failed. Sheridan's investigation shows that African medical practices were a primary resource for the vast majority of the enslaved population in the British Caribbean amidst the lack of European-trained doctors and the general neglect of slaves' health by shortsighted plantation owners.[1]

The building blocks of obeah existed through the practices of herbalists or weed-women. These individuals applied their traditional knowledge in innovative and rational ways. Interestingly, these weed-women were often misidentified by white planters as witches, as for instance in the figure of Esther in Edgeworth's "The Grateful Negro" (see Appendix C). Despite the occasional successes of herbal medicine, the epidemiological challenges were great. The failure of herbalists, doctors, and priests to apply herbal medicines to natural diseases created an ascending ladder of metaphysical last resorts for enslaved people of African descent. The next level from the herbalists was that of the diviners who could establish the identity of the malefactor who had presumably cursed or harmed the sufferer in some material way. From the diviner onward, suspects could be cursed by setting obeah on them, or by ultimately being confronted by the African

---

[1]    Richard B. Sheridan, *Doctors and Slaves: A Medical and Demographic History of Slavery in the British West Indies, 1680–1834* (New York: Cambridge UP, 1985) 70 and *passim*.

ritual of the poison test, a toxicological shibboleth that worked randomly but was understood as killing only the guilty.

One of the areas where effective traditional knowledge existed among enslaved Africans involved the curing of the debilitating disease called the yaws (or frambesia). The yaws was prevalent in West Africa and was brought over to the West Indies with the Middle Passage. It consisted of three stages: a) an incubation period where a mother yaw or single bodily eruption is revealed on the patient; b) a secondary stage when the yaws spreads all over the body over the course of several weeks or months; and c) a tertiary stage when the yaws attacks cartilage and facial bones, and causes major disfigurement. Yaws was highly contagious and degenerative, but if treated well with adequate rest and nutrition, rarely fatal. If treated properly, yaws would subside after the second stage. The effects of yaws were milder when undergone before puberty, and therefore some parents deliberately infected their children to immunize them.

Because of the similarity of the symptoms of yaws with those of syphilis, the malady was misunderstood and probably contributed to the myth of African hypersexuality. The breakout of the yaws could appear very repulsive, as the affected parts of the body, including the hair, turned white, and there was also a considerable white discharge from the infected areas. While the spirochyte that causes yaws is very similar to that which causes syphilis (they look the same under the microscope), yaws was much more contagious and also not spread principally through sexual activity, as was syphilis.

Thomas Trapham's tract on Jamaican health, published in 1679, systematically confuses the yaws with syphilis and concludes that these "venereal affects [are] most plentiful among the animal Indians, and the cursed posterity of the naked *Cham* [Ham]." Trapham links yaws to "a seminal taint monstrously corrupting first the spermatick parts" and proceeds to pontificate that the "venery" of the slaves is "significantly punished as well as naturally inflicted in the polluted Yawes."[1] Hans Sloane's

---

[1]    Thomas Trapham, *A Discourse of the State of Health of the Island of Jamaica* (London, 1679) 113–15.

influential 1707 text, *A Voyage to Jamaica*, rejects a generalized contagion hypothesis regarding yaws, instead insisting, "it is mostly communicated to one another by Copulation."[1] In 1766, William Hillary was much more appreciative of the detailed indigenous herbal knowledge for cures of the yaws that Africans "keep as a Secret from the white People, but preserve among themselves by Tradition." All the same, Hillary concludes that the white effluvia that dries on the Yaws "renders the Patient a disagreeable loathsome Sight: And now the Disease is become very infectious to those who handle or co-habit with them."[2] Edward Long suggests that the enslaved Africans had "no taste but for women; gormondizing, and drinking to excess; no wish but to be idle."[3] However, he also grudgingly observes that the "wonderfully powerful" herbs that Africans use to cure diseases "have foiled the art of European surgeons at the factories." This admission is prefaced with a laconic rejoinder that "Brutes are botanists by instinct," and Long goes on to discuss an instance from an American travel narrative of monkeys having been observed to have behaved as intelligent herbalists might.[4]

According to some statistics, about one-sixth of the enslaved population at any one time in eighteenth-century Jamaica was

---

[1] "Though this Disease is thought to be propagated by ordinary Conversation, or trampling with the bare Feet on the Spittle of those affected with it, yet it is most certain, that it is mostly communicated to one another by Copulation, as some other contagious Diseases are." Hans Sloane, *A Voyage to the Islands Madera, Barbados, Nieves, S. Christophers and Jamaica* (London, 1707) cxxvii.

[2] William Hillary, *Observations on the Changes of the Air ...* (London, 1766) 341–42.

[3] Long, *History of Jamaica* 2: 353.

[4] Long, *History of Jamaica* 2: 380. "*Esquemeling* relates, that when he and his companions were amusing themselves at Costa Rica with shooting at monkies, if one of them happened to be wounded the rest flocked about him, and while some laid their paws upon the wound, to hinder the blood from issuing forth, others gathered moss from the trees (or rather probably some species of styptic *fungus*) and thrust into the orifice, by which means they stopped the effusion. At other times they gathered particular herbs, and chewing them in their mouth, applied them as a poultice; all which, says he,'caused in me great admiration, seeing such strange actions in those irrational creatures, which testified the fidelity and love they had for one another.'

From what source did these monkies derive their chirurgical skill and knowledge? From the same, no doubt, whence the Negroes received theirs—the hands of their Creator; who has impartially provided all animals with means conducive to their preservation." *History of Jamaica* 2: 381.

incapacitated and unable to work because of the outbreak of the yaws.[1] The highly contagious and repulsive characteristics of the yaws resulted in the construction of "hothouses" or hospitals on a remote part of the plantation, where patients were kept away from white supervision. Most European physicians, afraid of catching the disease, left the care of these patients to their black counterparts. The beneficial aspects of the herbal medical knowledge were linked to myal, and there is evidence that the black doctors used traditional resources as well.[2] These doctors were extremely successful at dispensing sarsaparilla and other effective herbal remedies. Predictably, many of these herbal practitioners also suffered the ravages of the disease. This fact goes some way toward explaining the frightening appearance of many of the professors of obeah, who might have represented an alternative thaumaturgy, and indeed a popular science that competed with those doctors working within the plantation system.[3] As Alan Bewell warns us, the history of treatments of diseases under slavery can only be understood through a relational and differential model of disease, and the cultural negotiations that take place around disease that "frame" it for our understanding. We need to understand the pathogenic contexts that render diseases intelligible to observers and also take into account the perspectives of the patients, as well as the herbalists and doctors who treated patients according to different theories and treatment protocols. Obeah has to be placed within this framework for a fuller understanding of its medical scope, rather than just the speculations about it as religious belief-system.[4]

---

1   Michael Craton, *Searching for the Invisible Man: Slavery and Plantation Life in Jamaica* (Cambridge: Harvard UP, 1978) 126.

2   Monica Schuler, "Myalism and the African Religious Tradition in Jamaica," in Margaret E. Crahan and Franklin W. Knight, eds., *Africa and the Caribbean: The Legacies of a Link* (Baltimore: Johns Hopkins UP, 1979) 65–79.

3   But Richard Sheridan says that J.F. Nembhard's *A Treatise on the Nature and Cure of the Yaws* was a standard work available on every plantation. See Sheridan, *Doctors and Slaves* 69.

4   See Alan Bewell, *Romanticism and Colonial Disease* (Baltimore: Johns Hopkins UP, 1999) 2; Philip D. Curtin, *Death By Migration: Europe's Encounter With the Tropical World in the Nineteenth Century* (Cambridge: Cambridge UP, 1989); and Charles E. Rosenberg and Janet Golden, *Framing Disease: Studies in Cultural History* (New Brunswick, NJ: Rutgers UP, 1992) xxi.

Moseley, who wrote extensively about Three-fingered Jack, also produced a medical tract on the yaws.[1] It is to Earle's credit that, on two separate occasions in the novel, he speculates that practitioners of obeah played a central role in curing outbreaks of the yaws. Earle's explanation of the "wrinkled and deformed" appearance of the obeah-practitioner, Bashra, suggests that the lack of a regular method of treating the yaws in the West-Indies resulted in individuals such as Bashra being expelled from a plantation and their consequently greater deformity as a result of the lack of treatment. However, those ostracized sufferers of the yaws who survived ended up becoming skilled and venerated medical practitioners:

> Bashra was one of those deserted negroes, who, affected by a disorder [the yaws] prevalent in the West-Indies, are compelled to fly from the plantation on which they are engaged, and seek a retreat in the woods, where, unassisted, they are left to die or recover, at the will of Providence. This disorder is said to communicate so rapidly, that one single affected slave may in one day distemper the whole plantation.
>
> Those are the beings, who, in their seclusion, most frequently practice Obi. The more they are deformed, the more they are venerated, and their charm credited as the strongest.

"Wrinkled and deformed" and with "shrivelled feet," Bashra is associated with repulsive creatures including snails, lizards, and vipers. This direct link between obeah-practitioners and the yaws enhances the prophylactic power ascribed to these survivors who might have also had a mastery of traditional and indigenous knowledge. The religious power given by the slaves to the obeah-man might have been the conventional one accorded to a priest or healer in traditional African societies, but given the colonial horror expressed around this disease, there also arises a transgressive power and projections of miraculous actions and superhuman survival where moments of health and happiness were few and far between.

---

[1]   Benjamin Moseley, *A Treatise on Sugar with Miscellaneous Medical Observations* (also titled *Medical Tracts*) in which *No. 3: On the Yaws* (London: G.G. Robinson, 1799, 1800).

## Obeah in Literature

The first sustained literary treatment of obeah can be found in the fourth book of James Grainger's West India georgic poem, *The Sugar-Cane*, published in 1764 (see Appendix C). Grainger, a medical doctor who also wrote a tract on West Indian diseases, focuses on obeah as instrumental in causing—and occasionally curing—a litany of psychosomatic diseases that he observes among the enslaved Africans.[1] The suffering black's "imaginary woes" are "no less deadly" unless an obeahman engages "to save the wretch by antidote or spell." Grainger portrays obeah as a form of quackery "which ignorance and fraud / Have render'd awful." He ridicules the obeah rituals involving the use of mortuary items, fetish objects, and muttered incantations. Grainger scoffs at the alleged pharmacological inefficacy of obeah even as he documents the great psychological hold such practices have on slaves. A confused mixture of awe and condescension, Grainger's attitude exoticizes obeah while dismissing it.

While Grainger's version of obeah arises in the context of a georgic catalog of the conditions that need to be taken into account by plantation owners to improve the lot of their slaves (and hence also their agricultural property), many literary descriptions of a more anxious nature followed the outbreak of the French and Haitian Revolutions. Edmund Burke had famously described the French Revolutionaries in 1790 as "a gang of Maroon slaves suddenly broke loose from the house of bondage and therefore to be pardoned for the abuse of liberty to which [they] were not accustomed and ill-fitted."[2] The Romantic fascination with the irrational forces behind human revolutionary energies, evident in Burke's comparison, resulted in a plethora of vague references to obeah in the 1790s. Obeah became all that was mysterious, powerful, and sublime. Alan Richardson has therefore argued that:

---

[1]  James Grainger, *An Essay on the more Common West-India Diseases and the Remedies which that Country itself Produces by a Physician in the West-Indies* (London, 1764).

[2]  Edmund Burke, *Reflections on the Revolution in France* in Paul Langford, ed., *The Writings and Speeches of Edmund Burke*, vol. 8 (Oxford: Clarendon, 1978) 87.

the romantic concern with obeah ... grows out of British anxieties regarding power: the fluctuations of imperial power, the
power of slaves to determine their own fate, the power of demo-
cratic movements in France, in England, and in the Caribbean.
At the same time, the literary portrayal of obeah illustrates the
power of representation to generate, direct, or exorcize such
anxieties. The representation of obeah, that is to say, functions in
this period, rather like the practice of obeah itself.[1]

While literary representations of obeah had a powerful ideolog-
ical function that mapped colonial anxieties, the scope of these
representations in Britain is more limited than the full cultural
reach of the practice, of which historians are still only able to
provide a partial picture. Could it be possible that the fear of the
obeah-man as a witch was a religious placeholder for the much
greater secular threat of political independence posed by
Toussaint L'Ouverture and others like him? Michel-Rolph
Trouillot suggests that Europeans, with their limiting assumptions about alternative political traditions and other races, simply
did not possess the conceptual framework to apprehend the
revolutionary potential of the rebellion underway in Saint-
Domingue. Perhaps these mistaken assumptions resulted in the
sensationalist emphasis on the obscure aspects of practices such
as voudou and obeah. Deflecting attention from the insurrectionary politics of slave rebellion, colonists could relegate obeah
to the cultural space of primitive religion even as they suggested
that slaves were in need of Christianity.[2]

A plethora of scattered literary references does not always make
for a coherent picture regarding the cultural value of a practice such
as obeah. Obeah is often signaled by a series of recognizable stereotypes and conventions, as can be seen in the well-known
pantomime version of *Three-fingered Jack*, written by John Fawcett,
and with a full musical score by Samuel Arnold, that premiered in
Colman's Little Theatre in Haymarket on 2 July 1800 (see

---

[1]  Alan Richardson, "Romantic Voodoo: Obeah and British Culture, 1797–1807,"
  *Studies in Romanticism* 32 (Spring 1993) 5.
[2]  Michel-Rolph Trouillot, "From Planters' Journals to Academia: The Haitian
  Revolution as Unthinkable History," *Journal of Caribbean History* 25.1–2 (1991) 81.

Appendix C). The well-known Shakespearean actor Charles Kemble originated the role of Jack Mansong in blackface (until an accident led to his being replaced by Jack Palmer). The pantomime was a runaway hit, moving subsequently to Drury Lane, and then to Covent Garden for the next few decades (with the spectacle enjoying an initial unbroken run of nine years). The success of this melodramatic version of *Obi*, though it was mostly performed in Britain, reflects what Jean D'Costa calls a "distinctiveness of Caribbean genres [which] appears most clearly in drama."[1] *Obi* as pantomime suggests a Creole blend of British and African genres, including song, carnival, mummery, morris dancing, melodrama, and the celebratory spectacle of jonkonnu (or John Canoe).[2] Fawcett's *Obi* was converted into an even more racist melodrama in the 1820s and enjoyed quite a run in the provincial theaters, even while Earle's novel enjoyed a history of redaction and republication in both Britain and the United States alongside penny dreadfuls about Robinson Crusoe, Robin Hood, Dick Turpin, and Jack Sheppard throughout the first half of the nineteenth century. Meanwhile, Fawcett's *Obi* was followed by a farcical and unsympathetic treatment of obeah in *Furibond, or Harlequin Negro* (1807). By this time, the threat of Caribbean-wide slave rebellion had been contained and the British were on the verge of assuming moral superiority for having abolished the trade in slaves even if emancipation was still a few decades away. After formal emancipation was decreed in 1833 and realized by 1838, Thomas Frost converted *Obi* into a lengthy and turgid romance in 1851.[3]

---

[1] Jean D'Costa, "Oral Literature, Formal Literature: The Formation of Genre in Eighteenth-Century Jamaica," *Eighteenth-Century Studies* 27.4 (Summer 1994) 664.

[2] The festive celebrations that marked jonkonnu were sometimes seen as a benign alternative to obeah. The invocational language of obeah that influenced its literary representations in popular drama also reflect the strong influence of "cuss-cuss" or "tracing," a creative linguistic activity that D'Costa has identified as one of the earliest Jamaican literary genres, that combines Scots "flyting," Ashanti ritual imprecations, and the Twi form called *kasakasa*. See D'Costa, "Oral Literature," 667.

[3] The full stage directions are represented in the version in *Duncombe's British Theatre Vol. 59* (1825) and the more racist melodramatic versions in *Oxberry's Weekly Budget of Plays Vol. 1* (1843). There is also a spoken version of *Obi* produced by William Henry Murray in 1830. For a useful introduction to Fawcett, see Jeffrey N. Cox, ed., *Slavery, Abolition and Emancipation Vol. 5: Drama* (London: Pickering and Chatto, 1999). See also Thomas Frost, *Obi* (London, 1851). There is also the intriguing mention of a

Fawcett's protagonist is less noble than Moseley's and Earle's, as Mansong is accused of attempting to take the honor and life of his former master's daughter, Rosa (the equivalent of Harriet Mornton). Mansong ties up Rosa and imprisons her in his cave, whereas Earle, like Moseley, insists that Jack "would do no harm to woman, child, or any defenceless being." Unlike Earle, who had separated out the romantic subplot and ignored Jack's sexuality, Fawcett combines romance and revenge, thereby summoning the specter of inter-racial sex and murder that goes back at least to Shakespeare's *Othello* and *Titus Andronicus*. Fawcett's Mansong is a Machiavel when compared to Earle's romance hero. The pantomime protagonist is a manipulator of men and events, possessed with a native cunning and also a cynical disbelief in the very obeah rituals that he deploys to convince his interlocutors. In contrast, there is a moment when Earle's Jack "places but little confidence in the virtues of his Obi" after his capture, but this faith is revived after his daredevil escape and his renewed consultations with the obeah practitioner, Bashra. Earle's Jack also rewards the widow of a white prison guard he had killed and turns indiscriminately murderous only after the execution of his mother, following which "his depredations were dreadful, and he exercised cruelty with all the savage fury of a beast of prey." Fawcett's cynical Mansong is also more than matched by an intrepid and enterprising Rosa who dresses up as a boy and joins the search party for him, and who can also escape captivity with the requisite astuteness in order to protect her honor, as is conventional for the English stage at this point.[1]

---

Jamaican encounter between the historical Three-fingered Jack and an American actor Mr. Herbert, who sang so well that Jack refused to rob him. Bernard also says that theatrical costumes were stolen during his visit to Jamaica and "an Obeah man in a blue coat with silver lace trimmings could strike terror to any heart and command the awe of an entire township of natives." See John Bernard, *Retrospections of America, 1797–1811* (New York: Harper and Brothers, 1887) 135–36. See also Richardson Wright, *Revels in Jamaica 1682–1838* (New York: Dodd, Mead and Co., 1937) 191–92.

[1] The Jack-Rosa subplot may be a projective inversion of the predatory activities of white owners and overseers who translated their social power into sexual license to exploit their female slaves. Such exploitation is copiously illustrated in Thomas Thistlewood's journal regarding his life in Jamaica. See Douglas Hall, *In Miserable Slavery: Thomas Thistlewood in Jamaica, 1750–86* (London: Macmillan, 1989).

Earle's passive Harriet, in contrast, nearly dies from her uncon-summated love for William Sebald and suffers a joyless marriage with Captain Harrop. Rather than Rosa, it is Captain Harrop himself, the enslaver of Jack's parents, who is kidnapped by Earle's Jack and carried to the mountain hideout, where he is chained but also made to perform various domestic tasks, including the deliciously ironical one of having to nurse Jack back to health. After Jack's apprehension and death, Captain Harrop is found chained and starved to death in his mountain hideout—perhaps an indirect reference to the fact that Jamaican caves were often found to be old burial sites for Caribs.[1] This torture and starva-tion of Harrop is to be understood quite literally as successful revenge for the torture and execution of obeah-men, a standard practice since the Antigua trials of 1736, and spectacularly since Tacky's Revolt of 1760. Fawcett's and Earle's depictions of Jack Mansong roughly correspond to the anti-Jacobin projections and pro-Jacobin aspirations regarding figures such as Toussaint L'Ouverture. While Fawcett's Jack also alludes to German specters such as *Das Brockengespenst* and the stereotypical moun-tain brigands of Gothic melodrama explored in Wordsworth's experimental play, *The Borderers*, Earle's Jack is a straightforward popular hero who takes his place alongside his English equiva-lents, such as Robin Hood, Dick Turpin, and Jack Sheppard.[2]

Even more negative in its view of obeah-practicing maroons is Charlotte Smith's "The Story of Henrietta" in *Letters of A Solitary Wanderer*, also published, like Earle's and Fawcett's texts, in 1800. The luckless Henrietta, the daughter of a cruel planta-tion-owner, falls into the hands of Amponah, a slave who loves her, and escaping him, is captured by "savages, always terrible in their passions, and in whom the fierce inclination for European women was now likely to be exalted by the desire of revenge on

---

[1]  Sloane, *Voyage to … Jamaica* xlviii; Beckford, *Descriptive Account of the Island of Jamaica* 248.

[2]  Richardson sees Fawcett's Jack as a black Iago or anti-Jacobin version of a black Jacobin; to this portrait the much more positive depiction by Earle should be compared. See Alan Richardson, "Romantic Voodoo," 18–19. For the German suggestion, see Charles J. Rzepka, "Thomas De Quincey's Three-Fingered Jack: The West Indian Origins of the 'Dark Interpreter,'" *European Romantic Review* 8.2 (Spring 1997) 123, 133fn24.

a man so detested as [her] father." She also encounters "Obi women employed on their spells [who] discovered that some great misfortune was about to happen to [her]." While the Maroon general wishes to appropriate Henrietta sexually and install her as one of his wives, she escapes with the collusion of his other wives who do not wish to compete for their husband's favors with a fair-skinned rival. Henrietta eventually reunites safely with her lover Denbigh.[1]

This heightened literary presence of obeah in the late 1790s is no accident, especially when it is seen as a literary response to the voudou-inspired uprising of the slaves of Saint-Domingue in 1791. Unlike obeah, which kept its distance from Christianity and was derived from the Ashanti, Igbo, and Fanti sources originating in what is territorially present-day Ghana, voudou was derived from Fon and Yoruba elements originating from Benin, Dahomey, and the Bight of Biafra, and fully syncretized with Catholicism upon introduction to the Caribbean.[2] These important distinctions are sometimes ignored or conflated in the literary representations. While the literary representations of obeah in the Romantic period recuperate the crucial link between obeah practices and slave rebellion, they do so in order to scapegoat obeah into a dangerous and mystifying belief system that victimized credulous slaves into suicidal forms of behavior.[3] Identified as an African, rather than a New World religion, obeah was portrayed by authors such as Maria Edgeworth to be the obverse of Enlightenment.

Edgeworth's depiction of obeah in *Belinda* and "The Grateful Negro" is within the context of paternalistic and sentimentalist proslavery reformism. The use of obeah in *Belinda* is intended as

---

[1]  Charlotte Smith, *Letters of A Solitary Wanderer* (London, 1800) 114, 297, 303.

[2]  Roger Bastide describes several kinds of syncretism. There is the morphological type, involving the creation of a religious mosaic and the juxtaposition of artifacts; there is the institutional type, involving the reconciliation of liturgies and calendars; and there is the correspondence type involving the mythical and symbolic similarity of deities. See Roger Bastide, *African Civilizations in the New World*, trans. Peter Green (London: G. Hurst and Co., 1971). See also Margarite Fernández Olmos and Lizabeth Paravisini-Gebert, eds., *Sacred Possessions: Vodou, Santería, Obeah and the Caribbean* (New Brunswick, NJ: Rutgers UP, 1997).

[3]  Several of the plantation-owners testifying in 1789 claim to have lost many slaves to obeah-related deaths (see Appendix A).

comic relief demonstrating the credulity of Mr.Vincent's manservant Juba, who is terrorized by the Mary Wollstonecraft look-alike Harriot Freke and then subsequently demystified by a solicitous Belinda. The obeah plot in Edgeworth's short fiction, "The Grateful Negro" (see Appendix C) is more extensive, and intended as a didactic warning to the story's intended working-class audience regarding the recourse that slaves would have to indigenous cultural resources when rebelling because of ill-treatment by cruel planters.

Caesar, the "grateful Negro" of Edgeworth's title, exposes the obeah-inspired plot involving his fellow-slaves Hector and Esther, and helps vindicate the paternalistic slave-owning practices of the "good" master Edwards, named in tribute to the Caribbean historian Bryan Edwards. Caesar's switch of loyalty from his obeah-practicing fellow-slaves is motivated by his gratitude toward Edwards, his new master, who bought him to keep him from being separated from his wife and sent to Mexico to pay his previous owner's debts. Caesar's gratitude triumphs over all previous obligations and all desires for revenge against slaveowners and overseers. By didactically representing this conversion of Caesar's sentiments by trust (one of the key scenes in the short story being that of Caesar's master trusting his slave with the use of a sharp knife in his presence), Edgeworth also suggests that this new trust takes precedence over earlier confidences that Caesar was keeping about the impending slave rebellion planned by Hector (who bears some resemblance to Jack Mansong in his Koromantyn emphasis on revenge as a virtue). The rebellion, however, devastates the "bad" slave-owner's plantation even as the "good" one's properties are spared by his eloquence and humane treatment of slaves.

Edgeworth's narrative effort around obeah manages to remove enslaved persons from the sphere of their political insurgency and protest and instead assimilates them to the sphere of their subjection to sentimental and moral education by benign planters. Slave psychology is parcelled between the stereotypes of Koromantyns such as the rebellious Hector and Eboes [Igbos] such as the docile Clara. According to Edgeworth's historical source, Bryan Edwards, Koromantyns possess a "firmness, both of body and mind; a ferociousness of disposition; but withal, activity, courage, and a stubbornness, or what an ancient Roman would have deemed an elevation, of soul, which prompts them to enterprizes of difficulty and danger; and enables them to meet death, in its most horrible shape, with fortitude or indifference." This description encapsulates the kind of mentality ascribed to obeah-practitioners and slave rebels who are political leaders. Their presumed victims, such as the credulous Clara, correspond to the type of the Eboe: "the great objection to the Eboes as slaves, is their constitutional timidity, and despondency of mind; which are so great as to occasion them very frequently to seek, in a voluntary death, a refuge from their own melancholy reflections." However, "if their confidence is once obtained, [Eboes] manifest a great fidelity, affection, and gratitude, as can reasonably be expected."[1]

The humanitarian treatment of slaves by farsighted planters such as Edgeworth's Edwards results in the continuation of an ameliorated slavery under the values of paternalism and sentimentalism, whereas the inhumane management techniques of Jefferies are responsible for the destruction of his fortunes by vengeful slaves, and pose a general threat to the survival of slavery as an institution. The point of Edgeworth's story is to suggest that planters who express charity toward their slaves and inculcate them into feelings of gratitude—in other words, the practice of Christianity—is a preferable alternative to planters who neglect their slaves and thereby allow sorcery, revenge, and armed insurrection—or the practice of obeah—to flourish. Christianity paradoxically enables the continuation of a kinder and gentler form of slavery, even as obeah can be blamed for the general conflagration of Caribbean landed property by slave insurrections.[2]

Matthew Lewis' discussion of obeah in *Journal of A West India Proprietor*, written in 1815–17 (see Appendix A), is in line with this running theme of the danger of obeah, but occurs at a moment when its political threat appears to be on the wane. Obeah frustrates Lewis's attempt to impose order and efficiency

---

[1]  Bryan Edwards, *The History, Civil and Commercial of the British West Indies Vol. 2* (London, 1793) 74, 89.

[2]  For a more extended discussion, see George E. Boulukos, "Maria Edgeworth's 'Grateful Negro' and the Sentimental Argument for Slavery." *Eighteenth-Century Life* 23.1 (1999) 12–29.

on his plantations. Lewis sees obeah as turning into a standard excuse for laziness, and shifting blame onto others. His slaves rely too much on quack remedies and spells, to the point that when he receives complaints about one of his slaves called Adam being an obeahman, he decides to

> make it a crime even so much as to mention the word Obeah on the estate; and that, if any negro from that time forward should be proved to have accused another of Obeahing him, or of telling another that he had been Obeahed, he should forfeit his share of the next present of salt-fish … and should never receive any favour from me in future.

Rather than sell or transport Adam, Lewis's pragmatic solution is to Christianize the accused and "see what effect 'white Obeah' will have in removing the terrors of this professor of the black." Adam's christening is celebrated just as Lewis is about to leave for England.

Lewis represents obeah in several registers—the managerial (as above), but also in terms of the comic, the prophetic, and the gothic. Comedy dominates in his report of the existence of a bandit called Plato who was also "a professor of Obi." Plato is revealed to be a ladies' man and his "retreat in the mountains was as well furnished as the haram of Constantinople." His banditry is expended in satisfying the female desires for fripperies that arise within this harem, and at the same time he keeps wishing to add to his collection of females. Plato's weakness for women is matched only by his taste for rum, which eventually proves to be his undoing. When Plato is eventually captured, he predicts that "his death should be revenged by a storm, which would lay waste the whole island, that year" and also tells his gaoler "he had taken good care to Obeah him before his quitting the prison." Sure enough, after Plato's execution, Savannah-la-Mar had the most violent storm in its history, and meanwhile, the gaoler fell mysteriously sick and pined away to his death. For Lewis, this romantic mystery-making concerning Plato is supplemented by an account of the apprehension of an obeahman on his estate, caught with the standard "Obian bag" of fetishes. The obeahman was convicted and transported to the general satisfaction of "persons of all colours—white, black, and yellow." The consumerist aspect of obeah—also decried earlier by the Parliamentary depositions—comes to the fore in Lewis's comic account. By appearing to be a customized practice that plays off individual shortcomings and rivalries, obeah is discredited in the eyes of slaves as well as slave-owners because of what the Parliamentary Report called its "irresistible agency." Depositions come from all quarters concerning obeah practices, and the sale of medicines and charms is something that Lewis translates "in plain English" as "nothing else than rank poisons." Whether poison or cure, delusion or diabolism, obeah's irresolvable ambivalence is maintained when the episode ends performatively with Plato's prophecies coming true, even though Lewis began his account with skepticism. Savannah-la-Mar was destroyed by the combination of fire, flood, hurricane, and earthquake on 3 October, 1780. Lewis jovially attributes this significant event to Plato's agency.[1]

At the other end of the scale, Lewis's gothic poem, "The Isle of Devils," written on his voyage out, but placed between the accounts of the two voyages, makes full sensationalist use of terror, mystery, monstrosity, rape, and diabolism reminiscent of obeah practices and also his earlier gothic bestseller, *The Monk*. The poem rewrites the Caribbean romance of Shakespeare's *The Tempest* from the perspective of Irza, a monstrous character who loosely resembles Caliban. In a more demystificatory vein, Thomas Campbell's poem, *The Pleasures of Hope* (1799), references the flight of "Wild Obi" as the departure of "the evil spirit of the African" when confronted by the blinding light of Truth and Enlightenment reason. A similar comparison would lead a sarcastic Shelley to describe Wordsworth's conversion to the "white Obi" of Christianity in his preface to *Peter Bell the Third*. Obeah inspired a number of Romantics and their followers including Thomas De Quincey, Samuel Taylor Coleridge, William Wordsworth, William Shepherd, Walter Scott, Henry Wadsworth Longfellow, and Charles Baudelaire. Perhaps it even

---

[1]   There were six major hurricanes that hit Jamaica in the early 1780s, and Lewis could also be referring to any one of those.

played a role in Melville's decision to change the title of his classic novel from "Mocha Dick" to "Moby Dick."[1]

After emancipation, obeah's literary fortunes took the form of anthropological curiosity about folkloric rites (as in Sir Hesketh Bell's *Obeah: Witchcraft in the West Indies* or Zora Neale Hurston's *Tell My Horse: Voodoo and Life in Haiti and Jamaica*).[2] Obeah could be represented as a residual primitivism and a general turn to the irrational among the formerly enslaved population of African descent, even though these practitioners were still sought out secretly by whites. Jean Rhys's novels document this continuing underground status for a banned practice well into the twentieth century (for instance, *Wide Sargasso Sea*). However, Rhys references a somewhat confused mixture of obeah and kenbwa (quimbois) existing in her native island of Dominica obeah alongside Catholicism, which in that context was more receptive of obeah than British Protestantism (even in the manner that Catholicism was much more receptive of voudou in Haiti). More recently, Kenneth Ramchand dismisses "obeah and cult manifestations" in the West Indian novel as being "associated with socially depressed characters."[3] But it is worth asking if a longer and more complex history of the reception of African religious practices is being repressed in literary culture under symptoms of the melancholic lack of assimilation to more Europeanized mainstream values. From the beginning, obeah was devalued as the sign of racial recidivism to African practices. It is hence ironic that the earlier charges of witchcraft, magic, and fetishistic mistakes of agency can, in the twentieth century, be imputed to the mere subjective and psychological inadequacy of pathological individuals.

---

[1]   Thomas Campbell, *The Pleasures of Hope* (Edinburgh: Mundell and Son, 1799) 27, 77; see also Alan Richardson, "Romantic Voodoo;" Charles J. Rzepka, "Thomas De Quincey's Three-Fingered Jack;" and Helen P. Trimpi, "Demonology and Witchcraft in Moby-Dick," *Journal of the History of Ideas* 30.4: 558–62.

[2]   Sir Hesketh Bell, *Obeah: Witchcraft in the West Indies* (1889; Westport, CT: Negro Universities P, 1970); Zora Neale Hurston, *Tell My Horse: Voodoo and Life in Haiti and Jamaica* (New York: Perennial Library, 1990).

[3]   Kenneth Ramchand, *The West Indian Novel And Its Background* (London: Heinemann, 1970, 1983) 123.

## Conclusion

Through Earle's novel and the rich context around it that this introduction and the appendices point toward, we can see how obeah became a rich repository of the anxieties and projections by the slaveowners and British cultural discourse about the Caribbean at large. At the same time, the category leads us directly to considering the acts of resistance by enslaved Africans through religious, medical, cultural, and political forms of association. Looked at from one perspective, the focus on obeah is symptomatic of the larger problem of planter absenteeism in the Caribbean, a phenomenon that, according to some scholars, created a void at the apex of the colonial slaveholding structure.[1] As an inverted and compensatory mirror image of this absenteeism, obeah symmetrically alleges the presence of an orchestrating native intelligence posed as a threat to the indifferent or absent planter. An inordinate excess of agency is therefore ascribed to this ill-defined but much feared category of obeah. In the post-emancipation period, however, obeah is relegated to the status of an anthropological curiosity, as the cultural residue of exotic beliefs and practices no longer presented a political threat. The shifting status of obeah makes it function as a test case for understanding the manner in which fissures inhabit colonialist literary texts, and how the deepest processes of making meaning can connect the colonial archive with the literary text. During

---

[1]  One such estimate in 1835 suggests that 70–80% of Jamaican plantations were managed by attorneys and surrogates, but this is because absenteeism grew very quickly by the time of emancipation. Bernard Martin, *Jamaica As It Was, As It Is, And As It May Be* (London, 1835). However, allegations of absenteeism could also be misconstrued, as the phenomenon did not always lead to the additional abuses it has been blamed for. There were different kinds of absenteeism—local, temporary, and permanent—and absentees (such as Matthew Lewis) were sometimes in the forefront of humanitarianism and innovation. See Frank W. Pitman, "The West Indian Absentee Planter as a British Colonial Type," *American Historical Association Pacific Coast Branch Proceedings* (1927) 113–27; Lowell J. Ragatz, "Absentee Landlordism in the British Caribbean, 1750–1833," *Agricultural History* 5 (1931) 7–24; Orlando Patterson, *The Sociology of Slavery* 33; and Douglas Hall, "Absentee-Proprietorship in the British West Indies to about 1850," *Jamaican Historical Review* 4 (1964) 15–35. For a judicious assessment of the complexity of absenteeism, see Philip Morgan, *The Early Caribbean* (Omohundro Institute for Early American History and Culture, forthcoming 2006).

most of the period of slavery, obeah was an utterly confused category in the life of the slaves and the slaveowners, elevated to secret religion or dismissed as ultimate delusion; meanwhile, within the context of plantation epidemics, the practice of myal-men reigned supreme as popular medicine and was also seen as a magical intervention or counter-obeah. As resistance mechanisms, both obeah and myal became the sign of rebellious agency, and the proof of the politics of despair at the heart of much slave rebellion. Obeah provides the perfect evidence for an Enlightenment discourse of the denunciation of fetishism that exposes the mistakes of agency made by slaves and slaveowners, but at the same time, these religious practices cannot just be dismissed as primitivism from a secular modern perspective, as obeah might have had the scientific upper hand over some of the European medical techniques of the time. Obeah, therefore, can be read variably as medicine, symptom, fetish, or trope, suggesting a full-blown information system that named pharmacological knowledge, political conspiracy, religious practice, or literary construction.

Rather than exoticize, reify, or dismiss obeah as past observers did, we might learn from reading the strangeness of obeah that arises from its role, not just as a representation, but as a literary substitute or deflective presentation that performs various processes—religious, political, medical, and cultural—otherwise harder to document, describe, and understand. From the colonialist denunciation of the so-called "professors of obeah," we can glean indications that help mount a critical reversal of sorts, one that professes obeah to be the very entry-point into those difficult questions of how enslaved persons resisted their domination through resort to varying mechanisms of resistance. Reading obeah afresh can pose for us new questions about beliefs and practices—as well as facts and fictions—of life under slavery. These questions merit further investigation, whether they pertain to acts of faith, demonstrations of science, or accusations of delusion among enslaved Africans.

William Earle's *Obi* manages to address seriously some of these aspects of obeah, even as other aspects elude the generic containment of sentimentalist abolitionism he provides for the phenomenon. The revenge tale the author promises is rendered anticlimactic by the ultimate defeat of Three-fingered Jack, whose body parts are successfully exchanged for the advertised bounty. However, the subtler point made by the novel is that even if Jack appeared to be a superhuman hero, he was ultimately a man who would succumb to the forces ranged against him. These forces supporting colonial slavery in the Caribbean were much more powerful than a single man or a particular rebellion. Skirting the line between hagiography and realist history, Earle allows for a celebration of obeah-inspired banditry and emphasizes the reality of frequent defeat suffered by slave rebels. At the same time, Jack's revenge succeeds in so far as Captain Harrop's death by starvation is portrayed as having been deserved. Earle's decision to opt for the genre of family romance rather than describe Jack more overtly as a precursor of full-fledged political rebellion produces definite limitations, as does his reduction of Jack's rebellious companions to a few depoliticized characters such as Amri, Bashra, and Mahali, and his silence respective to the historical evidence regarding Jack's wife and other fellow-rebels that were mentioned in the newspaper reports. Written before abolition and emancipation, Earle's text aims to provide us with an entertaining concoction of religion, politics, and romance. This novel should continue to intrigue literary scholars of the African diaspora as well as the more casual readers who may chance upon it.

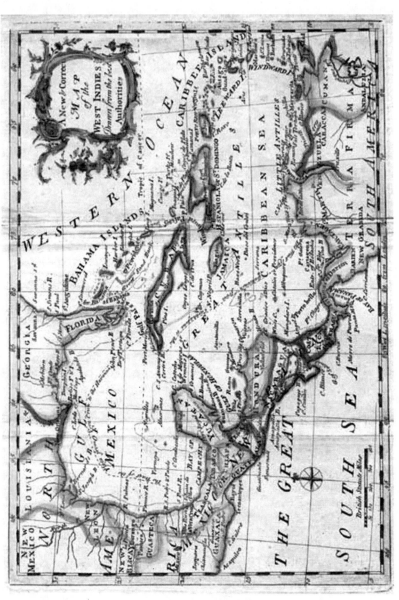

"A new and correct map of the West Indies drawn from the best authorities," John Gibson (1762). Reproduced by courtesy of Duke University Libraries.

# Timeline of Historical and Literary Events Surrounding New World Slavery, Abolitionism, and Obeah, 1492–1838

| Historical Events | Literary Events |
|---|---|
| 1450 Portugal establishes African-European slave trade. | |
| 1492 Columbus arrives in Caribbean. | |
| 1509 Jamaica becomes a Spanish colony. | |
| 1527 First African slaves brought to Brazil by the Portuguese. | |
| 1596 | Sir Walter Ralegh, *The Discoverie of the Large, Rich, and Bewtiful Empyre of Guiana*. A travel narrative of Ralegh's expedition. |
| 1610 | William Shakespeare, *The Tempest*. One aspect of the play is the relationship between an exiled Italian Duke and his slave, a native islander. |
| 1655 English navy captures Jamaica. | |
| 1657 | Richard Ligon, *A True and Exact History of the Island of Barbadoes*. |
| 1661 | Edmund Hickeringill, *Jamaica Viewed*. |
| 1670 Control of Jamaica formally transferred to England under the Treaty of Madrid. | |
| 1672 Establishment of the Foundation of the Royal African Company, which made Jamaica one of the biggest slave markets of the world. | |

| | |
|---|---|
| 1684 | Thomas Tryon, *Friendly Advice to the Gentlemen-Planters of the East and West Indies.* |
| 1688 | Aphra Behn, *Oroonoko.* One of the first fictional descriptions of a slave rebellion in the Caribbean. |
| 1698 | Edward Ward, *A Trip to Jamaica.* |
| 1709 | William Walker, *Victorious Love: a Tragedy.* |
| | Anonymous, *A Speech Made by a Black Guardaloupe.* |
| 1711 | Richard Steele, from *The Spectator,* no. 11. Popular account of a tragic love story between Inkle and Yarico, in which a young Indian maid is sold into slavery by her avaricious English suitor. |
| 1713 | Treaty of Utrecht signed between England and Spain, containing the secret "Asiento Clause," granting the British South Sea Company the rights to supply the Spanish colonies. |
| 1719 | Daniel Defoe, *Robinson Crusoe.* One of the most influential texts in world literature that features the theme of slavery in the Caribbean. |
| 1720 | William Pittis, *The Jamaica Lady: or, the Life of Bavia.* |
| 1729 | John Gay, *Polly.* Sequel to *The Beggar's Opera,* in which Macheath is transported to the West Indies and becomes a pirate. |
| 1730– 1739 | First Maroon wars in Jamaica. In 1739, Governor Trelawny signs a treaty with the leaders |

| | | |
|---|---|---|
| | of the Maroons recognizing their autonomy. | |
| 1735 | | Anonymous, "The Speech of Moses Bon Saam." An early abolitionist tract, it is unclear if it is a fabrication of a British abolitionist or the genuine speech of a Maroon leader. |
| 1736 | Slave revolt in Antigua. | Robert Robertson, *The Speech of Mr. John Talbot Campo-bell*. Response to "The Speech of Moses Bon Saam," it provides a sophisticated defense of slavery. |
| 1738 | | Frances Seymour, *The Story of Inkle and Yarico* and *An Epistle from Yarico to Inkle, After He had Left her in Slavery*. |
| 1740 | Discovery of longitude. | Charles Leslie, *A New and Exact Account of Jamaica*. |
| 1741–42 | | *The Fortunate Transport: or the Secret History of the Life and Adventures of the Celebrated Lady of the Gold Watch*. |
| 1751 | Vol. I of the French *Encyclopédie* published by Diderot and d'Alembert. | David Hume, *Enquiry Concerning the Principles of Morals*. |
| 1753 | British Museum chartered. | |
| 1754 | | Nathaniel Weekes, "Barbados, A Poem." |
| 1756 | Beginning of the Seven Years' War in Europe. In the Caribbean, the primary theater of conflict is Cuba, which the British win from the Spanish (but later return). A significant number of white settlers in Jamaica are involved in the attack on Jamaica.<br><br>William Pitt becomes Prime Minister. | |

| | | |
|---|---|---|
| 1757 | | Edmund Burke, *A Philosophical Inquiry into the Origin of Our Ideas of the Sublime and Beautiful.* |
| 1760 | Tacky's Rebellion in Jamaica. Tacky was widely thought of as an obeah practitioner, so this rebellion produced the first widespread awareness of the practice.<br><br>Jamaican Assembly passes a law outlawing obeah. | Laurence Sterne, *The Life and Opinions of Tristram Shandy, Gentleman* 2 vols. of 7. A heterodox clergyman, Sterne employs sentimentality to criticize slavery in later vols.. |
| 1763 | End of Seven Years' War marks British dominance of settler colonies and trade in the New World and India. | *The Peregrinations of Jeremy Grant, Esq; the West-Indian.* |
| 1764 | | James Grainger, *The Sugar-Cane.* Grainger's mock-epic poem refers to obeah as a kind of disease that afflicts slaves.<br><br>James Grainger, *Bryan and Pareene.* A ballad on West Indian life.<br><br>Samuel Foote, *The Patron.* |
| 1766 | | Sarah Scott, *The History of Sir George Ellison.* Scott's novel contains a description of plantation slavery. |
| 1767 | | John Singleton, *A Description of the West-Indies: A poem in four books.* |
| 1771 | | Richard Cumberland, *The West Indian: A Comedy.* |
| 1772 | Landmark case of Somerset v. Stewart, concerning an American slave who escaped in England. Lord Mansfield held that slavery could not be enforced in the English courts while the slave was in England. Understood by many as outlawing slavery in England *de facto*. | |

| | | |
|---|---|---|
| 1773 | | Peter Pindar, *Persian Love Elegies.* |
| 1774 | | Edward Long, *History of Jamaica.* Very influential racist account of Jamaican plantation society. |
| | | Francis Williams, *Carmen, or an Ode.* |
| | | Janet Schaw *Journal of a Lady of Quality* (1774–76). |
| 1775 | American War of Independence begins. | Edmund Burke, "Speech on Conciliation with America." |
| | | Samuel Johnson, *A Journey to the Western Islands.* |
| 1776 | Declaration of American Independence. | Adam Smith, *Wealth of Nations.* Edward Gibbon, *Decline and Fall of the Roman Empire.* |
| 1777 | | Henry Mackenzie, *Julia de Roubigné.* Anti-slavery text in the sentimentalist tradition. |
| 1778 | Scottish court case of Joseph Knight, an African purchased in Jamaica who petitioned for his freedom. In line with the Somerset decision, the Lords of Session declared in favor of Knight's petition. | |
| 1780 | Jamaica is terrorized by the slave bandit Jack Mansong, widely known as Three-fingered Jack. John Dalling, Governor of Jamaica, issues a Proclamation and offers a substantial reward for the head of Three-fingered Jack or members of his "gang." | |
| | Tremendous hurricane ravages Barbados, Saint Lucia, Martinique, Dominica, and Puerto Rico, killing well over 22,000 people. | |
| 1783 | Treaty of Versailles: Britain recognizes American independence. | |

| 1785 | Invention of the first cotton mill and Cartwright's power loom. | |
|---|---|---|
| 1786 | | Dorothy Kilner, *The Rotchfords.* An ethical primer that relates the consequences of the title family giving sanctuary to a runaway slave child. |
| | | Robert Burns, *Poems Chiefly in the Scottish Dialect.* |
| 1787 | Official start of abolitionist movement with the establishment of the Association for the Abolition of Slavery. | Anonymous, *Adventures of Jonathan Corncob.* Sometimes called the first American novel, it includes a satirical depiction of slavery in Barbados. |
| | | George Colman the Younger, *Inkle and Yarico: An Opera in Three Acts.* Comic opera based on an account first popularized in Richard Steele's 1711 *Spectator* piece. |
| 1789 | French Revolution begins. | Thomas Day, *The History of Sandford and Merton.* Best-selling work teaching the virtues of charity toward Africans. |
| | | William Blake, *Songs of Innocence.* Includes the poem "Black Boy" dealing with the themes of racism and Christian salvation. |
| 1790 | | William Beckford, *Remarks on the Situation of Negroes in Jamaica.* |
| | | William Beckford, *A Descriptive Account of the Island of Jamaica.* |
| | | Edmund Burke, *Reflections on the Revolution in France.* Burke describes the French Jacobins as a "gang of Maroon slaves, suddenly broke loose from the house of bondage." |

| | | |
|---|---|---|
| 1791 | Start of the Haitian revolution. Though Touissant L'Ouverture later becomes the best-known leader in this movement, a voudou priest named Boukman played a critical role in initiating early uprisings. | Thomas Paine, *The Rights of Man*. |
| 1792 | Denmark is the first European country to abolish the slave trade. | Robert Bage, *Man as He Is*. Includes the tragic story of a black servant and former slave whose wife commits suicide after being raped by their tyrannical master. |
| | | Anna Mackenzie, *Slavery, Or the Times*. MacKenzie's novel features a black hero who falls in love with an English woman. MacKenzie's novel is abolitionist, but she relies heavily on stereotypical representations of black subjects. |
| | | Mary Wollstonecraft, *Vindication of the Rights of Woman*. |
| 1793 | Louis XIV is executed. | Bryan Edwards, *History, Civil and Commercial, of the British Colonies in the West Indies*. Edwards' account is footnoted in Earle's novel. |
| | | William Godwin, *Political Justice*. |
| 1794 | Britain, Holland, and Prussia sign Treaty of Hague against France. | William Blake, *Songs of Experience*. |
| | The new French government abolishes slavery in St. Domingue, leading to cooperation between Toussaint L'Ouverture and the new French government. | |
| 1795 | Second Maroon War. The Jamaica Assembly transported many of the Maroons involved in the four-month struggle to Sierra Leone. | William Wordsworth begins "The Three Graves," described by Coleridge as inspired by Edwards' 1793 account. |
| 1796 | | Elizabeth Helme, *The Farmer of Inglewood Forest*. Features several |

benevolent female characters who manumit slaves whenever they can.

1797     William Shepherd, "The Negro Incantation," a poem referring to Tacky's Rebellion as described by Edwards, appears in *Monthly Magazine*.

Bryan Edwards, *A Historical Survey of the French Colony in the Island of St. Domingo*. Edwards' is an inflammatory account of the Haitian revolution, with particular emphasis on the Black Jacobins' treatment of white colonists.

1799     Benjamin Moseley, *Treatise on Sugar*. Contains an account of Three-fingered Jack.

Thomas Campbell, *The Pleasures of Hope*. Refers to obeah as "the evil spirit of the African."

1800     William Earle Jr., *Obi; or, the History of Three-fingered Jack: in a series of letters from a resident in Jamaica to his friend in England*.

John Fawcett, *Three-fingered Jack,* a pantomime, is performed in London for the first time. Though the plot of the pantomime is similar to that in Earle's novel (and both are derived from Moseley's narrative), there are some discrepancies.

Charlotte Smith, "The Story of Henrietta." A Gothic tale in which obeah plays a part.

| | | |
|---|---|---|
| 1801 | | Maria Edgeworth, *Belinda*. A novel with several references to obeah. |
| 1802 | Toussaint L'Ouverture is captured by French troops and sent to Fort de Joux prison in France, where he dies in 1803. | Maria Edgeworth, "The Grateful Negro," a short story set in Jamaica during a slave revolt. Edgeworth's short story is reprinted in 1804 in *Popular Tales*. |
| | The French reintroduce slavery. | Wordsworth writes "To Toussaint L'Ouverture," a sonnet lamenting reports of Toussaint's death. |
| 1803 | British ally with Haitian Revolutionaries in conflicts with the French. | |
| 1804 | British House of Commons votes to abolish Atlantic slave trade, but this is modified following the intervention of the pro-slavery lobby. | |
| | Saint-Domingue (Haiti) gains independence from French rule. | |
| 1807 | Great Britain abolishes Atlantic slave trade. | *A Description of Furibond; or, Harlequin Negro*, a pantomime figuring Jamaican magic, is performed in London. |
| 1809 | | James Montgomery, *The West Indies*. An abolitionist epic poem in which obeah plays a central part. |
| 1814 | | Jane Austen, *Mansfield Park*. A narrative set in England in which the primary source of the wealth which drives the plot is Sir Thomas Bertram's 'property' in Antigua. |
| 1815 | | Matthew Gregory Lewis begins keeping a journal of his experiences in Jamaica, published in 1834 as *Journal of a West India Proprietor*. |

| 1821 | | Mary Sherwood, *Dazee, or the Recaptured Slave*. Narrative set in Sierra Leone after the abolition of the slave trade. Deliverance from slavery is likened to Christian rebirth. |
| --- | --- | --- |
| 1826 | | Cynric Williams, *A Tour Through the Island of Jamaica*. Contains references to obeah. |
| 1833 | British Emancipation Proclamation decrees full emancipation for all slaves in the British Empire by 1838. | |
| 1835 | | R.R. Madden, *A Twelve Month's Residence in the West Indies*. |
| 1838 | Slavery in the British Empire formally comes to an end. | |

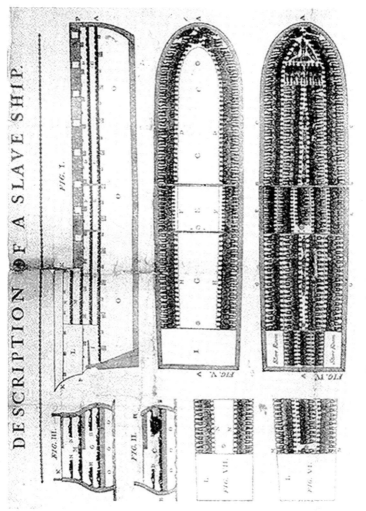

"Description of a Slave Ship," J. Phillips (1780).

# A Note on the Text

This edition is based on the British Library copy of the first edition published by Earle and Hemet in London in 1800. However, as the British Library copy is slightly damaged (the advertisement and frontispiece are missing and a couple of pages are torn at the edges resulting in the loss of text), the text has been reconstituted by consulting other copies at the University of Virginia and at the Institute for Commonwealth Studies, London. The same edition was also republished in Worcester, Massachusetts by Isaiah Thomas for B. and J. Homans in 1804.

There is a significant history of nineteenth-century republication and redaction of the text both in Britain and the United States. Often (though not always) these editions take the form of small chapbooks that reproduce summaristic chunks of text identifiable from the first edition, or from the account in Benjamin Moseley's *A Treatise on Sugar* (see Appendix A) sometimes accompanied with crude black-and-white or hand-colored woodcuts of Jack in costume, or his severed body parts. Sometimes these editions are individual publications for popular entertainment (for instance the 1825 edition by John Fairburn, *Wonderful Life and Adventures of Three-fingered Jack, the Terror of Jamaica!...Embellished with four coloured engravings*) or abolitionist propaganda (the undated *History and Adventures of Jack Mansong, the famous Negro Robber, and Terror of Jamaica* published at Otley by William Walker with a woodcut of Jack along with the Wedgwood motto, "Am I not a Man and a Brother?"). Other editions are found as items within series of pamphlets, juvenile books, or penny dreadfuls. As the pantomime version of *Obi* was also published in 1800, some of the editions attempt to synthesize both versions of the story, add further exploits, or provide a description of the drama or the lyrics of some of the best-known songs, duets, and choruses that were set to music by Samuel Arnold. Other than the various knock-offs of Moseley's, Earle's and Fawcett's versions, there is a somewhat different account authored also in 1800 by William Burdett, who claims to have lived on a Jamaican plantation. Burdett's version is entitled *Life and Exploits of Mansong, commonly called Three-finger'd Jack, the Terror of Jamaica. With a particular account of the Obi; Being the only true one of that celebrated and fascinating mischief, so prevalent in the West Indies.* Finally, there is a substantially longer novel on the topic, *Obi*, by Thomas Frost in 1851.

As spelling is inconsistent within the edition, it has been standardized to the most accepted form in 1800. Minor errors of typography and punctuation have been silently corrected.

Earle's original notes have been retained in the text and are identified by asterisks and daggers. Where necessary, editorial explanations of Earle's notes are included in square brackets immediately following the note.

# O B I;

OR, THE

# H I S T O R Y

OF

## *Three-fingered  Jack.*

### IN A SERIES OF LETTERS

FROM A RESIDENT IN JAMAICA TO HIS
FRIEND IN ENGLAND.

---

———————— Oh! ye who at your ease
Sip the blood-sweetened beverage! thoughts like these
Haply ye scorn: I thank thee, gracious God!
That I do feel upon my cheek the glow
Of indignation, when beneath the rod
A sable brother writhes in silent woe.

*Southey.*[1]

*Hear him!* ye Senates! hear this truth sublime,
HE WHO ALLOWS OPPRESSION SHARES THE CRIME.

*Darwin.*[2]

---

## London:

PRINTED FOR EARLE AND HEMET,
No. 47, Albemarle-ftreet, Piccadilly,

1800.

---

[1] From Sonnet III of *Poems Concerning the Slave Trade*, in *Poems By Robert Southey*, second ed. (Bristol, 1797) 56.

[2] From Erasmus Darwin, *The Botanic Garden; A Poem in Two Parts* (London, 1791) ll. 387–88 (in later editions ll. 449–50).

# ADVERTISEMENT.

I HAVE published these letters, which accidentally fell into my hands, with a view to commemorate the name of Jack, and place upon the list of heroes, one who, had he shone in a higher sphere, would have proved as bright a luminary as ever graced the Roman annals, or ever boldly asserted the rights of a Briton. His cause was great and noble, for to private wrongs he added the liberty of his countrymen, and stood alone a bold and daring defender of the Rights of Man. To him who shall applaud Jack through the varied scenes of his life; to him, whose heart shall sympathize in his misfortunes, who shall smile upon his deeds, at the same time he laments their cause, I dedicate the following pages.

W.E.J.[1]

---

[1] While Earle's full name appears to have been "William Earle, Junior," the designation "Junior" was used irregularly in subsequent republications of *Obi* in the nineteenth century.

# LETTER I.

DEAR CHARLES,

Jamaica.

A WHOLE week has your letter been lying open on my desk, ready for me to answer—a whole week have the above two words been written, as you may perceive by the difference in the shade of the ink and the cutting of my pen; for, three times has the dried standish[1] been replenished, and twenty times, at least, have I dipped into it, sometimes with a new pen, sometimes with a mended one—and still at this moment am I at a loss what to say to you in reply to your queries.

Now, you will think that, because I have written the above long sentence, my mind is wholly and exclusively engrossed by your business, and that I shall be able to go on in a regular steady way; but I tell you, Charles, it is no such thing; for, at the end of that very sentence, I stopped a full hour, unable to proceed—and now again do I stop short.

Try what I may, it will not do—but what is the matter? you will say. Jack!!! and his cursed three fingers!!!

I'll tell you what, Charles—I have just read your letter for the hundred and first time, and upon my soul, cannot see that the business it is about is of such great importance; so, with, or without your leave, I shall put off answering it, until I have eased myself of my insufferable burthen, by dispatching Jack, his three fingers and his Obi, and all that belongs to him; for, positively, I can think of nothing else.

And so it is with every body in the Island; go wherever I will, the name of Jack is perpetually buzzed in my ears. If I meet a friend in the street, it is no longer "How d'ye do?" but "Well, what news of Jack?" If any of my neighbours, calling his servant, says; "Jack, come here," I start and stare about, in expectation of seeing the three-fingered one make his appearance. Nay, there is

---

[1] A stand containing ink, pens, and other writing materials and accessories; an inkstand; also, an inkpot (*OED*).

not a *thing* called Jack, whether a smoke-jack,[1] a boot-jack,[2] or any other jack, but acts as a spell upon my senses and sets me on the fret at the bare mention of it. By heavens! it is too much, and I wish.....

Nay, I do not—I cannot find in my heart to form the same wish that most of the inhabitants here express every day. Jack is a noble fellow, and in spite of every cruel hard-hearted planter, I shall repeat the same to the last hour of my life. "Jack is a Negro," say they. "Jack is a MAN," say I.

—"He is a slave."

—"MAN cannot be a slave to MAN."

—"He is my property."

—"How did you acquire that property?"

—"By paying for it."

—"Paying! Paying whom?"

—"Him who brought him from Africa."

—"How did he get possession of him?"

—"He caught him there."

—"Caught! what? Like a wild beast?"

—"No, but he contrived means to convey him into his ship?"

—"Contrived! Then he brought him without his consent?"

—"Very likely."

—"And what is become of that robber?"

—"Robber! He is a very respectable man, who has left off trade, has married the daughter of a rich planter, and now lives very comfortably, after the fatigues of an industrious life."

—"What! Do they hang a poor hard-labouring man, who, driven by despair at the sight of his numerous family ready to starve for want of a bit of bread, takes advantage of a dark night, goes on the highway and frightens the traveller out of a few pieces of gold, and shall a daring ruffian, who is openly guilty of a crime more heinous in its nature and baneful in its effects, get respected by every body and pass his days in the peaceable enjoyment of riches acquired by such infamous means?"

---

[1]  An apparatus for turning a roasting-spit, fixed in a chimney and set in motion by the current of air passing up it (*OED*).

[2]  A contrivance for pulling off boots (*OED*).

—"I don't understand you; I never heard that the traffic[1] was infamous. Is it not authorised by all the nations of Europe, Asia and America? Have not regulations been made concerning it by all governments?"

—"Very true, but that does not make it more honorable. Prostitution is authorised, yes, for it is more than tolerated, by governments, many of which have also made regulations concerning it, but that does not make it less infamous."

—"Nay, you are going too far, and this is widely different."

—"Different!—By heavens! you will drive me mad."

And such, my dear Charles, is the daily altercation I have with the greatest part of the planters here, and what you have just read is a specimen of the various arguments brought on both sides of the question. As I know your sentiments upon the subject, I shall close it here and proceed to my narrative about three-fingered Jack, and as I have made it my business to collect every particular relative to him, I believe I shall have it in my power to give you a circumstantial account of all his actions. In fact, what I am now going to write is nothing more than a copy of what I had sometime ago begun to put into a regular story, out of several memoranda collected at different times. So, without lengthening this preamble, I thus begin:

Amri was a beautiful slave, the property of Mr. Mornton, of Maroons Town.[2] She was sanguinary in her temper; for, misfortune, or rather cruelty, had perverted a heart naturally inclined to virtue. She was torn from the arms of her husband, her family and friends, while in the may-day[3] of her life, from her native Africa.

She had vowed to curse the European race for ever; and had a son, in whose breast she never failed to nurture the baneful passion of revenge.

---

[1] With sinister or evil connotation: dealing or bargaining in something which should not be made the subject of trade, in this case slaves (*OED*).

[2] Maroons refers to a population of blacks, originally fugitive slaves, living in the mountains and forests of Surinam and the West Indies. The Maroons were very successful in establishing their own community to the extent that they had concluded treaties with the British and established a territorial jurisdiction in parts of the Jamaican mountains. While they were independent of the plantocracy, the terms of their truce also made them assist with the capture of slave rebels and runaways.

[3] Possibly in the sense of "prime of life."

She taught him to despise his groaning companions, complaining under their labor, meanly submitting to the christian whip, and then pusillanimously venting their griefs in half-suppressed sighs.

Jack had a soul, even in infancy, superior to such whining; he complained not of the daily labor heaped upon him, but of the tardiness of time.

Each night, when the grand luminator of the world hid his rays within the deep, he threw himself on his knees, and prayed to the great God of his country to ripen him to manhood, that he might shake off the yoke that pressed heavy upon him, and revenge the cause of his country and his parents. His youthful fiery soul led him to imagine himself the destroyer of all Europe; he saw in the warlike picture his fancy drew, the course he was to follow, and the transport of his heart was often visible by the uncommon hauteur of his manners. When assured of revenge, he would grin with a smile of malice, transparent on his cheek, at the overseer, while the merciless whip was lacerating his back.

He was of the most manly growth, nearly seven feet in height, and amazingly robust; bred up to hardihood, his limbs were well shapen and athletic; he could endure the most laborious toil, and would with ease perform the office of any two negroes within the plantation. His face was rather long; his eyes black and fierce; his nose was not like the generality of blacks, squat and flat, but rather aquiline,[1] and his skin remarkably clear. He discovered a great deal of expression in his countenance, and a very look of reproach from him would strike terror to his fellow-slaves. He was now two-and-twenty years of age, and every thing his fond but revengeful mother could wish him.

Returning from his labor to the small hovel, where he and his mother dwelt, after a heavy day of toil, he threw himself weary

---

[1] This passage is likely inspired by Aphra Behn's famed description in *Oroonoko: or the Royal Slave:* "His Face was not of that brown, rusty Black which most of that Nation are, but a perfect Ebony, or polish'd Jett. His Eyes were the most awful that cou'd be seen, and very piercing; the White of 'em being like Snow, as were his Teeth. His Nose was rising and *Roman*, instead of *African* and flat. His Mouth, the finest shap'd that cou'd be seen; far from those great turn'd Lips, which are so natural to the rest of the *Negroes*. The whole Proportion and Air of his Face was so noble, and exactly form'd, that, bating his Colour, there cou'd be nothing in Nature more beautiful, agreeable and handsome" (London, 1688) 33–34.

on the pallet of straw where he reposed. Amri arose, and clasped him in her arms.

"My son," cried she, "Now is the time arrived when you should contend for the rights of yourself and mother. Now is the time when you should revenge my cause. You are arrived to maturity, and, to inspire you to revenge my injuries, I will relate the misfortunes of my life."

Dear Charles, so much of the narrative was imparted to me by a negro, well acquainted with Amri, and I can assure you, for I have seen this three-fingered Jack, that he was every thing in soul and person requisite for the hero. Give me now a short pause. Sketch the man you would wish—a bold and daring fellow, ready to undertake any thing for the good of his country, inspired by a rooted revenge, on the strongest foundation villainy can fabricate, and Jack's the man to a point. I must break off. Adieu!

GEORGE STANFORD.


## LETTER II.

*The same to the same.*

DEAR CHARLES,

I RESUME my pen, and commence with the narrative of Amri. All impatience myself, I suspect you to feel as much. I set down her own words as near as memory can trace—mind that.

### MAKRO AND AMRI,

### AN

### *AFRICAN TALE.*

I am innocent of this blood, SEE YE to it.

"My son, your country borders on the Gambia,[1] and its inhabitants are distinguished from all others by the name of Feloops.[2] Remember that the spirit of our nation is, Never to forget an injury, but to ripen in our breasts the seeds of hate for those who betray us. We are to transmit our quarrels to our posterity, and it is incumbent on a son, from a sense of filial obligation, to resent the injuries done to his parents.

"You are the only son of my womb, the only offspring of the loins of Makro, and you shall be his avenger.

"Feruarue, the beloved of his country, lived in a hut, at whose base murmured the waters of the Gambia. I was his only daughter, and his sole delight. Makro's parents were deceased, and his hut adjoined ours. He was but two years my elder; I loved him, and he was the great friend of my father, so that our nuptials were soon solemnized; and I removed from my father's home to live with my dear Makro.

"How blest were we, my son! The God of our country smiled upon our stores; our herbage grew beneath our eye, and our lawful traffic with the vile Europeans, sanctioned by our virtuous Mansa,* answered our most sanguine expectations. Makro constantly attended the Korree,† and our cattle were as fine as any our nation boasted.

"One terrible day, my son, our God, we thought, seemed angry with us. He withheld his beams; the thunder roared above, and the tremendous lightning blighted the fruits of the earth. You were then but two months old within my womb. All nature at that moment seemed at variance, and the storm of rain drenched the Europeans' big ship; their sails were torn by the storm, and we heard them fire their terrifying guns, which we afterwards understood were signals of distress. Oh! what an hour was that! I stood

---

* For your information I shall subjoin notes, explanatory of such African words as may occur. King.
† A watering place where shepherds keep their cattle.

1 River 700 miles (1,130 km) long, rising on the Fouta Djallon, North Guinea, West Africa, and flowing generally northwest through Southeast Senegal then west, bisecting the country of Gambia, to the Atlantic Ocean at Banjul (*Columbia Encyclopedia*).
2 Perhaps Fulani, an ethnic group from present-day northern Nigeria. The rise of the Fulani empire occurs shortly after the period in which this text is set.

at our cabin door and saw one great swelling wave devour their ship, and they were for ever hurried from my sight. At that moment, with agonizing pity, I clasped my hands together, and wept their fate.

"Yes, indeed, I did weep the fate of those, whom with thee I am born to curse, such was *then* my generous unsuspecting nature. Well, the storm abated in its fury, till, at last, the waters gained their original calm, and the clouds above wore a more pleasing aspect.

"Makro, as was customary, was at the Korree, and, wishing to know if he was well, I paced the banks of the Gambia. As I looked upon the waters, I beheld floating to our shore a part of the ship rent in thousand twain by the merciless tempest. Lying, to all appearance dead, on this fragment of the wreck, were two Europeans, locked in each other's embrace. They were both young—one was scarcely fourteen. Imagine, my son, the emotions of a heart, ever ready to assist the distressed, on beholding such a scene. They were Europeans, and all Africa trembled at their name; they were my country's foes, but they were fallen; they claimed my pity, and I assisted them as though they had been my country's firmest friends—my heart could not view them in their real light.

"I hastened to the water's brink, and fast the fragment proceeded towards me; at length, it struck upon the shore, and I gave them all my aid. The captain of the sea-devoured vessel was soon recovered, and we both assisted to lead his nearly drowned boy to our cabin.

"I had got a small European bottle, with some brandy, which my Makro took from the despised of our nation, a Sonakee.* Captain Harrop, for so he was called, smiled upon the bottle, and giving some to his servant, he was soon recovered.

"My husband soon returned from the Korree, and entered our hut, while I was in the kindly office of renovating the drooping Europeans; he started back on beholding them, but I related the disastrous circumstance that called my mercy to their aid, and he also pitied them.

"By that time, when the glorious sun withholds his beams which are canopied over by the veil of night, they were both

---

* An unconverted native, one who drinks strong liquors, a drunkard.

perfectly recovered. Makro invited them to take some kous kous,* of which they ate most heartily, and much admired our Shea Toulou,† of which Makro placed plentifully before them. My son, noble was the blood that flowed in your father's veins. He was generous and humane, (in person thou art his model) of manly growth, of a fierce and intrepid disposition, commanding reverence from his countrymen, and dreaded by his country's foe. He was active and alert in times of war; lion-hearted, proud and generous, he would lead his men to victory, and was adored as the greatest war-captain of his country. In peace, he was gentle as the lamb, candid in his heart, and constantly exercised his time by a shepherd's employ.

"After our guests had eat[1] and were much refreshed, Makro bid them proceed to the European settlements on the Gambia, of which there are many, for the vile practice of purchasing slaves. I filled two soffroos‡ for them, but they most earnestly entreated to rest the night with us, and Makro, after some hesitation, consented to my preparing a temporary baloon†† for them. We all retired to our several pallets, and the next day Captain Harrop, was attacked by a violent fever. I attended him, and, indeed, I did as much as lay in my power to relieve his anguish.

"Oh! my son, I will pass over this part of my narrative: the hated remembrance of what I did for these vile white men rends my heart in twain. I sang him to his slumbers; I procured him a cooling drink; I added to his pallet, softened it for his weak frame, and cheered him in the hour of affliction. What was my reward? What was my recompence? Chains! Chains! my son, and life-closing slavery. Hear it, thou God of Africa, hear it! revenge,‡‡

---

* A dish prepared from boiled corn [Most often this North African dish, usually spelled couscous, is made from ground wheat or flour; "corn" usually means "wheat" at this time].
† Vegetable butter.
‡ A skin for containing water.
†† A sort of an apartment purposely for strangers.
‡‡ Revenge is supposed by several nations of Africa, particularly the Feloops, to be a god who presides at their birth, and gifts them with power, if the father is virtuous and injured; for then, the son is bound to revenge.

---

[1] Variant of eaten

nerve the arm of the son of Makro, and lend him thy invincible power; echo the groans of his country in his ears, and inspire him with thy malice. I have food at heart, aided by thee, to rouse his lion-soul from inactivity to revengeful slaughter. Then, reject not a distracted mother's prayer, but make him all her care-torn heart can wish!

"Captain Harrop recovered but slowly; he was wasted away to a mere shadow, and leaning on my arm for the benefit of pure air, he would walk out and view our herbage. 'Nature! nature!' would he cry, as he inspected our fertile fields, 'how profuse art thou, how lavish of thy bounty!'

"During his stay with us, he had taught me sufficient of his language to understand him, and I listened to what he said. I asked him, in unaffected ignorance, Who was nature? 'The great Creator,' answered he; 'He to whom you owe your being.' I did not rightly comprehend him, but he soon gave me to understand that I worshiped a false god.[1] I looked upon him with astonishment. He told me the glorious sun was but a substance created by his God, who was the great father of all. He told me of the enlivening power of the sun. 'I,' cried he, 'feel its warmth in my heart; its splendor inspires me with an active spirit to fulfill the duties of this life and enjoy society. You yourself,' applying to me, 'feel the same influence; the sun cheers the herbage of the field, when drooping; it sheds its enlivening rays, expands the opening leaf, which soon revels in prosperity. So the charitable man spreads his kindly rays around, revives the depressed, becomes a father to the orphan, a husband to the widow; by him are the afflicted comforted, the ignorant enlightened, and the poor relieved. Oh! Amri, a charitable man is the noblest work of God.'

"I was amazed to hear him speak; I thought him all virtue: how wretchedly was I deceived! Indeed, for the moment, he staggered my belief that I was doing right in worshiping, as he said, the servant of the real God. He made me remark the setting of the sun; I was charmed with what he said, and could for ever have listened to him. 'Behold,' said he, 'how complete are his works,

---

[1]  The Fulani people predominantly practice Islam. As a result of religious wars (1804–10), the Fulani established a Muslim empire in which they were the ruling elite.

and observe the gradual approach of night. The descent of yon bright orb is not into the sea, as you imagine; it goes to illumine other parts of this vast globe, which are hidden from your view. And now, behold, in proportion as its beams become more faint, night is spreading her grey curtain over the sky. Acknowledge the wisdom of the Creator here to be infinite, as the sudden transition from light to dark would, not only prove hurtful to the sight of man, but baneful to his interest, and derange the uniformity of creation. If,' continued he, 'you will with me observe the dawn of day, you shall contemplate the rise of the sun, which will prove a fund, not only of entertainment, but of instruction.'

"I readily assented, and we returned to our cabin. Makro was there already, and the captain's boy was instructing him in his language.

"At the approach of morning, captain Harrop tapped at my pallet's head, and besought me to rise. I did, and accompanied by Makro, we ascended a height where we could have an uninterrupted view of the vast expanse around.

"The grey clouds, which, the evening before, cast a gloom on the verdure, now were chased away by a vivid light, which, as it approached, grew more enlivening. The drops of dew that rested on the plants sparkled like so many pearls. I was wrapped in wonder and delight, for never before did I know how to discover those beauties which appeared to my astonished sight, and which Makro viewed with increased pleasure. How beautifully green did the vale beneath appear! how did my eye wander over hills, mountains, forests and meadows, that were watered by soft murmuring rivulets!

"The clouds were tinged and variegated with the sweetest colors; the light, insensibly increased, till the sun rising shot his first ray across the horizon; Makro clasped his hands in delight, as he beheld his slow approach. The eastern sky was previously clothed with purple, which, as the sun approached, gradually assumed a rosy tint, and gilded the hemisphere with blushing gold.

"Makro fell on his face, and embraced the earth in awful reverence; I followed his example; our instructor lifted us from the ground, we pressed him to our bosoms, and returned to our cabin, adoring the wisdom of the European, and earnestly entreating him never to leave us.

"He smiled; I thought it the smile of satisfaction and consent, and we heaped blessings on him.

"I need not add, my son, that we were happy; we blessed the accident that cast him on our shore, and eagerly sought every thing in our power to please him.

"Day followed day, and each brought something that endeared him to us the more. He was gay, lively, and would often teach me the songs of his country, at the same time commending my retentive memory.

"In short, two months soon elapsed in company of him who could so well instruct us how to adore the works of the infinite Creator of all things, and each day enliven our understandings by producing something new for us to admire.

"Oh! could we think it possible that the man who daily habituated our ears to tales of humanity could, while he grasped our hands in seeming friendly warmth, have a scheme in his head to blast our prospect of future peace, we who stood forward as his saviours! we could find no such deception in our own countrymen, and were not sufficiently acquainted with the character of the Europeans.

"Free from suspicion, we laid ourselves open to his cursed wiles, and became the dupes of our own credulity.

"Rendered more rational, we found beauties in nature which our countrymen could not discover; and Makro and myself would stroll far from our habitation, to again behold those scenes which he had taught us to delight in.

"One day, while reclining upon a hillock, we heard the sound of voices at a little distance from us. It was the two Europeans; and Makro, not understanding their language so well as myself, imposed on me a momentary silence, that he might listen to what they said; not from curiosity, for no such desire actuated our breasts, (then indeed we scarcely knew what it meant) but from the pure motive of learning whether we could understand them with facility.

"The captain's voice we first distinguished; his words, my son, are for ever impressed upon my memory, and I can with ease relate them.

"'William,' said he to his boy, 'I never can consent to be buried in this wild uncultivated spot, lost to my friends and to the world; reflect that it is for their own good, as much as for my benefit.

Have I not enlightened them, fertilized their minds, told them of the duties of this life, and how to enjoy society? What were they, when first we set foot on their shore? savages, dwelling with savages: I tell you, William,.....'

"'Sir,' interrupted the boy, 'have you a heart? but no, I am wrong, you are only trying whether the heart of your poor boy is softened by humanity. I am sure it is not, it cannot be your intention; I must not, I will not believe it.'

"'Peace, fool,' resumed the captain; 'you never knew me changeable in my determination.'

"He ceased; we soon understood he spoke of us, and that he was about to leave our country. Makro looked at me; I saw the manly tear upon his cheek; he sorrowed for the intended departure of the Europeans, who had gained our love, and he pressed me to his heart, the palpitation of which was almost too strong for our nature to support.

"They continued—

"'It is most fortunate,' rejoined the captain; 'the arrival of one of my own ships from Jamaica! it favors my views, and to-morrow shall see us on board.'

"'They will send their boat for us to shore, in the morning,' answered William.

"'Till then, peace,' added captain Harrop; 'a close mouth is a good safeguard.'

"We were both too much affected to accost them, for we expected they should reside with us for ever.

"'Ah!' sighed Makro, 'my dear Amri, our expectations were unnatural; do *we* not love our country? Say, could we leave it, our family and our friends? Oh! no—perhaps, in European plains, he may have a wife, who loves him dearly, and, Amri, I judge by myself, I could not leave thee.'

"This was sufficient; Makro silenced within my breast the upbraider that accused them of ingratitude.

"We returned home; they were there before us, and soon perceived in our countenance an unusual dejection.

"'My worthy friend,' cried captain Harrop, catching my hand, and wiping the tear from my cheek, 'are you not well? say, what has befallen you? Why this dejection?'

"I had not power to refrain uttering the cause of my grief, and replied, at the same time clasping his hand, while the tear glistened in my eye: 'I expected you would have resided with us for ever, and Makro and myself heard you say you were about to leave our country.'

"I saw a deadly paleness overspread his countenance, (I knew not then the cause) but recovering in a moment, he replied:

"'And does that distress you? Indeed, my gentle friends, it is essential to my own happiness; I have relatives in England that think me dead; I have large possessions, which, if I remain here, will fall into other hands. I have also a wife and children; these are strong arguments in favor of my return to a country to which I owe my birth. I am sure you cannot blame me; to you I owe my life, and my wife and children are bound to pray for you. If I idle my days here, I am of no service to them or my country, and then the life which you have preserved, your invaluable gift, is rendered useless.

"'In Europe, we live to assist one another, to share the labors of the day, and make life supportable. We barter our commodities more extensively than you do here, and the great exchange is diffusing round the world, like the generating sun, the rays of prosperity and affluence.'

"'Since it must be so,' I replied, 'I have no other alternative; may you be happy!' and placing a Saphie★ round his neck, 'may this preserve you in the hour of need! its virtue will protect you from the arms of the malignant, and O! when in your native country, do sometimes think of poor Amri and her husband Makro.'

"I was deeply affected, and William, the captain's servant, falling on his knees, and catching at the lappet[1] of his coat, cried: 'Master, have mercy!'

"'Silence, slave!' returned he, stamping his foot upon the ground and flinging him away. I saw him tremble, and his cheek was crimsoned with a malignant hatred; his eyes rolled furiously, and sparkled in anger.

---

★ An amulet or charm; a scrap of paper written on by a Mahomedan Priest, is enclosed in a horn, and sold at a high price to the natives. Bushreens (Mussulman, or Kafir) pagan natives, believe in the virtues of the Saphie, though they deny the religion.

---

[1] The flap or skirt (of a coat). Also, the lapel (*OED*).

"Makro rose from his seat.

"A something ran through my veins, and my blood was cold; a faintness seized my limbs, and my heart forgot its usual pulsation.

"William now regained his seat, and, hiding his face in his hand, cried: 'Most inhuman!' Harrop recovered himself, and, placing his hand upon his forehead, declared himself unwell; he embraced my husband, who stood by his side, with all the fervor of friendship, and assured him he could not order it otherwise; then shaking hands with his servant, begged his pardon for the harshness of his conduct. We soon retired to our several pallets."

Dear Charles, I must entreat a moment's patience, if my story interests you; if not, you will willingly consent without any entreaty.

My paper is filled, my pen worn to the stump—mind flagged—fingers cramped—and my little finger wears as fine a polish as an agate. Indeed, when I sat down, I did not think of entering so far into the narrative of Amri in this letter. Adieu!

GEORGE STANFORD.


## LETTER III.

*The same to the same.*

DEAR CHARLES,

I AGAIN resume my pen. Think not that I mean to revile my countrymen; those are not my countrymen, whose inhumanity is the subject of my page. They may be Britons born, but are not Britons at heart, and I disclaim them. There are thousands here that have hearts like rocks. Children, from their birth, tutored to inhumanity, and treat our fellow creatures worse than the dogs that lick the morsel beneath their table.

Oh fie! fie!

I shall proceed to delineate the character of an European West-Indian, in the narrative of Amri.

"In the morning, Makro would not go, as was customary, to the Korree, because he would witness the departure of his friend, and we took a walk for the last time, accompanied by captain Harrop, to view the surrounding plain.

"William waited on the banks of the Gambia for the arrival of the boat, and to give the captain notice.

"We arrived at the top of a hill, where we always made our observations, and a withered branch of a tree lay at our feet; he made us examine it.

"'Look,' cried he; 'here is another subject to admire; behold this tree flourishing, while an arm that was lopped from its side now withers on the ground.

"'This is a subject worthy of your minute attention. This arm, divested of nourishment, withers; the falling dew cannot revive it, nor the sun cheer it. Compare it to a limb torn from you or me; it needs must die, receiving no succour from the body, to which it once belonged. The blood that flows in our veins would no longer enliven that limb, and the place from whence it was torn would soon be covered by a growing skin.

"'Observe that tree; it has its veins as we have ours, and like it, we renovate life with a sustenance we gather from the earth.

"'We eat, and are eaten by creatures of the earth; thousands inhabit our mortal frame, and thousands inhabit the body of that tree. That receives a sustenance from the earth, and the spreading veins convey the sap of life to the remotest leaf of the same tree. Thus you see how complete is Nature in all her various performances.'

"This observation did but increase our agony at the idea of separation. I could have loved him, adored him. Ours were not weak minds, my son; they were pliant as the infant's, formed for instruction, gifted with retentive memory, and we looked upon the European as our great instructor.

"On looking in the plain beneath, we beheld a Caffila,* mastered by seventeen Slatees,† it was the most numerous I ever beheld, and came from a great way up the country.

---

* A caravan of slaves, from the interior of the country.
† Free black merchants, who trade in slaves, and with a small troop, well armed, march to the interior, either to purchase prisoners of war, or, if they fail in this, lay in ambush and take the inhabitants from their houses when asleep. Wars in Africa are much encouraged by the Europeans, and particularly the Dutch and English, and the number of slaves annually exported, are said to exceed 150,000 of those miserable people.

"Oh! my son, let pity warm your breast for the unhappy fate of your poor countrymen, and let a knowledge of their sufferings teach you how to revenge them!

"'Tis I would fan your bosom to a flame; 'tis I would rouse your inactive soul, and heap destruction on the christian race ..... but I will proceed in my narrative.

"Each Slatee had above fourteen slaves to his portion; some, prisoners of war; others, dragged from the bosom of their family; all manacled, a rope fastened each other by the neck, and a log of wood by the ancle. Thus were they torn from their homes by the infamous Slatees, and obliged to travel, fatigued and hungry, over sandy deserts, till they came to a proper market, where they were sold like cattle, and dispersed over the world.

"Such are the scenes we daily witness in Africa, such is the christianity of the Europeans who profess humanity.

"Captain Harrop was uneasy at the sight, and Makro, whose honest breast glowed with indignation, whose sparkling eye alone spoke the language of his heart, violently exclaimed against the horrible transaction. 'Are we not men?' did he cry; 'men as ye are? we vary in nothing but in color; we feel as you do, and are awake to same sense of pain; but still are we disposed by and among you like cattle.'

"Captain Harrop shook his head in token of dissatisfaction, and remained silent.

"By this time, the entire Caffila had passed us.

"One poor negro-woman remained behind; she was faint and could not walk, but she was mercylessly dragged along by two guides, with whips in their hands, who every now and then, spirited her with a lash. At length, exhausted, worn out with fatigue and bruises, she sunk down and expired in our presence.

"Her guide giving her a curse or two, accompanied by a few blows on the insensible body, walked on to join the Caffila, which had proceeded to some distance.

"This inhuman spectacle seemed sensibly to wound the feelings of our European instructor, who turned away his head, as we thought, in agony.

"We now silently proceeded down the hill, and were returning home, when we were roused by the firing of a gun at no great distance. 'Thank heaven! they are arrived,' cried captain Harrop, and we soon reached the banks of Gambia, but a short distance from our cabin, where a boat waited to bear him from our shores.

"On beholding captain Harrop, the boat's crew leaped on the strand, and hailed him with a loud huzza.[1]

"I shrunk back with terror, on beholding so many Europeans, and involuntarily clasped the hand of Makro.

"In the space of two minutes, another boat touched the shore; there were only two rowers on board.

"Captain Harrop took me by the hand; he trembled, he attempted to address us, but his voice faultered. 'Twas the trembling and faultering of a villain, and the compunction visible on his cheek, I misconstrued for an agonizing glow, occasioned by our separation. Alas! I soon found how much I was mistaken ..... well, well!

"Makro led me on to the boat, and captain Harrop shaking us both heartily by the hand, entered the one containing the two rowers only.

"I must say I was somewhat surprised, to find two touch upon our shores to carry away one man; but suspicion dwelt not within my bosom, and I did not wish to account for it.

"While Makro was examining the vessel, a gun fired, and on the signal being given, we were both seized, and forced into the boat. I fainted away, and was easily borne aboard the vessel. Makro, with reviving strength, struggled hard for liberty; his cause gave him twice the power of his adversaries, and he struck many to the ground. He seized a sabre from the side of one of his assailants, and dealt destruction with every blow.

"He had laid several of the Europeans powerless at his side, when one mercyless and well-aimed blow deprived him of his senses, and he fell. The weapon dropped useless from his hand, and buried itself in the streaming gore, while he, with irons round his ancles, hand-cuffed and chained to the boat, was conveyed on board the vessel, which, within an hour, set sail for Jamaica.

"On my first return to reason, I found myself with many other

---

[1]  A shout of exultation, encouragement, or applause; a cheer uttered by a number in unison; a hurrah (*OED*).

miserable wretches, deprived of liberty, confined within the narrow limits of a loathsome dungeon,[1] in a vessel bearing me from my native land, from my father and my friends. But where was Makro? surely, cried I, they have not deprived me of the only comfort their cruelty could leave me, or is he dead? I called upon his name, no answer was returned. Cruel! cruel! I uttered, and fell senseless on a pallet of straw.

"Several days elapsed, and I became more and more debilitated; my strength visibly declined, and the iron ring, which bound me by a chain to the wall, galled my ancles.

"I remember I asked the keeper, who brought the scanty allowance to our hold, to give me a bandage in mercy, for that my leg was so painful I could not support it much longer.

"'Bandage!' replied he; 'ha, ha, ha! I say, bandage indeed! may hap I may bring you a bit of salt, but it does not much signify, as to-morrow you will be allowed to stay an hour or two upon deck, for the benefit of the air.'

"Indeed, we needed it, for our prison was close to suffocation, and four of our companions were already dead.

"In about an hour after, he brought some salt, with which he rubbed my ancle, till overcome with excruciating agony, I fainted. When I recovered, I found my fainting had made no alteration in the continuance of his *job,* for he had bound it round with a piece of brown paper, and replaced the iron ring.

"The next day, we were ordered on deck; my enquiring eye looked around for Makro, alas! he was not there, nor could I see the perfidious Harrop.

"We had scarcely been an hour on deck, in the open air and enjoying the sea-breeze, when I heard a voice cry: Bring him on deck. I remembered the sound—'twas he—yes, yes, 'twas he whom, when dying upon a raft, I succoured. 'Twas he, who confessed he was indebted to me for life, and his gratitude was to throw chains over me, and drag me in bondage from my native country, to be made a slave.

"He came and examined the miserable captives; he stood before me; I could not speak, but lifted up my manacled hands,

[1]  Ship's hold.

and directed my eyes towards him. I saw the keen reproof cut him to the heart; he turned from me, and Makro was brought upon deck, chained to a broad plank, with arms and legs extended. His countenance was wan and emaciated; his hollow eyes were almost buried in their sockets; they were rivetted on me. I looked at him, and fast the tear rolled down his deadened cheek.

"'He has not eat these three days,' cried a boy, to the captain, 'nor will the whip compel him.' I soon understood it was Makro's resolve to die, and I ejaculated in heart I would not survive him.

"The boy, by the captain's order, brought a mess[1] for Makro; he stedfastly refused, and the boy, from his birth trained to inhumanity, struck him smartly across the thighs with a whip. Makro smiled contemptuously upon him. Oh! how did I long to clasp this faithful husband in my arms, to unfold to his heart that Amri would follow his heroic example.

"They then proceeded to new extremities with him; they forced his mouth, and keeping it extended with a gag, poured the loathsome beverage down his feverish throat; but no sooner did they extricate him, than he spit it back, accompanied by blood; for, in forcing their spoon into his mouth, they tore his throat in a most inhuman manner.

"Still he smiled and laughed to scorn their ineffectual means. This obstinacy got him another severe beating. I screamed, and was borne from the deck, while the operation was performing.

"The next day, when my allowance was brought, lest hunger should compel me to eat, I, without hesitation, overturned the bowl. This was observed by the keeper, who beat me till the blood streamed down my back, and I was deprived of feeling.

"In the evening, my bowl was replenished; my tongue and lips were parched by fever, and I endured an agony indescribable. I would have sacrificed every thing, but my love for Makro, for something to quench my immoderate thirst; but I obstinately persisted in my resolve, and again, lest excess of agony, in a moment of torpitude, should tempt me to taste the beverage, I overturned the bowl.

"The ensuing day, my fever raged more violent; our keeper

---

[1] A portion of liquid or pulpy food (*OED*).

came and, on observing my allowance spilt, and me dying, cursed me for my obstinacy, and went to give information to the captain.

"This day, we were ordered to pass on the deck; indeed the captain found us in so debilitated and deplorable a state, that he feared he should not be able to carry above half his complement to Jamaica,* and inhumanity gave way to private interest.

"Makro was on deck, but so weak, that he could not stand. He was now released from the plank to which he had previously been bound; his legs were unshackled, and his hands only were cuffed. Alas! he was so much enfeebled, that they need not fear him. I, myself, was not joined with the chain of slaves, but permitted to walk about, if my lacerated limbs would enable me. On seeing Makro, I tried to approach, but unable to support myself, I fell down. Stunned with the blow, I lay senseless, till captain Harrop himself lifted me up, and led me to my husband. I expressed my gratitude in the best manner I was able, and, to convince us of his generosity, he unbound us both. We fell into each other's arms; Makro pressed me, but faintly, to his bosom, and I prayed heaven to let us expire enfolded as we lay. Ah! why was that blessing denied us?

"Even Harrop's flinty heart was touched; even his bosom that knew not remorse dissolved for the moment, and the straying tear bedewed his cheek.

"Again was the mess brought before us, accompanied by the whip; Harrop found, to his infinite mortification, that force was of no avail, and he sought entreaty. The whip was thrown on one side, and thus spoke the monster, with syren[1] voice, accompanied by the tears of a crocodile. Oh! had heaven stamped an avoiding mark upon the forehead of dissimulation!—but I disdain to murmur; for I have a son that shall revenge me.

"'Son of Africa,' he cried, 'live and be happy; treat me not as your enemy, but look upon me rather as a friend, who strains

---

* It was the custom, though now, we believe, it is altered, for a planter to purchase one or two lots of slaves, and so round according to the bulk of the vessel and demand for slaves: the lot being made, the purchaser was obliged to abide by his chance traffic.

[1] One of several fabulous monsters, part woman, part bird, who were supposed to lure sailors to destruction by their enchanting singing (*OED*). Standard spelling is siren.

every nerve to serve you. When in your country, I strove to inform your mind; but you dwelt with heathens, and I regarded it as my duty to return the obligation you conferred upon me. I found my task but half complete, when I had taught you to admire the works of your Creator; what then remained was to introduce you to civilized society, of which you soon will become an ornament. If I used force, in compelling you from your shores, believe me, it has cost me much secret pain at heart; but nothing less could be done; for, I knew it would be useless to attempt to dissuade you from your native country.'

"Villainous depredator! could we heed his words? we were too much enlightened, to become his dupes a second time.

"When Makro understood that my present debilitated state proceeded from the want of sustenance, which was regularly served me, he requested of me that I would eat; but I refused even him who was as dear, nay dearer to me than life.

"On knowing the reason, he called for the bowl, and ate heartily, and I joined him. We had now been on deck near three hours, and our extreme languor, owing principally to the want of nourishment, gradually decreased. We could stand; as for me, I could walk; but Makro still preserved a great faintness.

"We were remanded to our dungeons, on the approach of evening, and now I was not chained by the leg as before, but by a belt which incircled my body, and hand-cuffed as usual.

"I now, for several days, ate my food regularly. I never saw Makro, who was confined in a separate dungeon, but when we were brought on deck, and I waited in eager expectation the approaching day. At length, it came; the very thought of his returning to his food made me regard life, the lassitude of my limbs decreased in consequence. Comparatively speaking, when I again came on deck, I was perfectly recovered, and so I expected to find Makro; but no; when my eyes beheld him, he was more languid than before.

"Harrop had us both unbound; my appearance pleased him, we were left to ourselves, and enabled to converse more freely.

"Makro, in a faint and dying voice, thus addressed me: 'Live, Amri; as you love me, live for my sake. I shall never reach the place of our destination, and, I do entreat you, attend to the last words of your dying husband. I will no longer take aught to nourish life; I am sickened by the weary load, rendered loathsome by the vile Europeans. I daily receive the lash for my obstinate perseverance; but I mock their cruelties, I scorn their wiles, and am prepared to die. Oh! Amri, I beseech you, live; live, as you love me; live to revenge my death. Take this girdle from my loins, and keep it in your possession. If the being to whom you are to give life, be male, let him wear it from his earliest birth, and whisper in his ear, till manhood dawns, what he owes to his country. Inspire his young bosom with revenge; tutor his early mind how to hate the European race; teach him, in his childhood, to lisp curses on their name, and blast their progeny for ever. You shall find the seeds you sow ripening as he grows in years, and expand into a flame; be this your task. Say, Amri, that you will do this, and I die contented.'

"He paused—

"I clasped him to my arms; I could not bear the idea of separation, and remained incapable of returning him an answer, though the necessity of my living, to give birth to one who might revenge his wrongs, struck me most forcibly.

"'Ah!' rejoined he, 'is it possible? and can Amri refuse my last request? Then, indeed, death, thou art most acceptable.

"'Amri, 'tis not that I fear to live, but I have resolved never to acknowledge a master. I do not seek death because I fear to buffet[1] with those Europeans, it is because I never can own a superior but my Creator. Man was His noblest work, and I am a man. He did not make slaves of one half of this globe, nor order the black to bend subservient to the white man's yoke; nor will I, a created being like them, be bought and sold, and toil like a beast of burthen, that they may enjoy the fruits of my labor. My beloved Amri, if you refuse me my last request, I shall think the white men are not the only cruel beings.'

"I dried my tears, loosened the girdle from his loins, and answered:

"'My beloved Makro, I will obey you in every thing: yes, may our God grant me a son to revenge your cause, and I will instil

---

[1]   To deal blows, fight, contend, struggle (*OED*).

into him hatred to the Europeans, and if he revenge you not, he shall receive his mother's curse.'"

Amri, overcome by her emotion, ceased her narrative, and Jack, rising hastily from his seat, brought down a sabre which he had concealed in the thatch, the slaves not being allowed to possess arms of any description. He drew it, and swore, with exulting fury, to merit his Creator's curse if he revenged not the cause of his parents.

Dear Charles, I must conclude this letter, with a promise to commence early to-morrow morning. It is now near midnight, and I have been so much taken up with the narrative, that I observed not how the hours fled. Adieu!

GEORGE STANFORD.


## LETTER IV.

*The same to the same.*


DEAR CHARLES,

JOY beamed in the eyes of Amri, as she beheld the darling of her heart, the offspring of Makro, in the strength of youth, with the sword of vengeance drawn in his hand. Fire shot from his eye and spoke the language of his soul; how blest was the fond doting mother!

Amri embraced him and proceeded.

"Your father was satisfied with my answer; he grasped my hand; but, exhausted by too great an exertion, he sunk back, and my arms received him.

"Captain Harrop now approached; he had listened to the preceding conversation, and was confounded. He entreated to be heard; he caught hold of the hand of Makro, and, in the most supplicating manner, begged our pardon, at the same time, declaring, with the most solemn asseveration,[1] that he would

---

[1] Emphatic confirmation of a statement; a word or phrase used to express confirmation; an oath (*OED*).

grant us both liberty when we came on shore, and entreated Makro, in the most tender manner, to receive his food.

"Your father smiled upon him.

"'Menial inhuman wretch!' he exclaimed, 'I am beyond thy power. Hardened European, thou seest one struggling in death, who doth defy thee; hadst thou a heart, thou wouldst feel how deservedly I despise thee. But for myself and Amri, thou hadst perished long since. Do not think I recal this to incite thee to mercy; I ask it not; I scorn it. Take away thy beverage; it is encompassed round with slavery, and I will rather die than live a dog, and own a cursed European for my master.'

"His voice faultered; the bowl was brought him, which he threw to the other side of the vessel.

"I was then divided from him; they bared his back, and stripping him to the waist, he received five hundred lashes.

"The first three hundred he supported with heroic fortitude, laughed, sung, and spit upon the captain alternately, who stood near him. My bosom was almost callous to feeling; I beheld the cruel infliction without a sigh, till I saw his head sink upon his breast, and his limbs forget their use. I would have flown to him, but the consolation of being near him, in his last moments, was denied me. He was now taken down, and brought to the side of the deck. His body lay almost at my feet, but I could go no nearer to him. I prayed, I supplicated the inhuman monsters, but in vain. Oh! in what a mangled situation was his body; the flesh was pulverized on his back, and stopped the flowing of the blood. They applied salt to his wounds, and the excruciating agony for a moment revived him. He begged to be raised from the ground; this was granted, and he supported himself against the main mast; but, too enfeebled to stand unassisted, a young lieutenant, who witnessed, with tears in his eyes, the horrid transaction, ran to give his aid.

"Makro beckoned Harrop to come near him; he did, and, seizing a pistol from the belt of the lieutenant, he shot him.

"Harrop fell, bathed in his blood.

"Immediately the ship was in confusion; the negroes set up a loud shout; the sailors ran to the assistance of their captain, and Makro clasped his hands together in token of resignation, then exclaimed: 'God of my country I come. Amri, farewell! Look to a meeting in Africa's plains.'* He then fell to the ground, and, lifting up his eyes to heaven, expired.

"The negroes, who beheld his cruel fate, trembled with apprehension, and each suspected his turn was next.

"I fell upon my knees, and humbly entreated I might be permitted to approach him. Cruel barbarians! they even refused me this simple request, and we were remanded to our dungeons. I resolutely refused to stir, till I was permitted to embrace the lifeless body of my Makro. They applied the whip to my shoulders, and in the midst of my supplications, tossed him over to the ocean, and hurried me away to confinement.

"Oh! remorseless wretches! did ye possess one spark of pity in your bosoms, ye could not have denied me such a demand. Each day furthered one or other of us to eternity, and I fancied my time as fast approaching, but I sought to cheer life, for the sake of revenge. I daily ate my allowance, and endeavoured to lose the remembrance of the cruelties exercised on Makro, since they depressed my spirits, and impaired my health."

"But what of Harrop?" demanded the impatient Jack, while a presaging anxiety distorted his countenance; "say, was the pistol to his heart?"

"Alas! he recovered."

Jack dwindled from his attitude of suspense; his soul had been roused with eager hope, and now was dashed with the bitterness of disappointment.

"The enfeebled arm of Makro, took but an unsteady aim; the whizzing ball shot through Harrop's side," continued Amri, "and he was conveyed from the deck; but he soon recovered, and, at the conclusion of our voyage, he was perfectly well.

"We fast approached our destination, and a few days more landed us on the shores of Jamaica. The slave cargo was considerably lessened, being, as captain Harrop himself acknowledged, when we set sail, above four Hundred; now we were reduced to

---

\* It is the general belief of African slaves that, when they die, they return to their own country.

less than half the number.[1] Thus, by severe treatment, they become enemies to themselves, and sacrifice thousands of poor souls, who, were they used kindly, would labor harder for their employers, and even with cheerfulness. But the European fools, though avarice is the leading feature of their hearts, are not aware how they destroy the gratification of this passion. Humanity would rather aid than diminish their schemes, and, were they to heal the wound in the negro's bosom, inflicted by those who tore him from his home, they would find how much more to their advantage it would be, than inhumanly whipping them. The worm will turn, if trod upon, and the weakest animal is prone to revenge.

"Need then the white men wonder if we seek redress? Are we not sanctioned by the laws of Nature? If they inflict the wound, shall we not heal it? Yes, we will, and the healing balm shall be revenge.

"We had no sooner entered Morant Bay,[2] than the sailors sent up a loud shout. This aroused me in my dungeon, and soon after we were all lotted,[3] and standing on the deck, awaiting the approach of our purchasers.

"In a few moments, the vessel was thronged with Europeans.[4] My companions thought them a herd of cannibals,[5] and their yell

---

[1] Although mortality rates of slaves on the Middle Passage were higher earlier in the eighteenth century, by the end of the century "British slave ships were losing an average 5 percent of their human cargoes." James Walvin, *Black Ivory: A History of British Slavery* (London: Fontana, 1993) 54. Of course, exceptional overcrowding on individual ships could lead to much greater losses even at this point in time.

[2] Body of water on the southeast shore of the island and home of an oft-used port. Gained notoriety later as the site for a significant riot on October 11, 1865 over economic strife in which 28 people were killed. "The measures taken to suppress the riot and to pacify the disaffected parish were effective but brutal... Five hundred and eighty men and women were killed, six hundred were flogged, and a thousand houses destroyed." *Short History of the West Indies,* by J.H. Parry and P.H. Sherlock (London: Macmillan & Co. Ltd, 1956) 241.

[3] Assigned by lot or as a lot, allotted, etc., as slaves were purchased in groups rather than individually.

[4] Typically, the slaves were brought ashore for purchase as allowing purchasers on board led to even greater disruption and panic among the slaves.

[5] This impression, which reverses the long-claimed European view that those of African descent were cannibalistic, also appears in *The Interesting Narrative of the Life of Olaudah Equiano.* When first taken aboard a slave ship, the title character echoes Jack's sentiments, "I asked them if we were not to be eaten by those white men with horrible looks, red faces, and loose hair." Werner Sollors, ed. (New York: Norton and Company, 2001) 39.

sunk to my heart. The white men thronged around us in flocks, and you may well imagine how frightened we were.*

"I was purchased, with several others, by my present master, and was branded on my breast[1] with the initials of his name.

"My son, I scorned to groan during the performance, but held my bosom with fortitude to receive the impression. The other poor wretches, who accompanied me, shrunk and writhed in the anguish of the moment. If in my then situation I sorrowed, it was for those unhappy beings who were incapable of firmness.

"We were soon dispersed amidst the elder negroes of the plantation, and in three months more, my son, you were born. Conceive my joy; I beheld you, while yet an infant on my knee, the avenger of Makro's wrongs. The transport of my heart was visible on my cheek, and each negro of our plantation, observing the pleasure I took in my child, wished me joy, and then the idea recurred to my heart: 'may he not be the saviour of our country! the abolisher of the slave trade!'

"Even our surly overseer smiled upon me, for the love I bore my infant. Oh! had he known the joy of my heart, or the more than maternal cause!"

Dear Charles, again I drop my pen. Could you feel as I felt when penning the death of Makro! I would that my paper could convey the agony of my heart. I more than once laid down my pen, and more than once my tears floated on the page; but again I resumed and followed Amri to the birth of her son, with her transport at the event. Adieu!

GEORGE STANFORD.

---

* The wisdom of the legislature of Jamaica has corrected this enormity in that Island, by enacting that the sales shall be conducted on shore. Edwards's West-Indies [Bryan Edwards, *History Civil and Commercial of the West Indies* (London, 1819).]

[1] Branding of slaves was extremely controversial by this time; by the 1790s, branding in Jamaica "is growing into disuse, and I believe in the Windward Islands thought altogether unnecessary." See Bryan Edwards, *History Civil and Commercial of the West Indies* (London, 1819) vol. 2, 54.

# LETTER V.

*The same to the same.*

DEAR CHARLES,

ADIEU to the impulse of the moment, to the feeling tear! I am a West-Indian again, and can proceed.

"By the time," added Amri, "you were five years old, you were esteemed the most valuable child on the plantation. You were strong and hearty; our God seemed to have endowed you with more than common strength, and I imagined he had gifted you with a power to revenge. The first words you lisped were curses on the white men, and the first bauble you took delight in was the sword. Nay, your strength was the talk and admiration of the whole plantation, and, at six years old, you commenced the labourer. This, so far from wounding, was a new sense of pleasure to me, a new transport to my bosom. I knew that labor would strengthen your young body, even to hardihood, expanding your supple joints, enlarging your bones, and nerving every fibre with acquired strength to aid that of nature.

"Your mind was moulded to my most sanguine wish; for, even at that age, you showed signs of a soul capable of great deeds. Once, when you idled at your work, and received the lash across your shoulder, you turned upon your persecutor and struck him, with all the heroic fire of your father glowing in your bosom, and transparent on your cheek. Though your back suffered for the daring outrage, I heeded not the incisions of the whip, but blessed the hour that I gave birth to such a darling treasure.

"Seven years had now elapsed, since I was torn by a rapacious monster from my native land, and I had bowed subservient to the white man's yoke. We had had frequent insurrections of the slaves, who, groaning beneath the despotic tyranny of their masters, with one accord, struggled hard to regain the so much wished-for liberty; but, for want of regularity in their proceedings, they failed in the execution of their plan, many lives were lost, and those that were emancipated from slavery, changed their life for one more precarious; they sought the mountains,[1] and lived by rushing on the unguarded whites who should by accident pass their den.[2]

"Daily were my ears habituated to some horrid murder committed by those frantic desperadoes. Oh! my son, how would I have rejoiced could I but have held thee up as their pattern and leader; but thou wast yet too young.

"Their lives were but of short duration; for, untutored to the method of arms, or each fearful of the other, they owned no leader, and left themselves open to the attack of their implacable foes.

"Mere petty ravages were frequent, and demanded the exertion of the Colony to suppress them, and a small troop of soldiery searched the woods. Two days had they lurked about, guarding each avenue, when finding that no one passed from the interior of the wood, and weary of the inactive employ, they boldly rushed forward and surprised a party of the rebels, who, at their approach, flew in all directions; but being closely pursued along the Savannah, they were all taken; some led the way to the cave of an Obi-Man,* who dwelt in a mountain near the lime Savannah.

"They were all brought to justice, and, to intimidate the other negroes of several plantations, were all executed.

"A separate day was appointed for the death of the Obi-Man, who was to be made a terrible example of, and executed in the presence of every slave.

"The day arrived.

"We all marched in procession to see the unhappy fate of our countryman.

"The wretched criminal was brought before us—Merciful God! I looked upon him and stared wildly in his venerable face—'It is—it must be,' I cried, ''tis my father Feruarue,' and screaming, I threw myself into his arms.

---

* Here, Earle reproduces about 50% of the selections from the House of Commons Sessional Papers of 1789 included in Appendix A. For the sake of avoiding unnecessary repetition, the reader is referred to that appendix.

---

[1] The mountains were known to be the territory of Maroon communities.
[2] Three-fingered Jack's banditry was alleged to take place on the road from Kingston to Morant Bay, near Cane River Falls, within the parish of St. Thomas in the southeast part of Jamaica.

"The negroes made a loud noise, and the planters present were astonished.

"Mr. Mornton pressed forward from among the rest; he knew me for his slave, and stopped the cruel executioners, who were about to tear my father from my embrace.

"It seems, upon a former trial, Feruarue had been exhorted to confess the tenure of his crimes, and how he affected the negroes, for which he was about to suffer.

"Thinking his confession would be of service to the colony, they had offered him life, which he refused. They had offered him freedom, this he likewise refused. They had put him on the rack,[1] he smiled at their tortures. They extended his legs and arms upon a wall, raised him from the ground about a yard, scorched the soles of his feet, and burnt him under the arm-pits; still he persevered, derided their tortures, and laughed at their preparations to agonize his frame, that they might rend from his soul a secret which he unhappily prized dearer than life.

"Mr. Mornton stopped the deadly proceedings against the sufferer, and thus spoke: 'Feruarue, the plantations have suffered greatly by you; it seems you have, by some hidden means, spirited up the negroes to a rebellion, and those that have refused to raise their hands against their masters have died in the most cruel manner by your means. Tell me how you have effected this; let me know how to avoid its pernicious consequences; and you shall be rewarded with life, and liberty to return to your own country, if it is your pleasure, accompanied by your daughter. If you refuse this, remember the most dreadful death awaits you.'

"'I defy your malice,' cried the bold Feruarue; 'bring me the torture, I'll show you a Feloop can keep a secret.'

"I implored; he was obstinate, and refused.

"'My daughter,' he cried, 'soon as I heard you had been seduced from your native country, I went to the Benlany* and implored some European monsters who were present to give me

---

* A sort of stage serving as a town-hall.

---

[1] An instrument of torture formerly in use, consisting (usually) of a frame having a roller at each end; the victim was fastened to these by the wrists and ankles, and had the joints of his limbs stretched by their rotation.

back my child, and six picked slaves should ransom her. They eagerly accepted my most liberal offer, and the next day I brought them on board their vessel.

"'Designing fiends! They laid us all in chains, and immediately put to sea.

"'My daughter, I know I must use brevity in my narrative, for the European tygers are anxious for their prey. I need not recount to you my sufferings during our voyage; you must be well acquainted with the unhappy lot of a slave, when at sea.

"'I was brought to their market, and sold. In my heart I secretly vowed revenge, and for that purpose, studied Obi.

"'I acknowledge I spirited up the slaves to rebellion; I acknowledge I struck terror to the hearts of many that refused their aid, but how I effected this remains with me, and with me shall expire.'

"'Hold,' cried Mornton; 'once more we put the question, confess and live; persist and die.'

"'Die, as a Feloop,' answered Feruarue; 'these infirm limbs shall yet display strength in torture. What shall I confess? that I have made the pallid Europeans tremble at my power; this is the only confession congenial to my soul, and I will make ye feel its force. What shall ye expect from a son of Africa? Revenge. You drag us from our homes, make slaves of us, and gall us with your whips. What does the African think of? Revenge.'

"'And do ye wonder, if, with hearts torn, souls subjected, that once knew peace and liberty, need ye wonder, if, with desperate resolution, and with one accord, we struggle to regain the land most dear to us, and the liberty we sigh for? Europeans, you feel not as we do; we, who, when in our land, were great and noble as ye are,.....' he sunk his head upon my bosom, and ere I could clasp him to my heart, he was dragged away, sighing 'farewell, my Amri! farewell!' He was covered over with the farrago of his weak and impotent charms, and a rope was slung round his waist.

"'Confess,' cried the executioner—

"'That I have been just,' added Feruarue, and immediately he was slung up above fifteen feet from the ground. A rapid fire burnt beneath him, whose volley of flame ascending scorched his withered frame.

"At that moment, all the remaining sparks of humanity

perished in my bosom; the Europeans plucked the remnant grain of mercy from my heart, and left nought behind but fury, rancour, and revenge.

"Oh my son! to behold the placid resignation of the dying man, to see the tear of anguish most acute, rolling down his furrowed cheek! was not that enough to steel my heart against those men, those European robbers?

"Feruarue called upon me. 'Amri,' said he, while with a forced serenity he suppressed the groan, for it is not to be supposed but he felt the fire's scorching heat; 'Amri,' said he, 'do you not rejoice? I go to my own country; may I meet thee there soon!'

"I could not answer; but the clasping of my hands spoke the agony of my heart.

"My father kept his eye upon me; at that moment, I thought of thee, my son, and the anticipated revenge; my bosom swelled with exultation, and my heart was rendered callous to all sense of feeling. Feruarue still looked at me, and I returned him the same stedfast gaze, till, at length, I saw the devouring flames incircle his whole body. 'Mercy! mercy !' I cried. Lost to all hope I rushed into the ravaging fire, to die with my father, but I was denied my eager wish, and snatched from the death I sought."

During the latter part of the narrative, Jack's eye sparkled with envenomed fury; his anxiety became so great, that, in the impulse of the moment, he grasped a tremendous club, as if about to rush upon his prey.

The soul of a hero was visible in him, and his expressive countenance displayed a mind and strength capable of performing a great and glorious achievement.

The club he wielded seemed to shrink in his Herculean gripe.

Amri proceeded to the conclusion of her narrative. "When I awoke to reason and to the knowledge of my situation, I found myself stretched upon a miserable pallet, with thee by my side. The flames had scorched me, and I endured excessive pain, but I consoled myself with the idea that first endeared me to life.

"Mr. Mornton procured me good medical assistance, and I rapidly recovered.

"At this time, Yamkee, the old negro on whose ground I lived, died, and bequeathed her little spot to me.* Now I became more capable, and had a greater opportunity, to tutor you how to hate the white men.

"My son, I had heard such things exist as good Europeans, men of great worth and charitable disposition, whose tender humanity has sought to redress our grievances, alleviate our sufferings, and lighten the load of slavery. Alas! no such men inhabit our Island; but Yamkee informed me our master Mornton was most humane and good. Good, in truth! If he heals our wounds, for whose sake is it? Is it for ours, or his own benefit? do we not work? do we not labor, till, jaded, we fall upon the ground, exhausted and fatigued? Then what is our reward? What? when, overcome by the labor of the day, we flag, the whip to cheer us on.

"One day, our planter's pride gave all a holiday, to celebrate his birth, and another day to celebrate the wedding of captain Harrop. This man did wed with our master's daughter; that was a day of joy, but not to me: could I celebrate the nuptials of that man? I could with pleasure celebrate his death.

"This day of joy; when all the negroes of the plantation were making themselves merry, I solitarily traversed the uncultivated country, most wretched and unhappy. This was a severe blow to my heart. I was distracted to hear of the happiness of this inhuman monster, who broke my peace, and made me most miserable.

"Oh! that I had had an opportunity to dash his matrimonial cup with poison! it was the sincerest wish of my heart.

"I pursued a long winding course up the mountain; lost in thought, buried in my own reflections, my busy mind was disturbed by the sound of voices near. I heard one singing; I listened attentively, and thus a female in soft delicate voice sang. The melody of her notes echoed through the foliage, and the soft breeze carried the airy measure to my ear.

---

\*   It is customary, nay, in fact a constant use in Jamaica, to dispose the newly imported negroes among the domesticated slaves of the plantation, who, in the first instance, are allowed a small portion of ground, which they cultivate for their support, after the labor of the day is completed for their masters. When they die, they have the privilege of bequeathing it to whom they please; but, surely, 'tis a cruelty to oblige them to support a newly imported negro, on a spot of ground matured by their own hard labor. [Known as a provision-ground; allotted to slaves in the West-Indies for the growing of food-stuffs (*OED*).]

POOR white man came to Ora's shore,
Where wild beast howl and lions roar;
He came, and faint beneath a tree,
Most piteous begg'd for charity.
Ah! poor white man, why didst thou roam?
   Sad Ora pities thee.
Why leave thy friend, why leave thy home,
   To deal with bad Slatee?

I'll give thee milk, I'll give thee corn,
I'll give the Saphie[1] in the horn,
I'll shield thee from the venomed lake
And guard thee 'gainst the rattle-snake,
If thou wilt bring me Sambo[2] good,
   Whom wicked Slatee sell;
Say ninety bars* and pass the wood.
   For I love Sambo well.

Oh! give me milk, Oh! give me corn,
I need no Saphie in the horn;
And in change I'll give to thee
Thy Sambo good and liberty.
I need thy care, I need thy food,
   For, faint beneath this tree,
I cannot walk and pass the wood
   To give thy love to thee.

Then good white man he eat his fill,
He cross the wood, the vale, the hill,
He cross the lake and cross the moor,

---

*   Nominal Money, value two shillings or thereabout sterling money.

---

1   A charm, particularly associated with the Ashanti people of what is now central Ghana.
2   One term in the lexicon used to refer disparagingly to slaves. The favourite homology for a slave was the woman or wife, then the minor child or an animal. Other terms for slaves were the apprentice, the pauper, the harlot, the felon, the actor, and the complex image of the Southern "Sambo" or Caribbean "Quashee" (*Encyclopædia Britannica*).

And comes unto the Slatee's door.
Oh! goodly Slatee, let me see
 The slaves you have to sell,
And thy price will pay to thee
 For Sambo, if he dwell.

Ah! good white man, so soon he come,
And cross the wood brings Sambo home.
Oh! Ora's heart high in glee,
And joy in white man's face I see.
Then good white man he to me say,
 'I go my friend, farewell!
'We part, for now I haste away,
  'In other lands to dwell.'

But no, I leave the lions roar
And seek with white man other shore;
With white man who beneath a tree
Did ask of Ora charity.
'Twas white man cheer'd my aching heart,
 And Ora grateful be:
Ah! white man, we will never part;
 I'll tramp the world with thee.

"There was music in the air, and a sweetness in the style of singing, to which my ear was but little accustomed, but the subject was contrary to my heart.

"I had half a mind to enquire of the singer if her ballad was drawn from life, though I was in no mood to hear a voice declare in praise of an European's virtues, and proceeded homewards.

"Since that period, nothing material has happened; a constant round of uninterrupted slavery has engrossed the whole."

———————————

So much for the tale of Amri; read it Charles, and blush for your countrymen. Adieu!

GEORGE STANFORD.

# LETTER VI.

*The same to the same.*

DEAR CHARLES,

I HAVE just breakfasted, and indeed I was so fatigued from the over night, that I did not resume my pen so soon as I could have wished this morning.

As I have not the power of writing sufficiently well to impress you with the subject, do read a little slower; indeed the badness of my scroll will not suffer you to read fast, but I mean think a little more, and I dare say you will soon learn what I wish to express.

Amri concluded her narrative; Jack embraced his mother, and resolutely swore to accomplish whatever she should dictate.

"Now then," cried the sanguinary Amri, "the eventful moment dawns, and, Harrop, look to it.

"In a cell, near Mount Lebanus, dwells the sequestered Bashra; to him must you apply for Obi, my son, and thither will we proceed this night, while the whole plantation is rocked in slumber; now, follow me."

She rose, and turning upon Jack, "There was a time, when Amri would have instructed you in the more mild and gentle persuasion of humanity; but," added she, "as you value your country, spurn the hated feeling, and let revenge light you to your prey."

Closely hid from the most penetrating eye, by the thick foliage of interwoven trees, stood the small sequestered hut of the Obiah-practitioner, Bashra, wrinkled and deformed.* Snails drew their slimy train upon his shrivelled feet, and lizards and vipers filled the air of his hut with foul uncleanliness.

His dwelling was the receptacle of robbers, and he gave them Obi, to protect them from the wounds of their assailants.

---

\* Formerly there was no regular method of treating yaws in the West-Indies. It was the custom, when a negro was so afflicted, to send him from the plantation, to recover at random, and it often contracted the limbs of the wretched sufferer, and made them much deformed.

It was here that fugitive negroes ran, to revenge themselves on those that did them any injury;* and here came the self-deluded Amri, with her aspiring son—to this horrible cell of iniquity. Bashra was astonished at the noble appearance of the hero-minded Jack, and embraced him with all the fervor of a father.

He prepared an Obi for him, of more than common qualities, a purpose preparation, that should stand by him in time of need, and the arms of his foe should fall defenceless from their grasp; in short, the charm possessed such rare virtues, that it was to answer every wish of its possessor.†

Amri was well pleased, and she herself slung the Obi horn round his neck.

Now was Jack his mother's pride. With strength superior to the boasted virtues of his Obi, though he placed the greatest confidence in them, he prepared to revenge his parents and oppose the destroyers of his country's peace. But then, how to begin the war? could he alone stand against the united efforts of a whole Island?

He did not imagine it, and looked for other means.

They returned, well satisfied, to their hovel, devising how they should set the slaves in open rebellion, and extirpate the European race.

The matter could not but appear difficult; but Jack, whose bosom burnt with an eager desire to command, thought those but trivial obstacles, and determined to strike the blow, with resolution on his side, which would partly insure success.

He resolved to speak to the private ear of those groaning slaves, and holding advantageous views before them, link them to one firm and resolute body.

---

*  Obi, for the purpose of bewitching people, or consuming them by lingering illness, is made of grave-dirt, hair, teeth of sharks and other animals, blood, feathers, egg-shells, and images in wax, the hearts of birds, livers of mice, and some potent roots, weeds and bushes, which the Europeans are at this time ignorant of, but were known for the same purposes to the ancients. *Moseley on Sugar, &c* [Benjamin Moseley, *A Treatise on Sugar* (London: G.G. and J. Robinson, 1799) 171; see Appendix A.]

†  "I," says Dr. Moseley, "saw the Obi of the famous negro robber, Three-fingered Jack, the terror of Jamaica, in 1780. It consisted of a goat's horn, filled with a compound of grave-dirt, ashes, the blood of a black cat, and human fat, all mixed into a kind of paste.

"A cat's foot, a dried toad, a pig's tail, a slip of virginal parchment, of kid's skin, with characters marked in blood on it, were also in his Obiah-bag."

Jack, capable himself of performing great deeds, never once admitted the possibility that all men were not like him; he fancied the negroes would take the same firm interest in the cause that he himself did; but, upon trial, he found how grievously he was mistaken.

He followed the next day's toil with unremitting zeal; indeed, the hopes of liberty inspired him, and the labor was light on his hands.

Towards the approach of evening, as he wiped the sweat from his brow, an European stood by his side whom he knew not.

The white man thus accosted him: "Friend, you must be deemed a material acquisition to the plantation of Mr. Mornton."

Jack returned his question with a look.

"But you feel a pleasure in cultivation, that fully rewards your labor. The sun shines and assists you in your toil; a glorious opportunity presents itself to you to contemplate the various beauties of Nature, and the soft zephirs that play around you keep your body in a moderate degree of warmth.

"How happy is your situation, how truly enviable! You can contemplate the vast expanse before you, and can say in private to your heart: 'My God, I have answered the end of thy creation; for I, with the sweat of my brow, diffuse thy beneficence around, extract from the earth the produce thereof, and help to render the comforts of life complete.'

Jack answered not, and he continued.

"And how grateful it is to the heart to say, I too have done my best to render you, lords of creation, happy; no doubt ye feel the force of my argument, and have thought as I do. Remember you command the voice of gratitude, and—"

"An European, and talk of gratitude!" were the first words Jack uttered: "do ye feel the expression in your heart? do ye know how to show it? What white man will say to the African, to thee I owe my life? Gratitude is an expression used by *your* countrymen, but practised by *mine*, who are unacquainted with its name."

"Friend, thou art somewhat severe upon the men of Europe; we do profess gratitude, and—" "never practice it," added Jack.

"Nay, to show it is not merely nominal with us, I declare here that I owe my life to a daughter of Africa, who with the tender arm of humanity, snatched me from a watery grave, and to her I am for ever bound in gratitude."

"Well, Sir?"—Jack's heart struggled in his bosom—"and how did ye express it?"

"She was a wild untutored being, bred up in native simplicity, in the bosom of Africa; she was ignorant, and I matured her understanding; her good heart was incircled by weeds of a savage growth; I plucked them by the roots and implanted in their stead seeds of a more refined nature; by my daily perseverance, and the susceptibility of a heart that owned all tender feelings from her birth, they soon expanded and ripened into blossom. I felt a pleasure in the culture of her mind, such as you must feel, when raising from the ground a nutriment to life. And now, the time arrived when I was about to leave her country; she, with an expanded mind, was become weary of a place, where nothing dwelt but savage ignorance, and in return for her saving my life, I have brought her to happier climes, accompanied by the partner of her heart; to climes, where the virtues born in our bosom are more refined than in the savage bowels of Africa."

Jack, whose breast was warmed with many a sigh which he had suppressed, now spoke: "I had parents, Sir, who were born in Africa, possessing all the barbarous virtues of their country, without European refinement; one in particular, which proved a vice to their interest, a damned vice, the source of all their succeeding misery, which hurried one to the grave, leaving the other now a wretched slave. They snatched from the shattered remnants of a tempest-beaten vessel, two helpless beings, Europeans, Sir, both in the agonies of death, and ready to expire in each other's arms. This was a scene, which, to hearts that would not harm a thing of heaven's creation, was most distressing. My mother hurried to the waves that bore the floating fragment; she drew them on shore, gave them all possible assistance, and conveyed them to her hovel, where by her care and attention they were soon recovered."

A tear stood in Jack's eye, and he exclaimed: "Why does the agonizing sweat of vengeance alone chafe my cheek? Why doth this nerved arm handle the spade, when it should wield the sword? My parents shielded those hapless monsters, in the bosom of their hovel, for full three months, when they were severed from their country. And what was the reward, the thanks they received for their liberality? You shall hear; chains and slavery! Those European monsters, in friendly mask, dragged them from their home. My father fought for liberty and struggled hard, till overpowered by numbers, he was forced to yield to the superiority of his foes. During their voyage, my father was most basely murdered by those relentless savages; my mother heard his dying groans, and would have followed him; but he forbid her to die, for his sake, for her sake, for the sake of revenge, which he expected from her offspring. She lived, was sold a slave here, in Jamaica sold, and gave me birth.

"Look to me, Europeans; tremble at the name of Jack, for he will revenge his father, and banish humanity from his heart, to accomplish its fondest wish."

He concluded with a look of resolution.

The European stood mute; his blood was stagnated, the color faded from his cheek, and his lips quivered. During this pause, an overseer came up, saying: "Captain Harrop, my master wants you." "Captain Harrop!" repeated Jack; the name was in his head—engraven in his heart. "Captain Harrop!" Every lineament in his face bespoke the knowledge of that hated name. He stood in an attitude of horror mingled with resentment; his hands were clenched, every limb shook with rage, every fibre in his frame quivered.

Captain Harrop was nearly fainting; he trembled; his body was covered with a cold sweat; his brow was palsied and the corrosive drops of terror trickled down his cheek.

Jack's trembling was occasioned by exerted strength; the muscles of his manly limbs were all in action, and his whole frame was convulsed with a lion's fury.

The overseer was astonished, on beholding the various emotions in the countenance of each. He struck Jack across the shoulders with the whip; Jack was insensible to the blow. He again repeated: "Captain Harrop, my master wants you."

This aroused Jack from his torpitude, and captain Harrop, recovering, replied: "I attend you."

They proceeded towards the plantation-house, and Jack stood like a tyger meeting his prey, ready to dart upon it. He maintains his ground, while its eyes are watching him; but no sooner are they withdrawn, than bounding forward he seizes the victim, and satiates his fury in its blood. So Jack rushed forward to his foe and seized his arm with a most powerful gripe.

A groan of anguish escaped the lips of Harrop.

This scene was a mystery to the overseer, who interfering, endeavoured to withdraw the arm of Harrop from the grasp of his antagonist. His endeavours were vain, and making use of his authority, he again struck Jack most severely with his whip.

Jack, with the disengaged arm, felled the overseer lifeless to the ground, and now captain Harrop became the sole object of his fury. Jack had no weapon, but with the other hand he lifted up his daunted foe, and prepared to dash out his brains.

Several negroes and overseers, who had been distant witnesses of the foregoing scene, arrived just in time to save his life. Jack was precipitating him to the ground, with all his vengeance, aided by the exertion of gigantic strength; the negroes fell to the ground, to receive the falling body of Harrop and prevent the impending injury; down he came, and the interfering slaves were scattered lifeless all around.

Jack was immediately seized by a strong party, who were arriving from all quarters. The whole plantation was in the utmost state of alarm, and many were terrified at his menacing looks.

Captain Harrop was very much bruised, and they were leading him away; no word had been spoken during this scene, and Jack first broke the pause. "Harrop," said he, "if my speechless rage any ways surprised thee, learn that Makro *was* my father, and Amri is my mother: keep the remembrance in thy heart, for I, their son, shall yet encompass revenge."

The captain was led away, and all the negroes flocked round Jack, who thus addressed them: "Countrymen and slaves, ye who daily feel the galling yoke of the Europeans, 'tis to ye I address myself, 'tis to ye I speak. Suffer not your tender offsprings to labor beneath a foreign sun; suffer not your wives, your mothers, to sink under the load of unnatural and disgraceful slavery.

"Rise, and reassume your rights. Throw off the chains that incircle ye, and oppose the enemies of your country man to man. What is there a desperate and firm mind cannot accomplish?

Remember the struggle is for liberty; to destroy the power of our enemies, to regain the privileges of our native land.

"Who is there would not, for the sake of themselves, their wives, their children and their country, rise into a firm body, cemented by the ties that bind us to each other? Who is there would not rise to repel the bold invaders of those rights dear to an African, and to every man who loves his country and his tender offspring?

"'Tis to ye I speak, for ye and not for myself. I have no wife, no family, no relation among ye, saving a loving mother, whose injuries rise to my heart.

"I am a single desolated being, ready to catch at an opportunity, wherein I can benefit the distressed of my country. If I die, no one bewails my loss, saving this loving mother; if I live no one is benefited by it, no one of ye, my brethren. The fruits of my labor and yours go to pamper the sordid appetites of the rich and proud, and not to relieve the distresses of the poor and needy, either of this country or ours.

"And then, let me ask you, what are our rewards, when the sweat of our brow drops upon the land in streams and clogs the earth? if we delay, the inhuman blow and more disgraceful whip. Are we not treated like dogs and worked like mules? and by men, as *we* are, who vary only with us in color—yes, my countrymen, let me add, in heart.

"They come to our shores, in Africa, and with deceitful tongue, delude us to their grasp; others more openly encourage a traffic with beings, if possible, more inhuman than themselves, the vile slatees, who plunder their countrymen, and sell them to their country's foes.

"And then, do they not encourage broils and intestine wars, setting our African princes to rebel against each other, to devastate our country of her sons by murder and united slavery? Need I exhort you to take up arms against the Europeans? Oh no, you have felt their tyrannical power as I have felt it, have groaned beneath the yoke, and have but awaited an opportunity that you might shake it off."[1]

---

[1] There are parallel thoughts in the speech that Jack makes here and the well-known speech of Oroonoko rousing his countrymen:

Jack paused; he was surrounded on every side by attentive negroes; those that had at first seized him gave up their hold, in attention to what he said, and when he finished, loud huzzas rent the air. There was one among them of a noble soul, of fine form, with fierce and penetrating eye; onward he came, with steady step and lion-hearted; he set the great example, with intrepid firmness. He grasped the hand of Jack, and thus Mahali spoke: "Nine annual suns have cheered the herbage of the field, since Mahali was dragged from his native clime; nine annual suns have, as they displayed their splendor, heard Mahali's groans, accompanied by vows of revenge; but now the moment dawns, the mist evaporates that incircled me, and I throw off the yoke.

"Countrymen, ye that do espouse the cause we fight for, now throng around, and let the reverberation of Liberty ascend to heaven, and reach on earth the gaudy dwellings of our tyrant masters."

Jack returned Mahali the friendly gripe. The overseers fled in every direction, fearing a rebellion, and thinking to suppress it ere it gained a head.

The loud shouts of the negroes were heard at a great distance, and thirty troops from the colony came down upon them with fixed bayonets; the affrighted negroes set up a loud yell and fled, while Jack, heated with rage, called to them aloud.

"Rascals! cowards! do ye fly then? I spurn you, and will seek the woods alone, there will I torment these vile Europeans. Traitors to your country, your trust and your liberty, I despise you, abject as ye are, I disclaim you; I loath you more than your enemies, under whose whip you would rather die than by one exertion shake off the thing ye hate.

---

And why, *said he,* my dear Friends and Fellow-sufferers, shou'd we be Slaves to an unknown People? Have they Vanquish'd us Nobly in Fight? Have they Won us in Honourable Battel? And are we, by the chance of War, become their Slaves? This wou'd not anger a Noble Heart, this wou'd not animate a Souldiers Soul; no, but we are Bought and Sold like Apes, or Monkeys, to be the Sport of Women, Fools and Cowards; and the Support of Rogues, Runagades, that have abandon'd their own Countries, for Rapin, Murders, Thefts and Villanies: Do you not hear every Day how they upbraid each other with infamy of Life, below the Wildest Salvages; and shall we render Obedience to such a degenerate Race, who have no one Humane Vertue left, to distinguish 'em from the vilest Creatures? Will you, I say, suffer the Lash from such Hands? (184–85).

"Hence, ye base and sorry crew, hence, ye have deceived me, I thought all men loved liberty."

Jack was without arms, and the soldiers were upon him; there was no possibility of making an escape, and resistance would have been madness; he submitted himself a prisoner, and was put under a strong confinement.

Well, Charles, we have followed our hero to a confinement, from whence nothing but heroism or the treachery of the guard can extricate him. I can assure you, in Jamaica, we have many Newgates,[1] and many bold[2] fellows confined in them.

I am right weary of my pen, I must beg another pause, and to-morrow I shall be at my desk ere the sun has shot his first ray. Adieu!

GEORGE STANFORD.


LETTER VII.

*The same to the same.*

DEAR CHARLES,

ACCORDING to promise I am seated at my desk ere the sun has deigned to gild the hemisphere with his morning radiance, ere the nightly ravages of the prowling racoon are ceased. I have passed but a sleepless interim. The image of Jack haunts me, and I am loath to drop my pen, until I have concluded his history. Say what you will, he is a noble fellow, and deserves the admiration of all free-born men.

Amri was distracted, when she heard of this misfortune; she flew to consult with Bashra, who was confounded; but, assuring her of the virtue of his Obi, he pacified the earnest mother, who trembled for her darling son.

---

[1]  The name of a celebrated London prison (pulled down in 1902–3), used more generally in British English to refer to any prison.

[2]  Bold is intended in the pejorative sense: audacious, presumptuous, too forward (*OED*).

On the second day of his imprisonment, Jack took his trial. "What," demanded the judge "could actuate you to such a deed?" "What?" retorted Jack, with the words of his heart in his eyes, "do you ask a slave what can urge him on to assume his native liberty? do you ask the man heart-broken, galled by repeated insults, whose back is daily gored by the lacerating whip, do you ask that man what can urge him to revenge? Think you we do not mingle with our groans curses on your race? or think you our hearts are callous to all feeling? Mistaken man, we feel as ye do. Think you we are dogs? again mistaken; in the eye of the great Creator, we are as ye are; but the scalding tear shall now no longer chafe my cheek, nor the sweat my brow. I know that I am to die; proceed to the execution of your office, ye men of justice, for I am prepared to die, with the native fortitude of my country. If you have mercy, dispatch me quick; I ask it, I beseech it of you; I lived but to revenge; the deity of my country proved false to me, and....." He paused; a sudden recollection crossed his brain, the manly tear started from his eye; "These drops" he continued, "are not the drops of weakness, I have a hapless wretched mother. As you shall expect a reward in the world to come, as you shall expect to be forgiven, when you appear before the great tribunal, protect her, cheer her oppressed heart, and I will, even in the hour of death, entreat mercy for my persecutors. Oh! agony of my heart, do I leave her in the power of voracious tygers? Look on me Europeans; Jack defies your malice; he invites your tortures; they shall not draw a groan from his heart; but the thoughts of my mother being open to your barbarities weigh heavy upon it, and more bitter anguish than all the cruelties you can exercise on my body."

Overcome with grief he sunk into the arms of his guard, and was borne back to his confinement.

He was cast for death; he was to be slung up by his waist, forty feet from the ground, to a gallows, exposed to the sun's burning heat and to those noxious insects of the West-Indies, that infect the body even to putridity, for three days, receiving no sustenance; on the fourth, he was to be taken down, and the soles of his feet seared, and under the arm-pits, then to receive five hundred lashes, have his heart and entrails burnt before him, to be quartered, and his quarters to be hung in four several parts of the Island, to strike terror to the slaves.

This sentence was heard with horror through all the plantations in the Island, but Jack listened to it with a firm indifference, and now he placed but little confidence in the virtues of his Obi.

On the fifth day from that of trial, Jack was to suffer. Three were already elapsed, and he was not without some hopes of making his escape. His prison windows were strongly grated with iron bars, those he found easy to tear asunder; but then a leap of thirty feet presented itself, and two centinels beneath to encounter. Jack knew that by remaining where he was he was sure to die, and if he was to make a desperate attempt he had the means of escape, though the event was hazardous. They had neglected manacling Jack; either they saw no occasion, or more probably, it was want of thought. His resolution was made, and on the fourth night, when the men were retired to their couch,[1] and no hum was heard, save the chattering of the centinels beneath, who were every now and then nodding on their post, Jack tore up the grating from the window, and viewed the height he had to leap; 'twas fearful, but Jack was no midnight robber, he trembled not at the waving of a bow or at the sight of danger, and with a massy bar in his hand, down he plunged.

The ground received him unhurt, but the centinels were aroused.

"Who goes?" demanded one.

"A friend," replied Jack.

"Make yourself known, we dare not suffer any person to pass; speak, or we fire."

It was very dark, the centinels did not see Jack leap, though they heard the descent, nor did they once conceive it possible for their prisoner to break the bars or leap so frightful a precipice.

Jack returned no answer, but was proceeding forward.

"Answer who you are, or we are bound to fire," repeated the centinel, who presented his musket, and his comrade came up

---

[1] A frame or structure, with what is spread over it (or simply a layer of some soft substance), on which to lie down for rest or sleep; a bed (*OED*).

by the side of Jack. Thus situated, he lifted his ponderous bar and struck the centinel who stood near him dead at his feet. The other fired; his shot whizzed under Jack's ear, who now rushed forward and beat his brains out.

He now took their cartridge boxes and muskets, and, lest the report of the gun should occasion immediate pursuit, he hid himself among the bushes.

He listened, but all was still and silent, and being anxious for this mother's safety, he resolved to see her.

His approach to the plantation of Mr. Mornton was dangerous; but he was acquainted with every winding of the road, filial affection prompted him on, and in a short time he entered the hovel of his mother.

Amri was stretched upon her pallet, in an agony of grief and bathed in tears.

Jack entered silently; he hung over her, and the fond smile was upon his cheek. Oh! what an exquisite satisfaction to his heart, to behold his mother's despair for her lost son, and to be able thus to soothe her sorrow!

Jack had a noble soul; his breast might have harboured every endearing virtue, and, though when an infant, they were destroyed to gratify a mother's revenge, still honor was his idol. He possessed great sensibility, and could not help bewailing the fate of those centinels who fell by his hand, although in self-defence.

After indulging in a pleasant reflection, he leaned over her pallet, tapped her gently on the shoulder, and cried in an affectionate voice: "Mother!"

She rose on hearing the well-known sound, and with a shout of joy threw herself into his arms.

Fair reader, have you a son? you alone can imagine their transports. Amri's bosom, though dead to every other feeling, still expanded to her son, and her heart, rendered callous by the malevolence of fortune, beat as strongly for him, as the British fair's who cherishes maternal affection for a virtuous offspring.

When their transports were in part abated, Jack related the method of his escape, and thus revived his mother's fears. She trembled for his safety, and he himself advised a retreat, but no supplication of his mother's could prevent his persevering in an instant revenge on captain Harrop. "This may be," he cried, "the last opportunity, and I will not lose it."

Though it was the nearest wish of Amri's heart to gratify that passion, still she valued the life of her son too much, to endanger it at the moment when he had rescued it; but Jack, flushed with the hopes of victory, persisted, and in the midnight hour she led him to the gaudy abode of captain Harrop.

Sleep dwelt not beneath his canopy; peace was a stranger to his guilty bosom, and if with opiates he invited the soporific god, frightful dreams and fancies would rouse him from the repose he could not enjoy.

Captain Harrop ever viewed the coming night with pain, for he could not rest, and passed the sleepless time in watching.

Jack stood before the portal of his mansion; no human eye beheld him, and he sought admission by force. The door repelled his utmost strength; he tried to break open the windows, they too refused him admission; but casting his eye above, he beheld a casement open; a ladder was only wanting and one he found tied with strong ropes to a gate before the house. He drew his sabre, cut the ropes asunder, and fixing it to the window, ascended, while Amri beneath sent up prayers to heaven for the protection of her son.

He got in at the window; a taper burned at the further end of the apartment, placed by fortune to guide him to his prey.

He listened—

He heard some one near him groan in disturbed slumber; his heart beat in trepidation: another groan succeeded, and he beheld Harrop stretched on a mattress near him. "Oh! Spare me, spare me," uttered the wretched man. "Mercy, mercy! yes, I will be just, but spare me." A cold sweat hung on his distorted brow; he writhed and twined about in anguish.

Jack viewed him with terror; the groans that proceeded from his heart made Jack's soul tremble; but time was precious, and he called on him by name; "Captain Harrop, arise." The guilty man started from his couch, and, uttering a scream, fell fainting at his feet.

"The lion preys not upon carcases."

Jack could not lift his arm against him; it sunk nerveless by his side. Had Harrop been a man, Jack had had no need of fire added to his impetuous soul; but his foe was cowardly and most pitiful, and Jack could not stab him.

He heard the heavy bell toll, and the grey streaks of morning were visible at the horizon; he lifted Harrop from the ground, who in the humblest terms sued for mercy; Jack heard approaching footsteps; with his left hand he slung the victim on his shoulder, in his right he brandished the gleaming sabre, and thus he descended.

The ladder broke beneath his feet, and he fell to the ground— Harrop was stunned.

Amri, who had waited in trembling anxiety, now blessed the Almighty providence that protected him, and, on beholding Harrop, the remembrance of her injuries rose to her heart, and she could have plunged Jack's sabre to the hilt, to search the soul of her enemy: but Jack begged his mother, as she regarded his and her own safety, to return home; no time was to be lost, and she fled to her hovel. He with his two guns, and captain Harrop braced upon his shoulder by one nervous arm, and his sabre in the other, for self-defence, flew on the wings of speed.

Mount Lebanus[1] was the place intended for his habitation; he had observed in former travels a cave almost hid from the human eye; the ascent to it was steep and dangerous; he knew every turning in the mountain, and that there was but one road to it.

To this spot he determined to owe his future safety; he climbed the rugged mountain with the burthen upon his back, though often forced, weary of his load, to rest himself and gather new strength.

Harrop still remained insensible; Jack proceeded, came up to the mouth of his cave, and no longer heeding his pursuers, if there were any, entered the gloomy abode.

A plague on't, Charles! What a number of interruptions have I had since I first sat down to write? but I cannot help it. Adieu!

GEORGE STANFORD.

---

[1]  Peak of 1, 751 feet located in the St. Thomas region of Jamaica.

# LETTER VIII.

*The same to the same.*

DEAR CHARLES,

IN pursuance of my task, I have once more taken my seat at my desk; and, as I have a little more leisure on my hands at present, than I usually have, I shall take up a portion of your time in saying something for myself. I do not know what to call it, whether a defence, or—but, to state heads—*Imprimis*, I am no author.[1]

*In secundis*, I am writing solely for your amusement.

Now to proceed with order. *Imprimis*, being no author, I must request your indulgence for all the faults..... But what need is there? I repeat it again and again. *Imprimis*, I am no author.

*In secundis*, or secondly, as I am writing for your amusement only, to enforce my former request in my solution of *Imprimis*, I must demand the aid of a few tears to soil my paper..... Soil, did I say? let me scratch out the word, I mean, a tear from the heart, to glitter on my page, like the dew of morning on the tender rose bud.

Oh! how rich is the tear of sensibility! not all the fancied pleasures of man can equal the soft emotions of the heart, when engendering the sympathizing drop. Not all the luxury and pageantry of pomp can equal the dazzling lustre of the pearly dew, glowing on the cheek, at the misfortunes of man.

Jack was a man! The precepts of his country were instilled into his heart, and he did no wrong. Conscience smote him not; he knew it not. He was not hardened, for he was awake to feeling. He would do no harm to woman, child, or any defenceless being. He was not dead to the ties of nature, for he loved his mother. He was not dishonorable, for he would not lift his hand against a son of Africa. He loved his countrymen, and the stream of consanguinity flowed warmly to his heart. The men of Europe

---

[1] It was a common literary convention in eighteenth-century sentimental novels for the author to express his inadequacy as a narrator. The sentimental novel, as popularized by Sterne in *Tristam Shandy* and *A Sentimental Journey* and by Mackenzie in *The Man of Feeling*, along with others, gave importance to direct expression of feeling—hence the emphasis on tears.

were his foes, and he would hunt the world to revenge himself on the sanguinary sons of the white cliffs. From this short sketch I would have you say with me:

Jack was a Man!!

Jack was a Hero!!!

The mouth of his cave was concealed by a heavy tree that had sprung its root full fifteen feet beneath, at whose base ran murmuring a cooling spring. One untrodden and narrow path led to it. Its windings were intricate, and would have bewildered the most wary traveller. No one dared to attempt its course while Jack was master of Lebanus.

The cave ran to an amazing distance, and its descent into the earth exceeded one hundred feet. 'Twas here that Jack brought the guilty Harrop, who on his knees implored his mercy.

Mercy! Jack knew it not; he had expunged the feeling from his heart, and resolved that the wretched Harrop should be a slave to him in his seclusion.

Jack had never considered how, thus buried from the world, he could live.

He was in want of many things, which he could not plunder from the unwary European, and to make the interior of his cave his dwelling, he was in want of fire, for many purposes, as well as to compose himself to his slumbers;* those he could not procure from the traveller; but on recollection, he determined to apply to Bashra.

Bashra was one of those deserted negroes, who, affected by a disorder† prevalent in the West-Indies, are compelled to fly from the plantation on which they are engaged, and seek a retreat in the woods, where, unassisted, they are left to die or recover, at the will of Providence.

This disorder is said to communicate so rapidly, that one single affected slave may in one day distemper the whole plantation.

Those are the beings, who, in their seclusion, most frequently practice Obi. The more they are deformed, the more they are venerated, and their charm credited as the strongest.

---

\* The slaves of the West-Indies cannot sleep without fire in their hovel.

† Vide Yaws, a disease described by Dr. Hort, in his medical observations added to Treatise on sugar.

When the negroes, the next day, assembled to their labor, and saw the unhappy centinels weltering in their blood, they instantly caused an alarm, which in a few hours was general through the whole Island, and every mouth was filled with the name of Jack, and the astonishing disappearance of captain Harrop.

There was an immediate pursuit ordered; but the expedition proved unsuccessful; they had searched the whole Island, and every spot where human being could inhabit; (Jack heard the footsteps of his pursuers beneath his cave, and loading both his muskets, stood prepared to meet their attack) but he was no where to be found.

The Court of Assembly met, and they summoned Amri to appear before them. She came, and fortitude along with her. They exhorted her to tell if she knew where Jack was concealed. "Every avenue," cried they, "is guarded, and he must fall into our hands."

"Must!" replied Amri, with all the force of expression; "must fall into your hands! then why summon a poor weak mother before your mighty council, to betray her son?"

"Resign him to the hands of Justice," added the former, "and we will give you life and freedom; but, if you persist, and we should find you are an accomplice, you shall know the rigor of our laws, and how severely you will suffer."

"Yes," returned this heroic woman, "I know, I well know the severity of your justice; do with me as you please; I am defenceless and in your power. But as for him, learn that he is beyond your malice; learn from me that he possesses an Obi, shall sink you all to very nothingness."

The few slaves that were present, at the name of Obi, gave a dreadful scream and fell upon their faces; even the council were alarmed. They well knew what a panic the science had occasioned for many years among the slaves, and to be thus revived, was to fill the Island with fresh terrors.

Amri was placed upon the rack; but she obstinately persisted in secrecy, though she earnestly declared she was no accomplice in his escape, nor did she know whither he was fled. She was discharged.

At the entrance of the woods around strong guards were placed, but Jack avoided their utmost diligence.

Wearied with their search, and often wounded by the negro robbers that infested the woods, they returned.

Jack, for the first two days of his enlargement,[1] hungered in his cave, a free and solitary prisoner. On the third, he ventured forth, having previously bound his captive, and visited the cave of Bashra, watchful of every step he took, and armed with two guns loaded and his sabre. A band of robbers were assembled there, and Jack appeared before them. They knew him, and vowed to own him as their leader; but Jack scorned assistance; his countrymen had failed him on the onset. Bashra filled Jack's horn with his Obi; and gave him an ointment, with which he rubbed the brows of his countrymen that they might not betray him! he likewise gave to those deluded people a charm of less magnitude, and they confided[2] in his magic skill.

Bashra concluded his ceremonies, and a loud blast from the echoing horn struck their ears. The robbers were affrighted, and Jack alone grasped his sabre with firmness. The blast was repeated, but more faintly, and three distinct but feeble blows were given with the flat of a sword on the hollow sounding rock, by way of signal. "It is our comrade," repeated the robbers, and they climbed the ascent from Bashra's cave.

They soon returned, bearing a negro on their shoulders, wounded and bloody. The dying man opened his eyes, and casting them on Jack, uttered: "Oh! let me die at the feet of the avenger of our nation." Jack was amazed; the wounded man was placed on the ground before him; he embraced the feet of Jack—

'Twas Mahali!

"Mahali!" Jack raised him up—and met his warm embrace; the blood gushed from his wounds, and Jack committed him to the care of Bashra.

Mahali was brave, Mahali was unfortunate, and Jack was compassionate and generous. Mahali was a Feloop, and Jack loved his countrymen.

Our hero received from Bashra a lamp, some oil and ammunition, and thus furnished, returned to his cave.

---

[1] Release from confinement or bondage (OED).

[2] To trust or have faith; to put or place trust, repose confidence in (OED).

Harrop was faint and pale with hunger; he again fell upon his knees before Jack, and implored him for food. "Wretch!" he replied, "barbarous inhuman savage! what mercy canst thou expect from me? Me, whom thou hast robbed of his family? What mercy canst thou expect from the son of that man, whose injured blood cries aloud to his Maker for vengeance? If life can be an indulgence, then thou shalt have it; but thou shalt curse the miserable load. Thou shalt implore me to divest thee of that, painful in itself, and hourly inflicting wounds to thy soul, by a retrospect on thy past life."

"Oh!" cried Harrop, "let humanity be the guide of your bosom; true, I have erred, and I acknowledge a just punishment is due; but temper your justice with mildness; humanity is a sovereign balm to the heart of man, and blest is he that possesses it. If you will unbind me and let me return to my family, I do most solemnly promise to obtain your pardon and your freedom."

"I despise thy offer; this is thy abode during the residue of thy days; here shalt thou linger and be my slave. Perfidious wretch! were I so inclined, could I give credit to thy promise? Hast thou not broken every tie that can bind man to man? Hast thou not forfeited all confidence in thy word or oath? Thou and thy pallid brethren may call Jack a robber, bold and daring; but they shall not call him a fool."

"By all my hopes of salvation in the world to come, by my hopes of pardon, I will be punctual to my word," replied the lost Harrop. "Hear me, thou just Being, at whose tribunal I shall one day appear; if I prove false, may thy infinite mercy be denied me!"

"No more," returned Jack; "I will never tread in confidence the plains, where sickly Europeans dwell; nor will I put any trust in thee: here be content to pass the remainder of thy days." Saying this, he dashed Harrop from him on the ground.

The cave was noisome, dark and dismal; a stifling vapour proceeded from the earth, and the lamp burnt but dimly. Jack plucked some wood, which he burnt to air it, and made himself a couch of grass which he covered with plantain leaves.

Several days had elapsed, and no discovery had been made of where Jack existed. The governor proceeded to his last resource, and offered a large reward for his apprehension. This reward was alluring, and many of the negroes would have tried to obtain it; but every one feared to venture against Jack, who possessed so powerful an Obi. Numbers, who were enemies to Jack, and had in their speech upbraided him, now fancying he had overheard them, thought themselves affected by him, and a great depopulation took place.

But Quashee, a brave black of Scots-Hall, Maroons-town, on the promise of that liberty which was dear to him, resolved to try the effect of an expedition. He communicated his design to several of the townsmen, and the next day was appointed.

Quashee was returning the same night to his wife; the church-bell had struck the hour of twelve, and it was very dark. His road lay near the hovel of Amri, and he heard persons in earnest conversation. Curiosity prompted him to listen, and he soon distinguished the voice of Jack; it was the parting word "farewell," he heard him utter.

Quashee would have instantly raised an alarm, but it was impossible to profit by it, and he chose the cooler method of watching him.

It was not for want of courage, for had Quashee been armed, he would have attacked him: but Jack had his two guns and sabre.

He saw Jack ascend the craggy steep of Mount Lebanus, but lost sight of him all of a sudden. No matter, Quashee had gained intelligence sufficient.

Accompanied by the towns-folks, on the morrow, Quashee set out upon his expedition, and arriving at the spot where he had lost Jack the evening before, they hid themselves among the bushes in expectation of their foe. Unfortunately for the party, Jack saw all their movements. He was standing on a small crag, cutting Plantains,* and concealed from their view by a number of branches that were entwined before him.

---

\* It may be some entertainment to the uninformed reader to know a little more of this fruit than merely the name. There are many species, but the two most remarkable are the Paradisaica, or Plantain-tree, and the Musa Sapientum, or Banana-tree. The first sort is cultivated in all the Islands of the West-Indies, where the fruit serves the Indians for bread, and some of the white people prefer it to the Yams and Cassada-bread.

Quashee's party consisted of seven, exclusive of himself. Eight was a fearful number, but the bold-hearted Jack was not to be

---

The plant rises with a soft stalk, fifteen or twenty feet high; the lower part of the stalk is often as thick as a man's thigh, diminishing gradually to the top, where the leaves come out on every side. These are often eight feet long and two or three feet broad, with a strong fleshy midrib and a great number of transverse veins, running from the midrib to the borders. The leaves are thin and tender, so that, when they are exposed to the open air, they are generally torn by the wind; for, as they are long, the wind has great power against them. These leaves come out from the center of the stalk, and are rolled up at their first appearance; but, when they are advanced above the stalk, they expand and turn backwards. As these leaves come up rolled in the manner above mentioned, their advance upwards is so rapid, that their growth may almost be discerned by the naked eye; and, if a fine line is drawn across, level with the top of the leaf, in an hour's time, the leaf will nearly be an inch above it. When the plant is grown to its full height, the spikes of flowers will appear in the center, which is often near four feet in length, and nods on one side. The flowers come out in bunches, those in the lower piles being the largest, the others diminishing in their size upward. The fruit, or Plantains, are about a foot long, and an inch and a half or two inches diameter. It is at first green, but, when ripe, of a pale yellow color. The skin is tough, and within is a soft pulp, of a luscious sweet flavor. The pikes of fruit are often so large as to weigh upwards of forty pounds. The fruit of this sort is generally cut before it is ripe; the green skin is pulled off and the heart is roasted in a clear fire for a few minutes, and frequently turned. It is then scraped and served up as bread. Boiled Plantains are not so palatable. This tree is cultivated on a very extensive scale in Jamaica, without the fruit of which, Dr. Wright says, the Island would scarcely be habitable, as no species of provision could supply their place. Even flour, or bread itself, would be less agreeable, and less adapted to the support of the laborious negroes, so as to enable them to do their business or keep in health. Plantains also fatten horses, cattle, swine, dogs, fowls, and other domestic animals. The leaves being smooth and soft, are used as dressings after blisters. The water from the soft trunk is astringent. Every other part of the tree is useful in different parts of rural economy. The leaves are also used for napkins and table-cloths, and are good food for hogs.

The second sort differs from the first, in having its stalks masked with dark purple spots and stripes. The fruit is shorter, straighter and rounder. The pulp is softer and of a more luscious taste. It is never eaten green, but when ripe. It is very agreeable, either eaten raw, or fried in slices as fritters, and is relished by all ranks of people in the West-Indies. The fruit of the Banana-tree is four or five inches long, of the size and shape of a middling Cucumber, and of a high grateful flavour. The leaves are two yards long, and a foot broad in the middle. Bananas grow in great bunches, that weigh a dozen pounds and upwards. When the natives of the West-Indies undertake a voyage, they make provision of paste of Banana, which, in the case of need, serves them for nourishment and drink. For this purpose they take ripe Bananas, and having squeezed them through a fine sieve, form the solid fruit into small loaves, which are dried in the sun, or in hot ashes, after having previously wrapped them up in leaves of Indian flowering rice. When they would make use of this paste, they dissolve it in water, which is very easily done, and the liquor, thereby rendered thick, has an agreeable acid taste imparted to it, which makes it both refreshing and nourishing.

intimidated; he fired from his place of concealment, and it proved a good shot.

The whole party were alarmed; Jack fired again, and it took effect. The towns-folks now fled in every direction; one alone was bold enough to remain with Quashee.

Jack drew his sabre and leaped down upon them; Quashee prepared for the combat. They began the contest and the towns-man drew from his belt a pistol and shot Jack. The ball pierced his shoulder, and the sabre dropped from his hand; but, like a lion who feels his courage revive when his blood sprinkles the plain, so Jack sprang upon his antagonist, and Quashee rolled in the sand.

Jack regained his sabre; the towns-man felt it to his heart. The struggle was renewed, and fire flashed from their sabres; the sweat poured down their foreheads; but Jack was faint with loss of blood; he was but a child to himself in the contest, and Quashee evidently gained ground. Jack with his left hand grasped the arm of his antagonist, and wielding his sabre, was about to let it drop with fury on his head, but Quashee, by a well aimed blow, deprived him of two of his fingers, and Jack lost his hold. Invigorated by the blow, he gave one fierce thrust, and the sabre of his adversary was shivered into atoms. Jack scorned advantage, and threw away his own; but Quashee was conquered, and he fled. Faint for loss of blood, wearied with the fight, Jack regained his sabre, and returned to his cave. He had destroyed all means of pursuit, and blockading every avenue leading to his cave, direct or indirect, he was in no fear of a surprise.

He threw himself on his couch, weary, faint and dejected; then extracting the ball from his shoulder, bound up his wound with a Plantain leaf, and sunk to a refreshing sleep.

GEORGE STANFORD.

# LETTER IX.

*The same to the same.*

DEAR CHARLES,

NOW, while Jack is in a sound slumber, I will present you with a sketch of captain Harrop the West-Indian Slave-Merchant, a man who has gained no inconsiderable fortune by this Man-traffic.

Henry Harrop was an only son, and his father concentered all his hopes in the darling boy. He was ambitious even in youth, servile, and, to aid his schemes, deceitful. He had a smooth tongue, which gained him the good will of all. Artful and cunning, he could disguise the sentiments of his heart with the greatest ease, and his father, who bore the best character in the Island of Jamaica, whose humanity was daily praised by every one, thought him a good and virtuous youth. The elder Harrop was born in London; but a near relation leaving him a small plantation, he quitted his native country at the age of twenty-one for Jamaica. He was too humane and charitable to thrive like most Planters. His slaves only knew they existed under such a yoke, but they never felt it, and they loved their master. Mr. Harrop was of a weak constitution; his health visibly declined, and at the age of forty-two, left this world for a better one. Thousands mourned his loss; even the poor negroes poured forth the effusions of a grateful heart, and his grave was daily watered by those who had felt his bounty, and whom he had ruled with the mild rod of humanity. He had married at an early age, and his wife had long since known the celestial bliss which he now sought.

Henry Harrop was just two-and-twenty years of age when his father died, and sole heir of a tolerably good estate, though not half enough to satisfy his avarice. About this time, the insurrection broke out of the Koromantyn, or Gold-Coast negroes, and he, by his cunning, was chiefly instrumental in bringing the offenders to justice. When the riots were suppressed, there was not half a sufficiency of slaves imported to stock the Island. Harrop, on this consideration, disposed of his property, converted it into money, and fitted out two vessels for the slave trade, to sail for Africa. This scheme was exceedingly productive, and in two voyages he made more than cent per cent[1] of the money he had expended.

About this time, his aunt, an elderly widow lady, residing in England, dying, left him half her property, and the other half to an only son, William Sebald. Harrop was appointed his guardian, and the property was invested in his hands.

William was a young man of great sensibility and tender feelings. He had been bred up in an affectionate manner, and was not fit for the occupation he was intended for.

Captain Harrop being now his guardian rather chose to have him under his own immediate eye, and without consulting his inclination, had him bound apprentice to himself.

William Sebald was unacquainted with the nature of his employment; at least, he knew not the miseries that were daily heaped on those unhappy beings, or the inhuman means by which they were obtained. At the age of twelve, he made his first voyage, and was shocked at the barbarous proceedings of his countrymen. On his return, he entreated his master not to take him any more, but Harrop insisted, and in an authoritative tone commanded him to obey. Poor William was almost heart-broken; his tears were unavailing, and, ere he had completed his fourteenth year, he had made his second voyage to the coast of Africa.

Just as they entered the mouth of the Gambia, a violent storm arose, which drove them to and fro for many hours; at length, the ship split against a rock. William flew to the arms of Harrop, with the idea of death before him. They fainted in each other's arms, and were born on a fragment of the vessel, directed by providence to the protection of the generous Amri. William was grateful to the saviours of his life, but Harrop conceived a hellish plot in his heart, which he waited an opportunity to put in execution.

They had been near three months with the Africans; Harrop knew of several British settlements on the banks of the Gambia, but he could not undertake the journey to them, so much did he dread the natives, who, though they chiefly deal with Europeans, yet seek every opportunity to murder them. He saw

[1] One hundred percent.

no possibility of regaining his country; by his flattering tongue, he had gained the hearts of the two unsuspecting Feloops; but, while he remained here, he was ruining his own interest; trade was his idol, and there was no relief to his busy mind.

One day, as he paced the banks of the Gambia, not far from the hovel of Makro, for he dared not trust himself, he descried an European vessel in the river. This was the greatest joy to his heart. He waved his handkerchief, they on board obeyed the signal, and the long boat was sent to shore. Lucky accident! the vessel was his own, arrived but lately from Jamaica, and manned by Mr. Mornton for the service.

He learned that the crew of the ship-wrecked vessel were nearly all saved, being taken up by a sloop of war; but the captain and William were missing, and in the next ship bound for Jamaica, they sailed and carried the tidings of their loss. Upon this, Mornton took Harrop's affairs in hand, and sought an heir to his property. There was in the Island a great dearth of slaves, and he manned the inactive vessel upon his own account.

Harrop was all joy; he went on board immediately, and the crew greeted him with a loud huzza.

The lieutenant, who had taken the command of the ship, had been treating for slaves with an old Slatee; but this not being able to obtain the price, had taken them to a better market.

Harrop resolved to make up for lost time, by taking a good cargo back, and without hesitation determined his compassionate friends should make part of it. William's blood freezed with horror in his veins, when Harrop, on gaining the shore, informed him of his intention, but he had not power to alter the cruel resolution of his master. He was distracted and in an agony of despair. He saw the saviours of his life cruelly forced from their own shores, from those shores where they exercised humanity to the remorseless being, whose ungrateful heart could think of no return for their hospitality, but chains and slavery. Look down, ye angels, upon earth, and say, is not this the office of the damned?

William, overcome by the sensations of his heart, sunk into a lingering fit of illness, nor did he recover till his arrival in Jamaica.

As he stepped his foot upon land, he solemnly vowed to heaven never more to go to sea, upon so nefarious a trade.

William was now but on the eve of fifteen, and he looked with tortured eye on the four remaining years of a painful servitude.

Harriet Mornton was an only daughter; she was two years younger than William, and could always dispel the gloom that settled on his brow. In short, love was then in its infancy, but it expanded by daily intercourse and ripening years. If William was not present, Harriet felt an unaccountable uneasiness; if Harriet was absent, William would heave many an unmeaning sigh. By the time that William was eighteen, he found how painful it was to be from her company; he endeavoured to discover the reason, but love is so intricate a sentiment, so imperceptibly stealing, that ere it is discovered, it is irrecoverably interwoven in the heart. Mr. Mornton was very wealthy, and Harriet was to inherit all. He sought for a husband equal in riches, and avarice was the prevailing feature of his heart.

Unfortunately for the young couple, at this critical juncture, captain Harrop, determined to quit the sea-faring trade, made a proposal to the planter for the hand of his fair daughter. This was accepted with avidity by the avaricious Mornton, without once consulting the happiness of his daughter. Indeed the plan was prosecuted in so private a manner that the young lovers had never any suspicion of the transaction, and she, a lovely girl of sixteen, was to be sacrificed to a man of thirty-four, but nearer forty in constitution; a man whose heart was unacquainted with any flame, but the love of aggrandizement; a man dead to every tender feeling, proud and remorseless.

Harrop discovered, as he thought, the dawning passion of the young couple, and prepared a plan, ere he avowed his love, to put a stop to their success. Artful and cunning, he knew the only means to eradicate their passion, baneful to his interest, was, by secrecy on his side, to imperceptibly bring proofs of the inconstancy of her swain, and gain her love by the deceitful mask of undesigning friendship.

No one understood the human heart better than captain Harrop. "If," said he, "I discover my passion for her at once, I shall lose her confidence, and she will put no belief in me; but, if, as a friend, I interest her heart, gratitude will inspire that, which if not thus undermined, would turn to hatred."

Captain Harrop had business in England; this was a favourable opportunity to commence his design, and William was dispatched to execute the commission. The lovers were almost broken-hearted. "Oh! William," sighed the affectionate maid, sinking upon his shoulder. "My dearest Harriet," cried he, while tears almost choaked his utterance, "I shall soon return, and then we will never part again."

"Oh! but, when far distant, will William love me as he loves me now?"

"Can my Harriet doubt my constancy? no, I here solemnly swear never to marry any but you."

"And I," cried she, in the fulness of her heart, "never to have any other husband."

They fell into each other's arms, and their tears mingled together. William with a sudden frantic resolution, tore himself away and entered the ship. Harriet stood on the beach, and her heart swelled with grief, as the receding vessel lessened from her view.

He had been gone from her near three months, and she had not heard from him. She could not believe him inconstant, but she thought it unkind. Every day was passed in eager expectation and anxious solicitude for the arrival of a vessel from England. Harrop, without hinting his love, paid her the most unremitting attention, and indeed soon gained her confidence so entirely, that one day she ventured to disclose her passion to him. Harrop, on the recital, with a well feigned tear and extreme agitation, alarmed her heart. She eagerly enquired the cause of his emotion; but, as if tears denied what he would say, he shook her affectionately and with energy by the hand; then, turning from her, took the handkerchief from his pocket to hide his grief. As he did this, a letter fell as unperceived by him, and he precipitately left the room. She called after him to take the letter, but he was out of hearing.

The direction was the hand-writing of William, and curiosity prompted her to inspect its contents. She trembled as she unfolded it; but imagine her emotions when she read the following words.

SIR,

The only apology I have to offer for delaying so long answering your last letter, is my usual thoughtlessness, joined to a number of engagements, that have taken up the greatest part of my time. I hope you will forgive this want of attention, especially when I assure you that your affairs have not suffered by any kind of neglect, and that I have done every thing that lay in my power to settle things to your wish. I shall shortly give you every information you require, and hope it will meet with your approbation. I would have done it with this, but some of the persons concerned are out of town, and not expected for some days. Meanwhile, I endeavour to pass my time as agreeably as business will permit. Shall I tell you that Love contributes his share in my amusements? Yes, the daughter of a rich merchant, with whom I occasionally became acquainted, is the dear enchanter that renders my stay here as happy as I can possibly wish. She has completely won my heart, and given me hers in exchange, which I value more than riches and kingdoms. I mean shortly to make my applications in form to her friends,[1] and from what I have already seen, have every reason to hope that success will crown our wishes. My next will bring you further intelligence; meantime I remain, Sir, Your humble servant,

WILLIAM SEBALD.

Dear Charles, adieu!

GEORGE STANFORD.


LETTER X.

*The same to the same.*

DEAR CHARLES,

HARRIET read the letter of her faithless William with horror and surprise. She could scarcely believe the clear proof of his perfidy. She read it again, the tears flowed down her cheeks and

---

[1]  One's relatives or kinsfolk (*OED*).

she fainted. This made so deep an impression upon her heart, that for many months her life was despaired of. A violent fever attacked her; a delirium succeeded, during which she frequently called on her ingrate by name; and thus Mornton first became acquainted with the loves of William and Harriet.

With the best medical assistance the Island could procure, she gradually recovered, and after an illness of twelve months, she was able to take the air. Harrop now continued his assiduity, and the unsuspecting Harriet became his easy dupe.

Mr. Mornton, eager to have so wealthy a son-in-law as captain Harrop, spoke his mind to his daughter in the following terms.

"My Harriet, I know it is the wish of your heart to see your father happy."

She bowed—

"I have no progeny but you; you are my only child and will inherit all my wealth; and to make that child comfortable and happy in this life is all my wish. Captain Harrop is a good man, and a rich man; him have I chosen as your partner for life, and....."

"Stop," cried the almost frantic daughter, falling upon her knees; "let me value captain Harrop only as a friend. I never can look upon him as my husband. As you love the peace of mind of your daughter, do not think of such a match; do not, I implore you. My heart has already found a partner; one I thought formed to make me happy, but ....."

"How, in disobedience to my will, have you dared to think of any one but the man of my choice?"

"Captain Harrop is old enough to be my father; but William Sebald ..... and indeed appearances may be deceitful; I cannot be persuaded that he does not love me."

Mornton bit his nether lip in rage; he seized his daughter by the hand, while a deadly frown distorted his brow. "As you expect to enjoy your father's love, think of no other but the man of my choice. Remember, I will be obeyed, and two days shall see your marriage ceremonies completed. I am resolved, and no power on earth can alter my fixed determination." Thus saying, he left the apartment, and she, bathed in tears, flung herself on a sopha; she knew the implacability of his temper, and that it was vain to entreat.

At this moment, Harrop entered; a dissembling smile played upon his cheek, which he soon changed for sorrow mingled with surprise.

"How! in tears, my lovely Harriet?" cried the perfidious monster. "Let me dry that moistened cheek; it is not fit it should be damped by sorrow." She had no other resource, and throwing herself on her knees before him, entreated he would not persist in a marriage so contrary to her wish. She assured him she loved another, and if he obtained her hand, he never could her heart.

Harrop, inured to the sea, and naturally of no very tender feelings, was sufficiently satisfied with that; provided he enjoyed her property, he was little anxious as to her love. "My dearest Harriet," he returned, "you have deprived me of what alone made my life supportable. I thought to have spent the residue of my days in matrimonial bliss, and you were the object of my heart. Oh! distracting moment! how have I cherished the fond delusion! I interwove this dear hope with the thread of my future life, and you have cruelly cut it asunder." He called a tear to his aid, which was ever ready at command. Harriet now was in an agony of grief; she knew there was no alternative, and Harrop wiping the tear from his cheek, resumed: "Vain man! how dost thou delude thyself with fancied joys? thou fillest to the brim in imagination the cup of bliss, nor canst conceive how it shall be dashed with bitters; but thou art born to error and I am doomed to despair." He left the room in violent agitation.

Harriet was amazed; she knew not of his passion, nor ever imagined that he regarded her till now.

In two days, Harrop led her to the hymeneal[1] altar. At the close of the ceremony, she fainted, and was borne home by her attendants; but it was too late to repine; she was cast away from her William for ever.

In about three weeks after their marriage, William returned from England; how much was he surprised to find his Harriet wedded with Harrop? He was distracted, and he penned the following letter, which he delivered to her servant the ensuing day.

---

[1] Pertaining to marriage.

## DEAR MADAM,

I WOULD have said dear Harriet, but you have cruelly deprived me of the privilege..... But I do not mean to upbraid you; I only wish to take a last farewell, and then to quit the habitable part of the world for ever. I would die, but that would be offending my Creator, and taking away that which he gave and he alone has a right to take away. The world has no charm for me; you proved false, and my hopes are blighted. Little did I think, when I received your letter in England, that you were playing false with me. Indeed I thought it another proof of my Harriet's love. I have your letter before me now; have you forgot the contents? Oh Harriet! could I expect this of you? could I conceive that you would thus break my heart? well! well! When I was in England, I fondly looked forward to the happy moment when I should call you mine. Oh! had absence cherished love in your breast as it did in mine, I should not now have to call my Harriet cruel. And when I set foot on this shore, my heart brimful of joy, little did I expect this..... But whither am I wandering? my brain is a chaos; I would proceed, but my pen, as if by instinct, traces the cause of my anguish on the paper. Adieu! I will endeavour, in seclusion, to forget that I once loved you.

Farewell! Farewell for ever!

## WILLIAM SEBALD.

When she had read the contents of this letter, she fell into violent fainting fits, and Mornton entered the apartment at the moment. He read the letter, and endeavoured to console his daughter. William was sent for, but he was nowhere to be found, and sixteen years had elapsed and they had never heard from him. When Harrop found his wife had discovered his perfidy, he pleaded the violence of his attachment, and avowed the forgeries, knowing that deception in the present instance, would be but to blacken her opinion of him.

Harriet, now Mrs. Harrop, endeavoured to live happy with her husband; she soon perceived the monitor in his bosom that disturbed his peace, and endeavoured to cheer his harassed mind.

Often times would he, when by her side, leap from the couch, and give a violent scream, while the big drops of sweat hung upon his brow. At first, she was very much alarmed, but soon was habituated to it by the frequent repetition.

She endeavoured to eradicate all remembrance of William from her bosom; to think still of him she knew was criminal.

Harrop was cruel and of a vindictive imperious temper; but, to serve his own turn, he could mask it with the most artful deceit, and he would often smile upon his amiable wife, while the most bitter venom was rankling at his heart. This however he was compelled to suppress; for, latterly, he had felt much of the gnawing reprover, conscience. He could not sleep; his nights were restless and his days gloomy; but Mrs. Harrop, whose bosom owned every virtue, paid him every attention. She pitied him, and wept when she reflected on his unpardonable cruelties. Surely such a being was not capable of exciting love in as fair a bosom as ever nature moulded. She was all gentleness and virtue, and humanity in her bosom shone as bright a gem as the female heart can harbour. She was a kind indulgent mother to the poor; she relieved their distresses, and shed a tear at their misfortunes.

At night, Harrop would often traverse the various apartments, instead of seeking refreshment in bed. It was on one of those nights, when, laid upon a sopha, his eye lids were pressed by the soporific god,[1] and betrayed by him into a frightful dream, that Jack surprised him. Mrs. Harrop was in a room not far distant, and hearing voices, she hurried on her bed gown. Harrop screamed, and 'twas her footsteps Jack heard; but what was her surprise, on coming into the apartment, to find it vacated, and hear one give a groan beneath the window. She answered by a loud scream, and fainted; but no one heard her, and she remained nearly two hours deprived of reason.

When she recovered, she was so weak and exhausted, that she had scarcely power to speak. She crawled to her chamber, where she sunk upon her couch, and was so overcome by her feelings that she had not power to give the alarm.

When the servant discovered her in the morning, she was

---

[1]  God who tends to induce sleep.

more dead than alive, and a long fit of illness kept her confined to her couch for many months.

By this time, I make no doubt Jack has awoke from his slumber; so I shall conclude my letter. Adieu!

GEORGE STANFORD.


## LETTER XI.

*The same to the same.*

DEAR CHARLES,

I HAVE given you the preceding account, because the parties are greatly concerned in our history, and I shall have to mention them in a little time; not from the interest the tale possesses, for I do not think there is sufficient in it to keep a reader of modern romance from yawning over the page; but to return to Jack.

He had received two severe wounds, and captain Harrop was his nurse. Thus this man was compelled to assist Jack, who, aware of the treachery of his guest, never brought his arms to the interior cave where he dwelt, and it was impossible for Harrop to ascend, having a heavy chain to his leg, which Jack carefully inspected very often, to see that it received no damage.

Traps were laid every where for Jack, but he escaped or avoided all. His battle with Quashee was related by the townsfolk, and the negroes trembled at his name. Even Quashee feared him, and thought his Obi was most powerful. Thus, in spite of all, Jack could roam at large; and the negroes and all the inhabitants were terrified at the name of Three-fingered Jack!

When recovered from his wounds sufficiently to venture abroad, Jack sought the cell of Bashra. There was but one man on earth who could claim a place in Jack's heart; it was Mahali; they were linked together by their country and their misfortunes. Jack entered the cell of Bashra; Mahali flew to the arms of his friend, and was flattered by the confidence he reposed in him; for, Jack trusted no man, needed no assistance, and fought all his battles alone; but Jack wanted to know the history of his countryman, and Mahali began in these words:

"I am a Feloop by birth, possessing all my country's principles, with a bosom burning with rage at all its wrongs. My narrative is but short and varied by few incidents; but my days of misery have been long, and my grief manifold; to the ear of a countryman I will relate a few of those scenes that have cankered the hearts of many.

"I dwelt, from my infancy, in a hut with my venerated parents, who were happy in me, and thought the sun had shot his ray of prosperity at my birth. I grew to manhood, and was the only joy of their heart. I would hunt the lion with stout heart, and always come off conqueror. In short, I was deemed the most expert hunter, considering my age. We all knew the European demand for slaves, and even in my earliest infancy trembled at the name; and as these white robbers would excite us to war against each other, I kept a trained band of my countrymen constantly ready for the fight, and was their acknowledged leader.

"Zimbo, another African chief, but of another tribe, frequently made war against me, and was as often beaten. At last, ashamed of his numberless losses and repeated defeats, he mustered an immense troop and made another desperate attempt.

"The battle was the most furious ever witnessed; they were double our numbers; but our countrymen were brave and hardy; the blood of our foes streamed on the ground, and thousands of slain impeded the progress of my troops, who were again conquerors. My small troop had suffered considerably by the contest, and, at the close of the battle, when each army was retiring from the combat, and our men were fainting with fatigue, each too much wearied to renew the fight, an infamous Slatee (my blood curdles at the recollection), who had lain in ambush, awaiting the issue, sprang upon both parties, killed, slaughtered, and made a great conquest.

"I called upon my men to renew the fight; but, weakened as we were, resistance was vain, and they fled. I followed them, let me not add, 'with shame be it said;' for, revenge infused her fire in my bosom, and I resolved with doubled force to subdue this foe to humanity. I entered the hut where my parents dwelt, but a small distance from the field of battle; the village was in flames, and my countrymen were perishing beneath the sword of the rapacious enemy. My father was bound hand and foot, and the blood gushed from his many wounds. It appeared the Europeans had spirited Zimbo to a war with us, and in the absence of the heroes of our town, had come to plunder us of our effects and drag away our friends.

"The lion in my soul was roused by the horrible carnage I saw before me, and with gleaming sabre I thickly dealt the blows of vengeance. The blood of the Europeans sprinkled our hovel; my father burst from his chains and fought like a Feloop, till a cruel pistol from the hand of a sailor shot him through the head. When I saw my father fall, I dropped the sword from my hand, and clasped his lifeless body. I loved my father, and 'twas filial affection that subdued me. I beheld my parents both streaming in blood by my side; I beheld, and fainting, sunk upon their bodies cold in death.

"The miseries of war were not half so dreadful as the dying groans of the poor helpless wretches, who were not able to contend with the blood-hounds of Europe; those savages came with fire and sword to devastate our town.

"On my recovery, I found myself in the caravan of the infamous Bendab, a Slatee; I offered forty chosen slaves for my ransom, but this was refused; and Bendab, with triumph, informed me that I, in his power, was better than a hundred picked slaves of my country.

"The caravan now slowly came to the banks of the Gambia, where we were disposed of among the English vessels, and with galling chains round my ancles, and my hands manacled, I set sail for Jamaica with a number of other unhappy wretches, miserable as myself.

"We arrived at Jamaica, after a prosperous voyage, and I was sold in the first lot with seventeen others, men and women. We were then conveyed to our plantation, and branded on the breast with the name of our purchaser.

"But, first, on the deck of that vessel that bore me from my country, I fell on my knees, and swore by the great God I worshiped, and in the face of my masters, that I would have revenge. The overseer stood close by my side, and was placing his small troop to march in order to the plantation. On hearing my declaration, he struck me across the shoulders with a yambo[1] cane. My heated soul was roused by the indignity, I got up from the deck, like lightning darted on the pallid wretch, and enfolding him in my manacled grasp, hurled him with exerted strength to the bosom of the waves. My fellow slaves, in the transport of the moment, sent up loud huzzas in token of my triumph.

"A boat was put out to take up the overseer, and it succeeded. You may guess my reward; I received five hundred lashes. I scorned to groan, and bore it with the inherent fortitude of my country. Since that time, I have eagerly looked forward to revenge; I blessed the moment when I saw you stand up to assert your country's right, but cursed the cowardly wretches that hustled me away and feared to oppose the terror and destruction of their nation."

Mahali ceased.

So will I. Adieu!

GEORGE STANFORD.


## LETTER XII.

*The same to the same.*


DEAR CHARLES,


QUASHEE anxious to obtain the reward acquainted the Governor with his expedition and the failure; at the same time, informing him that Amri was an abettor of Jack's, for he had seen him come out of her hovel. Upon this, a guard was commanded to lay in ambush for Jack, and several nights had elapsed, when, at length, he appeared at the door, armed with his guns and sabre. This was an eventful moment. The undaunted manner of Jack,

---

[1]  Possible variant of jambo—A name given in different parts of the East Indies and Malay Archipelago to several species of Eugenia (family Myrtaceæ), and their fruits (*OED*).

when he entered his mother's hut, gave a check to their courage, and they shrunk awhile from the attempt; but they were many and conquest seemed easy. The moon emerged from beneath a cloud; the door of Amri's hovel was half closed, and they could see to the interior. They observed Jack in close converse with Amri, and leaning on his two guns; his sabre was undrawn. As they wanted to spare his life, and likewise not to endanger their own, they stood some time consulting on the best method of attacking him.

Quashee was not one of them, or the bold-hearted fellow would not long have deliberated. One proposed to fire through the door; this was agreed on as the easiest way, and the foremost fired.

Jack saw himself betrayed, but the shot had missed, and he issued forth.

He returned the shot, and instantly heard a groan. At this moment, the friendly moon, under covert of a cloud, refused her light. The party fired in a volley; Jack was wounded, and an alarum bell was rung throughout the plantation; but Jack drawing his sabre, put himself on the defensive, and speedily retreated towards Lebanus, pursued by the party.

As he ascended the bewildering path that led to the mouth of his cave, he fired and the shot succeeded; again he fired, and the enemy struck with terror fled in all directions.

The next day, the whole Island rung with Jack's last exploit. Some asserted that the shots passed through his body and left no trace behind; nay, all unanimously declared that it was as idle to attempt to shoot Jack as to wound a shadow. Not one of the negroes but trembled at the name of Three-fingered Jack, and many of the Europeans believed in the fancied virtues of his Obi. But Jack was not invulnerable, as was proved by Quashee, who wounded him in several places, and deprived him of two of his fingers. If there was any part of Jack invulnerable, it was his heart, and that was open to every attack, save that of cowardice.

Jack was not to be intimidated; he feared not death; his cause was noble; he fought for the liberty of his countrymen; he fought to revenge a father, and this endowed him with a strength superior to the vaunting of his antagonists.

Amri was again summoned before the House of Assembly, and still refusing to give information, received sentence of death.

The execution was suspended for three days, and in the mean time various tortures were prepared.

One tremendous night, when the loud thunder howled through the mountains, and the scorching lightning blasted the foliage of the bending tree, Jack was prowling abroad and met a poor woman staying alone. She had lost her path, and thus accosted our hero: "For mercy's sake, Sir, do direct a poor woman in the road to Moore-town, for I have lost my way. I have not much to give you, but you shall have all I have got, if you will protect me from that daring robber, Three-fingered Jack, who would take my life, if he was to meet me."

"Would he?" replied Jack, "and for what reason would he take thy life?"

"Because I am a white woman, Sir, and he holds people of my color in such mortal hatred!"

"Fear nought," cried Jack; "together let us walk, and he will no more harm thee than I shall."

"I am a poor soldier's wife, Sir," said she, after a long pause, during which they had continued in the road through the blue mountains[1] that overlook Nanny-town; she now found herself out of danger and gained more confidence—"I am a poor soldier's wife, Sir, and my little hovel is in Moore-town. Alas! Sir, I have six children, and I find it very difficult to maintain them; but, thank heaven, there are plantains for them in abundance; his infinite mercy will not let them starve."

"But your husband?"

"Alas! Sir, he is dead."

"Dead!"

"Oh dear, yes, Sir; I forgot to tell you, I am a widow; Three-fingered Jack killed my husband."

"Three-fingered Jack! Ay? how did he do that? tell me, good woman."

"I will, Sir. I was born in a little village in England, and lived happily there. Edward was a farmer's boy; he loved me, and we were married. Two years passed, Sir; Edward labored hard to maintain me, but his means were ineffectual, and we had two children.

---

[1] Range of limestone mountains in the eastern end of Jamaica that reaches 7,400 feet.

"Edward was an orphan, a parishboy;[1] he had no relation, no friend, and the villagers abused him for marrying, saying what business had such a vagrant to populate the world and impoverish the village by a set of squalling brats. These cruel sayings cut my poor Edward to the heart, and one day, when a recruiting party entered our town, he in despair enlisted, and with the money gave bread to our infants. He enlisted and ....." "Sold himself for a slave," added Jack. "No," replied the woman, rather nettled at the word; "though, alas! in a short time, cruel orders came that he must leave England for Jamaica. I would not be separated from him, I loved, and followed him."

"Well!"

"Here we lived four years, and indeed far happier than in England; but we were getting rich and longed to see our native country, and Edward was about to purchase his discharge, that very day, when..... "

She could say no more.

"Conclude," cried Jack, on the tip-toe of suspence. "Three-fingered Jack, Sir, (he was not then so called) spirited up the slaves to a rebellion; but they, as our towns-folk said, wanting a stout heart, which *he* was master of, fled, when our troops approached and took him prisoner. He was sentenced to death, confined in a strong prison, and my husband was his guard. One night, he and his fellow were on duty, and ..... "

"I have heard your story before, good woman; 'tis said Jack escaped, and murdered them both, was it not so?"

"Ay, dear me, they were both found in the morning weltering in their blood."

Jack mused.

After a pause, the woman continued.

"The mother of Three-fingered Jack dies on the second morning, Sir."

"Dies?"

"You seem agitated, Sir."

Jack's blood was cold at his heart; his mother's death served

---

like a thunderbolt and stagnated the flow of blood, reason, life and all for a moment.

At length, they arrived at her hovel; she entreated him to walk in; he did, and seated himself. She refreshed him with the juice of a Banana, and gave him some dried fish. Jack was sensibly affected with her generosity and gave her a purse; useful to her, the contents were dirt to him. She counted over the gold again and again; she went to embrace him, and he presented her his three-fingered hand. On the discovery, she uttered a wild scream and fainted. Jack soon recovered her, smiled at her fears, presented her his three-fingered hand again, which she cordially shook, and he left her.

Dear, Charles, confess humanity was not estranged from the heart of the bold marauder. Adieu!

GEORGE STANFORD.

## LETTER XIII.

*The same to the same.*

DEAR CHARLES,

I AM going to give you a specimen of my poetry, and proclaim in lofty strains the valor, the fidelity and affection of the noble negroes, Jack and Mahali.

> There, on yon rock, whose frowning head defies
> The furious tempest thundered from the skies,
> Where waves the sally, bending 'neath the blast;
> There on yon crag, uprearing high its crest,
> Where from the caves the trembling waters roar,
> And o'er yon steep its foaming billows pour;
> 'Twas there Mahali in distraction stood
> And mingled with his tears the foaming flood.
> See, on yon tam'rind-tree, where hangs the sword
> That blood of Europe's pallid sons have gor'd,
> A hero's hand the conqu'ring steel obey'd,

And slaughter'd hosts have gasp'd beneath its blade.
'Tis now neglected, waving in the wind,
While on yon crag Mahali lies reclin'd.
Rouse him, ye spirits, guardians of the brave;
Give to his unstrung arm the restless glave;[1]
Bid him revenge and seek the bloodless plain,
Revenge his friend, revenge his parents slain.
Is't for the woodland hero that you sigh;
Mahali, forth, nor let his mother die.
Rouse, ye inactive, rush upon the foe,
And bear down all before your giant blow.
Thus roar'd the cat'ract, as it foaming fell:
Mahali heard it echoed from the dell;
He heard, and, rising with intrepid haste,
Close to his arm the rough hewn buckler brac'd;
His left equip'd, and ready for the fight,
His sabre brandish'd in his faithful right.
Now from his cheek he dash'd the briny tear
Forth to the waterfall to mingle there.
As the young tyger, roaming for his prey,          ⎫
Bounds through the waste, and goring all the way,   ⎬
Bleeds the fell victim to his thirst allay,        ⎭
With pride beholds the havock he has made,
Midst those by sound security betray'd,
Or on the mountain that o'er tops the plain,       ⎫
Exulting, learn new carnage to obtain,             ⎬
And marks the spot for fresh gor'd bodies slain.   ⎭
Mahali stood and held the gleaming glave
That damn'd the coward and appall'd the brave.
But see, the sun, now sinking in the west
Leaves heaven's vault in gayest purple drest;
And, while the eve its shortning rays invade,
It slow descends and leaves a length'ning shade;
The breeze is hush'd; soft Zephirs gently sigh
And ev'ning purple clads the mysty sky;
The feathery choristers adjourn their song

---

[1]    A sword; esp. a broadsword (OED).

And to their leafy pillow fluttering throng.
Mahali paus'd; he felt the calm controul
Pervade his frame and sink his moody soul,
While thus the torturer doubt his pow'r display'd,
And he his sad anxieties betray'd.
The negro came, the terror of the Isle,
The daring robber with predicting smile,
Two polished guns his manly shoulders grac'd
And his left side a trusty sabre brac'd.
Around his neck the horn was careless slung;
His bag* in front and four stout pistols hung.
He proud approach'd; his glory-beaming eye
Reproved Mahali for the cherish'd sigh.

Pshaw! all bombast! I will continue in my old track, and I dare say you will like it better.

Mahali threw himself into the arms of his friend and bathed him with his tears.

Mind, Charles, those were not tears of weakness, but drops from the heart, the tears of friendship in its purest garb.

Jack was not insensible of the cause that produced those marks of the most generous love; he embraced Mahali, and thus addressed him: "Cheer thee, my friend, nor sink beneath the weight of sorrow not thine own. Thy tears make grateful impressions upon my heart. Oh! Mahali, think not that Jack will tamely live and see his mother perish beneath the arm of the executioner. No, I will die with her. Let the European savages take my life, take a life that they have rendered irksome to the bearer." He felt overcome by the agony of his mind. Both were too much agitated for a time to speak. After a pause, Jack resumed: "But I will die as I have lived, a terror to my foes. They shall find that I will not tamely yield my life. Tomorrow dawn, will Amri be led forth to the fatal pile,[1] and I will follow, and die in attempting her rescue."

"Ah!" cried Mahali, "and thinks my friend so unworthily of me, that he has not permitted me to accompany him."

---

* His Obi-bag.

---

[1] A heap of wood or faggots on which a sacrifice or a person is burnt (*OED*).

"Mahali!"

"But as you value my friendship, I will insist on sharing your danger. You have roused the tyger in my heart, and my sword shall never lay useless in its scabbard, when it can be drawn to serve my friend."

Tears for a time choked Jack's utterance. Oh! heaven-inspired gratitude, transcendant maid, what an influence hast thou over the hearts of thy votaries!

Jack, after a struggle, answered: "Mahali, ask not of me to take thee to thy death; I cannot; my soul forbids the thought. No, live to lament my fate and tell the world my wrongs."

"Ah!" resumed Mahali, "surely 'tis most cruel to refuse thy friend his last request; be assured I never can or will survive thee."

"Mahali, I demand it of you; do not make my last moments miserable; give me some hope that I shall not sink unlamented to the grave."

"Oh! my friend, you do me wrong to think my heart will remain unbroken; I once more do assure you that my life is so closely interwoven with yours, that the same blow which deprives you of existence will also be my death."

"Mahali"—Jack could say no more, he fell upon his bosom, exclaiming: "We will die together."

Oh! thou great Creator, look down upon those *unenlightened savages!* see them entwined within each other's arms, while the mingled tear of friendship, the grateful effusion of two noble hearts, deprives each of the power of speech. But these are *savages* and worship an imaginary god; they are black men, and slaves, unworthy of the appellation of men. Ye sons of christianity, versed in enlightened schools, that teach you to distinguish and to adore the great Creator, emulate their great example, for ye have no such heroes among you.

The cock, with his clarion note, proclaimed the swift approach of morning; already were the twilight clouds dispersed, and Aurora[1] appeared in all her virgin majesty. Jack and Mahali were equipped for the combat.

---

[1]   Personified, the (Roman) goddess of the dawn, represented as rising with rosy fingers from the saffron-colored bed of Tithonus (*OED*).

The fanning breeze but gently waved the bough, and the sparkling dew rested on the damask rose's cheek. The glorious sun appeared streaking the heavens with his morning rays; and nature, in her sweet simplicity, could not dispel the heart-felt melancholy that clouded the faces of the negro friends. At length, the hollow sounding of the muffled drum, heard from afar and echoing the hills, aroused them from their torpor.

Amri was to be executed near Banana River, in the parish of St. David's; thither they proceeded, and soon arrived the procession; the hollow-rolling drum disturbed the morning silence, and, as proceeding in dismal echo, smote the ears of Jack and Mahali. Mournful prelude to the ensuing scene.

First, arrived at the stake a file of soldiers, pacing their way to the solemn music that uttered death in solemn breathings that froze the heart's blood and gave the soul to melancholy; next followed, marching two and two, the negroes from the several plantations in Kingston and Spanish-town; then the unhappy victim drawn in a sledge, and followed by the negroes of Mr. Mornton. When the cavalcade halted at the spot, Amri was taken from the sledge, and bound to the stake; a priest, in christian mercy, implored rest for her soul, and his pious office prepared her mind to meet her fate with fortitude. This was the only indulgence that could be allowed, and the indulgence least needed. Amri wanted not fortitude; the heroic woman was prepared to die, and no crime she had committed damped that ardor with which she was now about to seek the presence of her Creator. On the signal given, the torch was put to the faggot, and a volume of flame instantly incircled the body of the hapless victim.

At this moment, a breathless negro rushed from the ranks, with drawn sword bore down all before him, hastened to the pile and cut away the ropes that fettered Amri to the stake; the soldiers fired in a volley; Mahali flew, bearing the burden on his back. The affrighted negroes set up a loud yell, and the soldiery prepared to follow him; but, a nobler heart opposed their progress than ever inhabited the bosom of an European; Three-fingered Jack appeared, and with a pistol felled the foremost. Three-fingered Jack! Three-fingered Jack! checked the dismayed party, as from his belt he drew another pistol, and held up his three-fingered hand to the gaze of the multitude. "Let no man advance, as he values his life," uttered he, in dreadful and menacing tone. "Let no man advance, as he dreads this all powerful Obi, which renders me immortal, and devotes him to death." "Fire," cried the commanding officer of the corps, "Present, fire." But Jack mingled with the negroes, who feared to seize him, and rushed upon the guns of the soldiery. At this moment, unperceived, Jack escaped, to the no small mortification of the officer, and astonishment of the bewildered negroes. The soldiery imbibed a spark of their credulity, and could not be prevailed upon to pursue him to the Blue Mountains. Jack, breathless and in haste, sought Mahali, whom he soon found in the path leading to his cave, bleeding and supporting the expiring Amri. The last breath was trembling on her lips when Jack appeared; she opened her eyes, beheld her son, who with filial ardor grasped her hand, and she expired. Heaven received her amidst a choir of angels.

Mahali was very faint; a train of blood had marked his progress, and as he lay, supporting the breathless body of Amri, he felt a deadly weakness stealing upon him; but he, with the warmth of friendship at his heart, was regardless of his situation, and Jack was too much immersed in heart-broken and silent grief to observe Mahali. And now life prepared to gush from his wounds, amid the crimson torrent drained from his veins; he sunk backwards; Jack still remained insensible; and now Mahali breathed slower; he lisped forth the name of Jack; it was in his heart, upon his tongue; he was about to utter it, but the heart's blood ascending to his mouth choaked the word, and poured itself in gushing streams down his breast.

Jack now took cognizance of the situation of his friend: "Mahali," he cried, but 'twas too late, his soul had taken its flight; his eyes were sealed in death. "Mahali," Jack repeated; alas! the woods alone returned thy voice. Jack was in an agony of grief, manhood forsook him, desperation seized his heart, and he was about to plunge the dagger in his bosom; a confused mist appeared before his eyes, a faint shriek pierced from his bosom, and he fainted upon the bleeding bodies of his friend and mother.

Dear Charles, it is with difficulty I can suppress my tears;

accuse me not of weakness, but be assured I would rather have that laid to my charge, than the want of feeling. Adieu!

GEORGE STANFORD.

## LETTER XIV.

*The same to the same.*

Dear Charles,

I AGAIN resume my laborious task, but not with the same pleasure shall I now trace the subsequent life of our hero. With a heart callous to every feeling, suggesting every means of a horrible revenge, his depredations were dreadful, and he exercised cruelty with all the savage fury of a beast of prey.

But, first, let me inform you that the poor woman of Mooretown, whom Jack conducted through the Blue Mountains, was present at the death of Amri, and the only one that dared to follow him to his retreat. She knew Jack, she knew him to be generous, and, unperceived by him, arrived at the ascent leading to his cave, and secreted herself. The distressing scene before her eyes made her rush forward, regardless of danger, to the assistance of our hero, who then had fainted on the bleeding body of his friend. Indeed Jack's heart was perhaps agonized more by the death of Mahali than of his mother. This good woman, in whose bosom glowed fair gratitude, gave him every assistance and he recovered in her arms.

He opened his eyes; she had a phial of wine in her pocket, and she poured some down his throat. He drank heartily, and this lent him fresh vigor; but when he was recovered, he stared around him most horribly, and in deep-sounding hollow voice exclaimed, while his eyes pourtrayed the mingled agony of his heart: "Are you not afraid that I should kill you?" "Alas! no, Sir," answered the poor woman; "you killed my husband, but I am sure you would not harm me." "Did I kill him? Oh Mahali! Mahali!" added he, turning his eyes upon the dead body of his friend; then continuing to the woman: "There, go you now; go now."

"Sir, I think I had better not leave you?"

"Not leave me? would you betray me then?"

"Alas! no, Sir; but you seem so wild, that I fear to trust you."

"Go, go, then; do not trouble me."

She went away unwillingly, and returning on the morrow, found Jack still in the same place, clasping the infected bodies, already putrid from the heat of the climate. She endeavoured to drag him away, but all in vain, till he heard the report of a gun at a distance. This aroused him from his lethargic torpor; the report of a musket spoke revenge to his heart; he started from the ground, and seizing a pistol from his belt, was about to descend the mountain, when a young officer stood before him. Jack drew his sabre; the soldier declined the combat, expressing a wish to be heard, but Jack plunged the sabre to his heart.

Let me pass over the unheard-of-cruelties that succeeded. The poor woman felt the sharpness of his poignard; numbers of innocents fell beneath his rapacious sword, and black men alone were spared.

It was the beginning of December 1780, when he attacked a small party of negroes, carrying rum. He charged them to surrender; the poor fellows dropped upon their knees and begged for mercy. At this moment, a wild being rushed down a mountain's craggy steep; Jack smiled at the frantic appearance of the rash intruder: his hair was long and black, and hung scattered down his lacerated shoulders; his beard was neglected, torn and dishevelled; alas! melancholy was depicted upon his cheek, and his hollow eyes rolled in wild and vacant gaze; his dress was torn and his flesh often with it; you could not distinguish what his habiliments once were, for they bore the resemblance of nothing made by the hand of man: he grasped a large club, and down he came into the plains beneath. "Hold your unlawful hand," he cried; "stop not those men, but let them go their way, or find an enemy in me."

"First, ere I raise my hand against thee," cried our hero, "learn that thou wilt combat with Three-fingered Jack; let my name strike terror to thy heart, and do thou return in peace."

The wild man now raised high his club, and Jack throwing away his sabre, thrust in upon him. The affrighted negroes set up a loud yell, and ran away. Jack pressed him to his bosom, with the gripe of a Greenland bear; but the wild man was powerful, and dropping his club, seized his antagonist rudely by the throat. This was a severe contest; thrice the earth received them entwined in each other's grasp; and the starting blood strained from the veins, mingled with their sweat, and poured in rivulets down their bodies: but see, the wild man grasps him with fury round the waist, and Jack is thrown with violence some yards back. Up he is again, and like a tyger darts upon his foe. They close; Jack stoops from his gripe, and clasping him by the thigh, throws him with gigantic strength lifeless to the ground, and thus remains master of the field.

Never before did Jack meet with so powerful an adversary; he leaned against a tree to recover strength, then catching at the booty returned to his cave.

This pitiable being was an inhabitant of the woods around, and often seen by the traveller; no one harmed him, for he was senseless, and when he met the enquiring eye of him that passed the mountains, he would dart away and hide himself from their sight.

> High on a rock, or on the mountain's brink,
> Or in the vale, or 'neath a plantain tree,
> Or sometimes bending o'er the rippling brook,
>     He sheds the burning tear.

> His heart is cold, but yet he often sighs;
> Despair has trac'd her lines upon his cheek,
> But he's as gentle as the fresh yean'd lamb,
>     Nor will not harm the worm.

> Poor soul! He eats the unskin'd plantain;
> Unsettled in his mind he seldom rests;
> But when he does, 'tis on the pebbled ground,
>     Or in a noisome cave.

> His cloaths are rent in thousand thousand twain;
> They do not shield his body from the storm;
> His bosom bare its fury does invite—
>     Alas! poor William's crazed.

Oft have I seen him, with chalky stone,
Engrave his mistress' name upon the ground;
Or on the tree, or on the pointed rock,
    The name of Harriet lives.

I've seen him sitting by the margin'd lake,
With pensive mood and solitary gaze;
Have heard him in the deepest anguish say:
    "It was not always thus.

"Once thou wast merry and thy heart was gay;
Alas! where William trod, dame fortune smiled,
And deck'd the sport with choicest pleasures too,
    Till love had broke his heart.

"She was mercenary and inconstant;
William was poor, but then he was honest,
And his gay heart was virtuously inclin'd—
    But 'tis wretched cold now."

He lay for some time insensible, extended on the ground; but a humane wanderer passing the spot, and seeing his situation, generously lent his aid. He soon recovered, and opening his languid eyes fixed them on the countenance of the benevolent youth. He bore the age of thirty on his forehead, but his beard was not the growth of seventeen. A lovely expression beamed from his intelligent eye, and the fairness of his skin was heightened by the livid color that revelled on his cheek. His hair was of the sweetest auburn, and playful ringlets wantoned down his shoulders. He was rather below the common size, but his whole air and gait was lovely and interesting. The maniac looked upon him in wonder, and his gaze was returned with equal astonishment. At length, the names of "Harriet" and "William" trembled from their lips, and in a moment they were incircled in each other's arms. Harriet, overcome by her emotions, fainted, and William, at that instant every painful recollection subsiding, carried her into a friendly hovel that stood not far distant, and anxiously watched over her. Every other grief forsook his bosom, and hope once more became the inmate of a breast, that had long been torn by conflicting passions, and soul-devouring melancholy.

It may be necessary now to account for the sudden appearance of Mrs. Harrop. After the long absence of Harrop, and every one believing him dead, Mornton proposed another match for his unhappy daughter. I do assure you, Charles, love of wealth alone has raised him above insignificancy in our Island, though not above contempt and hatred. This man would sacrifice every thing to gratify his thirst for money, and, ere his daughter had attained her seventeenth year, her peace of mind had been destroyed to satiate his avarice. She long entreated him to decline his purposed match, and at last obstinately persisted in a refusal.

This was a severe stroke to Mornton's avarice; he expected her compliance, and even relied on his authority. She was a young and rich widow, and might marry the richest man in the Island, and the richest he selected. Finding entreaty of no avail, he resolved to use force, and prepared for the immediate completion of the nuptial ceremony; but, she gathering a knowledge of his design, resolved to fly from her importunate and disgusting lover, and at the same time from parental tyranny.

Dear Charles, what followed you already know; therefore, adieu!

GEORGE STANFORD.


## LETTER XV.

*The same to the same.*

DEAR CHARLES,

JACK's depredations became now so great and so atrocious, that Government was in a manner compelled to publish the following Proclamation.

## BY THE KING,

## A PROCLAMATION.

WHEREAS *we have been informed by our House of Assembly of this Island of Jamaica, that a very desperate gang of negro-slaves, headed by a negro-man slave, called and known by the name of Three-fingered Jack, hath, for many months past, committed many robberies, and carried off many negro and other slaves in the Windward-roads into the woods, and hath also committed several murders; and that repeated parties have been fitted out and sent against the said Three-fingered Jack and his said gang, who have returned without being able to apprehend the said negro, or prevent his making head again: And whereas our said House of Assembly hath requested us to give directions for issuing a Proclamation, offering a reward for apprehending the said negro called Three-fingered Jack, and also a further reward for apprehending each and every negro-man-slave belonging to the said gang, and delivering him or them to any of the gaolers in this Island: And whereas, we have since received another message from our said House of Assembly, requesting us to offer an additional reward of Two Hundred Pounds, as a further encouragement for the apprehending, or bringing in the head of that daring rebel Three-fingered Jack, who hath hitherto eluded every attempt against him: We, having taken the same into our consideration, have thought fit to issue this our Royal Proclamation, hereby strictly charging and commanding, and we do hereby strictly charge and command all and every* [one of] *our loving subjects within our said Island, to pursue and apprehend, or cause to be apprehended, the body of the said negro-man named Three-fingered Jack, and also of every negro-man slave belonging to the said gang, and deliver him or them to any of the gaolers of this Island. And we do at the instance of our said House of Assembly, offer a reward of One Hundred Pounds, and at the like instance a further reward of Two Hundred Pounds, to be paid to the person or persons who shall so apprehend and take the body of the said negro called Three-fingered Jack. And we do, at the instance of our said House of Assembly, offer a further reward of Five Pounds, over and above what is allowed by law, for the apprehending each and every negro-man slave belonging to the said gang, and delivering him or them to any of the gaolers of this Island, to be dealt with according to law.*

*Witness his Excellency, JOHN DALLING, Esq. Captain-General and Governor in Chief of our said Island of Jamaica, and other Territories thereon depending in America, Chancellor and Vice-Admiral of the same, at St. Jago de la Vega, the Thirteenth day of January, in the Twenty-first Year of our Reign, Annoque Domini One Thousand Seven Hundred and Eighty-one.*

JOHN DALLING.
*By his Excellency's Command,*
R. LEWING, *Sec.*
God save the King.

*House of Assembly, 29th Dec. 1780.*

*Resolved, That, over and above the reward of One Hundred Pounds offered by his Majesty's Proclamation for taking or killing the rebellious negro called Three-fingered Jack, the further reward of Freedom shall be given to any slave that shall take or kill the said Three-fingered Jack, and that the House will make good the value of such slave to the proprietor thereof. And if any one of his accomplices will kill the said Three-fingered Jack, and bring in his head and hand wanting the two fingers, such accomplice shall be entitled to his free pardon, and his freedom as above, upon due proof being made of their being the head and hand of the said Three-fingered Jack.*

*By the House,*
SAMUEL HOWELL, *Cl. Assem.*[1]

These proclamations were published by Governor Dalling, the 12th of December, 1780; and 13th of January, 1781. The reward of three hundred pounds, and liberty,[2] was a great inducement, and worked upon the hearts of many; but Jack's malefic Obi in the opposite scale, was a tremendous evil, and their courage failed them. But the bold and lion-hearted Quashee was not to be

---

[1]   Clerk of Assembly.
[2]   This pension awarded by the Jamaican legislature was still being paid as late as 1840, sixty years after Jack's killing: Clinton V. Black, *Tales of Old Jamaica* (London: Collins, 1966) 119.

intimidated by his imaginary spell, and, accompanied by another daring fellow, Sam, of Scots-hall, Maroons-town, they set out, determined to bring in the head and hand of Jack, or die in the failure of the expedition.

Quashee first got himself christened, and changed his name to James Reeder. A great party of the towns-people accompanied them, and the expedition commenced.

For many weeks were they lurking about and blockading the most inaccessible parts of the Blue Mountains, and near where Jack dwelt secluded from society and buried from the enquiring eye, but in vain. At length, wearied with this mode of bush-fighting, they boldly resolved to proceed to the mouth of his cave, and compel him to the fight.

The towns-folk were intimidated, and Quashee, Sam and a little boy, marched forward alone. They were well armed, and possessed an heroic boldness well suited to the nature of the enterprise. They had not proceeded far, before they discovered, among the weeds and bushes, the late impression of a human foot. Aware that the enemy was near, they slowly tracked the footsteps, making not the least noise, till, presently they discovered a smoke. This was a moment to prepare for life or death, and each seizing his musket, they came suddenly upon Jack before he perceived them.

Jack was seated over a blazing fire, at the mouth of his cave, roasting plantains. His looks were fierce, wild and terrible; up he started from the ground, and said he would kill them.

But Reeder told him that his Obi had no power over him, for that he was christened, and no longer Quashee, but James Reeder.

Jack started back in dismay; he was cowed; for he had prophesied that White Obi should overcome him, and he knew the charm, in Reeder's hands, would lose none of its virtue or power.

This was the first time he ever shrunk back in fear, and the first time he ever fled from his foe; but, with his cutlass in his hand, he threw himself down a precipice at the back of his cave.

Sam fired, and shot him in the shoulder, but Reeder's gun flashed in the pan,[1] and down he plunged headlong after him.

---

[1]   The pan was the part of a gun lock that held the gunpowder. A flash in the pan signified a sudden burst of light or fire, but no discharge.

The steep was thirty feet, and nearly perpendicular.

Jack now grasped his cutlass with resolution, and they commenced the bloody affray; the battle was fierce and long contested, and Jack's blood streamed down his back in floods from his wounded shoulder.

The little boy now reached the top of the precipice, and, with a good aim, shot Jack in the belly.

Sam, who did not lack courage, coolly took a round-about way to the field of action; but when he came to the spot where it had commenced, they had rolled, entwined in each other's grasp, down another precipice, in which fall they had lost their weapons.

Sam immediately descended, and likewise lost his cutlass amongst the weeds and bushes. When he came to them, they, though without weapons, were stoutly contesting the ground, and most fortunately for Quashee, Jack's wounds were deep and desperate, and he was in great agony.

Sam came up just time enough to save him from Jack's strangling grasp; he was then with his right hand almost cut off, and streaming with gore and gashes.

The ground was covered with Jack's blood, and he was further enfeebled by the stouter arm of death.

In this state, Sam knocked down Jack with a piece of rock, and when the lion fell, the two tygers got upon him, and beat his brains out with stones.

The little boy soon after found his way to them.

He had a cutlass, with which they cut off Jack's head and three-fingered hand, and carried them to Morant Bay; they then put their trophies in a pail of rum, and carried them in triumph to Kingston and Spanish-town, and claimed the rewards offered by the King's proclamation and House of Assembly.

Thus died as great a man as ever graced the annals of history, basely murdered by the hirelings of Government. No doubt in the end Jack died deservedly—had he died like a man. But who worked his passion to the pitch? Who drove him to the deeds of desperacy and cruelty? Oh fie! fie!!

I dare say you will wish to know what became of Harrop? I will tell you: starved to death in Jack's cave, and then only was he discovered.

William Sebald and Harriet were at length united, and have for many years enjoyed the sweets of a happy union.

Adieu!

GEORGE STANFORD.


FINIS.

# Appendix A: Historical Sources on Obeah

[The first extract in this appendix, from Benjamin Moseley's *A Treatise on Sugar* (1799), is an important source for the story of Three-fingered Jack and for the ideas concerning obeah that set the trend for a number of subsequent depictions. Born in Essex in 1742, Moseley received a medical education in London, Paris, and Leyden, and accepted the position of surgeon-general in Jamaica in 1768. He wrote several works examining the afflictions and treatments of his patients in the West Indies, including *Observations on the Dysentery of the West Indies, with a New and Successful Method of Treating it* (1781), *A Treatise Concerning the Properties and Effects of Coffee* (1775), and *A Treatise on Tropical Diseases and on the Climate of the West Indies* (1787). The second extract reproduces testimony collected from Jamaican planters for Parliamentary hearings on obeah in the House of Commons in 1789. These depositions reveal the manner in which obeah was regarded as a political threat as well as a cultural practice that needed to be managed under the institution of slavery. Several of the comments in these depositions reveal the white slaveowners' distorted understandings of African belief systems. The third extract features descriptions of obeah culled from Matthew Gregory Lewis's well-known *Journal of a West India Proprietor* (1834). Lewis, writing at a time when the perceived threat from obeah was diminishing, manages to represent the belief system in a number of literary modes. Known as Monk Lewis for his most famous work *The Monk* (1795), he was born in London in 1775. His father, Matthew Lewis, was the owner of large Jamaican estates, and his mother, who separated from her husband while Matthew Gregory was a boy, was an accomplished musician and a favorite at court. Following the death of his father in 1812, Lewis gave up his career as a prominent author and playwright influenced by both the new stream of romantic literature and German gothic literature. His focus became instead the exploration of his newfound wealth in frequent trips to his holdings in Jamaica. His commitment to his West Indian holdings was codified in his will, which dictated that whoever should possess the properties in the future be required to spend three months every third year in Jamaica to oversee the proper treatment of the slaves, none of whom was to be sold.]

## 1. Benjamin Moseley, *A Treatise on Sugar* (London: G.G. and J. Robinson, 1799)

The *yaws*[1] differs altogether from every other disorder, in its origin, progress, and termination.

Left to itself, it sometimes departs in 9, 12, 15, or 18 months, without leaving behind it any inconveniency. Sometimes it remains much longer, and ends in shocking nodes,[2] and distortions of the bones. Many are destroyed by it. No person is subject to it twice.

From want of care and proper management, the torments of the *yaws* surpass all description, from the *bone ache*,[3] and dreadful agonizing curvatures, and caries[4] of the legs, arms, collar-bones, wrists, and almost every other bone, and articulation in the body.

There is also, sometimes, a relic after the original malady is gone, called the *master yaw;* this is an inveterate ulcer, proceeding from the largest *yaw,* or chief determination of the eruption.

Generally, this distemper terminates in what are called *crab yaws.*[5] These are painful sores, or cracks in the feet, sometimes spongy, sometimes hard and callous.

There are two sorts of *yaws,* like the two species of *Farcy*[6] in horses; the *common yaws* and the *running yaws.*

The *common yaws,* without fever or indisposition, begins with small pimples, which soon increase, and appear in round, white, flabby eruptions, from about the size of a pea to that of a large strawberry, separately, or in clusters, in different parts of the body. These eruptions do not appear all at once; and, when some are declining,

---

[1]  Also called *frambesia,* the yaws is a chronic contagious disease characterized by raspberry-like lesions or tubercles on the skin. Caused by an organism similar to that which produces syphilis, the disease is spread through direct contact with the lesions of infected individuals, not through sexual contact. If left untreated, the yaws can result in severe disfigurement. For more information on the connection between the yaws and obeah, see introduction, 34–37.

[2]  Protuberances or knotty formations.

[3]  This term was associated with venereal disease, particularly syphilis.

[4]  Decay.

[5]  Crab yaws was known to attack the soles of the feet and palms of the hands, causing hardened ulcers.

[6]  A disease in horses and other animals similar to glanders, causing small tumors and hardened lymphatic vessels.

and others disappearing, a fresh crop comes out in a different part of the body. Sometimes a few doses of sulphur will force them out, when they are thought to be entirely gone from the habit.

The *running yaws* breaks out in spreading cutaneous[1] ulcers, discharging a great quantity of acrid corrosive matter, in different parts of the body. This is the worst sort.

The cure of the *yaws* is now understood by skilful practitioners. Inoculation is performed with success. Care soon removes the principal mischief of the distemper; and the *crab yaws* are easily cured in the manner which I have related in another publication.[*]

Formerly there was no regular method of treating the *yaws* in the West Indies. It was thought to be a disorder that would have its course, and, if interrupted, that it would be dangerous. It was then the custom, when a negro was attacked with it, to separate him from the rest, and send him to some lonely place by the sea side, to bathe; or into the mountains, to some Provision Ground,[2] or Plantain Walk;[3] where he could act as a watchman, and maintain himself, without any expence to the estate, until he was well; then he was brought back to the Sugar-Work.

But this rarely happened. A cold, damp, smoky hut, for his habitation; snakes and lizards his companions; crude, viscid[4] food, and bad water, his only support; and shunned as a leper; — he usually sunk from the land of the living.

But some of these abandoned exiles lived, in spite of the common law of nature, and survived a general mutation of their muscles, ligaments, and osteology;[5] became also hideously white in their woolly hair and skin; with their limbs and bodies twisted and turned, by the force of the distemper, into shocking grotesque figures, resembling woody excrescences, or stumps of trees; or old Egyptian figures, that seem as if they had been made of the ends of the human, and beginnings of the brutal form; which figures are, by some antiquaries, taken for gods, and by others, for devils.

---

[*] *Treatise on Tropical Diseases*, ed. 3, p. 519 [(London, G.G. and J. Robinson, 1795). This is Moseley's most significant work, which includes several accounts of the West Indian slaves' beliefs in the powers of obeah.]

---

[1] Occurring on the surface of the skin.
[2] A plot tended by slaves, where they tended their own produce.
[3] A plantation of plantains.
[4] Viscous or glutinous.
[5] Used here to mean bone structure.

In their banishment, their huts often became the receptacles of robbers and fugitive negroes; and, as they had no power to resist any who chose to take shelter in their hovels, had nothing to lose, and were forsaken by the world, a tyger would hardly molest them. Their desperate guests never did.[1]

The host of the hut, as he grew more misshapen, generally became more subtile;[2]—this we observe in England, in crooked scrophulous persons;[3]—as if Nature disliked people's being both cunning, and strong.

Many of their wayward visitors were deeply skilled in magic, and what we call the *black art,* which they brought with them from Africa; and, in return for their accommodation, they usually taught their landlord the mysteries of sigils,[4] spells, and sorcery; and *illuminated* him in all the occult science of OBI.[*]

These ugly, loathsome creatures thus became oracles of woods, and unfrequented places; and were resorted to secretly, by the wretched in mind, and by the malicious, for wicked purposes.

OBI, and *gambling,* are the only instances I have been able to discover, among the natives of the negro land in Africa, in which any effort at combining ideas, has ever been demonstrated.[5]

---

[*] This OBI, or, as it is pronounced in the English West Indies, *Obeah,* had its origins, like many customs among the Africans, from the ancient Egyptians.

OB is a demon, a spirit of divination, and magic. When Saul wanted to raise up Samuel from the dead, he said to his servants, "Seek me a woman (eminent for OB) that hath a familiar spirit."

His servants replied to him, "There is (a woman mistress in the art of OB) that hath a familiar spirit, at Endor."

When the witch of Endor came to Saul, he said to her, "Divine unto me (by thy witchcraft OB) by the familiar spirit, and bring me him up who I shall name to thee." I *Samuel, chap.* xxviii, v.7 and 8.

---

[1] Due to enforced quarantine, those afflicted with yaws were often circumstantially enabled to develop the knowledge of obeah practices and entertain those requiring their services in total privacy. The "professors," as Moseley later refers to them, possessed supernatural powers according to the majority of the slave population, but were feared by the white population for their effect on plantation societies.

[2] Cunning, artful, crafty.

[3] Those suffering from scrofula, also known as the King's Evil, a disease that causes chronic enlargement and degeneration of the lymphatic glands.

[4] An occult sign or device supposed to have mysterious powers.

[5] It is worth noting that both obi and gambling, the only instances of slaves exerting any "effort at combining ideas," threatened to upset the ideal stability of the plantation which would control both the spiritual and the economic resources of the slaves. Both practices might also suggest to the European eye a slave's misguided belief in

The science of OBI is very extensive.

OBI, for the purposes of bewitching people, or consuming them by lingering illness, is made of grave dirt, hair, teeth of sharks, and other creatures, blood, feathers, egg-shells, images in wax, the hearts of birds, and some potent roots, weeds, and bushes, of which Europeans are at this time ignorant;[1] but which were known, for the same purposes, to the ancients.

Certain mixtures of these ingredients are burnt; or buried very deep in the ground; or hung up a chimney; or laid under the threshold of the door of the party, to suffer; with incantation songs, or curses, performed at midnight, regarding the aspects of the moon. The party who wants to do the mischief, is also sent to burying-grounds, or some secret place, where spirits are supposed to frequent, to invoke his dead parents to assist him in the curse.

A negro, who thinks himself bewitched by OBI, will apply to an *Obi-man,* or *Obi-woman,* for cure.

These magicians will interrogate the patient, as to the part of the body most afflicted. This part they will torture with pinching, drawing with gourds, or calabashes, beating, and pressing. When the patient is nearly exhausted with this rough *magnetising,*[2] OBI[3] brings out an old rusty nail, or a piece of bone, or an ass's tooth, or the jaw-bone of a rat, or a fragment of a quart bottle, from the part; and the patient is well the next day.

The most wrinkled, and most deformed *Obian* magicians, are most venerated. This was the case among the Egyptians and Chaldeans.[4]

In general, *Obi-men* are more sagacious than *Obi-women,* in giving, or taking away diseases; and in the application of poisons. It is in their department to blind pigs, and poultry; and lame cattle.

---

the source of fortune, as both represented a sort of spiritual vice that fell far outside the realm of Christianity. It is interesting that Moseley goes on to immediately refer to obeah as a "science" as opposed to a belief system.

[1] Plantation owners were also ignorant of the healing powers of such natural resources and often called on the obeah professors to cure slaves who were afflicted with diseases that confounded modern medicine.

[2] To draw out or attract as a magnet does.

[3] Moseley uses the term "obi" to refer to different aspects of the practice. Here the term refers to the practitioner of obeah.

[4] Natives of Chaldea or the biblical Syria or Aramaia, associated with magical and oracular powers. In referencing this population of the Old Testament, there is an implicit link made between the foundations of Christianity and obeah practices.

It is the province of the *Obi-women* to dispose of the passions.[1]
They sell foul winds for inconstant mariners; dreams and phantasies
for jealousy; vexation, and pains in the heart, for perfidious love; and
for the perturbed, impatient, and wretched, at the tardy acts of time,—
to turn in prophetic fury to a future page in the book of Fate,—and
amaze the ravished sense of the tempest-tossed querent.[2]

Laws have been made in the West Indies to punish this *Obian*
practice with death; but they have had no effect. Laws constructed
in the West Indies, can never suppress the effect of ideas, the origin
of which, is the centre of Africa.

I saw the OBI[3] of the famous negro robber, *Three fingered* JACK,
the terror of Jamaica in 1780 and 1781. The Maroons who slew him
brought it to me.

His OBI consisted of the end of a goat's horn, filled with a
compound of grave dirt, ashes, the blood of a black cat, and human
fat; all mixed into a kind of paste. A black cat's foot, a dried toad, a
pig's tail, a flip of parchment of kid's skin, with characters marked
in blood on it, were also in his *Obian* bag.

These, with a keen sabre, and two guns, like *Robinson Crusoe,*[4]
were all his OBI; with which, and his courage in descending into
the plains and plundering to supply his wants, and his skill in retreat-
ing into difficult fastnesses,[5] commanding the only access to them,
where none dared to follow him, he terrified the inhabitants, and
set the civil power, and the neighbouring militia of that island, at
defiance, for two years.

He had neither accomplice, nor associate. There were a few
runaway negroes in the woods near Mount Libanus,[6] the place of
his retreat; but he had crossed their foreheads with some of the magic
in his horn, and they could not betray him. But he trusted no one.

---

[1]  It is interesting to note the gender role distinctions in the practice of obeah that
Moseley suggests. The obi-women seem to concentrate on futurology and sooth-
saying, while the men are more involved in the creation of obi for protection or
poisoning.

[2]  An inquirer; one who consults an occult practitioner.

[3]  Here "obi" refers to the accessories of Jack's sorcery.

[4]  Allusion to the passage in Daniel Defoe's classic where Crusoe arms himself: "My
Figure indeed was very fierce; I had my formidable Goat-Skin Coat on, with the
great Cap I have mention'd, a naked Sword by my Side, two Pistols in my Belt, and
a Gun upon each Shoulder" (London: W. Taylor, 1719) 300.

[5]  Mountain strongholds.

[6]  Also spelled Lebanus, located in the southeastern part of the island.

He scorned assistance. He ascended above SPARTACUS.[1] He robbed alone; fought all his battles alone; and always killed his pursuers.

By his magic, he was not only the dread of the negroes, but there were many white people, who believed he was possessed of some supernatural power.

In hot climates females marry very young; and often with great disparity of age. Here JACK was the author of many troubles:—for several matches proved unhappy.

"Give a dog an ill name, and hang him."

Clamours rose on clamours against the cruel *sorcerer*; and every conjugal mishap was laid at the door of JACK's malific[2] spell of *tying the point*,[3] on the wedding day.

God knows, poor JACK had sins enough of his own to carry, without loading him with the sins of others. He would sooner have made a *Medean* cauldron[4] for the whole island, than disturb one lady's happiness. He had many opportunities; and, though he had a mortal hatred to white men, he was never known to hurt a child, or abuse a woman.

But even JACK himself was born, to die.

Allured by the rewards offered by Governor DALLING, in a proclamation, dated the 12th of December, 1780, and by a resolution which

---

[1] Spartacus was born in Thrace during the Roman empire. It is believed that he deserted the Roman auxiliary legions and was then captured and sold into slavery to become a gladiator. Spartacus led his fellow slaves in escaping the gladiator's fate that awaited them and in defeating no fewer than seven Roman armies in their struggle for freedom. Spartacus was eventually captured by the Roman general Crassus in the Battle at Brundisium in 71 AD, a battle that also cost the slave leader his life. This reference to the slave general and the earlier reference to the literary hero Robinson Crusoe reveal a distinct admiration for Jack and the classically heroic qualities he embodies.

[2] Standard spelling is malefic, meaning baleful, producing ill effect.

[3] A Jamaican superstition in which an evildoer casts a spell over the married couple to make them unhappy.

[4] Medea was a devotee of the goddess Hecate and one of the most powerful sorceresses of the ancient world. This protofeminist classical figure, immortalized by Euripides and Seneca, sought to rectify her status as a betrayed wife and dispossessed mother by slaughtering her own children. Like the obeah practitioners, she also possessed the power to rejuvenate through the use of magical potions, concocted in her cauldron. The myth of Medea was reinvigorated in this period as a symbol of the ungovernability, gender role disruption, and redemptive potential of slave rebels and obeah professors. For a full discussion of the appropriation of the Medea myth in the West Indies' plantocracy, see Srinivas Aravamudan, *Tropicopolitans* (Durham: Duke UP, 1999) 315–25.

followed it, of the House of Assembly,[1] two negroes, named QUASHEE and SAM (SAM was Captain DAVY's son, he who shot a Mr. THOMPSON, the master of a London ship, at Old Harbour), both of *Scots Hall, Maroon Town*, with a party of their townsmen, went in search of him.

QUASHEE, before he set out on the expedition, got himself christianed,[2] and changed his name to JAMES REEDER.

The expedition commenced; and the whole party had been creeping about in the woods, for three weeks, and blockading, as it were, the deepest recesses of the most inaccessible part of the island, where JACK, far remote from all human society, resided,—but in vain.

REEDER and SAM, tired with this mode of war, resolved on proceeding in search of his retreat; and taking him, by storming it, or perishing in the attempt.

They took with them a little boy, a proper spirit, and a good shot, and left the rest of the party.

These three, whom I well knew, had not been long separated, before their cunning eyes discovered, by impressions among the weeds and bushes, that some person must have lately been that way.[3]

They softly followed these impressions, making not the least noise. Presently they discovered a smoke.

They prepared for war. They came upon JACK before he perceived them. He was roasting *plantains*, by a little fire on the ground, at the mouth of a cave.

This was a scene:—not where ordinary actors had a common part to play.

JACK's looks were fierce and terrible. He told them he would kill them.

REEDER, instead of shooting JACK, replied, that his OBI had no power to hurt him; for he was christianed; and that his name was no longer QUASHEE.

---

[1]    In Edwards' original note here, he quotes from the House of Assembly declaration on 29 December 1780: RESOLVED, that, over and above the reward of one hundred pounds offered by his Majesty's proclamation for taking or killing the rebellious negro called *Three fingered* JACK, the further reward of FREEDOM shall be given to any slave that shall take or kill the said *Three fingered* JACK, and that the House will make good the value of such slave to the proprietor thereof. And if any one of his accomplices will kill the said *Three fingered* JACK, and bring in his head, and hand wanting the fingers, such accomplice shall be entitled to his *free* PARDON, and his FREEDOM as above, upon due proof being made of their being the head and hand of the said *Three fingered* JACK.

[2]    Christened; converted to Christianity.

[3]    The Maroons were renowned as expert trackers. Part of the peace settlement following the Maroon Wars required Maroon men to assist plantation owners in seeking runaway slaves and in quelling revolt.

JACK knew REEDER; and, as if paralysed, he let his two guns remain on the ground, and took up only his cutlass.

These two had a desperate engagement several years before, in the woods; in which conflict JACK lost the two fingers, which was the origin of his present name; but JACK then beat REEDER, and almost killed him, with several others who assisted him, and they fled from JACK.

To do *Three-fingered* JACK justice, he would now have killed both REEDER and SAM; for, at first, they were frightened at the sight of him, and the dreadful tone of his voice; and well they might: they had besides no retreat, and were to grapple with the bravest, and strongest man in the world.

But JACK was cowed; for, he had prophesied, that *white* OBI would get the better of him; and, from experience, he knew the charm would lose none of its strength in the hands of REEDER.

Without farther parley,[1] JACK, with his cutlass in his hand, threw himself down a precipice at the back of the cave.

REEDER's gun missed fire. SAM shot him in the shoulder. REEDER, like an English bull-dog, never looked, but, with his cutlass in his hand, plunged headlong down after JACK. The descent was about thirty yards, and almost perpendicular. Both of them had preserved their cutlasses in the fall.

Here was the stage,—on which two of the stoutest hearts, that were ever hooped with ribs, began their bloody struggle.

The little boy, who was ordered to keep back, out of harm's way, now reached the top of the precipice, and, during the fight, shot JACK in the belly.

SAM was crafty, and coolly took a round about way to get to the field of action. When he arrived at the spot where it began, JACK and REEDER had closed, and tumbled together down another precipice, on the side of the mountain, in which fall they both lost their weapons.

SAM descended after them, who also lost his cutlass, among the trees and bushes in getting down.

When he came to them, though without weapons, they were not idle; and, luckily for REEDER, JACK's wounds were deep and desperate, and he was in great agony.

SAM came up just time enough to save REEDER; for, JACK had

---

[1]  Conversation, exchange of words.

caught him by the throat, with his giant's grasp. REEDER then was with his right hand almost cut off, and JACK streaming blood from his shoulder and belly; both covered with gore and gashes.

In this state SAM was umpire;[1] and decided the fate of the battle. He knocked JACK down with a piece of rock.

When the lion fell, the two tigers got upon him, and beat his brains out with stones.

The little boy soon after found his way to them. He had a cutlass, with which they cut off JACK'S head, and THREE-FINGERED HAND, and took them in triumph to Morant Bay.

There they put their trophies into a pail of rum;[2] and, followed by a vast concourse of negroes, now no longer afraid of JACK's OBI, they carried them to Kingston, and Spanish Town; and claimed the reward of the King's Proclamation, and The House of Assembly.[3]

**2. From** *House of Commons Sessional Papers of the Eighteenth Century, vol. 69. Report of the Lords of the Committee of the Council Appointed* **[by George III]** *for the Consideration of All Matters Relating to Trade and Foreign Plantations, Part I,* **1789 (Wilmington, DE: Scholarly Resources, 1975)**

A. Nos. 22, 23, 24, 25, 26

Whether Negroes called Obeah-Men, or under any other Denomination, practicing Witchcraft, exist in the Island of Jamaica?

By what Arts or by what Means, do these Obeah-Men cause the Deaths, or otherwise injure, those who are supposed to be influenced thereby; and what are the Symptoms and Effects that have been observed to be produced in People who are supposed to be under the Influence of their Practices?

Are the Instances of Death or Diseases produced by these Arts or Means frequent?

Are these Arts or Means brought by the Obeah-Men from Africa, or are they Inventions which have been originated in the Island?

---

[1] Ironic use of the term, as Sam is certainly not neutral, but just as much an enemy to Jack as Reeder.

[2] Rum would have been used for preservation so that the parts could be identified and the reward claimed.

[3] See introduction, 12–14. The reward for Jack's death was still being paid out as late as 1840, nearly sixty years after his death.

Whether any or what Laws exist in the Island of Jamaica for their Punishment, and what evidence is generally required for their Conviction?

Mr. Fuller, Agent for the Island; Mr. Long, and Mr. Chisholme. [Original marginalia.]

The term *Obeah, Obiah,* or *Obia* (for it is variously written), we conceive to be the Adjective, and *Obe* or *Obi* the Noun Substantive; and that by the Words *Obiah* Men or Women, are meant those who practice *Obi*. The Origin of the Term[1] we should consider as of no Importance in our Answer to the Questions proposed, if, in search of it, we were not led to Disquisitions that are highly gratifying to Curiosity. From the learned Mr. Bryant's[*] Commentary upon the word *Oph*, we obtain a very probable Etymology of the Term—"A Serpent, in the Egyptian Language, was called *Ob* or *Aub*."—"*Obion* is still the Egyptian name for a Serpent."—"Moses, in the Name of God, forbids the Israelites ever to enquire of the Daemon *Ob*, which is translated in our Bible, Charmer, or Wizard, Divinator aut Sortilegus."[2]—"The Woman at Endor[3] is called *Oub* or *Ob*, translated Pythonissa, and *Oubaious* (he cites from *Horus Apollo*)[4] was the Name of the Basilisk or Royal Serpent, Emblem of the Sun, and an ancient oracular Deity of Africa." This Derivation, which applies to one particular Sect, the Remnant probably of a very celebrated religious Order in remote Ages, is now become in Jamaica the general Term to denote those Africans who in that Island practice Witchcraft

---

[*] Mythology, Vol. I. p. 48, 475, and 478. [See Jacob Bryant, *A new system, or an analysis of antient mythology* (London: T. Payne, 1775–76).]

[1] For a discussion of the etymology of "obeah," see introduction, 23–25.

[2] See Deuteronomy 18: 10–11: "There shall not be found among you any one that maketh his son or daughter to pass through the fire, or that useth divination, or an observer of times, or an enchanter, or a consulter with familiar spirits, or a wizard, or a necromancer."

[3] From 1 Samuel 28:7. Before going into battle with the Philistines: "Then said Saul unto his servants, Seek me a woman that hath a familiar spirit, that I may go to her and enquire of her. And his servants said to him, Behold, there is a woman that hath a familiar spirit at Endor."

[4] The citation is from Horapollo 1.1.2. In citing this source, Bryant confuses the Greek cults in Pythia with African serpent cults and African ophiolatry. For a full discussion of ancient divination practices, see Bryant, vol. I, 473–90.

or Sorcery, comprehending also the Class of what are called Myal-Men,[1] or those who by means of a narcotic Potion,[2] made with the Juice of an Herb (said to be the branched *Calalue* or Species of *Solannum*)[3] which occasions a Trance or profound Sleep of a certain Duration, endeavour to convince the deluded Spectators of their Power to reanimate dead Bodies.

As far as we are able to decide from our own Experience and Information when we lived in the Island, and from the concurrent Testimony of all the Negroes we have ever conversed with on the Subject, the Professors of *Obi* are, and always were, Natives of Africa,[4] and none other, and they have brought the Science with them from thence to Jamaica, where it is so universally practiced, that we believe there are few of the larger Estates possessing native Africans, which have not One or more of them. The oldest and most crafty are those who usually attract the greatest Devotion and Confidence, those whose hoary heads, and a somewhat peculiarly harsh and diabolic in their Aspect, together with some Skill in plants of the medicinal and poisonous species, have qualified them for successful imposition upon the weak and credulous. The Negroes in general, whether Africans or Creoles, revere, consult, and abhor them; to these Oracles they resort, and with the most implicit Faith, upon all Occasions, whether for the Cure of Disorders, the obtaining Revenge for Injuries or Insults, the conciliating of Favour, the Discovery and Punishments of the Thief or the Adulterer, and the Prediction of future Events. Such is the Trade which these Wretches carry on at different Prices. A Veil of Mystery is studiously thrown over their Incantations, to which the Midnight Hours are allotted, and every Precaution is taken to conceal them from the Knowledge and Discovery of the White People. The deluded Negroes, who thoroughly believe in their supernatural Power, become the willing Accomplices in this Concealment, and the stoutest among them tremble at the very Sight of the ragged Bundle, the Bottle or the

---

1   For a discussion of myal-men, see the introduction, 28.
2   Referring to atropine and scopolamine, powerful hallucinogens found in plants of the genus Solanum.
3   Genus of plants commonly referred to as nightshade, noted for their narcotic or poisonous properties.
4   Natives of Africa is used here to distinguish these individuals from "Creole" slaves, or those born in the West Indies. It was widely believed that slaves born in Africa were potentially more dangerous as they had greater access to African traditions, languages, and religions.

Egg-shells, which are stuck in the Thatch or hung over the Door of a Hut, or upon the Branch of a Plantain Tree, to deter Marauders. In Cases of Poison, the natural Effects of it are by the ignorant Negroes ascribed entirely to the potent Workings of *Obi*. The wiser Negroes hesitate to reveal their Suspicions, through a Dread of incurring the terrible Vengeance which is fulminated by the *Obiah-Men* against any who should betray them; it is very difficult therefore for the White Proprietor to distinguish the *Obia Professor* from any other Negro upon his Plantation; and so infatuated are the Blacks in general, that but few Instances occur of their having assumed Courage enough to impeach these Miscreants. With Minds so firmly prepossessed, they no sooner find *obi set for them*[1] near the Door of their House, or in the Path which leads to it, than they give themselves up for lost. When a Negro is robbed of a Fowl or a Hog, he applies directly to the *Obiah*-Man or Woman; it is then made known among his Fellow Blacks, that *Obi is set* for the Thief; and as soon as the latter hears the dreadful News, his terrified Imagination begins to work, no Resource is left but in the superior Skill of some more eminent *Obiah-Man* of the Neighbourhood, who may counteract the magical Operations of the other; but if no one can be found of higher Rank and Ability, or if after gaining such an Ally he should still fancy himself affected, he presently falls into a Decline, under the incessant Horrour of impending Calamities. The slightest painful Sensation in the Head, the Bowels, or any other Part, any casual Loss or Hurt, confirms his Apprehensions, and he believes himself the devoted Victim of an invisible and irresistible Agency. Sleep, Appetite, and Cheerfulness, forsake him, his Strength decays, his disturbed Imagination is haunted without Respite, his Features wear the settled Gloom of Despondency; Dirt, or any other unwholesome Substance, becomes his only Food,[2] he contracts a morbid habit of body, and gradually sinks into the Grave. A Negro, who is taken ill, enquires of the *Obiah-Man* the Cause of his Sickness, whether it will prove mortal or not; and within what time he shall die or recover?

---

[1]  See the introduction regarding the distinction between *setting* and *pulling* obi, 19.

[2]  Dirt-eating and despondency were diagnosed as *Cachexia Africana*, the target of medical speculation at the time. There are currently several theories about the cause of soil-eating, which was more likely to occur in under-nourished women and children. In medical terms, the eating of earth or clay, known as *geophagy*, can be seen as a way to combat anemia due to iron deficiency while also potentially reducing gastric pain caused by hookworm. The practice can also be seen as a morbid craving to eat the inedible, known as *pica*, which can be symptomatic of certain intestinal diseases.

The Oracle generally ascribes the Distemper to the Malice of some particular Person by Name, and advises to set *Obi* for that person; but if no Hopes are given of Recovery, immediate Despair takes place, which no Medicine can remove, and Death is the certain Consequence. Those anomalous Symptoms, which from Causes deeply rooted in the Mind, such as the Terrours of *Obi*, or from Poisons, whose Operation is slow and intricate, will battle the Skill of the ablest Physician.

Considering the Multitude of Occasions which may provoke the Negroes to exercise the Powers of *Obi* against each other, and the astonishing Influence of this Superstition upon their Minds, we cannot but attribute a very considerable Portion of the annual Mortality among the Negroes of Jamaica to this fascinating Mischief.

The *Obi* is usually composed of a Farrago of Materials,[1] most of which are enumerated in the Jamaica Law,* viz. "Blood, Feathers, Parrots Beaks, Dogs Teeth, Alligators Teeth, Broken Bottles, Grave Dirt, Rum, and Eggshells."

With a view to illustrate the Description we have given of this Practice, and its common Effects, we have subjoined a few Examples out of the very great Number which have occurred in Jamaica; not that they are peculiar to that Island only, for we believe similar Examples may be found in other West India Colonies. *Père Labat*, in his History of Martinico, has mentioned some which are very remarkable.†

It may seem extraordinary, that a Practice alleged to be so frequent in Jamaica should not have received an earlier check from the Legislature. The Truth is, that the Skill of some Negroes in the Art of Poisoning has been noticed ever since the Colonists became much acquainted with them. Sloane and Barham,[2] who practiced Physic in

---

* Act 24. Sect. 10. passed 1760. [Following Tacky's Rebellion in 1760, which was led by a Jamaican believed to be an obeah practitioner, the Assembly of Jamaica outlawed the practice of obeah in Act 24 Section 10, passed on 13 December 1760 (see introduction, 18–23).]

† Tome ii. p. 59, 447, 499, 506. [Refers to Jean Baptiste Labat, *Nouveau voyage aux isles de l'Amerique* (Paris: G. Cavelier, 1728).]

---

1  Farrago: a confused group; a medley, mixture, hotchpotch.

2  Sir Hans Sloane, *A voyage to the islands Madera, Barbados, Nieves, S. Christophers and Jamaica, with the natural history of the herbs and trees, four-footed beasts, fishes, birds, insects, reptiles, &c. of the last of those islands* (London: T. and J. Egerton, 1707–25) and Henry Barham, *Hortus Americanus: containing an account of the trees, shrubs, and other vegetable productions of South-America and the West India Islands, and particularly of the island of Jamaica* (Kingston: Alexander Aikman, 1794).

Jamaica in the last Century, have mentioned particular Instances of it. The secret and insidious Manner in which this Crime is generally perpetrated, makes the legal Proof of it extremely difficult. Suspicions therefore have been frequent, but Detections rare: These Murderers have *sometimes* been brought to Justice, but it is reasonable to believe that a far greater Number have escaped with Impunity. In regard to the other and more common Tricks of *Obi*, such as hanging up Feathers, Bottles, Eggshells, &c., &c. in order to intimidate Negroes of a thievish Disposition from plundering Huts, Hog-styes, or Provision-grounds, these were laughed at by the White Inhabitants as harmless Stratagems, contrived by the more sagacious for deterring the more simple and superstitious Blacks, and serving for much the same Purpose as the Scarecrows which are in general used among our English Farmers and Gardeners. But in the Year 1760, when a very formidable Insurrection of the Cormantin[1] or Gold Coast Negroes broke out in the Parish of St. Mary, and spread through almost every other District of the Island; an old Coromantin Negro, the chief Instigator and Oracle of the Insurgents in that Parish, who had administered the Fetish or solemn Oath to the Conspirators, and furnished them with a magical Preparation which was to render them invulnerable, was fortunately apprehended, convicted, and hung up with all his Feathers and Trumperies[2] about him; and this Execution struck the Insurgents with a general Panic, from which they never afterwards recovered. The Examinations which were taken at that Period first opened the Eyes of the Public to the very dangerous Tendency of the *Obiah* Practices, and gave birth to the Law[3] which was then enacted for their Suppression and Punishment. But neither the Terror of this Law, the strict Investigation which has ever since been made after the Professors of *Obi*, nor the many Examples of those who from Time to Time have been hanged or transported, have hitherto produced the desired Effect. We conclude, therefore, that either this Sect, like others in the World, has flourished under

---

[1] Also "Coromantee," "Coromantyn," or "Koromantyn." The term describes an ethnic group of the Gold Coast, or more specifically people of the Akan-speaking region, located in present-day Ghana. See Richard Price, ed., *Maroon Societies* (Garden City, NY: Anchor Books, 1973). The Koromantyn were also seen as "frank and fearless:" Edwards, *History* vol.1, 90.

[2] Trifles, trash, rubbish; also in the sense of impostures or trickeries contemptuously applied to religious superstitions.

[3] Refers to Act 24, Section 10.

Persecution; or that fresh Supplies are annually introduced from the African Seminaries.[1]

A.
The Paper referred to in the preceding Account.

WE have the following Narratives from a Planter in Jamaica, a Gentleman of the strictest Veracity, who is now in London, and ready to attest the Truth of them.

Upon returning to Jamaica in the Year 1775, he found a great many of his Negroes had died during his Absence; and that of such as remained alive, at least One-half were debilitated, bloated, and in a very deplorable Condition. The Mortality continued after his Arrival, and Two or Three were frequently buried in One Day; others were taken ill, and began to decline under the same Symptoms. Every Means were tried by Medicines, and the most careful Nursing, to preserve the Lives of the feeblest; but in spite of all his Endeavours, this Depopulation went on for above a Twelvemonth longer, with more or less Intermission, and without his being able to ascertain the real Cause, though the *Obiah Practice* was strongly suspected, as well by himself, as by the Doctor and other White Persons upon the Plantation, as it was known to have been very common in that Part of the Island, and particularly among the Negroes of the *Papaw* or *Popo* Country.[2] Still he was unable to verify his Suspicions, because the Patients constantly denied their having any Thing to do with Persons of the Order, or any Knowledge of them. At length a Negress, who had been ill for some Time, came one Day and informed him, that feeling it was impossible for her to live much longer, she thought herself bound in Duty, before she died,

---

[1] Seminary here refers to a place where an art or science is cultivated, or from which that knowledge is propagated abundantly. The term also has an ironic connotation, as seminaries were the training sites for priests in the English mission services.

[2] It is difficult to determine the exact region to which this designation refers. The Popo people settled throughout Dahomey and Benin. It is also possible that it is referring specifically to Badagry town in Lagos State, southwestern Nigeria, which lies on the north bank of Porto Novo Creek, an inland waterway that connects the national capitals of Nigeria (Lagos) and Benin (Porto-Novo), and on a road that leads to Lagos, Ilaro, and Porto-Novo. Founded in the late 1720s by Popo refugees from the wars with the Fon people of Dahomey, Badagry was, for the subsequent century, a notorious disembarkation point for slave-trading ships bound for the Americas.

to impart a very great Secret, and acquaint him with the true Cause of her Disorder, in hopes that the Disclosure might prove the Means of stopping that Mischief which had already swept away such a Number of her Fellow-slaves. She proceeded to say, That her Step-mother (a Woman of the *Popo* Country, above Eighty Years old, but still hale and active) had put *Obi upon her,* as she had also done upon those who had lately died; and that the old Woman had practised *Obi* for as many Years past as she could remember.

The other Negroes of the Plantation no sooner heard of this Impeachment, than they ran in a Body to their Master, and confirmed the Truth of it, adding, that she had carried on this Business ever since her Arrival from Africa, and was the Terror of the whole Neighbourhood.—Upon this he repaired directly with Six White Servants to the old Woman's House, and forcing open the Door, observed the whole Inside of the Roof (which was of Thatch), and every Crevice of the Walls, stuck with the Implements of her Trade, consisting of Rags, Feathers, Bones of Cats, and a thousand other Articles. Examining further, a large earthen Pot or Jar, close covered, was found concealed under her Bed.—It contained a prodigious Quantity of round Balls of Earth or Clay of various Dimensions, large and small, whitened on the Outside, and variously compounded, some with Hair and Rags or Feathers of all Sorts, and strongly bound with Twine; others blended with the upper Section of the Skulls of Cats, or stuck round with Cats Teeth and Claws, or with Human or Dogs Teeth, and some Glass Beads of different Colours; there was also a great many Eggshells filled with a viscous or gummy Substance, the Qualities of which he neglected to examine, and many little Bags stuffed with a variety of Articles, the Particulars of which cannot at this Distance of Time be recollected. The House was instantly pulled down, and with the whole of its Contents committed to the Flames, amidst the general Acclamations of all his other Negroes. In regard to the old Woman, he declined bringing her to Trial under the Law of the Island, which would have punished her with Death; but from a Principle of Humanity, delivered her into the Hands of a Party of Spaniards, who (as she was thought not incapable of doing some trifling Kind of Work) were very glad to accept and carry her with them to Cuba. From the Moment of her Departure, his Negroes seemed all to be animated with new Spirits, and the Malady spread no farther among them. The Total of his Losses in the course of about Fifteen Years preceding the Discovery, and imputable solely to the

*Obiah Practice,* he estimates, at the least, as One Hundred Negroes.

B.

A Wainman (or Waggoner) belonging to the same Plantation happened to lose a Steer one very hot Day, on the Road leading to the Shipping Place. The poor Fellow, exceedingly vexed at this Accident, immediately went to a noted *Obiah-man,* who lived near the Spot, and after paying him the usual fee of 2 s. 6 d.[1] desired to know the Cause of his being so remarkably unfortunate, whilst the other Wainmen travelling the same Road, and on the same Day, had lost none of their Cattle? He concluded with petitioning for *Obi to be put,* that the other Wainmen might suffer equally with himself, or that *he* might not be so particularly distinguished for ill Luck.

C.

It may not be desirable that we should multiply Examples, to shew the Prevalence of this Superstition; we shall therefore only add one more, in order to display the Influence of it, over Negroes even of tender Years.—As a Gentleman was travelling not long since from Spanish Town to Kingston, in Jamaica, accompanied by his Servant (a Negro Boy of about the Age of 12 or 14 Years), who rode a little way before him, the Boy on a sudden stopped short, turned about in a very great Fright, and refused to proceed; his Master, surprised at all this, desired to know what was the matter with him? the Boy pointed with a Look of Anxiety to something on one Side [of] the Road, which at last his Master discovered to be nothing more than a Glass Bottle hung by the Neck upon a Stick which was fixed in the Ground. It was quite in vain for him to argue the Case; for neither Threats nor Persuasion could prevail upon his Servant to pass it, nor would he proceed an Inch till his Master had dismounted, and by breaking the Bottle destroyed the *Obi.*

The following Paper relating to the Obeah-men in Jamaica, was delivered by Mr. Rheder.

OBEAH-men are the oldest and most artful Negroes; a Peculiarity marks them, and every Negro pays the greatest Respect

---

[1] Two shillings, six pence (d. is from the Latin *denarius*). Twelve pence were equivalent to a shilling, and twenty shillings were equivalent to one pound sterling.

to them, they are perfectly well acquainted with medicinal Herbs, and know the poisonous ones, which they often use. To prepossess the Stranger in favour of their Skill, he is told that they can restore the Dead to Life; for this Purpose he is shewn a Negro apparently dead, who, by Dint of their Art, soon recovers; this is produced by administering the narcotic Juice of Vegetables. On searching one of the Obeah-men's Houses, was found many Bags filled with Parts of Animals, Vegetables, and Earth, which the Negroes who attended at the sight of, were struck with Terror, and begged that they might be christened, which was done, and the Impression was done away. In consequence of the Rebellion of the Negroes in the Year 1760, a Law was enacted that Year to render the Practice of Obiah, Death.

The Influence of the Professors of that Art was such as to induce many to enter into that Rebellion on the Assurance that they were to be invulnerable, and to render them so, the Obeah-men gave them a Powder with which they were to rub themselves.

On the First Engagement with the Rebels Nine of them were killed, and many Prisoners taken: Among the Prisoners was a very sensible Fellow, who offered to discover many important Matters, on condition that his Life should be spared, which was promised. He then related the Part the Obeah-men had taken, One of whom was capitally convicted and sentenced to Death.

At the Place of Execution he bid defiance to the Executioner, telling him that it was not in the Power of White People to kill him; and the Negro Spectators were astonished when they saw him expire. On the other Obeah-men, various experiments were made with Electrical Machines and Magic Lanthorns,[1] which produced very little Effect; except on one who, after receiving many severe Shocks, acknowledged his Master's Obeah exceeded his own.

I remember sitting Twice on Trials of Obea-men, who were convicted on selling their Nostrums,[2] which had produced Death. To prove the Fact, Two Witnesses are necessary, with corroborating Circumstances.

The following Paper was delivered by Mr. Fuller, respecting the Evidence generally required for the Conviction of Persons who have been tried on the Charge of practicing *Obeah.*

---

[1]  Instruments of torture.

[2]  Concocted remedies; used here ironically, as the medicine was said to produce death.

THE Gentlemen to whom this Question was particularly referred, having never sat upon, nor attended any Trial of this Kind, cannot, from their own personal Knowledge, take upon them to explain the Nature of the Evidence, which has been generally required for constituting a legal Conviction in such Cases.

Of the Jamaica Planters now in London, they have, after the most diligent Inquiries, been able to meet with only *One* who has attended any such Trials; and they regret exceedingly, that the Intelligence which they obtained from him did not appear sufficiently[*] pertinent.

The Clerks of the Peace in the several Parishes or Precincts of Jamaica, whose duty it is to attend these Trials to take Minutes of the Evidence, and to record the Proceedings in their official Rolls, might probably furnish very ample Information as to the Proofs which have generally operated to Conviction. But we do not know of any Person now in England who has acted in that Capacity, and therefore can offer nothing satisfactory on the Subject of the Question now proposed.

*Obeah Practice.*
*Jamaica, Case* I.

AMONG the Domestics of a Planter in the Parish of Vere, were Two Negresses who had suckled Two of his Children, and a Negro who served him in the Capacity of Butler or Waiting-man. The Infant which was nursed by One of these Women happened to die. Her Misbehaviour after this was such as obliged her Master to turn her out of his House, and she was ordered to work among the Field Negroes. The Butler, who was her own Brother, highly incensed at this, shewed some Symptoms of Discontent, which were not much regarded; but, in the course of a few Days, the Water of a Well from which the Family had their daily Supply, was observed to be very much discoloured, and intolerably fetid. His Master, imagining these might be the natural Effects of Stagnation, ordered the Well to be drawn till it was supposed to be nearly drained. But notwithstanding this Operation, the Water still continued ill-coloured, nauseous to the Taste, and offensive to the Smell. A Man was then let down,

---

[*]   Mr. Fuller has the Cases, which we collected, and they are annexed hereto.

who brought up a *white Fowl* in a very putrid State, without Beak or Claws, which had all been cut off. This Fowl was proved to have belonged to the Butler's Grandmother, residing upon or near the same Plantation. On further Examination, a large Quantity of *Indigo Seed*[1] was fished up from the Bottom of the Well. These Circumstances occasioned Suspicions of some mischievous Design. The Houses of all the Negroes were searched, and at one of them, inhabited by a near Relation of the Butler, a *Calibash* or Bowl was found, out of which a *greenish Liquid* had been recently emptied. This Circumstance brought to mind, that a Phial containing a Liquid of similar Appearance, had been noticed in the Butler's Pantry, who, upon the first Rumour of a Search, had conveyed it away. Still it was undecided upon whom the Suspicion ought to fall, till the Cook came voluntarily to his Master (apprehensive for his own Safety, if Poison should be privately thrown into any of his Dishes), and gave positive Information of "his having overheard the Butler threatening *Revenge,* and vowing that he would *buy some Obi to put for his Master.*"

Upon the Evidence of this Menace, the consequent Impoisoning of the Water, and the other Circumstances, the Butler was brought to Trial, convicted, and sentenced to Transportation. The Rectitude of his Sentence was confirmed by the Man's free Confession immediately before he was put on board Ship.

*Second.*

A valuable Negro had for his Wife a Negress who resided on a neighbouring Plantation. This Woman fell suddenly into a Decline, without any known Cause, and languishing for some Time, contracted at length a very morbid Habit of Body.[2] The Doctor who attended her, and tried a Variety of Medicines without any good Effect, declared it beyond his Power to afford her any Relief, and pronounced her incurable. When her Death was every Day expected, and after much Importunity to discover the cause of her Disorder, she was prevailed on to confess that her Husband, from a violent Suspicion of her Infidelity to him, and on her sturdy Denial

---

[1]  Indigo is used to produce blue dye. Indican is a natural glucoside of indigo that produces a light brown, bitter syrup with a slightly acidic reaction.

[2]  Depression.

of the Charge, had obliged her "to take Swear"[1] (as she called it), by drinking a Mixture of *Grave Dirt* and *Water*, accompanied with the usual Imprecation (that her Belly might swell and burst, and her bones rot, if she was guilty). She concluded with deploring the miserable End to which she had brought herself by denying the Fact, for that she really had been false to him. Intelligence of this Confession was given to her Husband's Master, who sent immediately for him, and representing the Peril in which he stood under the Law of the Land, which had declared the *Obiah Practice*, with *Grave Dirt*, a capital Offence, advised him to go directly to his Wife, and endeavour to cajole her into a Belief, that it was nothing more than a sly Contrivance of his own to get at the Truth: That the Mixture she had swallowed was not made with *Obiah Dirt*, but only with a little common Earth, which he had picked up on the Road, and therefore it was very harmless. The Fellow (who had owned the Fact to his Master) joyfully took his Advice, and acted his Part so well, that the poor Woman was completely duped a second Time, and recovering her Spirits, was soon restored to perfect Health.

If this Woman had died, the Evidence of her Declaration would not have been deemed sufficient for convicting her Husband of *Obiah Practice*; so that, in such Event, and without his own free Confession of the Fact, he would have escaped with Impunity. The singular Test of her Continence (it may be remarked by the way) so closely resembles the *Trial of Jealousy* by the *bitter Water* described in the Book of Numbers (Chap. 5),[2] as to point out something of a common Origin between them in the most ancient Laws and Customs of Africa.[3]

---

[1]  To take an oath.

[2]  From Numbers 5: 18–19 and 23–24: "And the priest shall set the woman before the Lord, and uncover the woman's head, and put the offering of memorial in her hands, which is the jealousy offering: and the priest shall have in his hand the bitter water that causeth the curse: And the priest shall charge her by an oath, and say unto the woman, If no man have lain with thee, and if thou hast not gone aside to uncleanness with another instead of thy husband, be thou free from this bitter water that causeth the curse ... And the priest shall write these curses in a book, and he shall blot them out with the bitter water. And he shall cause the woman to drink the bitter water that causeth the curse: and the water that causeth the curse shall enter into her, and become bitter."

[3]  This example in which obeah practices of African natives is compared with the Christian tradition is indicative of some persuasive tactics employed by plantation owners and their spiritual leaders to convert African slaves to Christianity. As seen in Earle's character of Quashee, slaves were led to see Christianity as "white obi" which had the power to defeat the "darker" powers of obeah.

Committee of the Council of the Island have returned no Answer
to these Heads of Inquiry.

## 3. From Matthew Gregory Lewis, *Journal of A West India Proprietor, Kept During a Residence in the Island of Jamaica* (London: J. Murray, 1834)

January 12 [1816]

In the year, [17]80, this parish of Westmoreland was kept in a
perpetual state of alarm by a runaway negro called *Plato*, who had
established himself among the Moreland Mountains, and collected
a troop of banditti, of which he was himself the chief. He robbed
very often, and murdered occasionally; but gallantry was his every
day occupation. Indeed, being a remarkably tall athletic young
fellow, among the beauties of his own complexion he found but
few Lucretias; and his retreat in the mountains was as well furnished
as the haram of Constantinople.[1] Every handsome negress who had
the slightest cause of complaint against her master, took the first
opportunity of eloping to join *Plato,* where she found freedom,
protection, and unbounded generosity; for he spared no pains to
secure their affections by gratifying their vanity. Indeed, no Creole
lady could venture out on a visit, without running the risk of
having her bandbox[2] run away with by Plato for the decoration of
his sultanas;[3] and if the maid who carried the bandbox happened
to be well-looking, he ran away with the maid as well as the bandbox. Every endeavour to seize this desperado was long in vain: a
large reward was put upon his head, but no negro dared to
approach him; for, besides his acknowledged courage, he was a
professor of Obi, and had threatened that whoever dared to lay a
finger upon him should suffer spiritual torments, as well as be physically shot through the head.

Unluckily for Plato, rum was an article with him of the first
necessity;[4] the look-out, which was kept for him, was too vigilant

---

[1]  That is, Plato did not lack for female companionship, but, like a Turkish royal, maintained a harem or seraglio of potential sexual partners.

[2]  A small box used to store hats, collars, caps, and other items.

[3]  A mockingly grandiose tone is used to refer to the members of Plato's "harem."

[4]  The trope of drunkenness as the fatal flaw in an otherwise powerful resistance leader
reiterates the notion of a spiritual vice that is also implicitly present in Plato's status
as an obi professor.

to admit of his purchasing spirituous[1] liquors for himself; and once, when for that purpose he had ventured into the neighbourhood of Montego Bay, he was recognised by a slave, who immediately gave the alarm. Unfortunately for this poor fellow, whose name was Taffy, at that moment all his companions happened to be out of hearing; and, after the first moment's alarm, finding that no one approached, the exasperated robber rushed upon him, and lifted the bill-hook,[2] with which he was armed, for the purpose of cleaving his skull. Taffy fled for it; but Plato was the younger, the stronger, and the swifter of the two, and gained upon him every moment. Taffy, however, on the other hand, possessed that one quality by which, according to the fable, the cat was enabled to save herself from the hounds, when the fox, with his thousand tricks, was caught by them.[3] He was an admirable climber, an art in which Plato possessed no skill; and a bread-nut tree,[4] which is remarkably difficult of ascent, presenting itself before him, in a few moments Taffy was bawling for help from the very top of it. To reach him was impossible for his enemy; but still his destruction was hard at hand; for Plato began to hack the tree with his bill,[5] and it was evident that a very short space of time would be sufficient to level it with the ground. In this dilemma, Taffy had nothing for it but to break off the branches near him; and he contrived to pelt these so dexterously at the head of his assailant, that he fairly kept him at bay till his cries at length reached the ears of his companions, and their approach compelled the banditti-captain once more to seek safety among the mountains.

After this Plato no longer dared to approach Montego town; but still spirits must be had:—how was he to obtain them? There was an old watchman on the outskirts of the estate of Canaan,[6] with whom he had contracted an acquaintance, and frequently had

---

[1]  Spirituous has the double meaning of containing alcohol and producing a lively, even volatile, effect.

[2]  A thick knife or chopper with a hooked end, used for pruning and cutting brushwood.

[3]  An allusion to the story of "The Fox and the Cat" in *Aesop's Fables*.

[4]  A large tree (*Brosimum alicastrum*) native to Mexico, Central America, and the West Indies, with round, greenish-yellow fruits of the mulberry family each with a large, edible seed.

[5]  Bill-hook.

[6]  The name of the estate is significant in its biblical echo of a promised land of freedom for the Israelites.

passed the night in his hut; the old man having been equally induced by his presents and by dread of his corporeal strength and supposed supernatural power, to profess the warmest attachment to the interests of his terrible friend. To this man Plato at length resolved to entrust himself: he gave him money to purchase spirits, and appointed a particular day when he would come to receive them. The reward placed upon the robber's head was more than either gratitude or terror could counterbalance; and on the same day when the watchman set out to purchase the rum, he apprised two of his friends at Canaan, for whose use it was intended, and advised *them* to take the opportunity of obtaining the reward.

The two negroes posted themselves in proper time near the watchman's hut. Most unwisely, instead of sending down some of his gang, they saw Plato, in his full confidence in the friendship of his confidant, arrive himself and enter the cabin; but so great was their alarm at seeing this dreadful personage, that they remained in their concealment, nor dared to make an attempt at seizing him. The spirits were delivered to the robber: he might have retired with them unmolested; but, in his rashness and his eagerness to taste the liquor, of which he had so long been deprived, he opened the flagon, and swallowed draught after draught, till he sunk upon the ground in a state of complete insensibility. The watchman then summoned the two negroes from their concealment, who bound his arms, and conveyed him to Montego Bay, where he was immediately sentenced to execution. He died most heroically; kept up the terrors of his imposture to his last moment; told the magistrates, who condemned him, that his death should be revenged by a storm, which would lay waste the whole island, that year; and, when his negro gaoler was binding him to the stake at which he was destined to suffer, he assured him that he should not live long to triumph in his death, for that he had taken good care to Obeah him before his quitting the prison. It certainly did happen, strangely enough, that, before the year was over, the most violent storm took place ever known in Jamaica; and as to the gaoler, his imagination was so forcibly struck by the threats of the dying man, that, although every care was taken of him, the power of medicine exhausted, and even a voyage to America undertaken, in hopes that a change of scene might change the course of his ideas, still, from the moment of Plato's death, he gradually pined and withered away, and finally expired before the completion of the twelvemonth.

The belief in Obeah is now greatly weakened, but still exists in some degree. Not above ten months ago, my agent was informed that a negro of very suspicious manners and appearance was harboured by some of my people[1] on the mountain lands. He found means to have him surprised, and on examination there was found upon him a bag containing a great variety of strange materials for incantations; such as thunder-stones,[2] cat's ears, the feet of various animals, human hair, fish bones, the teeth of alligators, etc.: he was conveyed to Montego Bay; and no sooner was it understood that this old African was in prison, than depositions were poured in from all quarters from negroes who deposed to having seen him exercise his magical arts, and, in particular, to his having sold such and such slaves medicines and charms to deliver them from their enemies; being, in plain English, nothing else than rank poisons. He was convicted of Obeah upon the most indubitable evidence. The good old practice of burning has fallen into disrepute; so he was sentenced to be transported, and was shipped off the island, to the great satisfaction of persons of all colours—white, black, and yellow.

January 28 (Sunday) [1816]

I shall have enough to do in Jamaica if I accept all the offices that are pressed upon me. A large body of negroes, from a neighbouring estate, came over to Cornwall this morning, to complain of hard treatment, in various ways, from their overseer and drivers, and requesting me to represent their injuries to their trustee here, and their proprietor in England. The charges were so strong, that I am certain that they must be fictitious; however, I listened to their story with patience; promised that the trustee (whom I was to see in a few days) should know their complaint;—and they went away apparently satisfied. Then came a runaway negro, who wanted to return home, and requested me to write a few lines to his master, to save him from the lash. He was succeeded by a poor creature named Bessie, who, although still a young woman, is dispensed with from labour, on account of her being afflicted with the *cocoa-bay*,[3] one of the most horrible of negro diseases. It shows itself in large blotches and swellings, and which generally, by degrees, moulder

---

1   Presumably, the man is secreted by slaves on Lewis' plantation.

2   Stones deemed to have magical properties, such as pyrites or meteorites.

3   Cocoa-bay, cocaby, or cacabay; a form of leprosy once prevalent in the West Indies.

away the joints of the toes and fingers, till they rot and drop off; sometimes as much as half a foot will go at once. As the disease is communicable by contact, the person so afflicted is necessarily shunned by society; and this poor woman, who is married to John Fuller, one of the best young men on the estate, and by whom she has had four children (although they are all dead), has for some time been obliged to live separated from him, lest he should be destroyed by contracting the same complaint. She now came to tell me, that she wanted a blanket, 'for that the cold killed her of nights;' cold being that which negroes dislike most, and from which most of their illnesses arise. Of course she got her blanket; then she said, that she wanted medicine for her complaint. 'Had not the doctor seen her?' 'Oh, yes! Dr Goodwin; but the white doctor could do her no good. She wanted to go to a black doctor,[1] named Ormond, who belonged to a neighbouring gentleman.' I told her, that if this black doctor understood her particular disease better than others, certainly she should go to him; but that if he pretended to cure her by charms or spells, or any thing but medicine, I should desire his master to cure the black doctor by giving him the punishment proper for such an impostor.[2] Upon this Bessie burst into tears, and said 'that Ormond was not an Obeah man, and that she had suffered too much by Obeah men to wish to have any more to do with them. She had made Adam her enemy by betraying him, when he had attempted to poison the former attorney; he had then cursed her, and wished that she might never be hearty again: and from that very time her complaint had declared itself; and her poor pickaninies[3] had all died away, one after another; and she was sure that it was Adam who had done all this mischief by Obeah.' Upon this, I put myself in a great rage, and asked her 'how she could believe that God would suffer a low wicked fellow like Adam to make good people die, merely because he wished them dead?' 'She did not

---

[1]  It was not uncommon for black men to serve the role of doctor on West Indian plantations. Often plantation owners specifically sought the counsel of black doctors in their knowledge of medicinal roots and herbs, largely unknown by their European counterparts. For a full discussion of the medical practices on West Indian plantations, see Richard Sheridan, *Doctors and Slaves: A Medical and Demographic History of Slavery in the British West Indies, 1680–1834* (Cambridge: Cambridge UP, 1985).

[2]  This statement reveals a prevalent anxiety on the part of plantation owners that black doctors were also obeah or Myal practitioners.

[3]  Derived from the Spanish pequeño or pequeñiño, meaning small, the term was used to refer to black children.

know; she knew nothing about God; had never heard of any such Being, nor of any other world.' I told her, that God was a great personage, 'who lived up yonder above the blue, in a place full of pleasures and free from pains, where Adam and wicked people could not come; that her pickaninies were not dead for ever, but were only gone up to live with God, who was good, and would take care of them for her; and that if she were good, when she died, she too would go up to God above the blue, and see all her four pickaninies again.' The idea seemed so new and so agreeable to the poor creature, that she clapped her hands together, and began laughing for joy; so I said to her every thing that I could imagine likely to remove her prejudice; told her that I should make it a crime even so much as to mention the word Obeah on the estate; and that, if any negro from that time forward should be proved to have accused another of Obeahing him, or of telling another that he had been Obeahed, he should forfeit his share of the next present of salt-fish,[1] which I meant soon to distribute among the slaves, and should never receive any favour from me in future; so I gave Bessie a piece of money, and she seemed to go away in better spirits than she came.

This Adam, of whom she complained, is a most dangerous fellow, and the terror of all his companions, with whom he lives in a constant state of warfare. He is a creole,[2] born on my own property, and has several sisters, who have obtained their freedom, and are in every respect creditable and praiseworthy; and to one of whom I consider myself as particularly indebted, as she was the means of saving poor Richard's life,[3] when the tyranny of the overseer had brought him almost to the brink of the grave. But this brother is in every thing the very reverse of his sisters: there is no doubt of his having (as Bessie stated) infused poison into the water-jars through spite against the late superintendent. It was this same fellow whom Edward suspected of having put into his brother-in-law's head the idea of his having been bewitched; and it was also in his hut that the old Obeah man was found concealed, whom my attorney seized and transported last year. He is, unfortunately, clever and plausible;[4] and I am told that the mischief which he has already done, by working

---

1  Salted cod; salt-fish with ackee (a vegetable) is still a national delicacy of Jamaica.
2  Meaning born in Jamaica, and having no connotation of color.
3  Another slave on Lewis' plantation who was the victim of the overseer's brutality.
4  In the sense of fair-seeming, but actually deceitful.

upon the folly and superstition of his fellows, is incalculable; yet I cannot get rid of him: the law will not suffer any negro to be shipped off the island, until he shall have been convicted of felony at the sessions;[1] I cannot sell him, for nobody would buy him, nor even accept him, if I would offer them so dangerous a present; if he were to go away, the law would seize him, and bring him back to me, and I should be obliged to pay heavily for his re-taking and his maintenance in the workhouse.[2] In short, I know not what I can do with him, except indeed make a Christian of him! This might induce the negroes to believe, that he had lost his infernal power by the superior virtue of the holy water; but, perhaps he may refuse to be christened. However, I will at least ask him the question; and if he consents, I will send him—and a couple of dollars—to the clergyman—for he shall not have so great a distinction as baptism from massa's[3] own hand—and see what effect 'white Obeah'[4] will have in removing the terrors of this professor of the black.

As to my sick Obeah patient, Pickle, from the moment of his reconciliation with his brother-in-law he began to mend, and has recovered with wonderful rapidity: the fellow seems *really* grateful for the pains which I have taken about him; and our difficulty now is to prevent his fancying himself too soon able to quit the hospital, so eager is he to return 'to work for massa.'

There are certainly many excellent qualities in the negro character; their worst faults appear to be, this prejudice respecting Obeah, and the facility with which they are frequently induced to poison to the right hand and to the left. A neighbouring gentleman, as I hear, has now three negroes in prison, all domestics, and one of them grown grey in his service, for poisoning him with corrosive sublimate;[5] his brother was actually killed by similar means; yet I am assured that both of them were reckoned men of great humanity. Another agent, who appears to be in high favour with the negroes whom he now governs, was obliged to quit an estate, from the frequent attempts to poison him; and a person against whom there is no sort of charge alleged for tyranny, after being brought to the

---

[1] The court.
[2] The plantation owner was responsible for the expenses of capturing a fugitive slave.
[3] A corruption of master.
[4] Meaning Christianity.
[5] Mercuric chloride or bichloride of mercury ($HgCl_2$), a white crystalline substance, which acts as a strong acrid poison.

doors of death by a cup of coffee, only escaped a second time by his civility, in giving the beverage, prepared for himself, to two young bookkeepers, to both of whom it proved fatal. It, indeed, came out, afterwards, that this crime was also effected by the abominable belief in Obeah: the woman, who mixed the draught, had no idea of its being poison; but she had received the deleterious ingredients from an Obeah man, as 'a charm to make her massa good to her;' by which the negroes mean, the compelling a person to give another every thing for which that other may ask him.

Next to this vile trick of poisoning people (arising, doubtless, in a great measure, from their total want[1] of religion, and their ignorance of a future state, which makes them dread no punishment hereafter for themselves, and look with but little respect on human life in others), the greatest drawback upon one's comfort in a Jamaica existence seems to me to be the being obliged to live perpetually in public. Certainly, if a man was desirous of leading a life of vice *here,* he must have set himself totally above shame, for he may depend upon every thing done by him being seen and known. The houses are absolutely transparent; the walls are nothing but windows—and all the doors stand wide open. No servants are in waiting to announce arrivals: visiters, negroes, dogs, cats, poultry, all walk in and out, and up and down your living-rooms, without the slightest ceremony.

Even the Temple of Cloacina[2] (which, by the bye, is here very elegantly spoken of generally as *'The* Temple') is as much latticed and as pervious[3] to the eye as any other part of my premises; and many a time has my delicacy been put to the blush by the ill-timed civility of some old woman or other, who, wandering that way, and happening to cast her eye to the left, has stopped her course to curtsy very gravely, and pay me the passing compliment of an 'Ah, massa! bless you, massa! how day?'[4]

February 25 [1818]
A negro, named Adam, has long been the terror of my whole estate. He was accused of being an Obeah-man, and persons notorious for the practice of Obeah had been found concealed from justice in his

---

[1]  Lack.
[2]  This is a mock-epic term for the water closet invoking the goddess Cloacina, who presided over the sewers in ancient Rome (from the Latin *cloaca* for sewer).
[3]  Permeable, and therefore visible to the eye.
[4]  Jamaican greeting, meaning "how do you do?"

house, who were afterwards convicted and transported. He was strongly suspected of having poisoned more than twelve negroes, men and women; and having been displaced by my former trustee from being principal governor,[1] in revenge he put poison into his water jar. Luckily he was observed by one of the house servants, who impeached him, and prevented the intended mischief. For this offence he ought to have been given up to justice; but being brother of the trustee's mistress she found means to get him off, after undergoing a long confinement in the stocks. I found him, on my arrival, living in a state of utter excommunication; I tried what reasoning with him could effect, reconciled him to his companions, treated him with marked kindness, and he promised solemnly to behave well during my absence. However, instead of attributing my lenity to a wish to reform him, his pride and confidence in his own talents and powers of deception made him attribute the indulgence shown him to his having obtained an influence over my mind. This he determined to employ to his own purposes upon my return; so he set about forming a conspiracy against Sully, the present chief governor, and boasted on various estates in the neighbourhood that on my arrival he would take care to get Sully broke, and himself substituted in his place. In the mean while he quarrelled and fought to the right and to the left; and on my arrival I found the whole estate in an uproar about Adam. No less than three charges of assault, with intent to kill, were preferred against him. In a fit of jealousy he had endeavoured to strangle Marlborough with the thong of a whip, and had nearly effected his purpose before he could be dragged away: he had knocked Nato down in some trifling dispute, and while the man was senseless had thrown him into the river to drown him; and having taken offence at a poor weak creature called Old Rachael, on meeting her by accident he struck her to the ground, beat her with a supplejack,[2] stamped upon her belly, and begged her to be assured of his intention (as he eloquently worded it) 'to kick her guts out.' The breeding mothers also accused him of having been the cause of the poisoning a particular spring, from which they were in the habit of fetching water for their children, as Adam on that morning had been seen near the spring without having any

---

[1]  The overseer of the plantation.
[2]  A name for various climbing and twining shrubs with tough, pliable stems found in tropical and subtropical forests, often made into a walking-stick or cane.

business there, and he had been heard to caution his little daughter against drinking water from it that day, although he stoutly denied both circumstances. Into the bargain, my head blacksmith being perfectly well at five o'clock, was found by his son dead in his bed at eight; and it was known that he had lately had a dispute with Adam, who on that day had made it up with him, and had invited him to drink, although it was not certain that his offer had been accepted. He had, moreover, threatened the lives of many of the best negroes. Two of the cooks declared, that he had severally directed them to dress Sully's food apart, and had given them powders to mix with it. The first to whom he applied refused positively; the second he treated with liquor, and when she had drunk, he gave her the poison, with instructions how to use it. Being a timid creature, she did not dare to object, so threw away the powder privately, and pretended that it had been administered; but finding no effect produced by it, Adam gave her a second powder, at the same time bidding her remember the liquor which she had swallowed, and which he assured her would effect her own destruction through the force of Obeah, unless she prevented it by sacrificing his enemy in her stead. The poor creature still threw away the powder, but the strength of imagination brought upon her a serious malady, and it was not till after several weeks that she recovered from the effects of her fears. The terror thus produced was universal throughout the estate, and Sully and several other principal negroes requested me to remove them to my property in St Thomas's,[1] as their lives were not safe while breathing the same air with Adam. However, it appeared a more salutary measure to remove Adam himself; but all the poisoning charges either went no further than strong suspicion, or (any more than the assaults) were not liable by the laws of Jamaica to be punished, except by flogging or temporary imprisonment, which would only have returned him to the estate with increased resentment against those to whom he should ascribe his sufferings, however deserved. However, on searching his house, a musket with a plentiful accompaniment of powder and ball was found concealed, as also a considerable quantity of materials for the practice of Obeah: the possession of either of the above articles (if the musket is without the consent of the proprietor) authorises the magistrates to pronounce a sentence of transportation. In consequence of this

---

[1]  Lewis owned several plantations in the West Indies.

discovery, Adam was immediately committed to gaol; a slave court was summoned, and to-day a sentence of transportation from the island was pronounced, after a trial of three hours. As to the man's guilt, of that the jury entertained no doubt after the first half hour's evidence; and the only difficulty was to restrain the verdict to transportation. We produced nothing which could possibly affect the man's life; for although perhaps no offender ever better deserved hanging; yet I confess my being weak-minded enough to entertain doubts whether hanging or other capital punishment ought to be inflicted for any offence whatever: I am at least certain, that if offenders waited till they were hanged by me, they would remain unhanged till they were all so many old Parrs.[1] However, although I did my best to prevent Adam from being hanged, it was no easy matter to prevent his hanging himself. The Obeah ceremonies always commence with what is called, by the negroes, 'the Myal dance.'[2] This is intended to remove any doubt of the chief Obeah-man's supernatural powers; and in the course of it, he undertakes to show his art by killing one of the persons present, whom he pitches upon for that purpose. He sprinkles various powders over the devoted victim, blows upon him, and dances round him, obliges him to drink a liquor prepared for the occasion, and finally the sorcerer and his assistants seize him and whirl him rapidly round and round till the man loses his senses, and falls on the ground to all appearance and the belief of the spectators a perfect corpse. The chief Myal-man then utters loud shrieks, rushes out of the house with wild and frantic gestures, and conceals himself in some neighbouring wood. At the end of two or three hours he returns with a large bundle of herbs, from some of which he squeezes the juice into the mouth of the dead person; with others he anoints his eyes and stains the tips of his fingers, accompanying the ceremony with a great variety of grotesque actions, and chanting all the while something between a song and a howl, while the assistants hand in hand dance slowly round them in a circle, stamping the ground loudly with their feet to keep time with his chant. A considerable time

---

[1]  Thomas Parr, reportedly born in 1483 and buried in Westminster Abbey after his death in 1635 at the age of 153.

[2]  While Myal and obeah were often conflated by European observers, Myal actually constituted a religious movement with African roots that held as one of its primary purposes the combating of obeah. In the Myal-dance, potential initiates were seemingly rendered lifeless and then revived. See the discussion of Myal in the introduction, 28.

elapses before the desired effect is produced, but at length the corpse gradually recovers animation, rises from the ground perfectly recovered, and the Myal dance concludes. After this proof of his power, those who wish to be revenged upon their enemies apply to the sorcerer for some of the same powder, which produced apparent death upon their companion, and as they never employ the means used for his recovery, of course the powder once administered never fails to be lastingly fatal. It must be superfluous to mention that the Myal-man on this second occasion substitutes a poison for a narcotic. Now, among other suspicious articles found in Adam's hut, there was a string of beads of various sizes, shapes, and colours, arranged in a form peculiar to the performance of the Obeah-man in the Myal dance. Their use was so well known, that Adam on his trial did not even attempt to deny that they could serve for no purpose but the practice of Obeah; but he endeavoured to refute their being his own property, and with this view he began to narrate the means by which he had become possessed of them. He said that they belonged to Fox (a negro who was lately transported), from whom he had taken them at a Myal dance held on the estate of Dean's Valley; but as the assistants at one of these dances are by law condemned to death equally with the principal performer, the court had the humanity to interrupt his confession of having been present on such an occasion, and thus saved him from criminating himself so deeply as to render a capital punishment inevitable. I understand that he was quite unabashed and at his ease the whole time; upon hearing his sentence, he only said very coolly, 'Well! I ca'n't help it!' turned himself round, and walked out of court. That nothing might be wanting, this fellow had even a decided talent for hypocrisy. When on my arrival he gave me a letter filled with the grossest lies respecting the trustee, and every creditable negro on the estate, he took care to sign it by the name which he had lately received in baptism; and in his defence at the bar to prove his probity of character and purity of manners, he informed the court that for some time past he had been learning to read, for the sole purpose of learning the Lord's Prayer. The nickname by which he was generally known among the negroes in this part of the country, was Buonaparte,[1] and he always appeared to exult in the appellation. Once condemned, the marshal is bound

---

[1]   A name of distinction in its connection to Napoleon Bonaparte.

under a heavy penalty to see him shipped from off the island before the expiration of six weeks, and probably he will be sent to Cuba. He is a fine-looking man between thirty and forty, square built, and of great bodily strength, and his countenance equally expresses intelligence and malignity. The sum allowed me for him is one hundred pounds currency,[1] which is scarcely a third of his worth as a labourer, but which is the highest value which a jury is permitted to mention.[2]

---

[1]   The state was required to compensate plantation owners for the value of slaves transported off the island.
[2]   Award.

# Appendix B: Accounts of Tacky's Rebellion (1760)

[The influence of obeah practitioners on Tacky's Rebellion led to various attempts to suppress the practice (see the introduction to this edition). Two of the most important sources for the discussion of the use of obeah during Tacky's Rebellion are Edward Long's *The History of Jamaica* (1774) and Bryan Edwards' *Observations on the Disposition, Character, Manners, and Habits of Life, of the Maroons* (1796). Long was born in 1734 in Cornwall and went to Jamaica as a young man where he established himself as judge of the vice-admiralty court in Jamaica. Health issues forced him to return to England in 1769, where he spent the rest of his life. Long's *History* became the chief source for future works on Jamaica, including Bryan Edwards' *The History Civil and Commercial of the British Colonies in the West Indies* (1793), which relied heavily on Long's information regarding maroon communities in Jamaica. Edwards was born in Wiltshire in 1743 and went to Jamaica as a young man under the care of his uncle, a wealthy merchant. Edwards successfully partnered in his uncle's business and soon gained ownership over the entire enterprise. He also inherited property in Jamaica, which, combined with his own successful business ventures, allowed him a leading position in the colonial assembly. *Observations on the Disposition, Character, Manners, and Habits of Life, of the Maroons,* supports the slave trade with certain restrictions.]

## 1. From Edward Long, *The History of Jamaica or, General Survey of the Antient and Modern State of that Island with Reflections on its Situation, Settlements, Inhabitants, Climate, Products, Commerce, Laws, and Government. In Three Volumes* (London: T. Lowndes, 1774)

After the pacification made with governor Trelawney,[1] no insurrection of moment occurred for many years. Some trifling disturbances happened, and some plots were detected, but they came to nothing;

---

[1]  Governor of Jamaica for sixteen years, Charles Trelawney's first major accomplishment in his administration was to establish a peaceful settlement that brought an end to the Maroon Wars in 1739. This agreement allowed the Maroons to exist independently in their own separate reserves, the chief capital of which is known as Trelawny Town.

and indeed the seeds of rebellion were in a great measure rendered abortive, by the activity of the Marons,[1] who scoured the woods, and apprehended all straggling and vagabond slaves, that from time to time deserted from their owners. But in the year 1760, a conspiracy was projected,[2] and conducted with such profound secrecy, that almost all the Coromantin slaves throughout the island were privy to it, without any suspicion from the Whites. The parish of St. Mary was fixed upon, as the most proper theatre for opening their tragedy.[3] It abounded with their countrymen, was but thinly peopled with Whites, contained extensive deep woods, and plenty of provisions: so that as the engaging any considerable number heartily in the scheme, would depend chiefly on the success of their first operations, they were likely to meet with a fainter resistance in this parish than in most others; and should the issue of the conflict prove unfavourable to them, they might retreat with security into the woods, and there continue well supplied with provisions, until their party should be strengthened with sufficient reinforcements, to enable their prosecution of the grand enterprize, whose object was no other than the entire extirpation of the white inhabitants; the enslaving of all such Negroes as might refuse to join them; and the partition of the island into small principalities in the African mode; to be distributed among the leaders and head men. A principal inducement to the formation of this scheme of conquest was, the happy circumstance of the *Marons*; who, they observed, had acquired very comfortable settlements, and a life of freedom and ease, by dint of their prowess. On the night preceding Easter-Monday, about fifty of them marched to Port Maria,[4] where they murdered the storekeeper of the fort (at that time unprovided with a garrison), broke open the magazine, and seized four barrels of powder, a few musquet-balls, and about forty fire-arms. Proceeding from thence to the bay, which lies under the fort, they met with some fishing-nets, from which they cut off all the leaden sinkers, made of bullets drilled. These Negroes were mostly collected from Trinity plantation, belonging to Mr. Bayley; Whitehall, and Frontier, belonging to Mr.

---

[1]  More commonly Maroons. One condition of the truce following the Maroon Wars was that the population track and return runaways.

[2]  Formed; the conspiracy refers to Tacky's Rebellion.

[3]  Long explicitly plots this event as a drama.

[4]  Port Maria is located on the northeast coast of Jamaica, approximately 35 miles north of Kingston and five miles east of Oracabessa.

Ballard Beckford; and Heywood Hall, the property of Mr. Heywood. Mr. Bayley had been called up by one of his domestics, and, mounting his horse, rode towards the bay, in hopes that, by expostulating calmly with the rebels, he might persuade them to disperse and return to their duty; but their plan was too deeply laid, and they had conceived too high an opinion of it, to recede.

Upon his nearer approach, he perceived they were determined to act offensively, and therefore galloped back with great expedition; a few random-shots were discharged after him, which he fortunately escaped, and rode directly to the neighbouring estates, alarming them as he went, and appointing a place of rendezvous. In this he performed a very essential piece of service to the white inhabitants, who before were strangers to the insurrection, and unprepared against surprize; but this notice gave them some time to recollect themselves, and to consult measures for suppressing the insurgents. In the mean while, the latter pursued their way to Heywood-Hall, where they set fire to the works[1] and cane-pieces,[2] and proceeded to Esher, an estate of Mr. William Beckford,[3] murthering on the road a poor white man, who was traveling on foot. At Esher they were joined by fourteen or fifteen of their countrymen. The Whites on that estate had but just time to shut themselves up in the dwelling-house, which they barricadoed as well as they could; unhappily they were destitute of ammunition, and therefore incapable of making any resistance. The rebels, who knew their situation, soon forced an entrance, murthered the overseer and another person, and mangled the doctor, till they supposed him dead; in this condition they drew him down several steps by the heels, and threw him among the other murthered persons: his limbs still appearing to move, one of the rebels exclaimed, that "he had as many lives as a *puss*;" and immediately discharged four or five slugs through his back, some of which penetrated the bladder. This gentleman was so dreadfully wounded, that the two surgeons, who afterwards attended him, were every day fatigued with the multi-

---

1   The sugar-works made up of the factory and mills.
2   Fields of sugarcane.
3   William Beckford is remembered as a historian whose principal works were comprised of observations of his time in Jamaica, particularly on the condition of the slave population. Beckford returned to London in the latter part of his life, where he died in 1799. He should not be confused with William Beckford, author of *Vathek*, who also had connections with Jamaica.

plicity of bandages and dressing, necessary to be applied upon almost all parts of his body; so that his recovery was next to miraculous.

After this exploit, they ravished a Mulatto woman, who had been the overseer's kept mistress; but spared her life, at the request of some of the Esher Negroes, who alledged, in her favour, that she had frequently saved them from a whipping by her intercession with the overseer; considering the hands into which she had fallen, this was thought an act of very extraordinary clemency; and, in fact, not owing really to any merit on her part, as the overseer had only chose to let his forgiveness appear rather to come through the importunity of another, than from the lenity of his own disposition. The doctor, notwithstanding his wounds, recovered afterwards. Yankee, a trusty slave belonging to this estate, behaved on the occasion with signal gallantry; he was very active in endeavouring to defend the house, and assist the white men; but, finding they were overpowered, he made his escape to the next estate, and there, with another faithful Negroe, concerted measures for giving immediate notice to all the plantations in the neighbourhood, and procuring auxiliaries for the white inhabitants. The rebels, after this action, turned back to Heywood Hall and Ballard's Valley, where they picked up some fresh recruits, so that their whole party, including women, increased to about four hundred. The fatigues of the opening of their campaign had so exhausted their spirits by this time, that they thought proper to refresh themselves a little before they renewed their hostilities; having therefore a good magazine of hogs, poultry, rum, and other plunder of the like kind, they chose out a convenient spot, surrounded with trees, and a little retired from the road, where they spread their provision, and began to carouse. The white inhabitants, alarmed by Mr. Bayley, had assembled in the mean time about 70 or 80 horse, and had now a fair opportunity of routing the whole body; they advanced towards the place where the rebels were enjoying themselves, and luckily discovered them by their noise and riot, or they might have fallen into an ambuscade.[1] The Coromantins did not exhibit any specimen of generalship upon this occasion; on appearance of the troop, they kept close in the wood, from whence they poured an irregular fire, which did no execution. The drilled bullets, taken from the fishing nets, described an arch in their projection, and flew over the heads of the militia. After

---

[1]    Ambush.

keeping their ranks for some time, it was proposed that they should dismount, and push into the wood; but on examining their ammunition, the militia found their whole flock, if equally divided, did not amount to more than one charge each man; they therefore held it more adviseable, for the major part to stand their ground on the reserve, while their servants, and some others well armed, advanced into the wood close to the rebels, several of whom they killed; a Mulatto man was said to have slain three with his own hand, and a brave North Briton[1] about the same number. The rebels, intimidated with this bold attack, retreated; but it was not judged proper at that time to pursue them.

During all these transactions, two Negroes, belonging to Mr. Beckford, having taken horse at the first alarm, were on the road to Spanish Town, and traveled with such expedition through very bad ways, that they brought the intelligence to lieut. governor Sir Henry Moore, by one o'clock the same day, who immediately dispatched two parties of regulars, and two troops of horse militia, by different routes, to the parish; orders at the same time were sent to the *Marons* of Scot's-Hall Town, to advance by another road from the Eastward, and a party from the Leeward Towns were directed to enter by the West. All these detachments were in motion as early as possible, and no measures could have been more effectually taken. The lieutenant governor happily possessed, in addition to great abilities, uncommon presence of mind, prudence, and bravery, a most consummate knowledge of the geography of the island, and of every road and avenue in its several districts. By this means, he was enabled to take every fit precaution, and form the most proper disposition of the forces, as well for reducing the insurgents, as protecting the estates in those parts, where the flame might be expected to kindle afresh. These detachments, by forced marches, soon made their appearance in St. Mary, and damped at once all the ideas of conquest, which at first had elevated the rebels. They kept in the woods, rambling from place to place, seldom continuing many hours on one spot; and when they perceived themselves close beset on all sides, they resolved to sell their lives as dear as possible. The *Marons* of Scot's-Hall behaved extremely ill at this juncture; they were the first party that came to the rendezvous; and, under pretence that some arrears were due to

---

[1]  A Scot.

them, and that they had not been regularly paid their head-money allowed by law, for every run-away taken up, they refused to proceed against the rebels, unless a collection was immediately made for them; several gentlemen present submitted to comply with this extraordinary demand, rather than delay the service; after which they marched, and had one engagement with the rebels, in which they killed a few. A party of the 74th regiment lay quartered at a house by the sea side, at a small distance from the woods; in the night the rebels were so bold, that they crept very near the quarters, and, having shot the centinel dead, retired again with the utmost agility from pursuit. Not long after this accident the regulars, after a tedious march through the woods, which the steepness of the hills, and heat of the weather, conspired to render extremely fatiguing, came up with the enemy, and an engagement ensued, in which several of the rebels were killed, and lieut. Bevil of the regulars wounded. The different parties continued in chase of the fugitives, and skirmishes happened every day; but in the mean while, the spirit of rebellion was shewing itself in various other parts of the island, there being scarcely a single parish, to which this conspiracy of the Coromantins did not extend. In St. Mary's parish a check was fortunately given at one estate, by surprizing a famous obeiah man or priest, much respected among his countrymen. He was an old Coromantin, who, with others of this profession, had been a chief in counseling and instigating the credulous herd, to whom these priests administered a powder, which, being rubbed on their bodies, was to make them invulnerable: they persuaded them into a belief, that Tacky, their generalissimo in the woods, could not possibly by hurt by the white men, for that he caught all the bullets fired at him in his hand, and hurled them back with destruction to his foes. This old impostor was caught whilst he was tricked up with all his feathers, teeth, and other implements of magic, and in this attire suffered military execution by hanging: many of his disciples, when they found that he was so easily put to death, notwithstanding all the boasted feats of his powder and incantations, soon altered their opinion of him, and determined not to join their countrymen, in a cause which hitherto had been unattended with success. But the fame of general Tacky, and the notion of his invulnerability, still prevailed over the minds of others, as that hero had escaped hitherto in every conflict without a wound. The true condition of his party was artfully misrepresented to the Coromantins, in the distant parishes; they were told that every thing went on prosperously, that victory attended them, and that nothing now remained but for all their countrymen to be hearty in the cause, and the island must speedily be their own. Animated with these reports, the Coromantins on capt. Forrest's estate, in Westmoreland, broke into rebellion. They surrounded the mansion-house, in which Mr. Smith, attorney to Mr. Forrest, with some friends, was sitting at supper; they soon dispatched Mr. Smith and the overseer, and terribly wounded captain Hoare, commander of a merchant ship in the trade, who afterwards recovered. Three other Negroes belonging to this estate made their escape privately, and alarmed the neighbouring settlements, by which means the white persons upon them provided for their lives, and took measures which prevented the Negroes on three contiguous estates from rising. A gentleman, proprietor of one of these estates, remarkable for his humanity and kind treatment of his slaves, upon the first alarm, put arms into the hands of about twenty; of whose faithful attachment to him, he had the utmost confidence: these were all of them Coromantins, who no sooner had got possession of arms, than they convinced their master how little they merited the good opinion he had entertained of them; for having ranged themselves before his house, they assured him they would do him no harm, but that they must go and join their countrymen, and then saluting him with their hats, they every one marched off. Among the rebels were several French Negroes, who had been taken prisoners at Guadaloupe, and, being sent to Jamaica for sale, were purchased by capt. Forrest. These men were the most dangerous, as they had been in arms at Guadaloupe, and seen something of military operations; in which they acquired so much skill, that, after the massacre on the estate, when they found their partisans of the adjacent plantations did not appear to join them, they killed several Negroes, set fire to buildings and cane-pieces, did a variety of other mischief, and then withdrew into the woods, where they formed a strong breast-work[1] across a road, flanked by a rocky hill; within this work they erected their huts, and sat down in a sort of encampment; a party of militia, who were sent to attack them, very narrowly escaped being all cut off. The men were badly disciplined, having been hastily collected; and falling into an ambuscade, they

---

[1]  Fortification.

were struck with terror at the dismal yells, and the multitude of their assailants. The whole party was thrown into the utmost confusion, and routed, notwithstanding every endeavour of their officers; each strove to shift for himself, and whilst they ran different ways, scarcely knowing what they were about, several were butchered, others broke their limbs over precipices, and the rest with difficulty found their way back again. This unlucky defeat raised the spirits of the Coromantins in this part of the country, and encouraged so many to join the victorious band, that the whole number soon amounted to upwards of a thousand, including their women, who were necessary for carrying their baggage, and dressing their victuals. This consequence shewed, how ill judged it was, to make the first attack upon them with a handful of raw, undisciplined militia, without advancing at the same time a party in reserve, to sustain their efforts, and cover their retreat. In suppressing these mutinies, the first action has always been of the utmost importance, and therefore should never be confided to any except tried and well-trained men. The winning the first battle from the rebellious party, usually decides the issue of the war; it disconcerts the conspirators, not as yet engaged, and who keep aloof, irresolute whether to join or not; and it intimidates all that are in arms, and most commonly plunges them into despondency: the reverse is sure to follow a defeat of the Whites on the first encounter; and nothing can add greater strength to rebellion, or tend more to raise the authority of the priests and leaders who have set it on foot. These remarks have been fully verified, in course of the present, and every other insurrection that has occurred in this island. The insurgents in St. Mary, who opened the campaign, were repulsed in the first conflict, and from that time grew disheartened, and diminishing in their numbers; their confederates in that parish looked upon their rout as ominous, and would not venture to associate with them in the undertaking, whilst those of Westmoreland, who would probably have given up the cause, if they had met with a severe check at their first outset, were now become flushed with a confidence in their superiority, and gathered reinforcements every day. However, they were not suffered to remain long in this assurance of success; a detachment of the 49th regiment, with a fresh company of militia, and a party of the Leeward *Marons*, marched to attack them. The regulars led the van,[1] the militia

---

[1]  The vanguard, or foremost troops.

brought up the rear, whilst the *Marons* lined the wood to the right and left, to prevent ambuscades. The rebels collected behind their fortification, made shew of a resolution to defend their post, and fired incessantly at their opponents, though with no other injury than wounding one soldier. The officer, captain Forsyth, who commanded the detachment, advanced with the utmost intrepidity, ordering his men to reserve their fire, till they had reached the breast-work; at which time, they poured in such a volley, that several of the rebels immediately fell, and the rest ran as fast as they could up the hill. A Mulatto man behaved with great bravery in this action; he leaped on the breast-work, and assaulted the rebels sword in hand. Having gained a lodgement, the troops declined a pursuit, and carelessly entered the huts, where they sat down to refresh themselves with some provisions, of which they found a large store; the rebels, perceiving this, discharged several random shot from the hill above them, which passed through the huts, and had very near been fatal to some of the officers: the *Marons*, upon this, penetrated the wood at the foot of the hill, and ascending it on the opposite side, and spreading themselves, suddenly assaulted the rebels in flank, who were instantly routed, and a great number killed, or taken prisoners. During the attack at the breast-work, Jemmy, a Negroe belonging to the late Mr. Smith, gave proof of his fidelity and regard to his master, whose death he revenged by killing one of the rebels, and other services, for which he was afterwards rewarded with his freedom, and an annuity for life, by the assembly. After this overthrow, the Westmoreland rebels were never able to act any otherwise than on the defensive; several skirmishes happened, in which they were constantly put to flight; their numbers were gradually reduced, and many destroyed themselves. About the time of their breaking out, several other conspiracies were in agitation: in the Vale of Luidas, in St. John's, the Coromantins had agreed to rise, ravage the estates, and murther the white men there; they fixed a certain day for commencing hostilities, when they were to break open the house at Langher's plantation, *and seize the fire arms lodged there;* after which, they were to slay all the Whites they could meet with, fire the houses and cane-pieces, and lay all the country waste. Three Negroes, who were privy to this machination, disclosed it to their overseer, in consequence of which, the ringleaders were taken up, and upon conviction, executed; others, who turned evidence, were transported off the island: and thus the whole of this bloody scheme was providentially frustrated.

In the parish of St. Thomas in the East, a Negroe, named Caffee, who had been pressed by some Coromantins there to join with them in rebelling, and destroying the estates and white inhabitants, declined at first being concerned; but recollecting that some advantages might be gained to himself by a thorough knowledge of their intentions, he afterwards pretended to have thought better of their proposals, and, professing his zeal to embrace them, he associated at their private cabals[1] from time to time, till he became master of the whole secret, which he took the first opportunity to discover, and most of the conspirators were apprehended.

Conspiracies of like nature were likewise detected in Kingston, St. Dorothy, Clarendon, and St. James, and the partizans secured.

In Kingston, a wooden sword was found, of a peculiar structure, with a red feather stuck into the handle; this was used among the Coromantins as a signal for war; and, upon examining this, and other suspicious circumstances, to the bottom, it was discovered, that the Coromantins of that town had raised one Cubah, a female slave belonging to a Jewess, to the rank of royalty, and dubbed her *queen of Kingston;* at their meetings she had sat in state under a canopy, with a sort of robe on her shoulders, and a crown upon her head.[2] Her majesty[3] was seized, and ordered for transportation; but, prevailing on the captain of the transport to put her ashore again in the leeward part of the island, she continued there for some time undiscovered, but at length was taken up, and executed. These circumstances shew the great extent of the conspiracy, the strict correspondence[4] which had been carried on by the Coromantins in every quarter of the island, and their almost incredible secrecy in the forming their plan of insurrection; for it appeared in evidence, that the first eruption in St. Mary's, was a matter preconcerted, and known to all the chief men in the different districts; and the secret was probably confided to some hundreds, for several months before the blow was struck.

Some persons surmised, that they were privately encouraged, and

---

1  Secret meeting of an insidious character often leading to conspiratorial activities.
2  This passage provides evidence that the slaves were reconstituting themselves according to African structures of royalty.
3  Long is being ironic here and perhaps derisive.
4  Communication of a secret or illicit nature.

furnished with arms and ammunition, by the French and Spaniards,[1] whose piccaroons[2] were often seen hovering near the coast; but there seems no just foundation for such an opinion: it is certain, the rebels found an easier means of supplying themselves with larger quantities of powder, ball, lead, and several stands of arms, on the different estates where they broke out; on some of these, they found two or three dozen musquets and cutlasses, which were not guarded by more than two or three white men. The planters, as I have before remarked, very imprudently kept these magazines,[3] which were by far too many for their necessary defence, and attracted the notice of the Coromantins, who are practised in the use of arms from their youth in their own country, and are at all times disposed for mutiny.

A fresh insurrection happened in St. James's, which threatened to become very formidable, had it not been for the activity of the brigadier Witter of the militia, and lieut. colonel Spragge of the 49th, who dispersed the insurgents, and took several prisoners; but the rest escaped, and, uniting with the stragglers of the other defeated parties, formed a large gang, and infested Carpenter's Mountains[4] for some time. Another party of twelve Coromantins in Clarendon, whom their master, from a too good opinion of their fidelity, had imprudently armed, at their own earnest intreaty, and sent in quest of a small detached band of rebels, of whose haunt he had gained intelligence, deserted to their countrymen, but were soon after surprized, and the greater part of them killed or taken. Damon, one of the Westmoreland chiefs, with a small gang, having posted himself at a place called Mile Gully in Clarendon, a voluntary party, under command of Mr. Scot and Mr. Greig, with three or four more, went in quest of them. They had a long way to march in the night, through the woods, and across a difficult country; but, having provided themselves with a trusty guide, they came up to the haunt about midnight, attacked the rebels without loss of time, killed the

---

1   Such a theory attests to the strained relationship between French, Spanish, and English planters and the larger political tensions among the three nations in their efforts to establish profitable plantation economies in the Caribbean.

2   Small pirate ships or corsairs.

3   Arms depots.

4   A range of mountains in southern Jamaica dotted with caves in which runaway slaves and rebels might hide.

chief, and one of his men, wounded another, and took two prisoners; for which service, the assembly made them a genteel recompence,[1] besides a good reward to the Negroes who assisted them in this enterprize.

The rebels in St. Mary's, under general Tacky, still maintained their ground. Admiral Holmes had dispatched a frigate to Port Maria, which proved of great use for the safe custody of prisoners, who were too numerous to be confined on shore, and required too large a party of militia to guard them; but after they were removed on board, where they were well secured, the militia were ready to be employed on more active service: no measure, therefore, could be more reasonable and judicious; and it was one good effect of the harmony then subsisting between the commander of the squadron and the lieutenant governor.[*] The rebels now thought only of concealing themselves, and made choice of a little glade, or cock-pit,[2] so environed with rocky steeps, that it was difficult to come at them; but, in this situation, a party of militia and *Marons*, with some sailors, assaulted them with hand grenades, killed some, and took a few prisoners. Soon after this, they suffered a more decisive overthrow; the *Marons* of Scot's-Hall, having got sight of their main body, forced them to an engagement; the rebels soon gave way, and Tacky, their leader, having separated from the rest, was closely pursued by lieut. Davy of the *Marons,* who fired at him whilst they were both running a full speed, and shot him dead. His head was brought to Spanish Town, and stuck on a pole in the highway; but, not long after, stolen, as was supposed, by some of his countrymen, who were unwilling to let it remain exposed in so ignominious a

---

[*] Two of the St. Mary's ringleaders, Fortune and Kingston, were hung up alive in irons on a gibbet, erected in the parade of the town of Kingston. Fortune lived seven days, but Kingston survived until the ninth. The morning before the latter expired, he appeared to be convulsed from head to foot; and upon being opened, after his decease, his lungs were found adhering to the back so tightly, that it required some force to disengage them. The murders and outrages they had committed, were thought to justify this cruel punishment inflicted upon them *in terrorem* to others; but they appeared to be little affected by it themselves; behaving all the time with a degree of hardened indolence, and brutal insensibility.

---

[1]  Good reward.
[2]  Jamaica is known for its steep "cockpit country" where rebels could live and elude capture.

manner. The loss of this chief,[*] and of Jamaica,[1] another of their captains, who fell in the same battle, struck most of the survivors of their little army with despair; they betook themselves to a cave, at the distance of a mile or two from the scene of action, where it was thought they laid violent hands on one another, to the number of twenty-five; however, the *Marons*, who found them out, claimed the honour of having slain them, and brought their ears to the lieutenant governor, in testimony of their death, and to entitle themselves to the usual reward. A few miserable fugitives still sculked about the woods, in continual terror for their fate; but at length, they contrived to send an embassy to a gentleman of the parish (Mr. Gordon), in whose honour they reposed implicit confidence, and expressed their readiness to surrender upon the condition of being transported off the island, instead of being put to death. This gentleman had a congress with their leaders unarmed, and promised to exert his endeavours with the lieutenant governor; on their part, they seemed well pleased to wait his determination, and gave assurance of their peaceable demeanour in the mean while. The lieutenant governor's consent was obtained; but under an appearance of difficulty, to make it the more desirable; and, upon intimation of it at the next private congress, they one and all submitted, and were shipped off, pursuant to the stipulation. The remains of the Westmoreland and St. James's rebels still kept in arms, and committed some ravages. In September therefore (1760) the lieutenant governor convened the assembly, and in his speech informed them, "That the various scenes of distress, occasioned by the insurrections which broke out in so many different parts of the country, would have engaged him sooner to call them together; but he was obliged to defer it, as their presence was so necessary in the several districts,

---

[*] He was a young man of good stature, and well made; his countenance handsome, but rather of an effeminate than manly cast. It was said, he had flattered himself with the hope of obtaining (among other fruits of victory) the lieutenant governor's lady for his concubine. He did not appear to be a man of extraordinary genius, and probably chosen general, from his similitude in person to some favourite leader of their nation in Africa. A gentleman, several years since, having set up in a conspicuous part of his plantation a bronzed statue of a gladiator, somewhat larger than the natural size, the Coromantins no sooner beheld, than they were almost ready to fall down, and adore it. Upon enquiry, the gentleman learnt, that they had discovered a very striking likeness between this figure and one of their princes, and believed that it had been copied from him.

[1] The captain seems to have been named in honor of the island.

to prevent the spreading of an evil so dangerous in its consequence to the whole island.

"That he had the satisfaction to acquaint them, his expectations had been fully answered, by the vigilance and bravery of the troops employed during the late troubles; that the many difficulties they had to encounter, only served to set their behaviour in a more advantageous light, and the plan now proposed for carrying on their operations, had the fairest prospect of totally suppressing, in a very short time, all the disturbers of the public repose.

"That the ready assistance he had received from rear-admiral Holmes, in transporting troops and provisions, and in stationing his majesty's ships where they could be of most service, enabled him to make use of such vigorous measures, and employ to advantage such a force, that, notwithstanding the formidable number of rebels which had appeared in arms, and the many combinations which were formed among the slaves throughout the island, *their projects were rendered abortive*, and tranquility again restored, where total destruction had been threatened.

"That nothing had been omitted to render the martial law as little grievous as possible to the inhabitants, although the long continuance of it could not fail of being severely felt by the community in general; but the public security required it; and to that, every other consideration gave place.

"That the care which had been taken to introduce a proper discipline among the militia, had now put them on so respectable a footing, that they only required the aid of legislature, to make them truly useful. The great defects of the last militia law were never more apparent than during the last misfortunes, when the private soldier was supported in disobedience of his commanding officer's orders; and, when called upon for his country's service, empowered, on the payment of an inconsiderable fine,[*] to withdraw that assistance, for which he was enlisted."

The latter part of the lieutenant governor's speech alludes principally to the conduct of several privates in the militia, and particularly the Jews, who refused to turn out and appear under arms on their sabbath, and other festivals or fasts, making a religious scruple of conscience their pretext, though it was well known that they never scrupled taking money and vending drams upon those days; others

---

[*] Ten shillings for non-appearance at muster.

willfully absented themselves, and paid the fine, which came to much less than their profits amounted by staying at home, and attending their shops.[1] I must not here omit a little anecdote relative to these people: one of the rebel leaders, having been taken prisoner in Westmoreland, was confined in irons, in the barrack at Savannah la Mar, to wait his trial. It happened that, on the night after his captivity, a Jew was appointed to stand centry over him: about midnight the rebel, after reconnoitering the person of his guard, took the opportunity of tampering with him, to favour his escape. "You Jews," said he, "and our nation (meaning the Coromantins), ought to consider ourselves as one people. You differ from the rest of the Whites, and they hate you. Surely then it is best for us to join in one common interest, drive them out of the country, and hold possession of it to ourselves. We will have (continued he) a fair division of the estates, and we will make sugar and rum, and bring them to market. As for the sailors, you see they do not oppose us, they care not who is in possession of the country, Black or White, it is the same to them; so that after we are become masters of it, you need not fear but they will come cap in hand to us (as they now do to the Whites) to trade with us. They'll bring us things from t'other side the sea, and be glad to take our goods in payment." Finding the Jew's arguments, in objection to this proposal, not so difficult to surmount as he had expected, he then finished his harangue with an offer, that, "if he would but release him from his irons, he would conduct him directly to a spot, where he had buried some hundred of pistoles, which he should have in reward." The Jew was very earnest to know whereabouts this hidden treasure lay, that he might first satisfy his own eyes, that what he had been told was true, before he should take any further step; but the prisoner flatly refused to let him into the secret, unless he was first set at liberty; which condition the Israelite was either too honest or too unbelieving to comply with, but the next day reported what had passed, to his officers.

The lieutenant-governor recommended to the house, the putting the island into a better posture of defence, and the passing such new regulations for remedying those defects in the laws, which the late calamities had pointed out, as might best seem adapted to prevent future attempts of the like nature.[2]

---

[1]  Long's anti-Semitism is visible here and in the anecdote following.

[2]  Refers to Act 24, Section 10.

The assembly immediately addressed him, to proclaim martial law, in order to put an end to the rebellion still subsisting in the Leeward part of the island. They transmitted the thanks of their house to admiral Holmes for the assistance he had given; who returned a very polite answer, and assured them, "that his greatest pleasure would consist in the execution of his duty against his majesty's enemies, and in giving the utmost protection in his power to the trade and commerce of the island."

They likewise expressed their most grateful sentiments of the lieutenant-governor's vigilance and conduct, which had so happily contributed to the reduction of the rebels in one part, and would, they hoped, very shortly effect their total suppression. For this end, they applied their deliberations, and received the proposals of William Hynes, a millwright by trade, who had been used to the woods, and very serviceable against the rebels in St. Mary's. He proposed that he should be empowered by the lieutenant-governor to beat up for volunteers, and raise among the free Mulattos and Negroes a party of one hundred shot;[1] with which he would march against the rebels in Westmoreland, and do his utmost to reduce them.

He desired to have two lieutenants and one ensign to be in subordinate command; that the reward for their service should be equal, and that his party should be furnished at the public expence with suitable arms and accoutrements, money to provide necessaries, and a stated premium[2] for every rebel they should take or destroy. This scheme was approved of, and a bill passed for carrying it into immediate execution. At the same time seven companies, of thirty men each, were draughted from the militia, and fifteen baggage-Negroes allotted to each company, making in all three hundred and fifteen, who were stationed by the lieutenant-governor in the most advantageous posts; and troopers were disposed in such a manner, as to carry dispatches to and from them, with the best expedition. The assembly granted 450 l.[3] to be divided among the Marons of Trelawny and Accompong Towns, in payment of their arrears due to them, and to encourage their future services. Captain Hynes, with his party, went in search of the rebels, and was four months on the scout; at last, after a tedious pursuit, he surprized them in their haunt, killed and took twelve, and the remainder were afterwards either slain or taken prisoners by other parties, or destroyed

---

[1]   One hundred soldiers.
[2]   Commission.
[3]   450 pounds.

themselves,[1] which latter was the catastrophe of the numbers;[2] for the parties of militia frequently came to places in the woods, where seven or eight were found tied with withes[3] to the boughs of trees; and previous to these self-murders, they had generally massacred their women and children. The assembly ordered 562 *l*. 12 *s*. 6 *d*.[4] to be paid captain Hynes, for his disbursements,[5] and as a recompence for his services. Thus terminated this rebellion: which, whether we consider the extent and secrecy of its plan, the multitude of the conspirators, and the difficulty of opposing its eruptions in such a variety of different places at once, will appear to have been more formidable than any other hitherto known in the West Indies; though happily extinguished, in far less time than was expected, by the precaution and judgement of the lieutenant-governor in the disposition of the forces, the prompt assistance of the admiral, and the alacrity of the regulars, seamen, militia, and Marons, who all contributed their share towards the speedy suppression of it. The lieutenant governor, under whose prudent conduct this intestine war[6] was so successfully brought to a conclusion, was a native of the island, and had a property in it at stake; but if this may detract any thing from the merits of his exertion, it proves at least, how much more may reasonably be hoped from the assiduity of a gentleman of the island, who is interested in its welfare, and in whom a perfect knowledge of the country is superadded to natural ability and public spirit, than from others, who, having nothing to lose in it, may be less anxious for its preservation. There fell, by the hands of the rebels, by murder, and in action, about sixty white persons; the number of the rebels who were killed, or destroyed themselves, was between three and four hundred. Few in proportion were executed, the major part of the prisoners being transported of the island.* Such as appeared to have

---

\*   Most of them were sent to the Bay of Honduras, which has long been the common receptacle of Negroe criminals, banished from this island; the consequence of which may, some time or other, prove very troublesome to the logwood cutters; yet they make no scruple to buy these outcasts, as they cost but little. It is difficult to find a convenient market for such slaves among the neighbouring foreign colonies; but, if possibly it could be avoided, these dangerous spirits should not be sent to renew their outrages in any of our own infant settlements.

---

1   Committed suicide.
2   Suicide contributed significantly to their defeat.
3   Creeping plant of Jamaica, *heliotropium fructosum*, used for making baskets.
4   562 pounds, 12 shillings, 6 pence.
5   Expenses.
6   Civil war.

been involuntarily compelled to join them, were acquitted; but the whole amount of the killed, suicides, executed and transported, was not less than one thousand; and the whole loss sustained by the country, in ruined buildings, cane-pieces, cattle, slaves, and disbursements, was at least 100,000 *l.* to speak within compass.

## 2. From Bryan Edwards, *Observations on the Disposition, Character, Manners, and Habits of Life, of the Maroons* in *The Proceedings of the Governor and Assembly of Jamaica In Regard to the Maroon Negroes* (London: J. Stockdale, 1796)

In the year 1760, an occasion occurred of putting the courage, fidelity, and humanity of these people to the test.[1] The Koromantyn slaves, in the parish of St. Mary, rose into rebellion, and the Maroons were called upon, according to treaty, to co-operate in their suppression. A party of them accordingly arrived at the scene of action, the second or third day after the rebellion had broken out. The whites had already defeated the insurgents, in a pitched battle, at *Heywood-Hall*, killed eight or nine of their number, and driven the remainder into the woods. The Maroons were ordered to pursue them, and were promised a certain reward for each rebel they might kill or take prisoner. They accordingly pushed into the woods, and after rambling about for a day or two, returned with a collection of human ears, which they pretended to have cut off from the heads of rebels they had slain in battle, the particulars of which they minutely related. Their report was believed, and they received the money stipulated to be paid them;[2] yet it was afterwards found that they had not killed a man; that no engagement had taken place, and that the ears which they had produced, had been severed from the dead bodies which had lain unburied at Heywood-Hall.

Some few days after this, as the Maroons, and a detachment of the 74th regiment, were stationed at a solitary place, surrounded by deep woods, called Downs's Cove, they were suddenly attacked in the middle of the night by the rebels. The centinels were shot, and the huts in which the soldiers were lodged, were set on fire. The

---

[1]  Refers to the Maroons.

[2]  To claim their bounty, Maroons produced severed body parts as evidence. Edwards, no fan of the Maroons, accuses them of deceit in this practice. In the next paragraph, he accuses them of cowardice and then goes on to charge them with cannibalism and eating rotten meat.

light of the flames, while it exposed the troops, served to conceal the rebels, who poured in a shower of musquetry from all quarters, and many of the soldiers were slain. Major Forsyth, who commanded the detachment, formed his men into a square, and by keeping up a brisk fire from all sides, at length compelled the enemy to retire. During the whole of this affair the Maroons were not to be found, and Forsyth, for some time, suspected that they were themselves the assailants. It was discovered, however, that immediately on the attack, the whole body of them had thrown themselves flat on the ground, and continued in that position until the rebels retreated, without firing or receiving a shot.

A party of them, however, had afterwards the merit (a merit of which they loudly boasted) of killing the leader of the rebels. He was a young negro of the Koromantyn nation, named Tackey, and it was said had been of free condition, and even a chieftain, in Africa. This unfortunate man, having seen most of his companions slaughtered, was discovered wandering in the woods without arms or clothing, and was immediately pursued by the Maroons, *in full cry.* The chase was of no long duration; he was shot through the head; and it is painful to relate, but unquestionably true, that his savage pursuers, having decollated the body,[1] in order to preserve the head as the trophy of victory, *roasted and actually devoured the heart and entrails of the wretched victim!**

The misconduct of these people in this rebellion, whether proceeding from cowardice or treachery, was, however, overlooked. Living secluded from the rest of the community, they were supposed to have no knowledge of the rules and restraints to which all other classes of the inhabitants were subject; and the vigilance of justice (notwithstanding what has recently happened) seldom pursued them, even for offences of the most atrocious nature.

In truth, it always seemed to me, that the whites in general entertained an opinion of the usefulness of the Maroons; which no part of their conduct, at any one period, confirmed.—Possibly their

---

\*  The circumstances that I have related concerning the conduct of the Maroons, in the rebellion of 1760, are partly founded on my own knowledge and personal observation at the time (having been myself present); or from the testimony of eye witnesses, men of character and probity. The shocking fact last mentioned was attested by several white people, and was not attempted to be denied or concealed by the Maroons themselves. They seemed indeed to make it the subject of boasting and triumph.

---

[1]  Beheaded.

personal appearance contributed in some degree, to preserve the delusion; for, savages as they were in manners and disposition, their mode of living and daily pursuits undoubtedly strengthened the frame, and served to exalt them to great bodily perfection. Such fine persons are seldom beheld among any other class of African or native blacks. Their demeanour is lofty, their walk firm, and their persons erect. Every motion displays a combination of strength and agility. The muscles (neither hidden nor depressed by clothing) are very prominent, and strongly marked. Their sight withal is wonderfully acute, and their hearing remarkably quick. These characteristicks, however, are common, I believe, to all savage nations, in warm and temperate climates; and, like other savages, the Maroons have those senses only perfect which are kept in constant exercise. Their smell is obtuse, and their taste so depraved, that I have seen them drink new rum fresh from the still, in preference to wine which I offered them; and I remember, at a great festival in one of their towns, which I attended, that their highest luxury, in point of food, was some rotten beef which had been originally salted in Ireland, and was probably presented to them, by some person who knew their taste, *because it was putrid*.

Such was the situation of the Maroon Negroes of Jamaica, previous to their late revolt; and the picture which I have drawn of their character and manners, was delineated from the life, after long experience and observation. Of that revolt I shall now proceed to describe the cause, progress, and termination; and if I know myself, without partiality or prejudice.★

---

★ It should not be omitted, that of late years a practice has universally prevailed among the Maroons (in imitation of the other free blacks) of attaching themselves to different families among the English; and desiring gentlemen of consideration to allow the Maroon children to bear their names. Montague James, John Palmer, Tharp, Jarrett, Parkinson, Shirley, White, and many others, are names adopted in this way; and I think great advantages might be derived from it if properly improved.

# Appendix C: Literary Treatments of Obeah

[This appendix includes additional literary treatments of obeah in poetry, drama, and fiction. These representations are useful contrasts to Earle's attempt to render obeah into literature. The first, James Grainger's *The Sugar Cane* (1764), initiates a confused description of obeah in terms of African exoticism, medical cure, and slave pathologies. Grainger was born in Scotland in 1721. He made the grand tour of Europe while completing his medical degree, then moved to London to join the Royal College of Physicians. He ventured to the West Indies in 1759 as the companion of a wealthy friend, where, following his marriage to a local heiress, he became manager of several of his father-in-law's sugar plantations. He also continued to practice medicine. Grainger's book-length georgic poem was considered innovative for its inclusion of highly technical terms in a classical poetic form, but was judged to be a failure in Britain where its attempt to create a colonial georgic was ridiculed. The second selection, from the pantomime *Obi; or, Three-Finger'd Jack* (1800) written by John Fawcett with a musical score by Samuel Arnold, was incredibly successful throughout the nineteenth century. Fawcett was born in 1768, the son of an actor, and became a respected actor himself enjoying his greatest successes in musical, comedic roles. He regularly performed at Britain's most popular theatres, including Drury Lane, Covent Garden, and the Haymarket, eventually becoming stage manager of the Haymarket and treasurer and trustee of Covent Garden. *Obi; or, Three-Finger'd Jack* became a highly successful pantomime after its debut in 1800, long continuing in repertoires of theatres in London and the United States. The pantomime saw only one performance in Jamaica, however, and even then only in altered form more than sixty years after its London opening. In the third selection, "The Grateful Negro," Maria Edgeworth uses the example of obeah in her didactic fiction to explore the themes of gratitude and servitude within a pro-slavery perspective. "The Grateful Negro" is a sentimentalist work that suppresses the political contexts of slave rebellion and instead proposes a paternalistic and moral alternative within which slaves might live peacefully with their masters. Edgeworth was born in Hare Hatch, Berkshire in 1768, the daughter of Richard Lovell Edgeworth, a respected educator, scientist, and politician of Anglo-Irish descent. She lived most of her life on her father's Irish estate surrounded by an extensive family. Many of her novels, tales, and short fiction offer implicit and explicit educational messages on a wide range of domestic and social issues. "The Grateful Negro," taken from her three-volume work *Popular Tales* (1804), is indicative of the fable-like tone adopted in much of Edgeworth's short fiction, intended to educate such disparate audiences as children and adolescents, the peasantry, and the aristocracy. Written as a didactic tale, it proceeds as many conservative abolitionist narratives do, expounding plantocratic paternalism and reciprocal gratitude by slaves as the preferred solution within a historical context of massive slave insurrections in the West Indies. In the manner of Thomas Day's interpolated tales in *Sandford and Merton,* the story prefers cardboard versions of virtue and vice, contrasting the generous planter, Edwards, with the tyrannical one, Jeffries, and the grateful slaves, Caesar and Clara, with the rebellious ones, Hector and Esther. Poetic justice means that one slave's gratitude and his master's paternalism are rewarded even as another master's extreme cruelty—and a violent insurrection by his rebellious slaves—are correspondingly punished. 'Edwards' is a straightforward tribute to his historical namesake, Bryan Edwards, whose *History of the West Indies* is the source for Edgeworth's footnotes on obeah.]

### 1. From James Grainger, *The Sugar Cane: A Poem. In Four Books* (London: R. & J. Dodsley, 1764) Bk. IV

NOR pine the Blacks, alone, with real ills,      365
That baffle oft the wisest rules of art:
They likewise feel imaginary woes;
Woes no less deadly. Luckless he who owns
The slave, who thinks himself bewitch'd; and whom,

In wrath, a conjuror's[1] snake-mark'd* staff hath struck!　　370
They mope, love silence, every friend avoid;
They inly[2] pine; all aliment[3] reject;
Or insufficient for nutrition take:
Their features droop; a sickly yellowish hue
Their skin deforms;[4] their strength and beauty fly.　　375
Then comes the feverish fiend, with firy eyes,
Whom drowth, convulsions, and whom death surround,
Fatal attendants! if some subtle slave
(Such, Obia-men are stil'd) do not engage,
To save the wretch by antidote or spell.　　380

　　IN magic spells, in Obia, all the sons
Of sable[5] Africk trust: — Ye, sacred nine![6]
(For ye each hidden preparation know)
Transpierce the gloom, which ignorance and fraud
Have render'd awful; tell the laughing world　　385
Of what these wonder-working charms are made.

　　FERN root cut small, and tied with many a knot;
Old teeth extracted from a white man's skull;
A lizard's skeleton; a serpent's head:
These mix'd with salt, and water from the spring,　　390

---

*　The negroe-conjurers, or Obia-men, as they are called, carry about them a staff, which is marked with frogs, snakes, &c. The blacks imagine that its blow, if not mortal, will at least occasion long and troublesome disorders. A belief in magic is inseparable from human nature, but those nations are most addicted thereto, among whom learning, and of course, philosophy have least obtained. As in all other countries, so in Guinea, the conjurers, as they have more understanding, so are they almost always more wicked than the common herd of their deluded countrymen; and as the negroe-magicians can do mischief, so they can also do good on a plantation, provided they are kept by the white people in proper subordination.

---

1　Magician, here meaning obeah-practitioner.
2　Inwardly.
3　Food.
4　Possibly referring to the yaws.
5　Black.
6　Invocation of the nine muses that reinforces, in content, the classical nature of the poem's form.

Are in a phial pour'd; o'er these the leach[1]
Mutters strange jargon, and wild circles forms.

 OF this possest, each negroe deems himself
Secure from poison; for to poison they
Are infamously prone: and arm'd with this,    395
Their sable country daemons they defy,
Who fearful haunt them at the midnight hour,
To work them mischief. This, diseases fly;
Diseases follow: such its wonderous power!
This o'er the threshold of their cottage hung,   400
No thieves break in; or, if they dare to steal,
Their feet in blotches, which admit no cure,
Burst loathsome out: but should its owner filch,
As slaves were ever of the pilfering kind,
This from detection screens;—so conjurors swear.[2]  405

## 2. John Fawcett, *Obi; or, Three-Finger'd Jack: A Serio-Pantomime, in Two Acts* (London: T. Woodfall, 1800)

PROSPECTUS.

SCENE—The Island of JAMAICA.

Act I.

SCENE 1.—A View of the extensive Plantations. The Planter's House, on one side; Great Gates, on the other. Preparations to celebrate the Birth-day of *Rosa*, the *Planter's* Daughter. *Captain Orford's* arrival, from England;—previously announced by his Black Boy, *Tuckey*, bringing a Letter. The *Captain's* introduction to *Rosa*, by her Father;—his admiration of her beauty;—his departure, after a short morning visit;—and his very speedy return, occasion'd by his being

---

[1] Generally spelled "leech," the word communicates the double meaning of one who practices medicine and one who attaches himself to another in order to extract gain. Doctors at this time also used leeches to draw blood from their patients, as blood-letting was a popular remedy for many ailments.

[2] This stanza relates to the use of obeah charms both defensively and offensively, i.e., the same charm will punish thieves who steal from the owner even as it protects the owner from detection if he is a thief.

stun'd by a blow, from THREE-FINGER'D JACK. *Rosa's* anxiety. Panick of the Slaves, at the name of *Jack*;—and the superior courage of the two Negroes, QUASHEE AND SAM.

SCENE 2. An Appartment, in the *Planter's* House. *Captain Orford* appears;—much recover'd from the blows he has received.—His profession of love to *Rosa*. The *Planter's* resolution to unite him with *Rosa,* in marriage.—Preparations for a Shooting Party.[1]

SCENE 3.—Inside of an *Obi-Woman's* Cave. Descent of *Negro Robbers,* into the Cave. Their Homage to the *Obi-Woman*, who presents them with *Obi*. The sudden and secret entrance of *Three-Finger'd Jack*. His rage at the Proclamation, issued against him. His *Obi-Horn* fill'd, by the *Obi-Woman;* and his Ceremonies to prevent the Negroes betraying him. Dance, and Carousal, of the *Negroes*. An Alarm. The mysterious disappearance of *Jack*, in consequence of it. Astonishment of the *Negroes*;—and their descent, still deeper, into the Cave.

SCENE 4.—*A Promontory*; with a view of the Sea; and a Boat, at Anchor. The *Planter, Captain Orford,* and *Tuckey,* with a Shooting Party. *Jack's* ascent, from the *Obi Woman's Cave*,—and his ambush. *Tuckey* cast into the Sea. *Captain Orford* wounded, and then captured, by *Jack*. Distress of the *Planter;* and terror of the *Slaves*.

SCENE 5.—*Montago Bay,*[2] in *Jamaica*. *Tuckey's* relation of *Captain Orford's* and his own, Adventure, with *Three-Finger'd Jack*. The *Planter's* dejection, and *Rosa's* grief. Proclamation of Reward, by the Officers of Government, for killing *Three-Finger'd Jack*. The two Negroes, *Quashee* and *Sam,* undertake to encounter him. They are join'd by *Tuckey*. *Quashee's* request to be christen'd, that he may overmatch *Jack*.

SCENE 6.—Outside of part of the *Overseer's* House, with Grounds adjacent. March. *Quashee's* and *Sam's* return from the Church, after the Christening of *Quashee*. Preparations for the Expedition against *Jack*. Rejoicings of the Slaves. A Negro Ball.

---

1   A hunting expedition; foreshadows the later expedition to hunt Jack.
2   More commonly spelled Montego Bay, located on the northwest coast of Jamaica.

ACT II.

SCENE 1.—An accurate representation of the Inside of a *Slave's Hut,* in *Jamaica. Quashee* and *Sam,* taking leave of their Wives, and Children. *Tuckey* with them. *Rosa* comes to them, in Boy's Cloaths; and obtains their consent to accompany them on their Expedition.

SCENE 2.—A Sea Beach. *Negro Robbers* prowling for Plunder. *Three-Finger'd Jack's* appearance among them,—their submission to him;— and his departure. The *Robbers* roused from their concealment, by the *Party* in quest of *Jack. Jack's* re-appearance; and the Robber's awe of his *Obi-Horn.*

SCENE 3.—*A Promontory;* with the Mouth of Jack's Cave. A violent storm of Rain, Wind, Thunder, and Lightening. *Quashee, Sam, Tuckey,* and *Rosa. Rosa's* fatigue. Her entrance into the mouth of the cave, for rest and shelter while the rest of the Party proceed. She is follow'd by *Jack.*

SCENE 4.—A Subterranean Passage. *Rosa* surprised by *Jack.* His intention of shooting her changed to making her his servant.

SCENE 5.—The Inside of Jack's Cave. *Rosa's* performance of menial offices for *Jack.* Her singing him to sleep. Her discovery of *Captain Orford's* being confined, and wounded, in the Cave;—whose escape, with her own, she effects, by stratagem.

SCENE 6.—An Apartment in the *Planter's* House. The Return of *Rosa,* and *Captain Orford* to the Planter.

SCENE 7.—*Mount Lebanus.*[1] Desperate fight, between *Jack,* and the Party employed to kill him. *Jack's* overthrow, and Death.

SCENE 8.—Subterranean passage. *Negro Robbers* bringing an account of *Jack's* Death, to the *Obi-Woman.* Capture of the *Robbers,* and *Obi-Woman,* by a Party of Soldiers.

SCENE LAST,—Publick Rejoicings, occasion'd by the Overthrow of *THREE-FINGER'D JACK.*

---

[1]   Located on the southeast side of Jamaica.

## CHARACTERS.

Captain Orford .................................................Mr. FARLEY.
Planter ..........................................................Mr. CAULFIELD.
Overseer .........................................................Mr. TRUEMAN.
Tuckey (the Captain's Boy) ...................................Master MENAGE.
Jack ..............................................................Mr. C. KEMBLE.
Quashee ..........................................................Mr. EMERY.
Sam ...............................................................Mr. I. PALMER.
Planter's Servants ...............................Mess.[1] ATKINS, WILKINS, &c.
Negro Robbers ...........................Mess. KLANERT, CHIPPENDALE, &c.

Rosa (the Planter's Daughter) ...............................Miss DE CAMP.
Quashee's Wife ................................................Mrs. MOUNTAIN.
Sam's Wife .....................................................Miss GAUDREY.
Obi-Woman ....................................................Mr. ABBOTT.

SONGS, &c.

ACT I.

DUET.—*Quashee's Wife and Sam's Wife.*
(Mrs. MOUNTAIN and Miss GAUDRY.)

THE White man come, and bring his gold,
 The Slatee[2] meet him in the bay;—
And Oh! poor Negro then be sold,—
 From home poor Negro sail away.

O, it be very sad, to see
 Poor Negro child and father part!—
But if White man kind massa be
 He heal the wound in Negro's heart.

CHORUS of NEGROES.

Good massa we find
Sing tingering, sing terry,—

---

[1]  Abbreviation for Messieurs, plural masculine French form of address.

[2]  Term for a slave trader.

When Buckra[1] be kind,
Then Negro heart merry.
    Sing tingering, &c.

TRIO.

We love massa; he be good;
 No lay stick on Negro back;
Much Kous-kous he give for food,
 And save us from Three Finger'd Jack.

CHORUS.
Good massa we find, &c.

OVERSEER.

BLACK ladies and gentlemen, please to draw near,
And attend to the words of your grand Overseer.
Leave work till to-morrow, my hearts, in the morning;
Be jovial and gay, for this is the day
That our master's, the good Planter's, daughter was born in.
 'Tis your Lady's birth day,
 Therefore we'll make holiday,
 And you shall all be merry.

CHORUS.
Sing tingering, &c.

AIR.—OVERSEER and CHORUS.
Swear by the silver Crescent of the night,
Beneath whose beams the Negro breathes his prayer;
Swear by your Fathers slaughter'd in the fight,
By your dear native land, and children swear;
Swear to pursue this traitor, and annoy him;
This Jack, who daily works your harms,
With Obi, and his magick charms—
 Swear, swear you will destroy him.

---

[1] Term for a white man.

CHORUS of Negroes.

Kolli, Kolli, Kolli! we swear all—
We kill, when he comes near us;
But no swear loud—for when we bawl,
Three Finger Jack he hear us.

DUET.—*Quashee and Wife.*
(Mr. Emery and Mrs. Mountain.)

*Quash.*   QUASHEE he load his gun,
   Me go kill Jack, dear,
  Hill will no cover fun
    When Quashee come back, dear.

*Wife.*—War no be certain, and gun no be true;
   Quashee shou'd Jack kill, my heart break for you!
   Sweet musick tink a tank, stay here delighting;
   No, go to battle, big Death come in fighting.

*Quash.*—Me go to battle will;—
    Musick no listen,—
   Men we will many kill,
    Now me newly christen.

*Wife.*—No go—Oh, no go—sweet Quashee, me pray—
   Droop so—me droop so, when you far away.
   Sweet musick tink a tang, stay here delighting:
   No go to battle—big death come in fighting.

*Quash.*—Me laugh at Obi charm—
    Quashee strong hearted,—

*Wife.*—Ah, me fear many harm,
    When you and me parted.

*Wife.* ⎰ No go. Oh, no go, sweet Quashee, me pray.
*Quash.* ⎱ Yes, go, Oh yes go, but long me no stay,

*Wife.*

Droop so, me droop so when { you / me } far away.

{ Sweet / Let } musick tink a tank { stay here / me no } delighting

*Quash.*

{ No / Yes } go to battle { big death come / men die } in fighting

FINALE.
*Quashee's Wife*—(Mrs. MOUNTAIN.)

We Negro men and women meet,
And dance and sing, and drink and eat,
        With a yam foo,[1] foo,—
And when we come to negro ball,
One funny big man be master of all.
        'Tis merry Jonkanoo.[2]

CHORUS.

Now we dance and sing and eat,
Yam, foo, foo, with a yam foo, foo.

*Quashee's Wife*—(Mrs. MOUNTAIN.)
Massa he poor Negro treat,
Give grand ball and Jonkanoo.

CHORUS.
Massa he poor Negro, &c.

*Quashee.*—(Mr. EMERY.)

QUASHEE now he Christen be,
    With a tick tick tack, with a tick tick tack,
And to-morrow Sam and he;
    They go kill Three Finger Jack.

---

[1]  May refer either to yam or fufu, a staple food that is a kind of dough made from plantains.

[2]  Traditional masquerade festival, occurring in the Christmas season; also meaning festivities more generally.

CHORUS.
Now we dance, &c.

*Quashee.*
Massa he poor Negro treat,
Give grand ball and Jonkanoo.

CHORUS.
Massa he poor Negro treat, &c.

*Sam's Wife*—(Miss GAUDRY.)

Jack he did good Captain wound;
Shoot him shoulder, hurt him back.
If by Quashee Jack be found,
Then good bye Three Finger Jack.

CHORUS.
Now we dance, &c.

*Quashee's Wife*—(Mrs. MOUNTAIN.)

Jack have charm in Obi-bag;[1]
Tom cat foot, pig tail, duck beak:
Quashee tear the charm to rag,
Make Three Finger Jack to squeak.

CHORUS.
Now we dance, &c.

ACT II.

SONG.
*Quashee's Wife.*—(Mrs. MOUNTAIN.)

MY cruel love to danger go,
    No think of pain he give to me;

---

[1]  The form of Jack's obi is not consistent throughout the pantomime. Here, his Obi-
horn has been turned into an Obi-bag.

Too soon me fear like grief to know,
    As broke the heart of Ulalee.[1]
                Poor Negro Woman, Ulalee!

Poor soul! to see her hang her head
    All day beneath the Cypress Tree;—
And still she sing my love be dead—
    The husband of poor Ulalee.
                Poor Negro Woman, Ulalee!

My love be kill'd! how sweet he smil'd;
    His smile again me never see;
Unless me see it in the child
    That he have left poor Ulalee.
                Poor Negro Woman, Ulalee!

My baby to my breast I fold,
    But little warmth, poor boy! have he;
His father's death make all so cold
    About the heart of Ulalee.
                Poor Negro Woman, Ulalee!

SONG.
*Rosa*—(Miss DE CAMP)

A Lady, in fair Seville City,
    Who once fell in love very deep,
On her Spanish guittar play'd a ditty,
    That lull'd her old Guardian to sleep.
                With a hoo, tira, lira, &c.

Her Guardian, not giving to dozing,
    Was thought the most watchful of men;
But each verse had so sleepy a closing,
    That he nodded, but soon woke again.
                With a hoo, tira, &c.

---

[1]  The name of Quashee's wife may be a play on the term ululu, which means a wailing cry or lament.

She touch'd the Guittar somewhat slower,
  Again he look'd drowsy and wise;
And then she play'd softer and lower,—
  Till gently she sealed up his eyes.
                With a hoo tira, &c.


AIR.

*Quashee's Wife*—(Mrs. MOUNTAIN.)
YOU never hear of Mandingo King?
  He lost dear daughter in the fight;
But she steal home to his tent at night—
  Then merry Black-man was Mandingo King.[1]


CHORUS.


For she steal home to his tent at night,
Then merry, merry blackman was Mandingo's King.
Mandingo King, oh, his heart was glad,
  He call his loving Subjects round;—
And say—"look here be dear daughter found,
  "Go dance to the Banja,[2] just like mad!"


CHORUS.
For she steal home, &c.


The king for signal throw big dart;
  Oh! then Black-men shout loud and clear;
And high they jump for his daughter dear,
  But none jump so high as her father's heart.


CHORUS.
For she steal home, &c.

---

[1]  The Mandingo people are a distinctive ethnic and cultural group of West Africa
    speaking closely related dialects of the largest language of the Mande subfamily.
[2]  The banjo derives from an African instrument called the bandore or banjore, a
    stringed musical instrument, played with the fingers, having a head and neck like a
    guitar, and a body like a tambourine.

FINALE.

WANDER now, to and fro,
    Cross the wide savannahs go;
Now no fright, Negro know,
    Tangarang, tan tang, taro.
Beat big drum—wave fine flag;—
    Bring good news to Kingston Town, O!
No fear Jack's Obi-Bag—
    Quashee knock him down, O!
Oh! through the dale, and over hill,
    The Negro now may go—
For charm be broke, and Jack be kill—
    'Twas Quashee gave the blow.

OVERSEER.

Here we see villainy
    Brought, by law, to short duration;
And may all Traitors fall
    By British Proclamation.

CHORUS.
Then let us sing
God save the King, &c. &c.

### 3. From Maria Edgeworth, "The Grateful Negro," *Popular Tales* (London: J. Johnson, 1804)

IN the island of Jamaica there lived two planters, whose methods of managing their slaves were as different as possible. Mr. Jefferies considered the negroes as an inferior species, incapable of gratitude, disposed to treachery, and to be roused from their natural indolence only by force; he treated his slaves, or rather suffered his overseer to treat them, with the greatest severity.

Jefferies was not a man of a cruel, but of a thoughtless and extravagant temper. He was of such a sanguine disposition, that he always calculated upon having a fine season, and fine crops on his plantation; and never had the prudence to make allowance for unfortunate accidents: he required, as he said, from his overseer produce and not excuses.

Durant, the overseer, did not scruple to use the most[*] cruel and barbarous methods of forcing the slaves to exertions beyond their strength. Complaints of his brutality, from time to time, reached his master's ears; but though Mr. Jefferies was moved to momentary compassion, he shut his heart against conviction: he hurried away to the jovial banquet, and drowned all painful reflections in wine.[1]

He was this year much in debt; and, therefore, being more than usually anxious about his crop, he pressed his overseer to exert himself to the utmost.

The wretched slaves upon his plantation thought themselves still more unfortunate when they compared their condition with that of the negroes on the estate of Mr. Edwards. This gentleman treated his slaves with all possible humanity and kindness. He wished that there was no such thing as slavery in the world; but he was convinced, by the arguments of those who have the best means of obtaining information, that the sudden emancipation of the negroes would rather increase than diminish their miseries. His benevolence, therefore, confined itself within the bounds of reason. He adopted those plans for the amelioration of the state of the slaves which appeared to him the most likely to succeed without producing any violent agitation or revolution.[†] For instance, his negroes had reasonable and fixed daily tasks; and when these were finished, they were permitted to employ their time for their own advantage or amusement. If they chose to employ themselves longer for their master, they were paid regular wages for their extra work. This reward, for as such it was considered, operated most powerfully upon the slaves. Those who are animated by hope can perform what

---

[*]  THE NEGRO SLAVES—A fine drama, by Kotzebue. It is to be hoped that such horrible instances of cruelty are not now to be found in nature. Bryan Edwards, in his History of Jamaica, says that most of the planters are humane; but he allows that some facts can be cited in contradiction of this assertion. [Durant resembles Paul, the overseer who ill-treats the slaves Ada, Lilli, Ayos, and Zameo in August von Kotzebue's *Die Negesklaven*, translated as *The Negro Slaves* (London: T. Cadell and W. Davies, 1796).]

[†]  History of the West Indies, from which these ideas are adopted — not stolen. [In *The History, Civil and Commercial of the British West Indies* (London, 1819), Bryan Edwards states: "I am certain, that an immediate emancipation of the slaves in the West Indies, would involve both master and slave in one common destruction" (vol.2, 179).]

---

[1]  According to J.B. Moreton's *West India Customs and Manners,* "White people of all ranks and denominations in Jamaica ... in general drink to excess, wines, spirituous and malt liquors" (London: 1793) 167.

would seem impossibilities to those who are under the depressing influence of fear. The wages which Mr. Edwards promised, he took care to see punctually paid.

He had an excellent overseer, of the name of Abraham Bayley, a man of a mild but steady temper, who was attached not only to his master's interests but to his virtues; and who, therefore, was more intent upon seconding his humane views than upon squeezing from the labour of the negroes the utmost produce. Each negro had, near his cottage, a portion of land, called his provision-ground; and one day in the week was allowed for its cultivation.

It is common in Jamaica for the slaves to have provision-grounds, which they cultivate for their own advantage; but it too often happens that, when a good negro has successfully improved his little spot of ground, when he has built himself a house, and begins to enjoy the fruits of his industry, his acquired property is seized upon by the sheriff's officer for the payment of his master's debts;[1] he is forcibly separated from his wife and children, dragged to public auction, purchased by a stranger, and perhaps sent to terminate his miserable existence in the mines of Mexico;[2] excluded for ever from the light of heaven; and all this without any crime or imprudence on his part, real or pretended. He is punished because his master is unfortunate!

To this barbarous injustice the negroes on Mr. Edwards's plantation were never exposed. He never exceeded his income; he engaged in no wild speculations; he contracted no debts; and his slaves, therefore, were in no danger of being seized by a sheriff's officer: their property was secured to them by the prudence as well as by the generosity of their master.

One morning, as Mr. Edwards was walking in that part of his plantation which joined to Mr. Jefferies' estate, he thought he heard the voice of distress at some distance. The lamentations grew louder and louder as he approached a cottage, which stood upon the borders of Jefferies' plantation.

This cottage belonged to a slave of the name of Caesar, the best negro in Mr. Jefferies' possession. Such had been his industry and exertion that, notwithstanding the severe tasks imposed by Durant,

---

[1] According to Edwards, "credit ... is oftentimes suddenly withdrawn, and the ill-fated planter, compelled, on this account, to sell his property at much less than half the cost" (*History,* vol.2: 289).

[2] The infamous Spanish silver mines worked by slave labor.

the overseer, Caesar found means to cultivate his provision-ground to a degree of perfection nowhere else to be seen on this estate. Mr. Edwards had often admired this poor fellow's industry, and now hastened to inquire what misfortune had befallen him.

When he came to the cottage, he found Caesar standing with his arms folded, and his eyes fixed upon the ground. A young and beautiful female negro was weeping bitterly, as she knelt at the feet of Durant, the overseer, who, regarding her with a sullen aspect, repeated, "He must go. I tell you, woman, he must go. What signifies all this nonsense?"

At the sight of Mr. Edwards, the overseer's countenance suddenly changed, and assumed an air of obsequious civility. The poor woman retired to the farther corner of the cottage, and continued to weep. Caesar never moved. "Nothing is the matter, sir," said Durant, "but that Caesar is going to be sold. That is what the woman is crying for. They were to be married; but we'll find Clara[1] another husband, I tell her; and she'll get the better of her grief, you know, sir, as I tell her, in time."

"Never! never!" said Clara.

"To whom is Caesar going to be sold; and for what sum?"

"For what can be got for him," replied Durant, laughing; "and to whoever will buy him. The sheriff's officer is here, who has seized him for debt, and must make the most of him at market."

"Poor fellow!" said Mr. Edwards; "and must he leave this cottage which he has built, and these bananas which he has planted?"

Caesar now for the first time looked up, and fixing his eyes upon Mr. Edwards for a moment, advanced with an intrepid rather than an imploring countenance, and said, "Will you be my master? Will you be her master? Buy both of us. You shall not repent of it. Caesar will serve you faithfully."

On hearing these words, Clara sprang forward, and clasping her hands together, repeated, "Caesar will serve you faithfully."

Mr. Edwards was moved by their entreaties, but he left them without declaring his intentions. He went immediately to Mr. Jefferies, whom he found stretched on a sofa, drinking coffee. As soon as Mr. Edwards mentioned the occasion of his visit, and expressed his sorrow for Caesar, Jefferies exclaimed, "Yes, poor devil! I pity him

---

[1]  The character of Clara may also be an allusion to Edwards' account of Tacky's rebellion, as he refers to "Clara, a most faithful, well disposed woman" (*History*, vol.2: 80).

from the bottom of my soul. But what can I do? I leave all those things to Durant. He says the sheriff's officer has seized him; and there's an end of the matter. You know, money must be had. Besides, Caesar is not worse off than any other slave sold for debt. What signifies talking about the matter, as if it were something that never happened before! Is not it a case that occurs every day in Jamaica?"

"So much the worse," replied Mr. Edwards.

"The worse for them, to be sure," said Jefferies. "But, after all, they are slaves, and used to be treated as such; and they tell me the negroes are a thousand times happier here, with us, than they ever were in their own country."

"Did the negroes tell you so themselves?"

"No; but people better informed than negroes have told me so; and, after all, slaves there must be; for indigo, and rum, and sugar, we must have."

"Granting it to be physically impossible that the world should exist without rum, sugar, and indigo, why could they not be produced by freemen as well as by slaves? If we hired negroes for labourers, instead of purchasing them for slaves, do you think they would not work as well as they do now? Does any negro, under the fear of the overseer, work harder than a Birmingham journeyman, or a Newcastle collier,[1] who toil for themselves and their families?"

"Of that I don't pretend to judge. All I know is that the West India planters would be ruined if they had no slaves, and I am a West India planter."

"So am I: yet I do not think they are the only people whose interests ought to be considered in this business."

"Their interests, luckily, are protected by the laws of the land; and though they are rich men, and white men, and freemen, they have as good a claim to their rights as the poorest black slave on any of our plantations."

"The law, in our case, seems to make the right; and the very reverse ought to be done — the right should make the law."

"Fortunately for us planters, we need not enter into such nice distinctions. You could not, if you would, abolish the trade. Slaves would be smuggled into the islands."

"What, if nobody would buy them! You know that you cannot

---

[1]   Birmingham was known for its expertise in handicrafts, particularly glass and pottery, while Newcastle was known for its coal mines.

smuggle slaves into England. The instant a slave touches English ground he becomes free.[1] Glorious privilege! Why should it not be extended to all her dominions? If the future importation of slaves into these islands were forbidden by law, the trade must cease. No man can either sell or possess slaves without its being known: they cannot be smuggled like lace or brandy."[2]

"Well, well!" retorted Jefferies, a little impatiently, "as yet the law is on our side. I can do nothing in this business, nor you neither."

"Yes, we can do something; we can endeavour to make our negroes as happy as possible."

"I leave the management of these people to Durant."

"That is the very thing of which they complain; forgive me for speaking to you with the frankness of an old acquaintance."

"Oh! you can't oblige me more: I love frankness of all things! To tell you the truth, I have heard complaints of Durant's severity; but I make it a principle to turn a deaf ear to them, for I know nothing can be done with these fellows without it. You are partial to negroes; but even you must allow they are a race of beings naturally inferior to us. You may in vain think of managing a black as you would a white. Do what you please for a negro, he will cheat you the first opportunity he finds. You know what their maxim is: 'God gives black men what white men forget.'"[3]

To these common-place desultory observations Mr. Edwards made no reply; but recurred to poor Caesar, and offered to purchase both him and Clara, at the highest price the sheriff's officer could obtain for them at market. Mr. Jefferies, with the utmost politeness to his neighbour, but with the most perfect indifference to the happiness of those whom he considered of a different species from himself, acceded to this proposal. Nothing could be more reasonable, he said; and he was happy to have it in his power to oblige a gentleman for whom he had such a high esteem.

The bargain was quickly concluded with the sheriff's officer; for Mr. Edwards willingly paid several dollars more than the market price for the two slaves. When Caesar and Clara heard that they were not to be separated, their joy and gratitude were expressed with all the ardour and tenderness peculiar to their different characters. Clara was

---

1   The popular interpretation of the Mansfield decision of 1772.

2   The smuggling of lace and brandy was a well-known occurrence in Jamaica.

3   For related maxims see Burton Stevenson, *Book of Proverbs, Maxims and Familiar Phrases* (London: Routledge and Kegan Paul, 1949) 1672–74.

an Eboe, Caesar a Koromantyn negro: the Eboes are soft, languishing, and timid; the Koromantyns are frank, fearless, martial, and heroic.[1]

Mr. Edwards carried his new slaves home with him, desired Bayley, his overseer, to mark out a provision-ground for Caesar, and to give him a cottage, which happened at this time to be vacant.

"Now, my good friend," said he to Caesar, "you may work for yourself, without fear that what you earn may be taken from you; or that you should ever be sold, to pay your master's debts. If he does not understand what I am saying," continued Mr. Edwards, turning to his overseer, "you will explain it to him."[2]

Caesar perfectly understood all that Mr. Edwards said; but his feelings were at this instant so strong that he could not find expression for his gratitude: he stood like one stupified! Kindness was new to him; it overpowered his manly heart; and, at hearing the words "my good friend," the tears gushed from his eyes: tears which no torture could have extorted! Gratitude swelled in his bosom; and he longed to be alone, that he might freely yield to his emotions.

He was glad when the conch-shell sounded to call the negroes to their daily labour, that he might relieve the sensations of his soul by bodily exertion. He performed his task in silence; and an inattentive observer might have thought him sullen.

In fact, he was impatient for the day to be over, that he might get rid of a heavy load which weighed upon his mind.

The cruelties practised by Durant, the overseer of Jefferies' plantation, had exasperated the slaves under his dominion.

They were all leagued together in a conspiracy, which was kept profoundly secret. Their object was to extirpate every white man, woman, and child, in the island. Their plans were laid with consummate art; and the negroes were urged to execute them by all the courage of despair.

The confederacy extended to all the negroes in the island of Jamaica,[3] excepting those on the plantation of Mr. Edwards. To them no hint of the dreadful secret had yet been given; their countrymen, knowing the attachment they felt to their master, dared not

---

[1] According to Edwards, "The great objection to Eboes as slaves, is their constitutional timidity, and despondency of mind" (*History*, vol.2: 89), while "Koromantyn are frank and fearless" (90).

[2] This statement by Mr. Edwards suggests that there may be a need for translation between Caesar and Mr. Edwards, or at least the perception of such a need.

[3] Many of the details concerning the conspiracy resemble those of Tacky's rebellion.

trust them with these projects of vengeance. Hector, the negro who was at the head of the conspirators, was the particular friend of Caesar, and had imparted to him all his designs. These friends were bound to each other by the strongest ties. Their slavery and their sufferings began in the same hour: they were both brought from their own country in the same ship. This circumstance alone forms, amongst the negroes, a bond of connexion not easily to be dissolved.[1] But the friendship of Caesar and Hector commenced even before they were united by the sympathy of misfortune; they were both of the same nation,[2] both Koromantyns. In Africa they had both been accustomed to command; for they had signalized themselves[3] by superior fortitude and courage. They respected each other for excelling in all which they had been taught to consider as virtuous; and with them revenge was a virtue![4]

Revenge was the ruling passion of Hector: in Caesar's mind it was rather a principle instilled by education. The one considered it as a duty, the other felt it as a pleasure. Hector's sense of injury was acute in the extreme; he knew not how to forgive. Caesar's sensibility was yet more alive to kindness than to insult. Hector would sacrifice his life to extirpate an enemy. Caesar would devote himself for the defence of a friend; and Caesar now considered a white man as his friend.

He was now placed in a painful situation. All his former friendships, all the solemn promises by which he was bound to his companions in misfortune, forbade him to indulge that delightful feeling of gratitude and affection, which, for the first time, he experienced for one of that race of beings whom he had hitherto considered as detestable tyrants—objects of implacable and just revenge!

Caesar was most impatient to have an interview with Hector, that he might communicate his new sentiments, and dissuade him from those schemes of destruction which he meditated. At midnight, when all the slaves except himself were asleep, he left his cottage, and went to Jefferies' plantation, to the hut in which Hector slept. Even in his dreams Hector breathed vengeance. "Spare none! Sons of Africa, spare none!" were the words he uttered in his sleep,[5]

---

1  The strong bonds and sense of community forged during the middle passage.
2  Used here to mean ethnic group.
3  Distinguished themselves.
4  Seen as a Koromantyn attribute.
5  Hector's dreams of revenge echo those of Three-fingered Jack.

as Caesar approached the mat on which he lay. The moon shone full upon him. Caesar contemplated the countenance of his friend, fierce even in sleep. "Spare none! Oh, yes! There is one that must be spared. There is one for whose sake all must be spared."

He wakened Hector by this exclamation. "Of what were you dreaming?" said Caesar.

"Of that which, sleeping or waking, fills my soul—revenge! Why did you waken me from my dream? It was delightful. The whites were weltering in their blood! But silence! we may be overheard."

"No; every one sleeps but ourselves," replied Caesar. "I could not sleep, without speaking to you on—a subject that weighs upon my mind. You have seen Mr. Edwards?"

"Yes. He that is now your master."

"He that is now my benefactor—my friend!"

"Friend! Can you call a white man friend?" cried Hector, starting up with a look of astonishment and indignation.

"Yes," replied Caesar, with firmness. "And you would speak, ay, and would feel, as I do, Hector, if you knew this white man. Oh, how unlike he is to all of his race, that we have ever seen! Do not turn from me with so much disdain. Hear me with patience, my friend."

"I cannot," replied Hector, "listen with patience to one who between the rising and the setting sun can forget all his resolutions, all his promises; who by a few soft words can be so wrought upon as to forget all the insults, all the injuries he has received from this accursed race; and can even call a white man friend!"

Caesar, unmoved by Hector's anger, continued to speak of Mr. Edwards with the warmest expressions of gratitude; and finished by declaring he would sooner forfeit his life than rebel against such a master. He conjured Hector to desist from executing his designs; but all was in vain. Hector sat with his elbows fixed upon his knees, leaning his head upon his hands, in gloomy silence.

Caesar's mind was divided between love for his friend and gratitude to his master: the conflict was violent and painful. Gratitude at last prevailed: he repeated his declaration, that he would rather die than continue in a conspiracy against his benefactor!

Hector refused to except him from the general doom. "Betray us if you will!" cried he. "Betray our secrets to him whom you call your benefactor; to him whom a few hours have made your friend! To him sacrifice the friend of your youth, the companion of your better days, of your better self! Yes, Caesar, deliver me over to the tormentors: I can endure no more than they can inflict. I shall expire without a sigh, without a groan. Why do you linger here, Caesar? Why do you hesitate? Hasten this moment to your master; claim your reward for delivering into his power hundreds of your countrymen! Why do you hesitate? Away! The coward's friendship can be of use to none. Who can value his gratitude? Who can fear his revenge?"

Hector raised his voice so high, as he pronounced these words, that he wakened Durant, the overseer, who slept in the next house. They heard him call out suddenly, to inquire who was there: and Caesar had but just time to make his escape, before Durant appeared. He searched Hector's cottage; but finding no one, again retired to rest. This man's tyranny made him constantly suspicious: he dreaded that the slaves should combine against him; and he endeavoured to prevent them by every threat and every stratagem he could devise, from conversing with each other.

They had, however, taken their measures, hitherto, so secretly, that he had not the slightest idea of the conspiracy which was forming in the island. Their schemes were not yet ripe for execution; but the appointed time approached. Hector, when he coolly reflected on what had passed between him and Caesar, could not help admiring the frankness and courage with which he had avowed his change of sentiments. By this avowal, Caesar had in fact exposed his own life to the most imminent danger, from the vengeance of the conspirators; who might be tempted to assassinate him who had their lives in his power. Notwithstanding the contempt with which, in the first moment of passion, he had treated his friend, he was extremely anxious that he should not break off all connexion with the conspirators. He knew that Caesar possessed both intrepidity and eloquence; and that his opposition to their schemes would perhaps entirely frustrate their whole design. He therefore determined to use every possible means to bend him to their purposes.

He resolved to have recourse to one of those persons* who,

---

* The enlightened inhabitants of Europe may, perhaps, smile at the superstitious credulity of the negroes, who regard those ignorant beings called *Obeah* people with the most profound respect and dread; who believe that they hold in their hands the power of good and evil fortune, of health and sickness, of life and death. The instances which are related of their power over the minds of their countrymen are so wonderful that none but the most unquestionable authority could make us think them credible. The following passage from Edwards's History of the West Indies, is inserted, to give an idea of this strange infatuation. [She goes on to quote a lengthy passage verbatim from Edwards' *History* reproduced in Appendix A 173–76.]

amongst the negroes, are considered as sorceresses. Esther, an old Koromantyn negress, had obtained by her skill in poisonous herbs, and her knowledge of venomous reptiles, a high reputation amongst her countrymen. She soon taught them to believe her to be possessed of supernatural powers; and she then worked their imagination to what pitch and purpose she pleased.

She was the chief instigator of this intended rebellion. It was she who had stimulated the revengeful temper of Hector almost to phrensy. She now promised him that her arts should be exerted over his friend; and it was not long before he felt their influence. Caesar soon perceived an extraordinary change in the countenance and manner of his beloved Clara. A melancholy hung over her, and she refused to impart to him the cause of her dejection. Caesar was indefatigable in his exertions to cultivate and embellish the ground near his cottage, in hopes of making it an agreeable habitation for her; but she seemed to take no interest in any thing. She would stand beside him immoveable, in a deep reverie; and when he inquired whether she was ill, she would answer no, and endeavour to assume an air of gaiety: but this cheerfulness was transient; she soon relapsed into despondency. At length, she endeavoured to avoid her lover, as if she feared his farther inquiries.

Unable to endure this state of suspense, he one evening resolved to bring her to an explanation. "Clara," said he, "you once loved me: I have done nothing, have I, to forfeit your confidence?"

"I once loved you!" said she, raising her languid eyes, and looking at him with reproachful tenderness; "and can you doubt my constancy? Oh, Caesar, you little know what is passing in my heart! You are the cause of my melancholy!"

She paused, and hesitated, as if afraid that she had said too much: but Caesar urged her with so much vehemence, and so much tenderness, to open to him her whole soul, that, at last, she could not resist his eloquence. She reluctantly revealed to him that secret of which she could not think without horror. She informed him that, unless he complied with what was required of him by the sorceress Esther, he was devoted to die.[1] What it was that Esther required of him, Clara knew not: she knew nothing of the conspiracy. The timidity of her character was ill-suited to such a project; and every thing relating to it had been concealed from her with the utmost care.

---

[1]  In the sense of being doomed.

When she explained to Caesar the cause of her dejection, his natural courage resisted these superstitious fears; and he endeavoured to raise Clara's spirits. He endeavoured in vain: she fell at his feet, and with tears, and the most tender supplications, conjured him to avert the wrath of the sorceress by obeying her commands whatever they might be!

"Clara," replied he, "you know not what you ask!"

"I ask you to save your life!" said she. "I ask you, for my sake, to save your life, while yet it is in your power!"

"But would you to save my life, Clara, make me the worst of criminals? Would you make me the murderer of my benefactor?"

Clara started with horror!

"Do you recollect the day, the moment, when we were on the point of being separated for ever, Clara? Do you remember the white man's coming to my cottage? Do you remember his look of benevolence—his voice of compassion? Do you remember his generosity? Oh! Clara, would you make me the murderer of this man?"

"Heaven forbid!" said Clara. "This cannot be the will of the sorceress!"

"It is," said Caesar. "But she shall not succeed, even though she speaks with the voice of Clara. Urge me no farther; my resolution is fixed. I should be unworthy of your love if I were capable of treachery and ingratitude."

"But, is there no means of averting the wrath of Esther?" said Clara. "Your life—"

"Think, first, of my honour," interrupted Caesar. "Your fears deprive you of reason. Return to this sorceress, and tell her that I dread not her wrath. My hands shall never be imbrued[1] in the blood of my benefactor. Clara! can you forget his look when he told us that we should never more be separated?"

"It went to my heart," said Clara, bursting into tears. "Cruel, cruel Esther! Why do you command us to destroy such a generous master?"

The conch sounded to summon the negroes to their morning's work. It happened this day, that Mr. Edwards, who was continually intent upon increasing the comforts and happiness of his slaves, sent his carpenter, while Caesar was absent, to fit up the inside of his cottage; and when Caesar returned from work, he found his master pruning the branches of a tamarind tree that overhung the thatch. "How comes it, Caesar," said he, "that you have not pruned these branches?"

---

[1]    Stained.

Caesar had no knife. "Here is mine for you," said Mr. Edwards. "It is very sharp," added he, smiling; "but I am not one of those masters who are afraid to trust their negroes with sharp knives."

These words were spoken with perfect simplicity: Mr. Edwards had no suspicion, at this time, of what was passing in the negro's mind. Caesar received the knife without uttering a syllable; but no sooner was Mr. Edwards out of sight than he knelt down, and, in a transport of gratitude, swore that, with this knife, he would stab himself to the heart sooner than betray his master!

The principle of gratitude conquered every other sensation. The mind of Caesar was not insensible to the charms of freedom: he knew the negro conspirators had so taken their measures, that there was the greatest probability of their success. His heart beat high at the idea of recovering his liberty: but he was not to be seduced from his duty, not even by this delightful hope; nor was he to be intimidated by the dreadful certainty that his former friends and countrymen, considering him as a deserter from their cause, would become his bitterest enemies. The loss of Hector's esteem and affection was deeply felt by Caesar. Since the night that the decisive conversation relative to Mr. Edwards passed, Hector and he had never exchanged a syllable.

This visit proved the cause of much suffering to Hector, and to several of the slaves on Jefferies' plantation. We mentioned that Durant had been awakened by the raised voice of Hector. Though he could not find any one in the cottage, yet his suspicions were not dissipated; and an accident nearly brought the whole conspiracy to light. Durant had ordered one of the negroes to watch a boiler of sugar: the slave was overcome by the heat, and fainted. He had scarcely recovered his senses when the overseer came up, and found that the sugar had fermented, by having remained a few minutes too long in the boiler. He flew into a violent passion, and ordered that the negro should receive fifty lashes.[1] His victim bore them without uttering a groan; but, when his punishment was over, and when he thought the overseer was gone, he exclaimed, "It will soon be our turn!"

Durant was not out of hearing. He turned suddenly, and observed that the negro looked at Hector when he pronounced

---

[1]   Thirty-nine lashes was considered the maximum; Durant is clearly violating the slave code.

these words, and this confirmed the suspicion that Hector was carrying on some conspiracy. He immediately had recourse to that brutality which he considered as the only means of governing black men: Hector and three other negroes were lashed unmercifully; but no confessions could be extorted.

Mr. Jefferies might perhaps have forbidden such violence to be used, if he had not been at the time carousing with a party of jovial West Indians, who thought of nothing but indulging their appetites in all the luxuries that art and nature could supply. The sufferings which had been endured by many of the wretched negroes to furnish out this magnificent entertainment were never once thought of by these selfish epicures. Yet so false are the general estimates of character, that all these gentlemen passed for men of great feeling and generosity! The human mind, in certain situations, becomes so accustomed to ideas of tyranny and cruelty, that they no longer appear extraordinary or detestable: they rather seem part of the necessary and immutable order of things.

Mr. Jefferies was stopped, as he passed from his dining-room into his drawing-room, by a little negro child, of about five years old, who was crying bitterly. He was the son of one of the slaves who were at this moment under the torturer's hand. "Poor little devil!" said Mr. Jefferies, who was more than half intoxicated. "Take him away; and tell Durant, some of ye, to pardon his father — if he can."

The child ran, eagerly, to announce his father's pardon; but he soon returned, crying more violently than before. Durant would not hear the boy; and it was now no longer possible to appeal to Mr. Jefferies, for he was in the midst of an assembly of fair ladies; and no servant belonging to the house dared to interrupt the festivities of the evening. The three men, who were so severely flogged to extort from them confessions, were perfectly innocent: they knew nothing of the confederacy; but the rebels seized the moment when their minds were exasperated by this cruelty and injustice, and they easily persuaded them to join the league. The hope of revenging themselves upon the overseer was a motive sufficient to make them brave death in any shape.

Another incident, which happened a few days before the time destined for the revolt of the slaves, determined numbers who had been undecided. Mrs. Jefferies was a languid beauty, or rather a languid fine lady who had been a beauty, and who spent all that part of the day which was not devoted to the pleasures of the table, or to reclining on a couch, in dress. She was one day extended on a sofa, fanned by four slaves, two at her head and two at her feet, when news was brought that a large chest, directed to her, was just arrived from London.

This chest contained various articles of dress of the newest fashions. The Jamaica ladies carry their ideas of magnificence to a high pitch: they willingly give a hundred guineas for a gown, which they perhaps wear but once or twice. In the elegance and variety of her ornaments, Mrs. Jefferies was not exceeded by any lady in the island, except by one who had lately received a cargo from England. She now expected to outshine her competitor, and desired that the chest should be unpacked in her presence.

In taking out one of the gowns, it caught on a nail in the lid, and was torn. The lady, roused from her natural indolence by this disappointment to her vanity, instantly ordered that the unfortunate female slave should be severely chastised. The woman was the wife of Hector; and this fresh injury worked up his temper, naturally vindictive, to the highest point. He ardently longed for the moment when he might satiate his vengeance.

The plan the negroes had laid was to set fire to the canes,[1] at one and the same time, on every plantation; and when the white inhabitants of the island should run to put out the fire, the blacks were to seize this moment of confusion and consternation to fall upon them, and make a general massacre. The time when this scheme was to be carried into execution was not known to Caesar; for the conspirators had changed their day, as soon as Hector told them that his friend was no longer one of the confederacy. They dreaded he should betray them; and it was determined that he and Clara should both be destroyed, unless they could be prevailed upon to join the conspiracy.

Hector wished to save his friend; but the desire of vengeance overcame every other feeling. He resolved, however, to make an attempt, for the last time, to change Caesar's resolution.

For this purpose, Esther was the person he employed: she was to work upon his mind by means of Clara. On returning to her cottage one night, she found suspended from the thatch one of those strange fantastic charms with which the Indian[2] sorceresses

---

[1]  The woody sugarcane plants catch fire easily when mature.
[2]  Most likely used here in the sense of native to the island, i.e., West Indian.

terrify those whom they have proscribed. Clara, unable to conquer her terror, repaired again to Esther, who received her first in mysterious silence; but, after she had implored her forgiveness for the past, and with all possible humility conjured her to grant her future protection, the sorceress deigned to speak. Her commands were that Clara should prevail upon her lover to meet her, on this awful spot, the ensuing night.

Little suspecting what was going forward on the plantation of Jefferies, Mr. Edwards that evening gave his slaves a holiday. He and his family came out at sunset, when the fresh breeze had sprung up, and seated themselves under a spreading palm-tree, to enjoy the pleasing spectacle of this negro festival. His negroes were all well clad, and in the gayest colours, and their merry countenances suited the gaiety of their dress. While some were dancing, and some playing on the tambourine, others appeared amongst the distant trees, bringing baskets of avocado pears, grapes, and pine-apples, the produce of their own provision-grounds; and others were employed in spreading their clean trenchers, [1] or the calabashes, which served for plates and dishes. The negroes continued to dance and divert themselves till late in the evening. When they separated and retired to rest, Caesar, recollecting his promise to Clara, repaired secretly to the habitation of the sorceress. It was situated in the recess of a thick wood. When he arrived there, he found the door fastened; and he was obliged to wait some time before it was opened by Esther.

The first object he beheld was his beloved Clara, stretched on the ground, apparently a corpse! The sorceress had thrown her into a trance by a preparation of deadly nightshade. [2] The hag burst into an infernal laugh, when she beheld the despair that was painted in Caesar's countenance. "Wretch!" cried she, "you have defied my power: behold its victim!"

Caesar, in a transport of rage, seized her by the throat: but his fury was soon checked.

"Destroy me," said the fiend, "and you destroy your Clara. She is not dead: but she lies in the sleep of death, into which she has been thrown by magic art, and from which no power but mine can restore her to the light of life. Yes! look at her, pale and motionless!

---

[1]  Wooden plates.

[2]  Belladonna, containing atropine, a highly potent and poisonous narcotic.

Never will she rise from the earth, unless, within one hour, you obey my commands. I have administered to Hector and his companions the solemn fetish oath,[1] at the sound of which every negro in Africa trembles! You know my object."

"Fiend, I do!" replied Caesar, eyeing her sternly; "but, while I have life, it shall never be accomplished."

"Look yonder!" cried she, pointing to the moon; "in a few minutes that moon will set: at that hour Hector and his friends will appear. They come armed—armed with weapons which I shall steep in poison for their enemies. Themselves I will render invulnerable. Look again!" continued she; "if my dim eyes mistake not, yonder they come. Rash man, you die if they cross my threshhold."

"I wish for death," said Caesar. "Clara is dead!"

"But you can restore her to life by a single word."

Caesar, at this moment, seemed to hesitate.

"Consider! Your heroism is vain," continued Esther. "You will have the knives of fifty of the conspirators in your bosom, if you do not join them; and, after you have fallen, the death of your master is inevitable. Here is the bowl of poison, in which the negro knives are to be steeped. Your friends, your former friends, your countrymen, will be in arms in a few minutes; and they will bear down every thing before them—Victory, Wealth, Freedom, and Revenge, will be theirs."

Caesar appeared to be more and more agitated. His eyes were fixed upon Clara. The conflict in his mind was violent; but his sense of gratitude and duty could not be shaken by hope, fear, or ambition; nor could it be vanquished by love. He determined, however, to appear to yield. As if struck with panic, at the approach of the confederate negroes, he suddenly turned to the sorceress, and said, in a tone of feigned submission, "It is in vain to struggle with fate. Let my knife, too, be dipt in your magic poison."

The sorceress clapped her hands with infernal joy in her countenance. She bade him instantly give her his knife, that she might plunge it to the hilt in the bowl of poison, to which she turned with savage impatience. His knife was left in his cottage; and, under pretence of going in search of it, he escaped. Esther promised to prepare Hector and all his companions to receive him with their ancient cordiality on his return. Caesar ran with the utmost speed along a by-path out of the wood, met none of the rebels, reached his master's house, scaled the wall

---

[1] Oath taken upon drinking a mixture of rum, blood, and grave-dirt.

of his bedchamber, got in at the window, and wakened him, exclaiming, "Arm—arm yourself, my dear master! Arm all your slaves! They will fight for you, and die for you; as I will the first. The Koromantyn yell of war will be heard in Jefferies' plantation this night! Arm—arm yourself, my dear master, and let us surround the rebel leaders while it is yet time. I will lead you to the place where they are all assembled, on condition that their chief, who is my friend, shall be pardoned."

Mr. Edwards armed himself and the negroes on his plantation, as well as the whites: they were all equally attached to him. He followed Caesar into the recesses of the wood.

They proceeded with all possible rapidity, but in perfect silence, till they reached Esther's habitation: which they surrounded completely, before they were perceived by the conspirators.

Mr. Edwards looked through a hole in the wall; and, by the blue flame of a caldron, over which the sorceress was stretching her shrivelled hands, he saw Hector and five stout negroes standing, intent upon her incantations.[1] These negroes held their knives in their hands, ready to dip them into the bowl of poison. It was proposed, by one of the whites, to set fire immediately to the hut; and thus to force the rebels to surrender. The advice was followed; but Mr. Edwards charged his people to spare their prisoners. The moment the rebels saw that the thatch of the hut was in flames, they set up the Koromantyn yell of war, and rushed out with frantic desperation.

"Yield! you are pardoned, Hector," cried Mr. Edwards, in a loud voice.

"You are pardoned, my friend!" repeated Caesar.

Hector, incapable at this instant of listening to any thing but revenge, sprang forwards, and plunged his knife into the bosom of Caesar. The faithful servant staggered back a few paces: his master caught him in his arms. "I die content," said he. "Bury me with Clara."

He swooned from loss of blood as they were carrying him home; but when his wound was examined, it was found not to be mortal. As he recovered from his swoon, he stared wildly round him, trying to recollect where he was, and what had happened. He thought that he was still in a dream, when he saw his beloved Clara standing

---

[1] "[W]hatever the prophetess orders to be done during this paroxysm is most sacredly performed ... as she frequently enjoins them to murder their masters, or desert to the woods." John Gabriel Stedman, *Narrative of a Five-Years Expedition to Surinam, 1772–1777* (1796; Amherst: U of Massachusetts P, 1971) 364.

beside him. The opiate, which the pretended[1] sorceress had administered to her, had ceased to operate; she wakened from her trance just at the time the Koromantyn yell commenced. Caesar's joy!— We must leave that to the imagination.

In the mean time, what became of the rebel negroes, and Mr. Edwards?

The taking the chief conspirators prisoners did not prevent the negroes upon Jefferies' plantation from insurrection. The moment they heard the war-whoop, the signal agreed upon, they rose in a body; and, before they could be prevented, either by the whites on the estate, or by Mr. Edwards's adherents, they had set fire to the overseer's house, and to the canes. The overseer[2] was the principal object of their vengeance—he died in tortures, inflicted by the hands of those who had suffered most by his cruelties. Mr. Edwards, however, quelled the insurgents before rebellion spread to any other estates in the island. The influence of his character, and the effect of his eloquence upon the minds of the people, were astonishing: nothing but his interference could have prevented the total destruction of Mr. Jefferies and his family, who, as it was computed, lost this night upwards of fifty thousand pounds.[3] He was never afterwards able to recover his losses, or to shake off his constant fear of a fresh insurrection among his slaves. At length, he and his lady returned to England, where they were obliged to live in obscurity and indigence. They had no consolation in their misfortunes but that of railing at the treachery of the whole race of slaves. Our readers, we hope, will think that at least one exception may be made, in favour of THE GRATEFUL NEGRO.

*March,* 1802.

---

[1]   Self-professed.
[2]   The brutal Durant.
[3]   The average plantation's value at this time was approximately 42,000 Jamaican pounds (30,000 pounds sterling). Edwards, *History* (Vol 2. 296).

# Select Bibliography

## Primary Texts

Anonymous. *Adventures of Jonathan Corncob, Loyal American Refugee. Written by Himself.* London: G.G.J. and G. Robinson and R. Faulder, 1787.

Austen, Jane. *Mansfield Park.* London: T. Egerton, 1814.

Bage, Robert. *Man As He Is.* London: William Lane at the Minerva Press, 1792.

Beckford, William. *A Descriptive Account of the Island of Jamaica.* London: T. and J. Egerton, 1790.

Behn, Aphra. *Oroonoko, or, The Royal Slave.* London: Will. Canning, 1688.

*Biographica Dramatica.* Vol. 3. London, 1812.

Blake, William. *Songs of Innocence and Experience.* New York: United Book Guild, 1794.

Bonhote, Elizabeth. *The Rambles of Mr. Frankly.* London: T. Becket and P.A. Dehondt, 1772.

Brooke, Henry. *The Fool of Quality.* London: W. Johnston, 1764–70.

Burke, Edmund. *A Philosophical Inquiry into the Origin of Our Ideas of the Sublime and Beautiful.* Philadelphia: D. Johnson, 1806.

Burke, Edmund. *Reflections on the Revolution in France.* London and New York: Macmillan, 1890.

Campbell, Thomas. *The Pleasures of Hope.* Edinburgh: Mundell and Son, 1799.

Cheap Repository Tracts. *The Black Prince.* Bath: S. Hazard, 1799.

Combe, William. *The Devil Upon Two Sticks in England.* London: Logographic Press, 1790.

Coventry, Francis. *The History of Pompey the Little; or, The Life and Adventures of a Lap-Dog.* London: M. Cooper, 1751.

Cumberland, Richard. *Henry.* London: Charles Dilly, 1795.

——. *John de Lancaster.* London: Lackington, Allen, and Co., 1809.

Cundall, F.S.A. Frank. "Three-Fingered Jack: The Terror of Jamaica." *West India Committee Circular* 45.816–18 (1930).

Day, Thomas. *Sandford and Merton.* London: John Stockdale, 1783–89.

Defoe, Daniel. *Robinson Crusoe.* New York: Scribner, 1957.

*Dunscombe's British Theatre.* Vol. 59. London, 1825.

Earle Jr., William. *Obi; or, The History of Three-fingered Jack: in a series of letters from a resident in Jamaica to his friend in England*. London: Earle and Hemet, 1800.

Edgeworth, Maria. *Belinda*. London: J. Johnson, 1801.

——. "The Grateful Negro." *Popular Tales*. London: J. Johnson, 1804.

Edwards, Bryan. *The History, Civil and Commercial, of the British Colonies in the West Indies*. London: J. Stockdale, 1793–1801.

——. 'Introduction' to *The Proceedings of the Governor and Assembly of Jamaica, in Regard to the Maroon Negroes*. London: J. Stockdale, 1796.

Fawcett, John. *Three-fingered Jack*. London: Woodfall, 1809.

Foote, Samuel. *The Patron*. London: T. Lowndes, 1781.

Frost, Thomas. *Obi*. London, 1851.

Galt, John. *Bogle Corbet; or, The Emigrants*. London: H. Colburn and R. Bentley, 1831.

Gay, John. *Polly*. London: John Bell, 1777.

Genest, John. *Some Account of the English Stage*. Vol. 7. London, 1832.

Godwin, William. *Political Justice*. London: Allen and Unwin, 1949.

——. *St. Leon: A Tale of the Sixteenth Century*. London: G.G. and J. Robinson, 1799.

Grainger, James. *An Essay on the More Common West-India Diseases and the Remedies which that Country Itself Produces by a Physician in the West-Indies*. London, 1764.

——. *The Sugar Cane: A Poem. In Four Books*. London: R. and J. Dodsley, 1764.

Hays, Mary. *Memoirs of Emma Courtney*. London: G.G. and J. Robinson, 1796.

Helme, Elizabeth. *The Farmer of Inglewood Forest*. London: William Lane at the Minerva Press, 1796.

*Henry Willoughby*. London: G. Kearsley, 1798.

Hickeringill, Edmund. *Jamaica Viewed*. London: B. Bragg, 1705.

Hillary, William. *Observations on the Changes of the Air, and the Concomitant Epidemical Diseases in the Island of Barbadoes*. London, 1766.

Hofland, Barbara Hoole. *Matilda; or, The Barbadoes Girl*. London, 1816.

*House of Commons Sessional Papers*. London: 1789.

Hume, David. *Enquiry Concerning the Principles of Morals*. London: A. Millar, 1751.

Johnstone, Charles. *Chrysal; or, The Adventures of a Guinea*. London: T. Becket, 1760.

Kilner, Dorothy. *The Rotchfords*. London: John Marshall, 1786.

LaVallee, Joseph. *Le nègre comme il y a peu de blancs.* Madras [Paris]: Buisson, 1789.

Lee, Sophia. *The Recess; or, A Tale of Other Times.* London: T. Cadell, 1783–85.

Leslie, Charles. *A New and Exact Account of Jamaica.* Edinburgh: R. Fleming, 1740.

Lewis, Matthew Gregory. *Journal of a West India Proprietor, Kept During a Residence in the Island of Jamaica.* London: J. Murray, 1834.

Ligon, Richard. *A True and Exact History of the Island of Barbadoes.* London: Peter Parker, 1673.

Long, Edward. *The History of Jamaica.* London: T. Lowndes, 1774.

Mackenzie, Anna Maria. *Slavery, or, The Times.* London: G.G.J. and J. Robinson, 1792.

Mackenzie, Henry. *Julia de Roubigné, A Tale.* London: W. Strahan and T. Cadell, 1777.

MacNeill, Hector. *Memoirs of the Life and Travels of the Late Charles Macpherson, Esq. In Asia, Africa, and America. Illustrative of Manners, Customs, and Character.* Edinburgh: Archibald Constable, 1800.

Madden, R.R. *A Twelvemonth's Residence in the West Indies During the Transition From Slavery to Apprenticeship.* Philadelphia, 1835.

Martineau, Harriet. *Demerara: A Tale, Illustrations of Political Economy* no. 4. London: Charles Fox, 1832.

——. *The Hour and the Man: A Historical Romance.* London: E. Moxon, 1841.

Melmoth, Courtney [Samuel Jackson Pratt]. *Liberal Opinions Upon Animals, Man, and Providence.* London: G. Robinson and J. Bew, 1775–77.

*Memoirs and Opinions of Mr. Blenfield.* London: W. Lane, 1790.

Moore, John. *Zeluco.* London: A. Strahan and T. Cadell, 1789.

Montgomery, James. *The Wanderer of Switzerland, the West Indies, and Other Poems.* Philadelphia: James P. Parke and Edward Parker, 1811.

Moseley, Benjamin. *A Treatise on Sugar.* London: G.G. and J. Robinson, 1799.

Opie, Amelia. *Adeline Mowbray; or, The Mother and Daughter.* London: Longman, Hurst, Rees & Orme, 1805.

*Oxberry's Weekly Budget of Plays.* Vol. 1. London, 1843.

Paine, Thomas. *The Rights of Man.* London: H.D. Symonds, 1792.

Pittis, William. *The Jamaica Lady: or, the Life of Bavia.* London: Tho. Bickerton, 1720.

Ralegh, Sir Walter. *The Discoverie of the Large, Rich, and Bewtiful Empyre of Guiana.* Ed. Neil Whitehead. Norman: U of Oklahoma P, 1997.

Saint-Lambert, Jean-François. *Ziméo*. Paris, 1800; trans. Weedon Butler, *Zimao, the African*. London: Vernor and Hood, 1800.

Saint-Pierre, Jacques-Bernardin de. *Paul et Virginie*. Paris, 1787; trans. Daniel Malthus, *Paul and Mary, an Indian Story*. London: J. Dodsley, 1789; trans. Helen Maria Williams, *Paul and Virginia*. London: G.G. and J. Robinson, 1795.

Scott, Sarah. *The History of Sir George Ellison*. London: A. Millar, 1766; abridged as *The Man of Real Sensibility*. Philadelphia: James Humphreys, 1774.

Sells, William. *Remarks on the Condition of the Slaves in the Island of Jamaica*. London, 1823.

Shakespeare, William. *The Tempest*. Ed. Alden and Virginia Vaughan. London: Arden, 1999.

Sherwood, Mary. *Dazee; or, The Re-Captured Negro*. London: F. Houlston and Son, 1821.

Sloane, Hans. *A Voyage to the Islands Madera, Barbados, Nieves, S. Christophers and Jamaica*. London, 1707.

Smith, Charlotte. *Desmond*. London: G.G.J. and J. Robinson, 1792.

———. *The Wanderings of Warwick*. London: J. Bell, 1794.

———. *The Letters of a Solitary Wanderer: Containing Narratives of Various Description*. London: Sampson Low, 1800–01.

Sterne, Laurence. *The Life and Opinions of Tristram Shandy, Gentleman*. London: R. and J. Dodsley, 1760–67.

———. *A Sentimental Journey Through France and Italy*. London: T. Becket and P.A. De Hondt, 1768.

*Supplement to the Royal Gazette* 2.67 (29 July 29–5 August 1780).

*Supplement to the Royal Gazette* 2.84 (25 November–2 December 1780).

*Supplement to the Royal Gazette* 2.87 (16–23 December 1780).

*Supplement to the Royal Gazette* 3.93 (27 January–3 February 1781).

Thelwall, John. *The Daughter of Adoption; A Tale of Modern Times*. London: R. Phillips, 1801.

Thomas, Ann. *Adolphus de Biron: A Novel, Founded on the French Revolution*. Plymouth: P. Nettleton, 1795.

Tonna, Charlotte Elizabeth. *The System: A Tale of the West Indies*. London: Frederick Westley and A.H. Davis, 1827.

Trapham, Thomas. *A Discourse of the State of Health of the Island of Jamaica*. London, 1679.

Tryon, Thomas. *Friendly Advice to the Gentlemen-Planters of the East and West Indies*. London: Andrew Sowle, 1684.

Walker, George. *The Vagabond*. London: G. Walker, and Lee and Hurst, 1799.

Walker, William. *Victorious Love: A Tragedy*. London: Ralph Smith, 1698.

Ward, Edward. *A Trip to Jamaica*. London, 1698.

Weekes, Nathaniel. *Barbados a Poem*. London: J. and J. Lewis, 1754.

Williams, Cynric. *A Tour Through the Island of Jamaica*. London: Hunt and Clarke, 1826.

Wollstonecraft, Mary. *Vindication of the Rights of Woman* (1792). London: Walter Scott, 1891.

## Secondary Texts

Allibone, Samuel Austin. *A Critical Dictionary of English Literature*. London: Trubner, 1859–71.

Aravamudan, Srinivas. *Tropicopolitans: Colonialism and Agency, 1688–1804*. Durham: Duke UP, 1999.

——, ed. *Slavery, Abolition and Emancipation Volume VI: Fiction*. London: Pickering and Chatto, 1999.

Baker, David Erskine. *Biographia Dramatica, or, A Companion to the Playhouse*. London: Hurst, Rees, Orme, et. al., 1812.

Barclay, Alexander. *A Practical View of the Present State of Slavery in the West Indies*. London, 1827.

Barry, Florence V. *A Century of Children's Books*. London: Methuen, 1922.

Bastide, Roger. *African Civilizations in the New World*, trans. Peter Green. London: G. Hurst and Co., 1971.

Bell, Sir Hesketh. *Obeah: Witchcraft in the West Indies*. 1889; Westport, CT: Negro UP, 1970.

Benveniste, Emile. *Problems in General Linguistics*, trans. Mary Elizabeth Meek. Coral Gables: U of Miami P, 1971.

Bernard, John. *Retrospections of America, 1797–1811*. New York: Harper and Brothers, 1887.

Bewell, Alan. *Romanticism and Colonial Disease*. Baltimore: Johns Hopkins UP, 1999.

Black, Clinton V. *Tales of Old Jamaica*. London: Collins, 1966.

——. *The Story of Jamaica: From Prehistory to the Present*. London: Collins, 1965.

——. *History of Jamaica*. London: Collins Clear Type Press, 1958.

Boulukos, George E. "Maria Edgeworth's 'Grateful Negro' and the Sentimental Argument for Slavery." *Eighteenth-Century Life* 23.1 (1999) 12–29.

Brathwaite, Edward Kamau. "The African Presence in Caribbean Literature." *Slavery, Colonialism and Racism*, ed. Sidney Mintz. New York: Norton, 1974.

Butler, Marilyn. *Maria Edgeworth: A Literary Biography*. Oxford: Clarendon, 1972.

Campbell, Mavis C. *The Maroons of Jamaica: A History of Resistance, Collaboration and Betrayal*. Granby, MA: Bergin and Garvey, 1988.

Carlyle, Thomas. *Chartism in Selected Writings*. Ed. Alan Shelstone. Harmondsworth: Penguin, 1986.

Chambers, Douglas. "'My Own Nation:' Igbo Exiles in the Diaspora." *Slavery and Abolition* 18.1 (1997) 72–97.

Chambers, Robert. *A Biographical Dictionary of Eminent Scotsmen*. Glasgow: Blackie, 1855.

Cox, Jeffrey N., ed. *Slavery, Abolition and Emancipation Vol. 5: Drama*. London: Pickering and Chatto, 1999.

Craton, Michael. *Searching for the Invisible Man: Slavery and Plantation Life in Jamaica*. Cambridge: Harvard UP, 1978.

———. *Testing the Chains: Resistance to Slavery in the British West Indies*. Ithaca: Cornell UP, 1982.

Cross, Wilbur L. *The Life and Times of Laurence Sterne*. New York: Macmillan, 1909.

Curtin, Philip D. *Death By Migration: Europe's Encounter With the Tropical World in the Nineteenth Century*. Cambridge: Cambridge UP, 1989.

D'Costa, Jean. "Oral Literature, Formal Literature: The Formation of Genre in Eighteenth-Century Jamaica." *Eighteenth-Century Studies* 27.4 (Summer 1994) 663–77.

Davis, David Brion. *The Problem of Slavery in the Age of Revolution, 1770–1823*. Ithaca: Cornell UP, 1975.

Day, Thomas. *Fragment of an Original Letter on the Slavery of the Negroes Written in the Year 1776*. London: John Stockdale, 1784.

Edgeworth, Maria and Richard Lovell Edgeworth. *Memoirs of Richard Lovell Edgeworth, Esq., Begun by Himself and Concluded by His Daughter Maria Edgeworth*, 2 vols. London: R. Hunter, 1820.

Ellis, Markman. *The Politics of Sensibility: Race, Gender and Commerce in the Sentimental Novel*. Cambridge: Cambridge UP, 1996.

Falconbridge, Anna Maria. *Narrative of Two Voyages to the River Sierra Leone During the Years 1791–2–3, In a Series of Letters*. London, 1794.

Faulkner, Peter. *Robert Bage*. Boston: Twayne, 1979.

Felsenstein, Frank. *English Trader, Indian Maid: Representing Gender, Race, and Slavery in the New World, An Inkle and Yarico Reader*. Baltimore: Johns Hopkins UP, 1999.

Ferguson, Moira. *Subject to Others: British Women Writers and Colonial Slavery, 1670–1834*. London: Routledge, 1992.

Fyfe, Christopher. *A History of Sierra Leone*. Oxford: Oxford UP, 1962.

Gaspar, David Barry. *Bondmen and Rebels: A Study of Master-Slave Relations in Antigua With Implications for Colonial British America*. Baltimore: Johns Hopkins UP, 1985.

Genest, John. *Some Account of the English Stage from the Restoration in 1660 to 1830*. Bath: H.E. Carrington, 1832.

Gignilliat, George Warren, Jr. *The Author of* Sandford and Merton: *A Life of Thomas Day, Esq*. New York: Columbia UP, 1932.

Goveia, Elsa V. *A Study on the Historiography of the British West Indies to the End of the Nineteenth Century*. Mexico: Instituto Panamericano de Geografía et Historia, 1956.

Greimas, Algirdas-Julien, and François Rastier. "The Interaction of Semiotic Constraints." *Yale French Studies* 41 (1968) 86–105.

Hall, Douglas. "Absentee-Proprietorship in the British West Indies to about 1850." *Jamaican Historical Review* 4 (1964) 15–35.

———. *In Miserable Slavery: Thomas Thistlewood in Jamaica, 1750–86*. London: Macmillan, 1989.

Handler, Jerome S. and Kenneth M. Bilby. "On the Early Use and Origin of the Term 'Obeah' in Barbados and the Anglophone Caribbean." *Slavery and Abolition* 22.2 (August 2001) 87–100.

Heilman, Robert Bechtold. *America in English Fiction, 1760–1800: The Influences of the American Revolution*. Baton Rouge, LA: Louisiana State UP, 1937.

Hulme, Peter. *Colonial Encounters: Europe and the Native Caribbean, 1492–1797*. New York: Methuen, 1986.

Hymes, D. *Pidginization and Creolization of Languages*. Cambridge: Cambridge UP, 1971.

James, C.L.R. *The Black Jacobins: Toussaint L'Ouverture and the San Domingo Revolution*. London: Alison and Busby, 1980.

Jameson, Fredric. *The Political Unconscious: Narrative As a Socially Symbolic Act*. Ithaca: Cornell UP, 1981.

Kelly, Gary. *The English Jacobin Novel, 1780-1805*. Oxford: Clarendon, 1976.

Knutsford, Viscountess Margaret Jean Trevelyan. *Life and Letters of Zachary Macaulay*. London: Edward Arnold, 1900.

La Barre, Weston. "Materials for a History of Studies of Crisis Cults: A Bibliographic Essay." *Current Anthropology* 12.1 (February 1971) 3–44.

Mackenzie, Henry. *A Review of the Principal Proceedings of the Parliament of 1784* in *The Works of Henry Mackenzie*. 5 vols. Edinburgh: Archibald Constable, 1808. 7: 177–400.

Morgan, Philip. *The Early Caribbean*. Omohundro Institute for Early American History and Culture, forthcoming.

Morrish, Ivor. *Obeah, Christ and Rastaman: Jamaica and Its Religion*. Cambridge: James Clarke, 1982.

Neale Hurston, Zora. *Tell My Horse: Voodoo and Life in Haiti and Jamaica*. New York: Perennial Library, 1990.

Olmos, Margarite Fernández and Lizabeth Paravisini-Gebert, eds. *Sacred Possessions: Vodou, Santería, Obeah and the Caribbean*. New Brunswick, NJ: Rutgers UP, 1997.

Parry, J.H. and P.H. Sherlock. *Short History of the West Indies*. London: Macmillan, 1956.

Patterson, Orlando. *The Sociology of Slavery: An Analysis of the Origins, Development and Structure of Negro Slavery in Jamaica*. London: MacGibbon and Kee, 1967.

Perrin, Noel. "Introduction." *Adventures of Jonathan Corncob, Loyal American Refugee. Written by Himself*. Ed. Noel Perrin. 1787. Boston: David R. Godine, 1976.

Phillippo, James M. *Jamaica: Its Past And Present State*. London, 1843.

Pitman, Frank W. "The West Indian Absentee Planter as a British Colonial Type." *American Historical Association Pacific Coast Branch Proceedings* (1927) 113–27.

Price, Lawrence Marsden. *Inkle and Yarico Album*. Berkeley: U of California P, 1937.

Ramchand, Kenneth. *The West Indian Novel And Its Background*. London: Heinemann, 1970, 1983.

Ragatz, Lowell J. "Absentee Landlordism in the British Caribbean, 1750–1833." *Agricultural History* 5 (1931) 7–24.

Rajan, Tillotama and Julia M. Wright. "Introduction." *Romanticism, History, and the Possibilities of Genre: Re-forming literature 1789–1837*. Cambridge: Cambridge UP, 1998. 1–20.

Richardson, Alan. "Romantic Voodoo: Obeah and British Culture 1797–1807." *Studies in Romanticism* 32 (Spring 1993) 3–28.

Romaine, Suzanne. *Pidgin and Creole Languages*. London: Longmans, 1988.

Rosenberg, Charles E. and Janet Golden. *Framing Disease: Studies in Cultural History.* New Brunswick, NJ: Rutgers UP, 1992.

Rzepka, Charles J. "Thomas De Quincey's Three-Fingered Jack: The West Indian Origins of the 'Dark Interpreter,' *European Romantic Review* 8.2 (Spring 1997) 117–38.

Sancho, Ignatius. *Letters of the Late Ignatius Sancho, An African.* Ed. Vincent Carretta. 1782. New York: Penguin, 1998.

Schuler, Monica. "Myalism and the African Religious Tradition in Jamaica." *Africa and the Caribbean: The Legacies of a Link.* Ed. Margaret E. Crahan and Franklin W. Knight. Baltimore: Johns Hopkins UP, 1979. 65–79.

Scott, Walter. *Biographical Memoirs of Eminent Novelists and Other Distinguished Persons,* 2 vols. Edinburgh: Robert Caddell, 1834.

Sharpe, Jenny. *Ghosts of Slavery: A Literary Archaeology of Black Women's Lives.* Minnesota: U of Minneapolis P, 2003.

Seaga, Edward. *Pocomania: Revival Cults in Jamaica.* Kingston: Institute of Jamaica, 1982.

Sheridan, Richard B. *Doctors and Slaves: A Medical and Demographic History of Slavery in the British West Indies, 1680–1834.* New York: Cambridge UP, 1985.

Simpson, George Eaton. *Religious Cults of the Caribbean: Trinidad, Jamaica, Haiti,* 3rd ed. Rio Piedras, Puerto Rico: Institute of Caribbean Studies, University of Puerto Rico, 1980.

Spinney, G.H. "Cheap Repository Tracts: Hazard and Marshall Edition." *The Library* 20.3 (December 1939) 295–340.

Sterne, Laurence. *The Letters of Laurence Sterne.* Ed. Lewis Perry Curtis. Oxford: Clarendon, 1935.

——. *Sermons of Mr. Yorick,* 2 vols. London: R. and J. Dodsley, 1760.

Stewart, John. *A View of the Past and Present State of the Island of Jamaica.* Edinburgh: 1823.

*Substance of the Report Delivered by the Court of Directors of the Sierra Leone Company on Thursday the 27th March, 1794.* London: James Phillips, 1794.

Summers, Montague. *A Gothic Bibliography.* New York: Russell and Russell, 1941.

Sypher, Wylie. *Guinea's Captive Kings: British Anti-Slavery Literature of the XVIIIth Century.* Chapel Hill: U of North Carolina P, 1942.

Trimpi, Helen P. "Demonology and Witchcraft in Moby-Dick." *Journal of the History of Ideas* 30.4 (1969) 558–62.

Trouillot, Michel-Rolph. "From Planters' Journals to Academia: The Haitian Revolution as Unthinkable History." *Journal of Caribbean History* 25.1–2 (1991) 81–99.

Turner, Mary. "Religious Beliefs." *A General History of the Caribbean Vol. 3: The Slave Societies of the Caribbean*. London: UNESCO, 1997. 287–321.

Umeh, John Anenechukwu. *After God is Dibia: Igbo Cosmology, Divination and Sacred Science in Nigeria*. London: Karnak House, 1997.

Walvin, James. *Black Ivory: A History of British Slavery*. London: Fontana, 1993.

Williams, J.J. *Psychic Phenomena of Jamaica*. New York: Dial, 1934.

———. *Voodoos and Obeahs*. New York: Dial, 1934.

Wright, Richardson. *Revels in Jamaica 1682–1838*. New York: Dodd, Mead and Co., 1937.